FLIGHT OF THE *MARINER*

Flight of the
Mariner

Paul Ware

Hodder & Stoughton

Copyright © 1997 by Paul Ware

First published in Great Britain in 1997 by Hodder and Stoughton
A division of Hodder Headline PLC

The right of Paul Ware to be identified as the Author of
the Work has been asserted by him in accordance with the
Copyright, Designs and Patents Act 1988.

10 9 8 7 6 5 4 3 2 1

A CIP catalogue record for this title is available
from the British Library

ISBN 0 340 68913 7

Typeset by Palimpsest Book Production Limited,
Polmont, Stirlingshire
Printed and bound in Great Britain by
Mackays of Chatham PLC, Chatham, Kent

Hodder and Stoughton
A division of Hodder Headline PLC
338 Euston Road
London NW1 3BH

CONTENTS

Chapter 1

SWORDSMAN

I'd like to try and keep hindsight out of this narrative if I can, and just tell it as it happened. The problem with that, of course, is where to begin. *With* hindsight, the events that precipitated much of what follows occurred before I was born, yet I couldn't have known about them, could I? *Without* hindsight, my story doesn't really begin until my eighteenth birthday, but to begin there is to dive in at the middle.

Very well, then: a compromise.

I was seven years old when my parents were the victims of a road traffic accident. My mother was killed outright, and my father was hospitalized for months. I know that he blamed himself for what had happened – wrongly, by all accounts – and although he eventually walked out of hospital as healthy as he had ever been, there were many ways in which he never recovered from that accident. Never really survived it.

Faced with the prospect of bringing up a child entirely on his own – ours was not a closely knit family – my father might easily have settled for the more 'sensible' option of having me fostered or adopted. That such a thing was suggested I know for a certainty, and equally as certain was my father's response to it. Despite the fact that this was the 1960s, and single-parent families were still enough of a novelty to appear strange – especially when the single parent concerned was the father – his determination to raise me himself grew from an obstinate pose to an unshakeable resolve.

And in the interests of historical accuracy – and as some small act of repayment – I must now record that the effort he put in was neither lost on me nor was it wasted.

An intensely physical man in every sense of the word, he was not much given to the finer feelings which, in those pre-feminist days, were still largely the province of women. So although he never failed to show me a gruff kind of affection, he was seldom loving or gentle towards me. I can recall no occasion, save on the day of my mother's funeral, that he ever hugged me, or that I ever saw him shed a tear.

Our relationship, such as it was, grew not out of shared confidences and trust, but out of time spent together and shared experiences. He found it impossible to relate to me as a child, perhaps even as his son, and treated me in much the same manner that he did his contemporaries. Faced with such a situation at so impressionable an age I did what any child would do and tried to copy everything that he did.

I grew up fast. And although my life remained deficient in many vital respects, there was no denying the rich variety that was present in those other areas where my father felt comfortable.

He had been an engineer in the army after the war and cars remained one of his great passions. I learned to drive in the field behind our house when I was twelve and the following year I stripped and rebuilt the remains of our old saloon and turned it into a hot-rod. It ran for twenty miles or so and then dumped most of its engine in that selfsame field, and although at the time it seemed like the end of the world to me I learned more from that one failure than from all the successes that followed it.

Engineering wasn't the only thing the army had taught my father, and he passed on to me every scrap of knowledge and experience that his brief time in the forces had brought him. And if that meant teaching me how to shoot (illegally) or drink (illegally) or fight (dirtily) then that was fine with him. Like I said, I grew up fast.

2

In a lot of ways it was a bit like something out of *Boy's Own*, except that I was already old enough to realize that as a life style it left a great deal to be desired. My father was no fool, and I think he saw the dangers even before I did. Academically he was a long way from being a genius. He had a natural aptitude for many things but his formal education had been interrupted by National Service and he had never found the time or the inclination to go back to it. He was not unhappy with this state of affairs, but where I was concerned he was determined that I should get all the chances that he had been denied. With a child's misplaced sense of loyalty to his only remaining parent I resisted all of his early attempts at making me into something that he wasn't. But the resistance was never more than token, because despite my love for him and, in the early days, for our peculiar life style, I enjoyed school and wanted to do well at it.

Once a mutually acceptable status quo had evolved we might have gone on like that for years, but two events were approaching that were destined to change my life forever. The first was a gradual change in my father. He had always been a strong drinker and, after my mother's death, something of a womanizer. But at what point he turned into an alcoholic I am still not certain. I was fifteen when I gained the first real inkling, but, foolishly, I ignored it, not realizing its significance. Over the next three years both the significance and the full horror of the situation would become impossible to ignore.

The second event was my introduction to the person who, had things turned out differently, might now be writing this account in my place.

Whenever I think of her I hear music. That's not meant to be poetic, it's just the way it is. I first saw her after hearing the most amazing piano playing I had *ever* heard; being a naturally curious person, I followed the sound of the playing to its source.

She was playing the ancient relic of an upright grand that stood in the school assembly hall, and playing it like I'd never imagined that worm-eaten old artefact could ever be played. She had also chosen what, at that time, I considered to be the best piece of piano music ever written, although I had no knowledge of its true pedigree. I knew it only from my father's embarrassingly old record collection, a ballad called 'Deep is the Night'.

(What she was actually playing, of course, was Chopin's Étude in E, arguably the greatest work ever written for the piano.)

Secure in my ignorance I stood transfixed as I watched her play in the empty hall, the sound reverberating through the entire school, itself deserted as this was the middle of the summer holidays. I myself was only there because I had been involved in an inter-school football match and had heard the music from the changing rooms. Everyone else had left, but earlier that day my father had been particularly unpleasant and I had delayed going home for as long as possible.

As I stood and watched her I tried to fathom out who she might be. She seemed too young to be a teacher, but was clearly too old for a student, even one attending the sixth-form college that formed an annexe to the school. She was slender, with reddish brown hair that didn't quite reach her shoulders, and a serious, not conventionally pretty face. She was wearing a silk blouse and one of those peasant-girl skirts that were popular at the time, and the longer I stared at her the more of an enigma she seemed to become.

She was reaching the end of her playing and I was on the point of stepping into the hall and introducing myself when a hand the size of a shovel landed on my shoulder. A voice said in my ear, 'What are you doing loitering around here, lad?'

I half turned and stared into the face of the school's senior history teacher, a heavy-set, loutish individual whose favourite pastime was intimidating first- and second-year pupils and, when he could, those higher up the school as well. I was an inch taller than him, but nothing like as stout. I won't say I could have snapped him in two like a rotten twig, but I wouldn't have been afraid to try either.

'Just listening,' I replied.

'Just listening, what?' he demanded.

I wondered if he wanted me to hit him. I guessed perhaps he did.

'Just listening—' I said, '—sir.'

4

'Well, "just listen" somewhere else,' he barked, and pushed me in the direction of the changing rooms.

Thinking dark thoughts I walked away, and I didn't see my mysterious piano player again until almost four weeks later. When I did I got the shock of my life. In fact, I had to work extremely hard to convince myself that it was the same woman, because although her physical appearance was unchanged her demeanour was unrecognizable from that of that first brief view I had had of her. She was, indeed, a teacher, and she took up a position at my own school at the start of the new term.

My first encounter with her was during an art lesson, and although I cannot now remember precisely what transgression had drawn me to her attention I recall quite clearly what the outcome was. She hauled me to the front of the class (I was five inches taller than her and outmassed her by about fifty pounds, but there was no arguing with that grip she had on my arm) and held up the piece of art I had been working on – a charcoal portrait, done from old photos and a vague, haunting memory, of my mother. She then gave the rest of the class a critique of the picture, one that was utterly scathing and yet clinically accurate into the bargain. The class fell about, and I was eventually returned to my seat, scarlet and ready to kill somebody; the picture was screwed up in my left fist.

And thus began my relationship with the woman whom I now knew as Mrs Catlin. Mrs! Her married life, according to popular rumour, had lasted barely six months, and she and her husband had been separated now for over a year. On that first day when I saw her, when it had seemed that the music she was playing had let me glimpse her soul, I had been convinced that she was one of the world's truly free spirits. The fact that I could have been so wrong seemed like an affront to everything I believed in.

In the months that followed, and for the remainder of my time in the fourth year, she was a constant thorn in my side, never giving me a hint of credit for doing something right and coming down on me like the wrath of God for the slightest lapse in the quality of my work. Had she taught only art this might not have been so bad, but unfortunately her teaching abilities were wide and varied. In addition to art she also taught English Lit, French and pure maths.

She also taught French and English Lit to A-level standard, which was doubly damning since I had planned to study both subjects in the sixth form. In a matter of months, Mrs Catlin had managed to become a total anathema to me, and had succeeded in becoming the only person in the world I actively hated.

On the last day of term at the end of my fourth year Mrs Catlin collared me in the art room and took me on one side. I wondered what unknown crime I had committed to deserve her wrath on the last day of the school year.

'Do you have any idea,' she asked me, 'of what you are going to do with the rest of your life?'

To say that I was taken aback would be an understatement. Everything about her manner suggested that this was a question she'd asked me a dozen times before without ever getting a satisfactory response. In fact, she'd never before expressed any interest in my future whatsoever.

'I've thought about it,' I replied, adding sarcastically, 'but I thought I'd try and pass my O levels first, if that's all right.'

'O levels aren't everything,' she snapped back, such an admission from her startling me. 'But at least you're on the right track. Now, what are you going to do over the summer?'

I started to answer, as usual putting my mouth into gear long before engaging my brain, and found myself stopped by a sudden surge of anger and bitterness. My plans for the summer had all been made months before, and involved spending a lot of time with my father and doing some camping and off-road motorcycling, which was my latest passion. But those plans had now effectively gone down the drain. My father's drinking had been getting steadily worse for weeks, with him sometimes spending whole nights away from home, and his perennial moodiness had taken on new and darker overtones that seemed to be punctuated by bouts of scarcely restrained violence. I found myself wishing more and more that I was old enough to leave home *now*, before he did something for which I might never be able to forgive him.

But there was no way I was going to explain all of that to Mrs Catlin, so I simply said. 'I guess I'll just take a long rest. Why, what do you care?'

'I give you a lot of latitude with your manner, Shaw,' she said warningly, 'But don't push it. And to answer your question, it's always of interest to me what my students do with their free time, particularly if all they do is waste it.

'Have you ever done any fencing?' she asked abruptly.

The question caught me completely off guard. 'I put one up round the back garden . . .' I began.

'Don't waste your humour on me,' Mrs Catlin snapped. 'You know what I mean. Now, have you or haven't you?'

I was momentarily lost for words; I had obviously misunderstood the question but she didn't seem inclined to believe that so I just said, 'Yes, sure.'

'Good,' she said, actually smiling for what I thought was the first time since I'd known her. 'Do you have your own equipment?'

I thought about the hundreds of pounds' worth of tools in our cellar but realized that they were all designed for engineering, not woodwork.

'No,' I said. 'Not really.'

'No problem,' Mrs Catlin said. 'I can get all we need. Is Saturday afternoon all right with you?'

Well, no, I thought, *it isn't; not if you're going to be there.* But I felt strangely cornered by her, overwhelmed by this uncharacteristically enthusiastic approach. So despite all my best efforts to do otherwise I found myself saying, 'Yes, fine. Saturday.'

'I'll meet you at the school gates at two o'clock,' Mrs Catlin said. 'We can use the gymnasium here; it will be more private.'

'Um, right,' I said. I wanted to add, *Wouldn't the woodwork room be better?* but I decided against it – I had a feeling it wouldn't go down too well.

'Right, off you go,' Mrs Catlin said.

I left the art room feeling very confused.

On Saturday I turned up on time. I hadn't seen my father since Thursday night and didn't really want to be in the house when he returned, which was my rationalization for why I had bothered to keep this appointment at all when normally Mrs Catlin was somebody with whom I wouldn't have voluntarily shared the same country. She met me at the school gates and I think we both got a shock. We had been used to seeing one another in our normal daily clothing, so for Mrs Catlin the shock shouldn't have been too unexpected – after all, who wears a school uniform on a Saturday? And although jeans, T-shirt and a leather biker's jacket may have been a rather radical departure from my weekday uniform it was not as outrageous as the fashions favoured by most of my class. My first view of Mrs Catlin in 'casual dress', however, was a real surprise.

At school she had always favoured a kind of gypsy appearance, sporting flouncy skirts with tasselled hems, primary-colour silk blouses, and hand-embroidered waistcoats. She also had a taste for cheap metal jewellery, particularly large bracelets and hair slides. I don't think anyone would have been surprised to learn that she lived in a painted waggon with only a black cat and a crystal ball for company.

Which meant that the sight of her, on that Saturday afternoon, wearing jeans, a T-shirt, and a black leather biker's jacket was a little too much to take.

She looked me up and down, making me suddenly self-conscious about the way I was staring at her, and said wryly, 'Well, well; who would have thought you'd have such good taste in clothes, Shaw?'

I struggled for a reply, then she grinned and we both laughed.

'Come on,' she said, turning and striding towards the front entrance of the school. 'I'm ready for a serious workout.'

I hurried to catch up and, feeling very foolish, said, 'This, uh, fencing, where did you say we were going to do it?'

'In the gym,' said Mrs Catlin. 'I brought a selection of blades, since I forgot to ask what you use. What *do* you use, by the way?'

Blades, I thought. *Fencing*, I thought. *Oh, hell.* Too late, I realized what she had meant.

Blushing from collar to hairline. I explained to her how I had misunderstood her original question. She looked at me as though I was an idiot, and the momentary truce in our undeclared war was over.

'You're just messing me about, aren't you, Shaw?' she said frostily. 'You're just trying to make a fool out of me and waste my time.'

8

'No,' I said, wavering between anger at the injustice of the accusation and an urge to defuse the situation that my own obtuseness had helped create. 'I really did misunderstand . . .'

'Right,' she snapped. 'Get down to that gym.'

'What are you . . .?'

'Move it, Shaw,' she said. 'I'm going to get something out of this afternoon.'

I went ahead of her down to the gym, to be confronted by a collection of equipment that looked like something from a cheap remake of *The Three Musketeers*. Yet at the first glimpse of those weapons I felt something inside me stir, something like the way I had felt when my father had first taken me shooting, or when I had first taken up archery – a sport my father found entirely unacceptable for a grown man. But this new feeling was a hundred times stronger than any I'd felt before, and far more compelling.

'Let's get you kitted up,' Mrs Catlin said, clearly still angry.

I endured the suiting-up in silence, realizing that any protests would only delay still further the moment when I could get my hands on one of those blades.

As soon as all the protective devices were in place I made for the rack that held the weapons and picked up the heaviest one there.

'Put that down,' Mrs Catlin snapped. 'I'm not trusting an épée to a total novice.' She handed me a much lighter blade. 'Take this and get the feel of it while I suit up – and try not to stab yourself, will you?'

I smiled condescendingly, pointing with feigned amazement to the capped point of the weapon. Mrs Catlin turned away with a look of disgust.

I took the weapon and went to the far side of the gym, where she had marked out what I assumed to be a conventional piste on the wooden floor. I'd watched a little fencing on television, and had some idea of what was involved. I flicked the blade around a little, and tried to find a natural posture. It wasn't easy; I knew that the real trick – like with archery – would be balance, and relied on my own fairly good sense of equilibrium to guide me.

Mrs Catlin returned presently and looked critically at the way I was standing. She walked around me, kicked my feet into slightly different positions, adjusted the set of my shoulders, and stepped back. 'Better?' she asked. I shrugged, but I knew what she meant; the slight change of body line had made the pose feel less clumsy.

She struck a pose beside me.

'Follow me,' she said, and executed a simple series of movements. I copied them. She looked at me and said, 'Shaw, you wouldn't be playing some sort of game with me, would you?' My expression must have reflected the genuine puzzlement I felt at her question because she just said, 'Follow me,' and executed another, slightly more complex series of moves.

We spent an hour doing seemingly (to me) meaningless exercises. They were all so simple and so obvious that going through them over and over struck me as a waste of time for both of us. In the end, I began to think that she was doing this to punish me. I stepped back from her, jabbing the point of my foil down onto the floor.

'This is boring,' I said.

She spun to face me.

'Boring?' she repeated. She studied her feet for several seconds; I could see that she was sweating, and wondered why – I hadn't even begun to raise my heart rate yet.

'Right,' she said at length. 'Put your mask on and defend yourself.'

I pulled on my mask and raised my blade. I had barely had time to blink before Mrs Catlin had rushed me. In a second my blade was clattering across the floor and her point was making an impressive dent in the padding over my heart.

She stepped back. 'Again,' she snapped.

I retrieved my weapon and took up a defensive stance. She rushed me, and this time it seemed almost that I could read her mind. *Yes*, I thought, *the blade will move thus and so, turning my own blade aside for a thrust to the midsection.* A fraction of a second later the manoeuvre was completed, and once again I was dead.

'Again,' Mrs Catlin said, this time not in anger but with a new, less brittle tone in her voice.

She came at me again, and this time I fended her off for all of ten seconds before her point took me in the sternum.

'Again,' she said, and she sounded almost pleased.

This time when she attacked I parried and counter-attacked. I had her on the run for several paces before she rallied and turned the tables on me. Her third attempt finally got through and took me in the throat.

She stepped back, watching me from behind her mask, then said, 'Again.'

The exchange this time lasted for several minutes, and was a fierce round of attacks and counters, with Mrs Catlin actually going on the defensive more than on the offensive. Still, it ended much as I had expected, with an extremely hard thrust to the solar plexus that actually winded me.

Mrs Catlin took off her mask and approached me. She was drenched in sweat, her hair matted to the side of her face. She pulled off my mask and swore softly in French, presumably thinking I wouldn't understand.

'You might at least pretend to be working hard,' she said.

'I am,' I told her. 'It just doesn't show on me. And anyway, you've been going easy on me.'

She brushed her hair back and glared at the clock on the wall. 'It's taken you less than two hours,' she said, 'to achieve what it has taken me over ten years to accomplish. All you lack is knowledge of the advanced techniques, but to be honest I think you'll work most of them out for yourself anyway, given time. Shaw, you are the most natural and intuitive fencer I have ever seen. Have you never suspected that you might have this kind of talent?'

I shook my head, surprised by what she had said. I didn't feel as though anything we had done that afternoon had been that spectacular – I hadn't won so much as a single exchange.

'Have you had enough?' I asked her.

'More than enough,' she said, 'for today at any rate. Let's clear this stuff away and then we can each take a shower – you may not need it, but I certainly do.'

We restored the gym to its normal appearance and then retired to the changing rooms. Twenty minutes later Mrs Catlin led me out of the building and locked the main doors behind her.

'Let me give you a lift,' she said.

I followed her round the side of the building to the staff car park and found myself staring at the only vehicle there: a year-old Suzuki GT750M. A pair of white full-face helmets was fastened to the pillion grab-rail with a safety chain.

'Uh, miss,' I said, 'whose is the "kettle"?'

Mrs Catlin laughed; obviously she was familiar with the water-cooled Suzuki's nickname.

'It's my brother's,' she said. 'He's on a field trip to France so I'm minding it for him.'

Mrs Catlin's brother, of whom she spoke fairly often in class, was an art lecturer at one of the nearby colleges. From what she'd said I would have thought a 2CV would have been more in his line.

She unfastened the helmets and gave me one. I pulled it on, wondering how I could get out of this without giving offence. As two-stroke triples from the 1970s go, the Suzuki is perhaps the least monstrous in terms of handling, and its smooth ride makes it seem a lot less ferocious in a straight line than a lot of its contemporaries, but that aside it's still a death-or-glory type of machine, and not something that should be in the hands of a novice.

Mrs Catlin levered the bike off its stand and swung her leg over the seat. She turned on the ignition and flicked out the kick-start lever. I was about to point out that the bike had an electric starter when she straight-legged the lever all the way down and brought the engine roaring into life; if the compression had kicked back I think she would have been sent twenty feet over the handle-bars. As an example of self-confidence and control, however, it had the desired effect: I climbed on behind her without a moment's hesitation.

Less than four minutes later we were pulling up outside my house. Mrs Catlin's riding style was like her appearance: utterly individual. I couldn't deny that she could handle the bike, but I was forced to wonder about the circumstances under which she'd learned. I suspected that a great deal of trial and error had been involved.

'I'd like to fence some more with you, Shaw,' she said as I handed back my helmet.

'Sure,' I said. I didn't want to seem too eager – I'd enjoyed

12

the fencing more than anything else I'd ever tried, but I didn't particularly want to spend my holidays hanging around Mrs Catlin. Then again, it might give me another chance to ride the Suzuki, even if only as a pillion.

'I'm tied up tomorrow,' she said, 'but I'm free Monday.'

'Fine,' I said. I hesitated, then said, 'Will you be on the "kettle" again?'

She handed back the spare helmet. 'I'll pick you up at two o'clock,' she said.

I nodded, and she slipped the bike into gear and was gone.

Chapter 2

DEATH

It seems strange now, looking back, to realize that the tragic circumstances that precipitated the main events of this narrative actually took another three years to develop. At the time it seemed like scarcely a matter of months, so rapidly did the time pass.

Even after the end of the summer holidays I continued to spend a lot of my free time with Mrs Catlin. At first it was just for fencing, but later we added a more generalized exercise routine to help improve both our standards with épée, foil and sabre. After that came hiking and rock climbing, then cycling which led, inevitably from my point of view, to motorcycling.

But with all that, there was never any sense that our time together was spent socializing. If anyone had suggested to me that I was Mrs Catlin's friend I would have been deeply shocked, and probably strangely amused in a disgusted kind of way. For while it was perfectly true that I enjoyed our activities it was always quite clear that she was the teacher and I the pupil, and that her only interest was in instructing me in those things for which I showed any aptitude. Our relationship at school, though less strained than it had been before that first summer, was still an abrasive one, and several of my class mates were astonished that I should voluntarily spend my spare time with someone who clearly thought so little of me. And I might have agreed, except that I was coming to realize that Mrs Catlin's outward show of emotion on any subject was very largely a smokescreen, a diversion to conceal her true thoughts and feelings until she had sorted them out and gained some kind of control over them. In some ways, I actually came to respect her for this, although it made her a difficult person to like and an almost impossible one to get close to. Mercifully, neither prospect held any kind of appeal for me.

I've said that Mrs Catlin was always careful to maintain our teacher/pupil relationship, and on the whole this was true. But there was one exception, and that was with our fencing. It became apparent to both of us in a very short space of time that my natural ability at this activity far outstripped hers, and that only her greater technical knowledge and experience gave her an edge over me. I was therefore extremely annoyed when, midway through our third lesson, she suddenly declared that she was not prepared to teach me anything further. Never having been known for my even temper, I threw down my mask and demanded to know why not. Mrs Catlin's own temper was often on a hair-trigger, especially where I was concerned, so I was surprised at how calmly she removed her own mask and at how carefully she chose her words in replying.

'Do you play the piano, Shaw?' she asked.

My mind was suddenly filled with music, and we were back in the empty assembly hall where I had first seen her. For a fleeting instant I forgot who she really was and saw her again as I'd seen her then. I found that my throat was very dry when I tried to answer her.

'No,' I said.

'I do,' she told me. 'But I can't read music. Can you read music, Shaw?'

I shook my head, not trusting myself to speak.

'I once asked a music teacher to teach me to read music,' she said, 'so that I could play things without having to have heard them first – I play by ear, Shaw; you know what that means?'

I nodded.

'Well, this music teacher asked me to play something for him,' she said. 'I did, and he said he wouldn't teach me to read music because if he did I'd lose the ability I already had – and that ability, in his opinion, was too precious to jeopardize. At the time I was angry with him, but looking back I think he was right. I enjoy playing because I feel that it comes from inside me; it's . . . spontaneous.' She looked at me. 'Your fencing,' she said, 'is like that. But it's about a thousand times stronger in you than my ability to play the piano is in me. Do you understand?'

I thought I did, but my mind was still full of music – and she said my ability was a thousand times stronger than *that*. It seemed incredible, and yet when I was fencing I did sense something of what she was saying.

Recovering myself somewhat, I asked, 'But how will I learn?'

She smiled.

'The same way I did,' she said, '—by practising.'

And so we practised. The method was simple, and, for me, frustrating. But it worked. Mrs Catlin introduced new moves and techniques into her own style and let me suffer defeat after defeat until I worked out counters to them. It made for some explosive sessions. But it worked.

When we were not involved in our more physical pursuits Mrs Catlin gave me private tutoring in the academic subjects that we each agreed would be the important ones for me to pass at O level. I don't think either of us knew where all of it was taking me, but the sense of achievement was sufficiently exhilarating to forestall any long-term commitments, at least until I had actually taken my O levels.

During this period I grew steadily more alienated from my father. In part this was due to the fact that Mrs Catlin had gradually taken his place as my companion in the activities that filled my free time, and for this I must accept the full responsibility. But it was equally as much my father's excesses with alcohol and women that drove a wedge between us, and for that I deny any fault on my part. In fact, I tried on several occasions to mend the rift that was growing between us, to have my efforts met with either sullen silence or a violence that was as startling in its venom as it was in its unpredictability. By the time my O-level results finally came in things had become so bad between us that I had no desire whatever to share the good news with him, and so I contented myself with joining my school friends for the traditional (and entirely unofficial) fifth-form party at the end of term. Yet I felt as out of place with them as I now did with my father, for their views seemed too narrow and immature to have anything to do with my own plans for the future. Yet if I could not share the pleasure of the moment with them, then who could I share it with? I suspected that the answer to that question should have been obvious, yet it somehow eluded me.

The next twelve months were the most gruelling I had ever spent, with Mrs Catlin a positive slave-driver both at school and in our private sessions. It was almost as though she could see something in the future, a prevision that was denied to me, something that frightened her and for which she was desperately trying to prepare me.

I do not believe that that something was the tragic event that occurred in the summer on my eighteenth birthday, yet in retrospect it seems as though both it and the real future that lay ahead of me were inextricably linked.

I had been dreading my eighteenth for months, convinced that my father was likely to do something stupid to commemorate the event, and for once he did not disappoint me. I had spent the day with Mrs Catlin, hiking on the moors where she lived and discussing the courses that I would take in the next year, my final one at school. We had disagreed quite a bit as I recall, which was nothing new, and eventually Mrs Catlin had demanded to see some work of mine from the previous term on which I was basing my argument. Since the work was at my house, and since Mrs Catlin refused to wait until the next day to see it, I agreed to take her over to my place there and then. Had I not done so, the remainder of this narrative might have been very different.

Mrs Catlin rode pillion with me on my new motorcycle, something she often insisted on doing as, she claimed, it helped improve my sense of responsibility. This may have been true, but personally I think the real reason was that she loved motorcycles and had been very disappointed when her brother had taken back the Suzuki.

We pulled up outside my garden gate just as the sun was going down. I realized straight away that something was wrong, because the front door was wide open and all the lights in the house were ablaze. From the back of the house I heard an explosive crash, mingled with the sound of breaking glass and some furious cursing that I instantly identified as having come from my father.

'You'd better wait out here,' I told Mrs Catlin and, hanging my helmet on the cycle's twist grip, headed straight towards the front door.

I saw my father come staggering down the hallway that led to the kitchen, the scene behind him one of wreckage and destruction. And, to my horror, I saw that there was a pistol in his right hand; I had never known that my father kept a gun in the house, although I knew that he kept several at the club where he was a member.

When he saw me standing in the open doorway he grinned, but the look in his eyes was far from cheerful.

'Well, well!' he roared drunkenly. 'If it isn't my son, the Man! Come to see your father, have you, boy? Come to collect your birthday present, eh? Like to see it, would you?'

I felt rooted to the spot with fear and loathing. I had never seen him so wild before, so totally unlike the brusque but kindly man I had known as a child. When had he changed so? And how had I failed to see it?

He waved the gun drunkenly in my direction, but I saw in his eyes that the anger was all directed inwards, that it wasn't me he hated nor me at whom he railed so ferociously, but at something within himself, something that he seemed to feel had betrayed him.

'Death, boy!' he cried, almost in tears. 'That's my gift. It's the only thing that's real. The only thing. Death! That's what makes you a man, boy: death. Not life; not living: dying! You can't be a man unless you know death. Unless you know how to die.' His eyes suddenly locked on mine and tears streamed down his face. He screamed, 'I know how to die!' and he thrust the muzzle of the gun under his chin and pulled the trigger. The report was deafening in the narrow hall and, feeling the gorge rise in my throat, I watched as his blood sprayed across the walls and ceiling through the ragged hole in the top of his skull. His body lurched forward and fell to the floor at my feet, the blood splashing across my shoes and the bottoms of my jeans. I turned and threw up, sinking to my knees and retching uncontrollably.

It can only have been seconds later that Mrs Catlin was beside me, her shoulder under my arm, shoving me to my feet. I felt the room reel about me, and I grabbed at her for stability. She winced at the pressure of my grip but said nothing until I was able to stand unaided.

'Stay there,' she said softly, and turned to the corpse at my side. I glanced down at it, and was struck by the utter unreality of the situation. That ungainly lump of bone and meat that lay there was no more my father than a side of beef would have been. Whatever my father had been had left those broken remains and gone – to a better place, I hoped, desperately, a place where his torment might be ended and he could find peace.

Mrs Catlin kneeled at the side of the body and, very carefully, took the gun from its fingers. She turned back to me and put the gun in my hand. I looked down at it stupidly.

'Wait outside,' she said to me.

I walked leaden-footed out of the front door. One or two curious neighbours had begun to gather at the garden gate. I walked towards them and they backed away, wary expressions on their faces. I heard someone say, 'He's got a gun,' and I raised the weapon, wishing someone would just take it from me. Someone screamed and the small crowd scattered, leaving me standing alone beside my motorcycle.

Mrs Catlin joined me seconds later, a small cardboard carton in her hand. I recognized it, without giving the thought conscious acknowledgement, as an ammunition carton.

She strode to the bike and levered it off its stand.

'Put that away,' she said, indicating the pistol. I looked at it, seeming to see it for the first time. It was a snub-nosed .357 revolver, a magnum, probably a Smith and Wesson. I unzipped my jacket and put the gun into the inside pocket. Mrs Catlin handed me my helmet. She thumbed the bike's starter and I climbed on behind her.

'Shouldn't we—?' I began to say, and she pulled away, riding past the little knot of people who had gathered at the end of the street and out onto the main road. I grabbed the handrail as she twisted the throttle to its stop, the bike's front end rising sharply; I wanted to protest, to tell her to stop, but the words wouldn't come. I closed my eyes, wishing that I could as easily close off the image that filled my thoughts, and surrendered myself to whatever Mrs Catlin had in mind.

Chapter 3

BEYOND THE BLIND SPOT

We rode for miles. At first I thought we were going to her house, but she missed both turnings that would have taken us there and, presently, we were out on the narrow, winding B roads far from town.

My mind had begun to settle down a little with the ride, and to gain some perspective on what had happened. Somehow, this flight from the scene seemed a kind of admission of a guilt that did not exist. Why were we running? What had we done wrong? And even if we were guilty of something, it seemed entirely out of character for Mrs Catlin to simply run away from a problem, however serious it might be.

'Mrs Catlin!' I yelled. 'Pull over!'

'Not yet!' she called back, and that seemed to be that.

We rode for almost two hours, well into the darkness of the autumn evening. It was a mild night and soon I could see a scattering of stars in the cloudless sky. Under different circumstances it might have been a very pleasant little jaunt into the countryside, with perhaps a night's camping ahead and some hiking to look forward to in the morning.

'Where are we going?' I demanded.

The bike coasted to a stop and Mrs Catlin killed the engine.

'Right here,' she said.

She waited for me to dismount and then climbed off, pulling the bike onto its stand.

'Look, miss,' I said shortly, 'I want to know what's going on here. Why have we done a runner like this? What have I done wrong?'

'Shaw—' she began, then hesitated; she pulled off her helmet and said quietly, 'Bear with me, please, Shaw. I know what I'm doing. Just . . . trust me. OK?'

I had taken off my own helmet and was ready for a serious argument if she didn't start producing some answers in pretty short order, but the look on her face in the moonlight was so pitiful that all my questions seemed to melt away. I'd never seen her look vulnerable before, and for a second it seemed as though she had lost far more today than I had. I shrugged and said, 'OK. What now?'

'We need to find somewhere to spend tonight,' she said. 'In the morning I'll explain everything. And, Shaw – I mean, everything. All right?'

I nodded.

'Scout around in those trees,' she said. 'I'll move the bike off the road.'

I was about to suggest that I was better equipped to handle the bike over rough ground, but thought better of it; it probably wasn't true and, besides, I could hardly send her off alone in the darkness to find us somewhere to camp. Feeling about as necessary as a walking stick to a fish I tromped off towards the trees she had indicated.

Even in the bright moonlight the country around us was largely indistinguishable and the small stand of trees was nothing more than a black silhouette against the skyline. I recalled that there was a small torch in one of the bike's panniers and turned to call out to Mrs Catlin to fetch it. A little circle of light was already bobbing up from the road behind me. I turned and waded into the undergrowth around the trees.

With no warning the ground suddenly gave way beneath my feet. I gave a yelp of surprise and slid down a rough incline for a distance of perhaps fifteen feet before hitting hard packed dirt. My knees buckled and I landed painfully on my backside, surrounded by total darkness with only a small patch of moonlight above me for orientation.

Seconds later I saw the light of the torch flash down through the opening and heard Mrs Catlin's voice.

'Shaw?' she called.

'I'm down here,' I replied, rather stating the obvious. 'Stay away from—'

A shower of dirt preceded Mrs Catlin's ungainly landing at my side.

'You were saying?' she gasped breathlessly.

'I was suggesting,' I told her, 'that you avoid the edge of the hole as the ground was rather loose and you might fall in.'

'Pity you didn't tell me quicker,' she said, getting up.

'Actually,' I observed, 'I had thought it would be self-evident to anyone with a modicum of common sense.'

Mrs Catlin shone the torch around in the darkness, muttering something about 'common sense' being a contradiction in terms, and then said, 'Let's have a look down this way.'

'We'll get lost,' I told her.

'In a hole in the ground?' she said.

'It's obviously a pothole of some kind,' I said. 'They sometimes go on for miles.'

'I know that,' she told me. 'So tie the end of this to something.'

She handed me a ball of twine that she had had in her pocket. I decided not to ask her why she was carrying a large ball of string around with her (she'd probably say it was in case she fell down a hole – I could tell she was in that kind of mood) and tied the end of it to a large root in the slope down which we had both fallen.

'Happy now?' Mrs Catlin asked.

'Not especially,' I told her.

She shone the torch in her face so that I could see how devastated this left her and then she turned and marched off into the darkness. Playing out the ball of string I followed her.

The ball was about three-quarters done with no end to the tunnel in sight when the slight tension in the string suddenly vanished. I snatched up the loose end and found that it was only about six feet long, the end looking like it had been cut clean through.

'Uh, Mrs Catlin—' I said, for she was marching on ahead of me, unaware of our potential difficulty.

'What is it, Shaw?' she called back over her shoulder. 'Have you stepped on a mole or something?'

I ignored the sarcasm and said simply, 'The string appears to have broken.'

Mrs Catlin turned and shone the torch directly onto the end of the string.

'It's been cut,' she said, looking at me accusingly.

'I didn't do it!' I told her. 'It must have been—' I was about to say that the ball must have been made up of two separate lengths of string, but I knew that that wasn't the case. The string had felt as though it had broken as I played it out. I was sure of that.

'Let's find the other end,' I suggested. 'I'll tie them together.'

We backtracked and easily found the length of string lying on the floor of the passage. I bent down to grasp the end of it and as my fingers touched it

I was standing about three feet further along the tunnel, my hand still reaching for the end of the piece of string that was now behind me.

I straightened up, thinking my eyes had played tricks on me in the semi-darkness. I turned and bent down to the end of the string

and it was nowhere in sight. I looked over my shoulder and saw that the end was three feet behind me once again.

I looked at Mrs Catlin. She had a puzzled expression on her face, the kind I had often seen her wearing when studying a piece of unusual art whose meaning escaped her.

'What's happening here?' I asked.

She shook her head. 'It's like . . .' she began, and faltered. She handed me the torch. 'You watch me,' she said, 'and see if you can make sense of it.'

I shone the torch on her as she walked toward the end of the string where it lay in the dirt. She bent down and her fingers almost touched it

but she was too far along; she had somehow missed it. She turned and reached for it again

and missed it by about three feet, yet I couldn't see how. Her fingers had been right on it and then . . .

'Blind spot,' I said slowly.

Mrs Catlin looked at me.

'Watch,' I said.

I stood upright and slowly walked toward the point in the passage marked by the neatly cut end of the length of string. Forewarned I still almost missed it but

there it was, like an all-over blind spot, as though for a tiny fraction of a second all sensory input was cut off. I turned back to Mrs Catlin.

'Did you see it?' I demanded.

'No,' she said, puzzled.

'No, of course not,' I said. 'If you had it wouldn't be a blind spot, would it?'

'You aren't making much sense, Shaw,' she told me, and I could tell that she was losing her patience.

'There's something in the tunnel,' I said, 'something right there where the string stops, that blanks out all sensation, both for anyone crossing it and anyone watching . . .'

'Preposterous!' Mrs Catlin said.

'So *you* explain it!' I snapped, striding forward and, in my annoyance, completely missing the odd sensation.

'I can't,' Mrs Catlin said, 'and I don't intend to try. Now come along; when you interrupted me with this nonsense I had just spotted daylight up ahead.'

27

She turned and walked away, ignoring my muttered complaints, and I was obliged to follow.

Twenty yards or so further on I too saw what I had originally thought Mrs Catlin had mistakenly referred to as 'daylight' – surely, I had thought, she meant 'moonlight'. Yet the fine golden ray that shone so brilliantly through a narrow gap in the passage ahead of us could, I realized, only be the light of the sun. Which was, of course, ridiculous.

I pressed along behind her and together we peered through the narrow gap, which ran from the floor of the passage to a point some twenty feet overhead; at its widest point, which was a foot or so above my head, it was just about wide enough for a person to worm through. The slightly lower section that we were trying to peer through was about eight inches wide and tapered down to a ragged point at its base.

I stared over Mrs Catlin's shoulder and felt my heart hammer in my chest at the sight that met my disbelieving eyes. Beyond the gap lay a landscape the like of which I had never even dreamed of. I appeared to be looking down the lush slope of a semi-tropical valley. Trees of an entirely alien shape and appearance marched away on all sides, and the ground around them was carpeted in a yellowish-green grass that was littered with the most gorgeous red and yellow flowers I had ever seen. A small river bisected the valley slightly to our left, its source somewhere below the level on which we stood. In the far distance, on a horizon that was wreathed in mist, I could make out a jagged line of purple mountains, their peaks capped with snow. And overhead, the sun, impossibly, was a brilliant shower of gold close to its zenith, the sky around it a dazzling, cloudless, cobalt blue.

I turned away from the gap and leaned against the side of the tunnel, too dazed to speak.

Presently, Mrs Catlin turned to me and said, far too briskly to be convincing, 'Well, Shaw, I don't know about you but I'm about ready to wake up now. What do you say?'

I waved my hands aimlessly and said, 'Sure, why not? It's the only explanation that makes any sense.'

I glanced at Mrs Catlin and found her pinching herself. It didn't seem to be doing any good.

'I've an idea,' I said brightly. 'Since we're obviously not going to wake up just yet why don't we take a closer look at that valley? After all, what harm can it do?'

'Absolutely none,' Mrs Catlin agreed. 'Would you care to go first?'

I turned to the gap and looked for some kind of foothold that would allow me to climb to the point at which I could squirm through it. Eventually I accepted Mrs Catlin's assistance and found myself halfway through the crevice and, rather startlingly, looking down a gently sloping rock face that didn't reach the floor of the valley for about thirty feet.

I turned to Mrs Catlin and, bracing my feet against the sides of the crevice, helped her to join me. In a moment she was beside me on the narrow ledge that abutted the crevice, her arms wrapped around me in a most uncharacteristic display of helplessness. I was shocked by how tiny and frail she felt, and for the first time realized that she was not entirely the iron lady she would have had people believe. We stood for a few seconds without moving, staring out at the valley of which we were suddenly a part, conscious of the heat of the sun on our warm clothing and the incredible fragrances that were carried to us on the light breeze.

'If this *is* a dream,' I whispered, 'then everything else I've ever seen must have been an illusion. Because this is the most real thing I have *ever* seen.'

Mrs Catlin seemed to become aware of my arms around her and promptly eased herself out of my grasp.

'Let's save the metaphysical debate until we've climbed down from here, shall we?' she suggested.

I resisted the urge to push her off the narrow ledge and instead explored the possibilities of a more dignified descent.

'Take off your shoes,' Mrs Catlin said, beginning to remove her own. 'This slope is solid enough for us to climb down barefoot if we're careful.'

I pulled off my shoes and socks and threw them down to the base of the slope. Then, side by side, we made our descent.

In a matter of moments we had reached the level ground and were pulling our shoes back on. I glanced back up the slope and confirmed something that I had suspected when I first stepped out onto the ledge: the crevice was situated part-way up the side of a huge cliff face. Its height was unguessable but was at least a couple of hundred feet, and probably a lot more. Its breadth stretched into the trees on both sides for as far as the eye could see.

'At least we won't get lost,' I said. 'This cliff must be visible for miles.'

Mrs Catlin nodded and walked off at right angles to the base of the cliff, her step slow and measured and her gaze sweeping the nearest trees, as though searching for something.

'What are you looking for?' I asked.

'Have you ever seen trees like these before?' she asked me.

There wasn't anything in that valley that looked remotely familiar, but the trees were definitely its most striking feature. They were tall, rangy things, as black as ink and gnarled and twisted like something pulled from a bonfire. Their branches, which were confined to the uppermost third of their height, grew in a funnel shape up and out from the trunk, and were covered in a dense mass of bottle-green leaves and purple flowers. They weren't the only trees in the valley, but they were the most prolific and by far the most striking. Yet even their more commonplace fellows did not seem at all familiar to me.

I said as much, then added, 'But there are probably hundreds of species of trees I've never seen. If this valley really is what it looks like I'd be very surprised to see the kind of trees we have back home.'

Mrs Catlin glanced back over her shoulder and asked me what I'd meant by that particular choice of phrase.

'Well, let's put it this way,' I said: 'I don't think we're in Kansas anymore.'

Mrs Catlin gave me a sardonic grin but said nothing.

'Let me put it another way,' I ventured. 'Wherever this place is, it isn't anywhere on Earth.'

The grin became a saccharine smile as she said, 'And am I then to take it that you are now accepting this as reality and not the product of one of our imaginations?'

'Well, I know I couldn't imagine anything as vivid as this,' I told her. 'And since I appear to have a full set of memories I doubt that *I* am a product of *your* imagination.'

Mrs Catlin dismissed my reasoning with a wave of her hand. 'I have a thorough imagination,' she told me. 'If I imagine a thing I supply it with a complete set of background details. You could quite easily be a product of my subconscious.'

I avoided suggesting that if that were the case she should seek psychoanalysis; I knew that she was merely being pedantic while she came to terms with what she already knew but found so unacceptable – that what I had just said was the plain and simple truth.

I pulled off my jacket and my sweater, and still felt over-dressed even in just jeans and a T-shirt. Mrs Catlin had taken off her own jacket and sweater and had unbuttoned her shirt to what I considered an indecent degree. Given the heat, however, I could hardly blame her.

I noticed, with a sick feeling, that the bottoms of my jeans were still caked in blood. And suddenly the realization of what the blood meant hit me with all the force of a runaway truck. My father – my *father* – was dead. Gone. The only person in my life that I could ever have truly said I loved. And the guilt was more than I could bear. I could feel the tears running down my face, and with a mounting sense of horror I heard myself begin to sob. Mrs Catlin half turned, and all I wanted to do was to run, to run and hide and not let her see me. But there was nowhere to run, and no one left to run to. Before I knew what I was doing I was on my knees in the soft, yellow grass and she was kneeling in front of me, her arms around me and my head buried in her shoulder. I wanted to die, but I knew that I wasn't likely to be that lucky.

Presently I drew back from her, not meeting her eyes, and she slowly arose and walked some distance from me, her back turned. I thanked her silently as I pulled myself together and then said, my voice almost as steady as I would have liked, 'What now?'

I saw her draw a breath, as though steeling herself to make a big decision.

'Shaw,' she said, 'this is real.'

I nodded, then realized she wasn't looking at me and said, 'I agree.'

Now she did look at me. There was an animation in her eyes I'd only ever seen there on a handful of previous occasions. There was also concern, which I knew was for me.

'I want to . . . look around,' she said, seeming to avoid a particular choice of phrase. 'And I don't mean just give the place a cursory once-over, I mean . . .'

'You want to explore,' I said, grinning at her childish excitement and at the same time sharing it.

She nodded, blushing like a schoolgirl on her first date. Part of this desire to explore was, I knew, an attempt to distract me from my grief, and I was grateful to her for that. But there was something else going on in her mind, something deeper that I didn't quite understand. What I did understand was her excitement at being here, now that we had begun to accept the truth of our situation – whatever that was – and it was an excitement I found I shared.

'So what are we waiting for?' I demanded enthusiastically. 'Let's explore!'

Chapter 4

REVELATION

We set off down the hillside towards the river, at the same time striking out away from the cliff face. The going wasn't particularly difficult, although once or twice we had to check the speed of our descent to prevent ourselves from reaching the river rather more precipitately than we might have liked.

As we walked we kept up a running commentary with one another on the flora and fauna all around us, trying to outdo one another at spotting something new or particularly interesting. And since everything was both new and positively fascinating it was a game whose novelty value never seemed to wane.

We reached the bank of the river about halfway through the afternoon, by which time the cliff was several miles behind us. I looked back at it and gained yet another perspective on its construction. Seen from this distance it looked almost like a dam, except that its surface was too uneven and too obviously natural to be man-made. It filled the valley like a great wedge, and at its summit was actually higher than the uppermost slopes of the valley sides, though whether the cliff extended beyond the limits of the valley sides I couldn't tell.

Mrs Catlin kneeled down on the grassy bank of the river and

peered down into the clear, swiftly moving water. The surface lay several feet below the level of the bank, and beneath it I could see silver shapes darting to and fro. Mrs Catlin placed her hand slowly into the water. I stood very still, trying not to breathe; with a flash of motion she flung a fish onto the bank, grinning from ear to ear – tickling fish was one of the few things *I* had taught *her*.

'Go and get some firewood,' she said, reaching into the water once more.

I collected some dry wood from amongst the surrounding under-growth and found a clear space close to the river bank where I began to build a fire. I used some straight twigs to make a spit for the fish and put them to one side ready for when Mrs Catlin had finished her 'angling'. I pondered on the various methods that I might use to get the fire started, but eventually convenience won out over ingenuity and I put my box of matches next to the spit in readiness.

Mrs Catlin eventually pulled three fair-sized fish from the river and used my penknife to clean them while I got the fire started.

'It will be dark soon,' she said, handing me the first fish. 'You'd better plan on keeping that fire lit until morning.'

I gave her a puzzled glance.

'Something moved in the bushes at the other side of the river while I was getting the last fish,' she said, adding, 'Something big but very stealthy. I almost didn't see it.'

I nodded, looking around me; suddenly, the idyllic landscape had taken on a menacing aspect.

The potential danger did nothing to dull our appetites, however, and the fish were delicious – though I, for one, thought they could have used some salt. By the time we had finished and I had stockpiled some additional firewood the sun had sunk low enough on the horizon for the treeline to cut off its light entirely. Mrs Catlin and I sat close together by our fire, neither of us speaking, each drinking in the alien sounds and smells around us, the darkness accentuating our non-visual senses and bringing the landscape into a new, different kind of focus. I don't think I had ever felt so alone in my whole life as I did at that moment, yet the feeling brought with it no accompanying sense of loneliness, which surprised me.

I looked across at Mrs Catlin, seeing the light of the fire making strange, constantly shifting patterns of shadows across her face, and I remembered a promise she had made earlier in the day, back in our old world.

'You promised me an explanation, miss,' I said quietly. 'I think I'm about ready for it.'

She looked at me; her eyes were amber in the firelight, alien, strangely catlike.

'Are you, Shaw?' she asked. 'Truly?'

I nodded.

She looked into the fire again and said quietly, 'Once upon a time, there was a beautiful young woman. She was an idealist, a visionary – a dreamer. She would have been a real child of the Sixties, except that at this time the Sixties were over a decade away. She was a source of constant distress to her parents, and spent some months in a mental home during her mid-teens because – the doctors said – she was suffering from delusions.

'The delusion she was suffering from,' Mrs Catlin said, 'was that on the North Yorkshire moors there was a cave through which it was possible to pass into another world.

'The doctors said she was a living example of the "Alice in Wonderland" complex, and put her on lots of drugs in order to bring her back down to reality. She was just clever enough to make them think they had succeeded.

'Later, she went back to the cave and found that it was only a cave after all. She settled down, got married, and started a family. She forgot all about the cave, the valley beyond it, and the foolish dreams she had had as a child.

'One night not long after the birth of her only son she felt an irresistible urge to go back to that cave, ostensibly to prove to herself once and for all that there really was no other world, no magic doorway to an alien land; the real reason, of course, was that the birth of her son had reawakened in her the dreams and fantasies she had cherished in her own childhood.

'She went back to the cave and found, to her considerable surprise, that the valley had come back. She spent months visiting the cave in secret; she never ventured into the valley, she just sat high up in the fissure in the cave wall and gazed at the other world. Then, one day, it was gone again.

'Over a period of several years she studied the appearance and disappearance of the valley, eventually finding a pattern to the manifestations. She plotted, to a high degree of accuracy considering she had no training in mathematics, when each appearance would occur, and for how long it would last.

'As I'm sure you can imagine, the urge to confide all of this to someone – someone who would not try to have her committed again – was irresistible. She found the right person quite by chance. A friend had asked her to babysit her eight-year-old daughter, and in the child she found the nearest thing to a kindred spirit she had ever met. She told the child everything, and the child believed her. The child kept the woman's secret, and she never once doubted the truth of what she had been told, even though she never saw the proof of it with her own eyes.'

Mrs Catlin turned and looked at me, and I felt a shiver run through me.

'—Until today,' she added. 'The woman, Shaw, was your mother. And the eight-year-old child was me.'

I stared at her in silence until she was forced to turn her gaze away.

'You've lied to me my whole life,' I said; I could scarcely believe how angry I felt.

'I've never lied to you,' Mrs Catlin said.

'You've not exactly been liberal with the truth!' I yelled, jumping to my feet.

Mrs Catlin was on her own feet in an instant.

'Get that tone out of your voice, Shaw,' she snapped. 'And sit right back down!'

I sat. Despite the alien jungle that surrounded us, and the revelations of the last few minutes, Mrs Catlin seemed incapable of abrogating her authority over me. Faced with some of the implications that this hinted at I felt my anger fading away, but not the feeling of betrayal that had sparked it.

Mrs Catlin sat down and looked at me intently until I found the strength to look back. I was astounded to see that there were tears in her eyes, although her features remained composed and, when she spoke, her voice was steady.

'Your mother,' she said quietly, 'gave me a dream. I built my whole life in such a way that when I eventually came here I would be ready for it. I have to say that I don't feel that time has yet come. But when your father . . .' She paused, then said, 'When I first met you as your teacher I didn't know who you were; it was a coincidence, Shaw, nothing more than that. But when I found out who you were and that your mother had died, I was determined that her dream would live on, not just in me, but in you too. My own parents had moved away from Yorkshire when I was nine – you were barely two years old, so it's no surprise you don't remember me – and I lost all contact with your family; I think my mother had never really approved of my friendship with your mother. At any rate, when I found out that you were her son, and that she had died before imparting her dream to you, that was when I became – well, obsessed, I suppose – with passing on all that I had learned to you. I had intended to tell you about the cave next year, when you'd finished your final exams; it didn't seem right to tell you any sooner. But I knew that the synchronization between the two worlds was functioning now, and when your father . . . did what he did, I made the decision on the spur of the moment that *now* was the time.

'I've never tried to deceive you, Shaw. I've only ever wanted what was best for you. If that sounds like a cliché then I'm sorry, but that's the way it is.'

She picked up some wood and threw it on the fire.

'What about all that stuff in the cave?' I demanded. 'And when we got here, why pretend not to know where we were? What was all that about?'

'Shaw,' she said wearily, 'you have to appreciate that until today I'd never seen this world. I'd believed in it, in my heart, but to be confronted with it like that – I was almost in shock when we got here, and because I hadn't had time to tell you about your mother I just, well, I suppose I just pretended to be as much in the dark as you were. And anyway, you figured it out pretty quickly for yourself, didn't you?'

'But the cave,' I said, 'the blind spot—'

'I knew nothing about that,' she said. 'Your mother never spoke of it. She believed that the fissure in the cave wall was the contact point between the worlds. I think now that she was wrong; the blind spot, as you call it, was the actual transition point. But I knew none of that at the time.' I opened my mouth to speak but she held up her hand to silence me.

'Let's get some sleep,' she said. 'If you're going to let this affect your decision about what we do tomorrow then I'd rather you made that decision in the morning, and not tonight.'

I stared at her as she settled down for the night. I was conscious of the fact that, in the pocket of my jacket, I still carried the pistol that she had taken from my father, and for the briefest of instants I toyed with the slightly sadistic idea of shooting her through both kneecaps and then leaving her here while I made my way home.

It was the thought of the word 'home' that banished any feelings of retribution from my mind.

I added a few green leaves to the fire, although I didn't really expect any predators to bother us in the night, and lay down some distance from Mrs Catlin – but not so far away that, should she awaken before morning, she would not be able to see me. I think I was asleep the moment my head touched the ground.

Chapter 5

TURNING POINT

We spent three days following the river in a direction that we had fairly arbitrarily designated as north. Its course followed an almost geometrically straight line, and its bank was, for the most part at least, fairly easily navigable. There were stretches where we had to track some distance inland in order to avoid impassable obstacles or perilously steep slopes, but these presented no real hardships and we'd both traversed more difficult country in the hills of our native Yorkshire.

We had a good many discussions during those three days, all of them concerning the revelations of that first night. Some of these 'discussions' were little more than arguments, ending with Mrs Catlin accusing me of being childish or with my stomping off to sulk for a couple of hours. Some of them were a bit traumatic in other ways, because we had both 'lost' my mother at an early age and memories of her were painful: the sense of a life that had been needlessly wasted was strong in both of us. But the majority of our talks were simply an examination of the ways in which Mrs Catlin had shaped both our educations and the probable uses to which we might put what we had learned. I think we were both taking it for granted that this world would be inhabited by some from of intelligent life, though neither of us ever stated the fact outright.

I think it was inevitable that the peace and tranquillity of our sur-roundings – and the persistent absence of Mrs Catlin's half-glimpsed predator – would lead us to become careless. What was surprising was that when we did make our first serious mistake it was over something that we were both perfectly capable of avoiding.

I was taking my turn at catching breakfast from the river when I heard a sudden cracking sound above me, followed by a furious rustling in the branches overhead. I didn't need to look to know what it was: a deadfall. A branch – a big one by the sound of it – that had been slowly rotting away at its juncture with the tree trunk was now finally breaking free of the tree to which it had been attached. I threw myself in what I hoped was the right direction to avoid a direct hit – a deadfall can kill – and lost my footing on the grassy bank. I slid most of the way to the edge of the river, regained enough of my balance to keep from going in head first, and then the partly rotted branch came crashing down directly in front of me. I was congratulating myself on my quick reflexes when the branch flopped over virtually into my arms, lashing me painfully across the bridge of the nose, and the next thing I knew, both the branch and I were hitting the surface of the water. In far less time than it takes to tell, I found myself being rapidly carried away by the current.

I clung to the branch desperately, gasping for air in the sur-prisingly cold water. I tried to get my bearings as the river sent me hurtling downstream, suddenly very much aware that it was carrying me further and further away from Mrs Catlin. And as innocuous as this country had so far proved to be – careless mistakes notwithstanding – I did not relish the prospect of either of us having to trek through it alone.

The river, as I was beginning to realize to my dismay, had something of an undertow, and more than once I felt my legs being sucked down, only my increasingly precarious grip on the tree limb saving me from going under. I was scrabbling for a better handhold when I chanced to glance back in the direction I had come. Mrs Catlin was standing on the river bank – miles away from me, it seemed, although in reality it can hardly have been more than a few hundred yards (I had not been in the water for quite as long as it had seemed) – and was gazing intently in my direction.

I attempted to wave, which proved to be a mistake. When my head broke surface again it was to witness the most insanely reckless act I had ever known Mrs Catlin to commit. She sprinted several feet along the river bank and dived in.

I stared incredulously at her pathetically tiny figure as she began to swim towards me, my own plight suddenly forgotten in the light of the far greater peril into which my former teacher had thrown herself. She couldn't possibly know how treacherous these waters were, and while I knew from past experience that she was an excellent swimmer she would have had to have been an Olympic contender and a lifeguard all rolled into one to have stood a chance of ever catching up to me.

Imagine my amazement, then, when bare minutes later she was clutching breathlessly to the log at my side.

'You idiot!' I yelled over the din of the river as it roared in our ears. 'Why didn't you stay on the bank?'

'I . . . can . . .' she gasped, 'swim . . . faster than . . . I can . . . run!'

I glared at her, and she grinned back at me.

'Sorry, Shaw,' she gasped, 'but when I saw you being swept away . . . I guess I don't get any brownie points for this, huh?'

I shook my head, wondering what on Earth could have possessed her. But she was still wearing that idiotic grin, like she'd done the most sensible thing in the world and couldn't understand why I was making such an issue out of it.

'Anyway,' she said, 'it looks like it's pretty academic now.'

She pointed downriver and as I followed her gaze I felt my heart sink. The river came to an abrupt apparent end a couple of hundred yards further on, a line of white water marking the top of a waterfall over which we could be hurled in a matter of seconds. It was impossible to tell what lay beyond the fall: it could have been a drop of only a few feet, or it could have been hundreds; and even if it was only a short drop, it could have been into rapids that would flay us alive.

'Swim!' I yelled, striking out for the nearer bank.

I don't have Mrs Catlin's grace in the water, but I have twice her muscle power, and had she not been with me I think maybe I could have made it – maybe. As it was, I could see that she would never reach the bank in time, and with a curse I changed course to intercept her.

'What are you—?' she cried.

I grasped one of her hands in mine.

'We're going over!' I yelled.

I caught a brief glimpse of her eyes above the surging water, wide and filled with sudden fear, and then my body was dashed bone-jarringly over smooth rocks, water engulfed me, and I felt a sinking sensation that had nothing to do with the river's undertow. We had gone over the waterfall, and the drop was rather more than a few feet.

The view was spectacular. Under almost any other circumstances it would have been a pleasure to look at it, but things being what they were I barely had time to give it a single glance. I had a brief impression of a bowl-shaped depression, several miles wide, covered with an assortment of bushes and small trees, and directly below us a lake that filled one corner of the depression, its shore a narrow strip of sandy beach.

That was as much as I had time to take in, because in the next instant we had hit the surface of the lake.

The turbulence of the waterfall eased our landing somewhat – without it I think we would have been killed – but not so much that the impact didn't drive from my lungs what little air was left in them. Tightening my grip on Mrs Catlin's hand, and fighting the near-irresistible urge to inhale no matter what the cost, I struck out for the calmer waters away from the base of the falls.

My head broke the surface and I gave a great shout, flooding my lungs with air. My vision was a mass of purple spots and there was a ringing in my ears like the inside of a bell tower, but at that moment my only thought was for the limp, seemingly lifeless woman who floated at my side.

I rolled over onto my back and pulled her face above the water. She wasn't breathing. I tilted her head back, pinched her nose, and gave her mouth-to-mouth. I felt my senses blur with the added effort, my own body badly deoxygenated. I thrashed about in the water to keep myself conscious and after several more attempts at reviving her I was rewarded with a great hacking cough from her and the feel of her body convulsing in my arms as her lungs began to work for themselves once more.

She spat out a great deal of water and began to move her arms weakly, assisting me in moving us slowly through the water. I found myself marvelling at the woman's sense of self-possession; her will-power was indefatigable.

We reached the nearer shore of the lake in a matter of minutes and, dragging ourselves out of the water, collapsed onto the narrow strip of beach.

It was some time before either of us felt like moving, but we were given little opportunity to enjoy our brief respite or our relief at having survived the plunge over the waterfall. For, as we lay there, I became aware that we were no longer alone. Opening my eyes, I found that we were now surrounded by a small group of people.

Chapter 6

TWO CITIES

My instinctive reaction, born of a mindless xenophobia of which I was instantly ashamed, was to reach for the gun in my jacket pocket. The jacket, of course, was lying on the bank of the river, probably several miles away now, and the gun with it.

I pushed myself slowly to my knees and regarded the little knot of people before me. To all intents and purposes they were human beings, men and women, a fact that somehow failed to reassure me: human beings. I reminded myself, were probably the most dangerous species my own world had ever produced.

The group surrounding Mrs Caltin and me was made up of six men and one woman. Further along the shoreline of the lake were a couple of dozen of their fellows, all of whom seemed largely unconcerned by the arrival of two strangers, two aliens, in their midst.

Aliens.

The word filled my mind like the tolling of a death knell. *They* were not the aliens here, we were. Outward appearances aside, these were not 'people' who surrounded us, but creatures; their seeming resemblance to Mrs Catlin and me was, in all probability, only of the most superficial kind.

And yet . . .

They seemed so normal-looking, and not in the least bit intimidating. In fact, the small group nearest us seemed as wary of us as I was of them.

They were all healthy-looking individuals – by human standards – though a trifle on the short side, the tallest of them being several inches shorter than myself. Their skins were a light tan colour, their hair dark brown or black. The men all wore beards, though these, like their hair, were trimmed quite short; the women were each endowed with a full head of hair, so long on some of them that it trailed almost to their ankles. The only garments that were in evidence were loin cloths and something that looked like a short waistcoat or vest, open at the front and tied in place with a single thong or lace; these were worn mostly by the women, although several of the men sported them as well. On their feet they wore low-strapped sandals. All of their garments appeared to be made from tanned leather.

Appeared. There it was again, that doubt. Their garments couldn't actually be leather, not unless this world's animal life included cows. Of course, since it seemed to include humans there was no reason why it *shouldn't* include cows too, but somehow the notion seemed faintly . . . ludicrous.

I nudged Mrs Catlin, who was so far blissfully ignorant of our audience. She rolled over slowly, looked up, and was bolt upright at my side in an instant.

'Shaw,' she said in an intense whisper, 'who are these people?'

I gave her a look and said, in the same stage whisper, 'Oh, I'm sorry, I forgot to ask. Hang on, I'll see if any of them is carrying a business card.'

Mrs Catlin returned my look with enough venom to poison a rattlesnake and muttered something unintelligible.

The small crowd around us were now doing a little muttering of their own, exchanging furtive glances with one another and pointing coyly at, I supposed, our clothing. Somehow, this wasn't quite what I'd been expecting from my first encounter with an alien race.

In an attempt at taking the initiative I got to my feet and held out my hand to the nearest of the men in the group. He looked at it with a hint of curiosity but not much else.

'David Shaw,' I introduced myself, adding, 'Explorer. Greetings from the people of Earth.'

The man turned to one of his fellows and spoke at some length in a language like none I had ever heard before. Then he turned back to me and said something that was clearly intended for my benefit yet meant no more to me than had his previous monologue.

I glanced at Mrs Catlin for guidance. She frowned and said, 'We appear to face a variety of choices.'

I must have looked puzzled.

She indicated the waterfall behind us.

'We can't go back the way we came,' she said, 'and without a local guide I doubt we'd find our way back to the cave via any other route.' She waited for this to sink in; it didn't take long. If we couldn't find the cave again then we were no longer explorers: we were immigrants.

'To find a reliable guide,' she went on, 'we really need to speak the local language – however poorly. To do that, we need to get these people to teach it to us. And the best way to do that is to assimilate some of their culture.'

I understood what she meant; learning the language idiomatically was probably our only option, and that would be easier if there was some kind of social set-up to draw on.

But . . . I shook my head in wonder. Now that she'd said it it seemed like the most obvious observation imaginable. Yet for her to have reached it within minutes of being faced with the necessity left me stunned: was she really that self-possessed? Or was I missing something in her reaction?

I looked around, groping for my own equivalent of her powers of reasoning.

'It doesn't look as though they've got much of a culture,' I said, indicating their clothing. 'But I know what you're getting at.'

'I'm glad to see you didn't sleep through all my lessons,' Mrs Catlin said sweetly.

'Only the truly dull ones,' I replied, admiration giving way to a more familiar irritation at the woman.

The little gathering around us was beginning to break up; it seemed as though our novelty value had worn off. The man to whom I had spoken was still looking at us with the nearest thing to interest I'd yet seen in these people, so I decided that he was the one on whom we would concentrate our efforts at becoming integrated into their group.

I walked slowly around him, knowing that he would be compelled to turn to keep me in view. When he was facing back towards the main body of the group further down the shoreline I began to walk towards them. Picking up on my initiative, Mrs Catlin moved around to the man's other side and then began walking parallel to me. Between us, we drew the man on. He seemed to get the idea pretty quickly, and soon we were walking through the ranks of his fellows, and drawing one or two genuinely curious glances from some of them.

I had wondered what they were doing here, since a cursory examination of the landscape around the lake revealed no obvious signs of habitation – and their activities at the water's edge seemed to be confined to some energetic fooling around. It was with a hint of disappointment that I realized that this was precisely what it did amount to. I had a sudden vision of Mrs Catlin and I ending up in the alien equivalent of a California beach-bum community, where work was a dirty word and 'hanging out' was the ultimate social achievement. It wasn't that I objected to such a lifestyle, it was just that I'd been hoping for something a little more exciting. As things turned out, I was to get my reckless wish, and to live to regret it.

The outing to the lake lasted almost until sunset, during which time Mrs Catlin and I joined in some co-ordinated swimming, played a game not unlike tag though with some physical rough-and-tumble that would have been more suited to American football, and listened to what I took to be a poetry recital – Mrs Catlin agreed with me on that one, and she had a better ear for such things than I have. It was after the recital that things started to break up and people began to make their way away from the lake via a well-beaten trail through the woods. Sticking close to our native guide, Mrs Catlin and I followed.

The path took us about a mile through the woodland which abruptly gave way to open savannah, a broad plain covered in lush yellow grass that grew to waist height in places and that stretched away for as far ahead as the eye could see.

And out on that golden plain, scarcely half a mile away, stood the last thing I had been expecting to see. I had expected that these people would have come from – at best – a village of crude but intelligently constructed wooden huts, perhaps surrounded by pens for livestock or a few fields planted with grains or vegetables. What I had never in my wildest dreams imagined was that our destination, and their home, would be a city.

I touched Mrs Catlin's arm.

'I don't understand,' I said quietly.

'I think I do,' she replied thoughtfully. 'But let's wait till we get a little closer.'

We moved out onto the plain and made our way through the grass towards the city. So springy and resilient was the grass that it left little or no trace of our passage, and gave no hint at all of the journey our companions must obviously have made through it earlier in the day.

As we drew closer to the city I began to see what it was that Mrs Catlin had deduced about it. That it was the home of our new-found friends was certain, but equally as certain was the fact that they had not built it. And the closer we drew to it the more convinced of this I became. By the time we had actually passed out of the grassland and were walking the deserted avenues of the ancient structure I no longer even believed that it had been built by their most remote ancestors, or by any recognizable ancestors of humanity. What it was about the place that made me believe it had been built by a non-human – and non-humanoid – race I couldn't have said with any degree of certainty. Perhaps it was the obsessive nature of the architecture – the place was all circles – or possibly it was the size and placement of doors and windows; more likely it was the cumulative impact of a hundred small details, many of them operating on a subliminal level, that served to convince me.

I have said that the city was all circles, and this was certainly the impression it gave. The taller buildings were regular cylinders, some of them over twenty storeys high, and the smaller ones were domes or flat-bottomed spheres. The doors and windows were all circular, and some of the doors were not at ground level. I wondered if this had been the dwelling place of a winged race, but I dismissed the idea instantly – fliers would not have felt comfortable out here in the open; it would have left them too exposed to air- and ground-based predators.

I voiced some of my thoughts to Mrs Catlin, and was pleased to find that she agreed with them.

'But be careful,' she advised, 'not to apply Earth logic to situations we find here. Analogues need not be exact, and we can't possibly hope to understand the psychology of any race on this planet – at least, not until we've learned the language. Perhaps not even then.'

I nodded, oddly depressed by what she had said. It seemed to me intolerable that we would always remain aliens in this world, yet why that should have been I couldn't have said with any degree of certainty. I felt an irresistible, quite inexplicable desire to feel myself a part of this world.

'Did you notice the construction of these buildings?' Mrs Catlin asked.

'Yes,' I said. 'All the circles . . .'

'No, no,' she interrupted impatiently, 'the actual construction. Look more closely.'

Not for the first time I resisted the urge to do her some physical violence, and strained my eyes to see what she had spotted that I had missed. I saw it almost immediately, and silently cursed myself for having let her beat me to it.

'No joints,' I muttered. 'Like each building was carved out of a solid lump of marble.'

'You think this is marble?' she demanded, gesturing to a building we were passing close to.

'Well, no,' I said. 'I just meant . . .'

'Let's try to maintain some kind of intellectual integrity, Shaw,' she said stiffly. 'If nothing else, it might keep us alive a little longer.'

I glanced around the silent city streets.

'You think we're in danger here?' I asked.

'Right now? Perhaps not,' she conceded. 'But ultimately? Yes, I believe so. There is something very disturbing about the set-up here, and I can't quite figure out what it is. But the underlying impression is definitely one of menace.'

'That's a bit melodramatic, don't you think?' I suggested.

To my surprise she gave me a rather bashful smile.

'Perhaps you're right,' she said. 'It's been a trying sort of day, and I may be jumping at shadows.'

We said no more as our little procession made its way deeper into the city, but with each deserted avenue that we passed and each bleak and featureless building that stared out at us from its ancient, darkened windows and doors I found myself placing greater and greater credence in what Mrs Catlin had said. The very fact of this city and its incongruous inhabitants indicated either some great natural catastrophe or some act of deliberate malevolence that had changed forever the course of intelligent life on this planet – and changed it, it seemed, for the worse. It wasn't quite like finding a bunch of Neanderthals living in the gutted remains of New York City – the natives were too obviously intelligent for that – but whatever it all meant, it wasn't likely to be a pretty story.

Our eventual destination turned out to be a vast plaza in what I guessed to be the centre of the city. It was an open, circular (naturally) space several hundred yards in diameter, and was bordered by some of the least conventional buildings I had yet seen. The circle motif persisted in them, but here it was worked upon and modified to produce an effect that was vaguely abstract. On the whole, it was more pleasing to the eye than the stark simplicity of the rest of the city.

In the centre of this plaza, and making an unlikely contrast with the magnificent structures around it was a smaller city: a city of tents. Constructions of animal hide and silk over wooden frameworks filled about half of the surface area of the plaza, and although they appeared incredibly primitive in such a setting there was no denying that a high level of craftsmanship had gone into their creation. There was no hint of the makeshift about them – the smallest one that I could see was as big as a bungalow – nor of anything primitive in either design or construction. And, also, their arrangement was not random or unruly but was clearly the result of careful planning and systematic execution.

As we neared the city of tents our group began to break up. I stuck close to my chosen representative, Mrs Catlin flanking him as casually as she could under the circumstances.

We reached what was clearly his own tent and he paused in the open entrance, regarding us closely. Then he made a short but seemingly friendly speech, walked into his tent, and closed the flap behind him.

'I thought this was getting a bit too easy,' I said dryly.

Mrs Catlin tapped her foot, her forehead creased in thought. She was far better travelled than I was and had had first-hand experience of dealing with foreign cultures, so I was more than willing to defer to her judgement where our next move was concerned.

'I think we camp out tonight,' she said at length.

'Why not in one of those buildings?' I suggested. The nights had been pleasant so far, but the idea of sleeping out in the open while surrounded by strangers made me a little nervous.

'No,' Mrs Catlin said. 'They seem to avoid using the buildings themselves, so we should do likewise – there may be some taboo associated with them, or perhaps they just think they're haunted. Either way, we don't want to upset anyone.'

I shrugged and followed her some little distance from the main body of the tents to a space close to one of the surrounding buildings.

'In the morning,' Mrs Catlin said, 'we need to work out who's in charge here. And how we go about obtaining some language lessons.'

Together we settled down on the hard stones of the plaza and did our best to get a good night's sleep, knowing that we were going to need all our wits about us on the following day. It was the worst night's sleep I'd had since leaving our own Earth, and the first one when I really would have felt better for having the reassurance of the gun at my side.

Chapter 7

EARNING OUR KEEP

We stayed in the ancient city for the better part of six months, and if its adoptive inhabitants had a full-time leader then they did a good job of hiding the fact. (We would, eventually, discover that there *was* a spokesperson for the group but that his official duties rarely made it necessary for him to identify himself. We were destined one day to meet him on a professional basis, but it would not be to our advantage.)

On the first morning of our stay at the camp Mrs Catlin and I found ourselves the subject of some kind of town-council meeting. The minutes were a bit difficult for us to follow, and I think we both experienced a moment of concern when the meeting finally broke up and a group of three men approached us.

'Whatever they do,' Mrs Catlin advised, 'offer no resistance. We need to learn all we can from these people. Making enemies is the last thing we want to do.'

'Just so long as they don't turn out to be cannibals,' I replied.

Mrs Catlin cast me a quick look to make sure I wasn't being serious, which made me wonder what we would do if it turned out I was right.

The men seemed friendly enough as they approached us, and at a gesture from one of them we followed the little group to a collection of tents set aside from the rest of the camp. I'd barely noticed these tents the night before – they were smaller and not quite so well made as the others in the city, and looked older; there was evidence of numerous repairs to many of them – but I had wondered briefly at their significance. As we neared them their occupants came out to confront us, and I was genuinely surprised at their appearance. That they were not of the same race as our hosts was instantly apparent, as was the fact that they clearly came from a mixture of racial backgrounds. There were about thirty in all, mostly men, and a cursory examination revealed them to be a mixture of blacks, Orientals, Asians and Caucasians, or rather their equivalents from this world's stock of humanity. They were dressed differently from the others we had already met, their meagre clothing seeming to be a mixture of brightly coloured cottons and silks. The men wore short kilts, wraparounds, held up by belts of knotted leather; the women wore overlapping, loosely layered skirts and brief, chiton-style tops, or no tops at all, a fact that at first caused me some consternation. I wondered briefly how the ultra-conservative Mrs Catlin would react to this latest development, but she seemed entirely oblivious to it. The most major difference in dress between these people and the others was a steel band, about an inch thick, that each wore just above his or her left ankle. Despite their relatively expensive-seeming garments, I don't think that there was an instant, from the moment I first saw these people, that I did not realize that they were slaves. Our hosts fell a long way in my estimations that morning, and never fully recovered.

One of the men who had brought us here to what I now realized were the slave quarters addressed one of the male slaves, an enormous black individual who looked like he'd been carved out of a piece of ebony the size of a station waggon. If our hosts had no nominal leader, I guessed at that moment that their slaves did.

From the manner of both our escort and the black I guessed that we were being put in his care but that we were not to become slaves ourselves. Somehow, this did not seem to me to be much of a distinction. I did not know at that time, of course, just what was the full significance of the bands that the slaves wore on their legs.

In a matter of moments Mrs Catlin and I had been left alone with the slaves, who began to edge slowly towards us.

'Any advice?' I asked Mrs Catlin.

'Sorry, Shaw,' she muttered, 'I seem to have run out of that particular commodity.'

The slaves closed in around us, their manner not overtly threatening but not particularly friendly either. One of them, a red-headed fellow about my height but built like Arnold Schwarzenegger, reached out to Mrs Catlin and tugged at the front of her shirt, as though trying to remove it.

'Knock that off,' I snapped, pushing his hands away.

'It's all right, Shaw,' Mrs Catlin said.

'No, it isn't,' I replied indignantly. 'They may not mind parading about half naked but that's no reason why we have to.'

The redhead, it seemed, hadn't much liked the way I had interrupted him, and he put himself directly in front of me, our bodies almost touching, and gave me the death-eye. I returned it without a blink; I'd played this game at school, and with people a lot bigger than he was. It didn't occur to me at the time, but at school I hadn't been putting my life on the line.

The black put a stop to things before they could develop, barking out an order to Red that sent him skulking away, but not before his expression had told me that I had just made an enemy for life.

The black dispersed the other slaves with a couple of sharp commands, all save one man and one woman. He pushed me towards the man and gestured for Mrs Catlin to accompany the woman. I didn't like the idea of our being split up, but Mrs Catlin went with the other woman without a backward glance, so that appeared to be that.

I accompanied my new guide to where half a dozen other male slaves were waiting and together we set off through the streets of the city. We were heading off at right angles to the avenue down which Mrs Catlin and I had made our entrance to the city of tents, so that in a matter of minutes I was completely lost. The table-top landscape upon which the city was built meant that it was possible to see for vast distances down the radial streets of the metropolis, but the circular nature of its intersecting avenues had a strangely disorientating effect upon my sense of direction, making visual alignment within the city quite difficult. Conscious of the fact that getting seriously lost could turn out to be more than a minor inconvenience I tried to work out the pattern by which the city had been built. It was what Mrs Catlin, in one of her more flippant moods, would have called a three-headache exercise, but as we neared the outskirts of the city I began to see the key to navigating within it: it was all a matter of nested and interlocking circles, punctuated by the lengthy radial streets I had noted earlier. The pattern was unbroken throughout the city: there were no tangents or chords to these circles, only radii and quadrants, with intersecting circles forming lens shapes where they crossed. And the buildings in each city 'block' reflected the shape of the block itself, as described by the pattern of the streets. I gave myself a mental pat on the back for my ingenuity, at the same time wondering just how much use my deductions would prove to be if ever I became separated from my guides – or if ever I elected to separate myself from them, a prospect which, at some point in the future, seemed inevitable. For now, Mrs Catlin and I needed our hosts and their slaves to teach us the local language and to assist us in finding our way back to the cave that would take us back to Earth, but beyond that, and a desire to learn as much of the customs of this land as was possible, I had no intention of remaining among them any longer than I had to – least of all as one of their slaves.

Close to the edge of the city we came upon a building that seemed to be our destination. It was a squat disc, barely two storeys high but a hundred yards wide or more, and filled an entire city block. Its entrance was a shallow arch, eight feet high at its apex and twenty feet wide at its base. The building appeared to have no other openings anywhere along its surface.

We entered and it was several seconds before my eyes adjusted to the gloom within. When they had, I beheld an enormous collection of earthenware vessels, obviously designed for carrying water and of a broad variety of sizes and shapes, littered indiscriminately across the floor. The largest vessel would have held perhaps ten gallons, the smallest only a few pints.

My companions each picked up a pair of vessels and trooped

back out into the street. I grabbed a pair of five-gallon jars, felt their weight, and thought better of it. One of the men gave me a malicious grin as I put them down and selected two slightly smaller containers. Empty, they weighed almost as much as the water they could hold. I noticed that none of the others present, not even one skinny individual who was a good head shorter than me, had any difficulty in hefting a pair of five-gallon jars each. I rather peevishly put it down to their lifestyle and, feeling considerably deflated, followed them out of the building. I had begun to guess now what our duties for today would comprise and, given the size of the vessels we were using and the number of people in the city, I did not look forward to the rest of the day with much enthusiasm.

We trekked out into the grasslands for perhaps half a mile before coming to our watering hole. It was a broad, slow-moving river that, I guessed, fed the same lake as the rather larger river into which Mrs Catlin and I had fallen on the previous day. There was evidence of a tributary to this river that had once fed the city directly but which appeared to have dried up long ago.

We filled our pots in the river and, without a moment's pause, set off back to the city.

Then we did it all again. And again. And again. And yet again throughout the whole of the morning. When we came back into the city for the last time before the midday break I was virtually on my knees.

The leader of the slaves found me in the vessel-storage building, propping up a wall that didn't need it and trying to remember how to breathe. He got me to my feet and walked me around the building slowly, holding me up as effortlessly as I might have supported a small child learning to take its first steps. Gradually, I began to come around, but I still could not walk unaided without reeling like a drunken sailor.

When I could breathe properly, he led me back to the camp and sat me down at one of the communal dining tables. I know that I ate like a starving man, but what it was I cannot even remember. I do recall that it was washed down with a sweet and utterly delicious red wine, and it was this alone, I think, that gave me the courage to face the prospect of the afternoon.

I was pausing between cautious sips of this wonderful beverage, with my head resting in my free hand and my eyes closed, the world of my other senses sliding in and out of focus in time to the pulsing ache in my muscles, when I felt a hand resting lightly on my shoulder. A soft voice said, in an almost musical lilt, 'Kondeo mai sukoki to, Shaw-jin?'

I glanced up in surprise, having caught what sounded like my own name in the otherwise meaningless jumble of words. My astonishment at finding that the speaker was Mrs Catlin could not be overstated. She smiled at my expression, and said, 'I asked if you wanted more wine, Shaw-jin.'

I nodded dumbly, only now realizing that my former teacher was, along with several of the women slaves, serving at the tables. She poured more wine into my goblet, avoiding my eyes but trying hard to suppress a grin.

'That's mighty impressive for one morning,' I told her. 'What's the "gin" bit mean?'

She shrugged.

'It's just an honorific,' she said coyly.

Someone a little way down the table called out to Mrs Catlin for more wine (I caught the word for 'wine' this time: *sukoki*) and she moved off without another word.

The afternoon was not quite so bad as the morning had been. The substantial lunch – and the sukoki – had restored both my strength and my spirits, and by the time we were ready to call it a day I was feeling no more than pleasantly weary. I followed the small retinue of slaves back to the city square and joined them for the evening meal.

I'd been too weary to notice at lunchtime, but I now saw that the whole camp shared the dining facilities equally, masters and slaves alike, and although it was the female slaves who did the serving everyone seemed to be eating from the same menu.

Mrs Catlin was serving once again, and seemed to have learned a whole new vocabulary. I knew that she was talented as a languages teacher, but I had never guessed quite what a facility she had for actually learning languages herself.

'Tonoko da,' she said as she served me.

I pointed to the bowl of stew in front of me and she laughed.

'No, no,' she said, 'that's *zhurba*. "Tonoko da" is a greeting; you know, "Hi, how are you?"'

'Ah,' I said. Her obvious enthusiasm was not meshing too well with my own rather less energetic mood.

'The usual response,' she said, 'is "Da tono", which means—'

'If it means "Eat up",' I said, picking up a spoon and attacking the zhurba, 'then I'm all for it.'

Mrs Catlin raised one eyebrow in a way that convinced me I was not likely to get a second helping and walked off without another word.

I cursed myself all through dinner, but my heart wasn't in it. There were times when Mrs Catlin had all the grace and empathy of a plateful of porridge. Like all intellectuals she had a tendency towards tunnel vision when she was caught up in some pet project, and those around her who didn't share her current obsession tended to get trampled underfoot.

I wondered, while digging into a second helping that I had managed with smiles and gestures to charm out of another of the serving women, what would happen after the evening meal was over. I hadn't seen the slave quarters on the previous night so I didn't know what the usual routine might be – or, indeed, if I was expected to be a part of it. For while it certainly seemed as though Mrs Catlin and I had become de facto slaves to our hosts there was something in the general mood of those around us that suggested that something else was, in fact, the case.

The routine following dinner was a fairly simple one: everyone did pretty much whatever he or she wanted. Some of our hosts went off to the lake; some wandered around the ancient city, looking at its numerous sights; some of the slaves took themselves off to another part of the river; and some, like me, just wanted to find a place to crash out for a few hours.

But before I did that I thought perhaps I should do a little fence-mending. Mrs Catlin may have acted thoughtlessly, but I'd been downright rude. I found her in an outdoor enclosure that was obviously a kitchen, doing the universal chores that follow any meal.

'Tonoko da, Catlin-jin,' I said, leaning on the fence that sur-rounded the kitchen and doing my best to look contrite.

She looked at me and flushed for no reason that I could think of; the other women in the enclosure giggled.

'Don't call me that!' Mrs Catlin said, casting a quick glance at the other women. 'It . . . it isn't appropriate.'

'Ah,' I said, implying a level of understanding that was entirely missing at that moment. 'Anyway,' I went on, 'I'm sorry I was a bit abrupt earlier. I guess I've had a long day.'

'Apology accepted,' Mrs Catlin said, adding, 'Feeble excuse dismissed out of hand. Help me with these things and we'll talk.'

We finished clearing away the kitchen utensils and then Mrs Catlin led me to a fairly large tent at one end of the slaves' camp.

'This is our accommodation until we've earned a place of our own,' she said. 'It's the quarters that new slaves get when the Ladden acquire them.'

'You've learned a lot,' I said, considerably impressed. 'Who are the Ladden?'

Mrs Catlin told me – or at least told me as much as she'd been able to pick up. Most of what she knew were names and routine phrases for daily activities, such as mealtimes, and half a dozen sentences that any tourist might want to know when contemplating a holiday in a foreign country. Nonetheless, for one day's work – and among a people who did not seem overly inclined to be forthcoming – it was quite an achievement.

Our hosts, it transpired, were nomads, gypsies, and they called themselves the Ladden. Mrs Catlin had already discovered this much, but in the weeks to come we would learn more. They had no fixed abode, but never ventured out of this one corner of the continent on which they lived. Instead, they spent large parts of the year wandering from one long-dead metropolis to another. These habitations of a previous, non-human civilization were to be found all over the Ladden's continent, although not in quite the profusion as here in this particular region. If the Ladden knew who had built these cities, or how long ago, or for how long they had stood deserted, they never saw fit to inform us.

The first thing we learned about the Ladden was that they

permitted no one to enjoy their hospitality who was not capable of paying for it, and to the Ladden there were only two forms of payment. They did no menial work themselves but kept their small band of slaves, made up of captured travellers from various other races, employed in such tasks. The slaves were jointly owned by the whole community and in return for their labours were permitted a high degree of freedom about the Ladden camp; they also, as I had already seen, shared in the communal meals to the same degree that the Ladden themselves did. The only restriction placed upon the slaves was that they were permitted to own no property whatsoever, which effectively prevented them from aspiring to the only other means of paying for their place at the Ladden table, which was to create works of art. The Ladden – whom I became convinced were the most egotistical people ever to live – considered themselves to be born artists, and did no other work whatsoever. At various times of the year they would make journeys to certain travelling markets and there exchange the products of their arts and crafts for tools and food and wines and, occasionally, new slaves. One of the principal duties of slaves, as I would soon learn, was to grow, forage or hunt for food between market visits. The richly-made clothing of the slaves was a bit of Ladden irony: caring nothing for their own sartorial elegance they dressed their slaves in garments that they themselves had made and that they could have sold for a higher price than the value of the slaves themselves.

Mrs Catlin told me as much of this as she already knew, adding a few logical speculations of her own. I was impressed, and told her so. At the same time, I was struggling to find a comfortable position in which to sit on the only furnishings to be found in 'our' tent, namely a straw mattress piled with woollen blankets. There were several such in the tent, and I could hardly complain at having been allocated the worst of the bunch as they were all pretty much the same.

Mrs Catlin noticed my discomfort and asked me what was wrong. I told her about my day, and about the rather pathetic way in which my body had stood up to it.

'I used to think I was reasonably fit,' I complained, 'but these guys are like demons. I don't think one of them raised a sweat today.'

'Take off your shirt and lie down,' Mrs Catlin said.

It was a measure of how tired I was that I did exactly that and never thought to ask what she had in mind. A moment later I found out. Mrs Catlin had massaged strained or aching muscles for me in the past but this was the first time she'd ever given me a proper body massage. Needless to say, she was thoroughly proficient, and I'm not ashamed to say that within five minutes of her starting I was fast asleep.

Chapter 8

INTELLIGENCE TEST

The weeks sped by with incredible rapidity. Our duties in the slave teams changed periodically, and I felt extremely smug on discovering when I was sent out on a hunting expedition that I knew more about setting snares and traps than any of my companions did. They knew a couple of basic trapping techniques, but seemed wholly ignorant of the principles behind them. They regarded my own efforts with considerable scepticism until they began to pay off. I became quite popular with the kitchen staff for a while, since I began providing them with more variety in game than they had ever seen.

Mrs Catlin was speaking the language like a native by the end of the third month, and I was only a few weeks behind her. We both began noticing oddities in the language, largely having to do with names and common nouns; they didn't seem to have evolved from the same source as the rest of the language. This city, for example, was called Hippom Ather, which supposedly meant Summer Home, yet when they spoke of it as a summer home (which, for these nomadic people, it was) they used the phrase *mir hal*. Then again they often called it Tokaida (pronounced as four distinct syllables: toe-ka-ee-da), but I came to believe that that was merely a generic term for whichever of these ancient cities they happened to be in at the time. Mrs Catlin theorized, and I could do little more than bow to her wisdom in such matters, that the spoken language of the Ladden – which they called simply the High Tongue – was a comparatively recent invention, and that they had once had a much different language that now survived only in their distinctive names and in a small handful of anachronistic verbs and adjectives. The fact that the Ladden claimed (possibly falsely) that there was only one spoken language on the whole planet tended to support this theory.

This planet, as both Mrs Catlin and I were simultaneously beginning to realize, was old, much older than our Earth. It seemed as though innumerable civilizations had risen and fallen here over many millennia. Some of them had achieved incredible levels of sophistication before collapsing, while others had barely begun to flourish before being wiped out. Evidence of this was apparent in all of the Ladden's folk tales and poetry and literature, but it would be many months yet before Mrs Catlin and I came to realize just how old this planet really was, and to what condition its dominant life form had deteriorated.

In some ways, the Ladden themselves were a very primitive people, yet the depth of their own cultural heritage, and their awareness of world history in general, was startling. Getting proper nouns out of them was hard work, but we eventually established that the country in which they lived, and in which we now found ourselves, was called Ragana-Se-Tor – although I had the feeling that this was actually one of their descriptive names, like Hippom Ather, and not a proper noun as such. The continent on which Ragana-Se-Tor stood had been, in relatively recent times, the seat of a mighty empire, and now bore the name of the city from which that empire had first spread: Thek. Mrs Catlin was convinced that much of the Ladden's language had been based on ancient Thekkish, though none of the Ladden was prepared to voice an opinion on this.

It came as something of a surprise to me to discover that the Ladden knew they lived on a planet; I had half-expected them to try and tell us – with absolute certainty – that the world was flat.

This was partly due to prejudice on my part, but was also born out of something I had heard the Ladden say on several occasions; they referred to the 'edge of the world', a place in the distant west, and seemed to mean it literally. All attempts at pinning down what they meant by this resulted in failure, which was doubly frustrating given how knowledgeable they obviously were in other matters of geography. I filed the matter away in my memory, hoping that one day I would learn the answer to it for myself.

As to the name of the planet itself, this presented a problem. When speaking of themselves as a species, the Ladden used the word Vinh. I interpreted this as being the equivalent of our word 'human', yet when speaking of the planet they would seem to apply the word not to themselves but to it. Phrases such as 'We are of the Vinh' or 'This is the Vinh world' had a different feel to them when spoken in the High Tongue to phrases such as 'We are the Vinh' or 'This is the world of the Vinh'. Their word for 'world', in a planetary sense, was Shushuan, pronounced with heavy emphasis on the last syllable, so for the lack of anything better that was what Mrs Catlin and I elected to call it.

Although our place in the social structure of the Ladden camp remained vague for several weeks – right up until the point, in fact, at which we erected our own tent and moved out of the new-slave quarters – there finally came a point at which we began to gain an inkling of what was going through the minds of our hosts.

As I have already said, the Ladden themselves did no work other than that directly associated with their artistic endeavours, but up until the events I am about to relate we could see no evidence that they ever did anything at all of a productive nature. That all changed one morning when, as the slaves gathered to be assigned their daily tasks, a man of the Ladden appeared and led Mrs Catlin and me away to a large tent in the centre of the camp. I felt some considerable unease at this point, since the whole atmosphere of the camp as we were led through it was one of excitement and expectancy.

Within the large tent were numerous tools, arranged around individual work areas, which at a glance I associated with pottery, weaving, carpentry, sculpting, painting, metal work and a host of other crafts, some of which were not so easy to identify. Our guide led us at an unhurried pace to each of the work areas in turn, inviting us – largely by sign language – to handle the various tools and, as it were, get the feel of them. I caught Mrs Catlin's eye as we examined a hand-powered potter's wheel.

'What do you make of this?' I muttered.

She glanced around at our guide, who was standing to one side, a carefully neutral expression on his face.

'It's a test,' she said simply.

'What of?' I asked.

'"Of what",' she corrected. 'Of our ingenuity, on one level – I think. But there's more to it than that.' She looked at the square top of the potter's wheel, then across at our stoney-faced guide. I saw the little groove appear between her brows that meant she was making a decision she wasn't too sure about. Then she picked up the small stick that lay next to the wheel and, inserting the point into the hole in one corner of the wheel, spun it around. She looked to our guide for a response, and he smiled with evident delight. 'OK,' Mrs Catlin muttered, 'so we know I know what this is for. Now what?'

'Make something,' I said.

'Don't be idiotic,' Mrs Catlin snapped. 'Why would they want . . .?' She looked at me suddenly, and I almost expected a little light to come on over her head. 'Shaw, you are a natural genius. Have I ever told you that?'

'Not that I can recall,' I said dryly.

Mrs Catlin pantomimed putting something onto the potter's wheel to show the Ladden that she understood what it was for. The Ladden directed her to the side of the tent where a number of large containers stood. He left her to examine the contents and seemed very pleased when she took a handful of clay from one of them. She returned to the potter's wheel, sat down behind it, and went to work.

The Ladden looked pointedly at me. *OK*, I thought, *so Mrs Catlin has just gone up in his estimations, but where does that leave me?* I glanced around the tent, looking, as much as anything, for inspiration. I was modestly proficient at half a dozen handicrafts, but I was no artist. I felt confident that Mrs Catlin could design a pot in her head and create it with her hands virtually simultaneously, but I had no such talents. I was on the point of giving up and resigning myself to a life of slavery for as long as we stayed in the Ladden camp when suddenly my gaze chanced to light upon what looked like a jeweller's bench. I walked casually towards it, not wanting to commit myself too thoroughly until I had had a better look at the tools that were neatly laid out on one side of the bench. My guide was on me in an instant, however, proffering a three-legged stool that had been under the bench for me to sit upon. Feeling decidedly cornered, I sat down and looked more closely at what it was that had caught my eye: a partially completed necklace, formed of gold and silver wire threaded with small objects that had no immediate significance – it was their lack of obvious definition that had prompted my interest.

My guide watched me closely as I spread the necklace out before me. It was not an especially delicate design, which was good because I was not particularly adept at fine detail work. Ignoring my overly inquisitive overseer, I reached into the pockets of my ragged jeans and dug out the few coins that had lain there since we had left Earth. I laid them out beside the necklace, matching them as far as possible for size and colour with the objects already incorporated into it, and realized that I was going to need more. With an irrationally deep-seated reluctance, I slipped off my wrist watch and laid it out with the change. Picking up a bladed tool from the collection beside me I prised the back case off the watch and carefully removed its innards.

I glanced up at the Ladden; his fascination was almost comical in its intensity.

I disassembled the works of my watch – saying a silent prayer of thanks that it hadn't been a digital one – and began to redesign the necklace in such a way that it could incorporate these paltry few remnants of my past life. Of course, I wanted it to do more than just incorporate them; if I was to impress these people as much as I knew Mrs Catlin was likely to, then I needed to have the necklace actually take on a whole new appearance, one which the Ladden would probably never have seen before. I picked up a small brace-and-bit and began to drill some holes in my collection of coins.

It was hours later before the Ladden would let me stop. I now had a small crowd of them watching me, and although I felt no animosity from any of them I couldn't judge exactly what the mood of the gathering actually was. Mrs Catlin's pottery had clearly been a big hit with them, but she had finished that long ago, and I was now the centrepiece of the evening's entertainment for the whole camp.

I had to admit that I was rather pleased with the work I had done. I had used the watch face, with its luminous hands and numbers, for the centrepiece of the necklace, surrounding it with an asymmetrical collection of gears and odds-and-ends from its own insides. On either side of the face I had placed coins and metal segments from the watch strap, incorporating into them the original parts of the necklace. It might have looked distinctly odd to earthly eyes, but to the Ladden it was something totally alien to their whole experience, and as such lost all of its seeming absurdity.

As soon as it was finished the necklace was passed around the group, and I had enough of an understanding of Ladden body language by now to know that they liked it. I caught sight of Mrs Catlin at the back of the group, giving my handiwork her own critical appraisal. She glanced over to me and, seeing me watching her, turned pointedly back to the necklace and looked at it even more closely. I noticed the Ladden nearest to me nudging one another and pointing at Mrs Catlin, and realized that she was playing a very dangerous game – they had accepted her on the strength of her pottery, so if she was seen to reject what I had made . . .

She looked slowly up at me, her face unreadable, and then gave me one of her rare, totally genuine smiles. A ripple of approval went around the rest of the group and I felt myself sag noticeably with relief.

Mrs Catlin made her way to my side and leaned on my shoulder, staring down at me. It was an unusually personal gesture, made all the more so by the fact that we were both tired and had let our guards down a little with one another.

'It is actually very beautiful, Shaw,' she said, and it took me a moment to realise she was talking about the necklace.

'I didn't see your pot,' I told her.

She pointed to a stand on which the pot had been placed for general examination. I was impressed: it was a kind of oriental temple jar, very simple but classically elegant. It had the stamp of her character all over it.

'You look exhausted,' she said.

'I am,' I told her.

She stepped aside and tugged me to my feet.

'Tomorrow will be interesting,' she observed as she led me through the crowd of appreciative Ladden and towards the tent flap.

'Oh?' I said, wondering how any day in this place could be anything else.

'Of course,' Mrs Catlin said. 'I mean, do we go back to slave duties, or will we be expected to start producing masterpieces to order?'

I gave her a very sceptical glance, but she was clearly being serious. I have to say I did not sleep very well that night.

Chapter 9

PUNISHMENT

In fact, we could not have become artists right away for the simple reason that we owned no materials. The clay, metal, wood, cloth and so on that the Ladden used was not, as I had at first thought, communal property. Each Ladden owned his or her own supply of the tools and materials needed for their art or craft, and we had only been given a free run of the craft tent that one time so that we could be tested as fully as possible. In the future, we would have to earn whatever tools and raw materials we needed, and the only way for us to earn them was to remain in the camp of the slaves. And so, for a time, we were content to stay there. We were so occupied with the business of learning the language that there was scarcely time for contemplating anything else. Until, that is, the events of which I will now speak: events that ended the dreamland period of our time with the Ladden and brought us back to the realities of the situation with a very nasty jolt.

It was towards the end of our stay in Hippom Ather, which as I have previously noted means 'Summer Home', and at a time when Mrs Catlin and I began to notice a slight but significant change in the weather. It was not so much that the days were getting colder, but rather that they were getting shorter, and the nights were not as

73

clement as they had been. In my still very broken High Tongue I had made enquiries about this, and gathered from the replies I received that the Ladden would soon be leaving the ancient city on the edge of the forest and heading for warmer climes. Neither Mrs Catlin nor I had yet been able to ascertain how the Ladden navigated, nor whether they possessed anything analogous to a compass, so it was difficult to know whether they would be heading north or south. Whichever it proved to be, the direction would take us away from Hippom Ather at right angles to the river valley in which we had arrived in this world, and thus, we reasoned, put us a considerable distance from our only means of returning home.

Mrs Catlin and I were discussing this in our tent on the night when things were destined to come to a head.

'I don't like the idea of just going off into who-knows-where with them,' I said.

'Nor do I,' Mrs Catlin agreed pensively, 'but what alternative do we have?'

'We could go home,' I observed.

She looked at me. This was something we hadn't discussed since our first day with the Ladden, but I think we both knew that it wasn't what we really wanted. One day – probably – we would have to return to Earth. But not yet. Not until we had seen more of this new world.

'Perhaps we should just go off on our own,' I suggested. 'I mean, it's not as if we were prisoners . . .'

The tent flap abruptly flew open and the leader of the slaves thrust his head through the opening. His name, as near as I could pronounce it, was P'nad, and although he was taciturn I had found him a personable enough individual. Actually, he reminded me a lot of myself.

'Come swiftly,' he said.

Mrs Catlin and I arose, exchanging worried glances.

We left the tent and found the whole of the Ladden camp assembled in the light of the larger moon. (There were three moons, but the other two were so small I hadn't even noticed them for the first month.) One of the Ladden was holding a strange-looking device, and I felt a curious sensation at seeing it – it was the first technological thing I had yet seen on this planet. Suddenly, and with an impact that staggered me, I realized that elsewhere on this world – perhaps even on this very continent – there might be an advanced race who would regard the Ladden as little more than aborigines or bushmen. Dazed at the sheer credulity Mrs Catlin and I had shown in assuming that the Ladden were the best this world had to offer, I gazed in desperate fascination at the device in the Ladden's hand.

It was a wand of sorts, several inches thick, and formed of interlocking crystals of various colours and degrees of opacity; it was, perhaps, eighteen inches long.

'A slave has escaped,' said the Ladden.

The other slaves, almost as one individual, instantly fell to one knee – not a gesture of obeisance, more like prayer – and touched the metal rings on their ankles. Some of them seemed close to tears; one woman wept openly. The atmosphere was very confusing; it was as though the Ladden had announced the death of a loved one.

'P'nad will return the slave,' the Ladden continued. 'He will take four others with him.' To P'nad he said, 'Take the shabo'on as well. This is a lesson they must learn.'

I recognized the word 'shabo'on', and although I knew it referred to Mrs Catlin and me I had never found a suitable translation for it. The nearest I could come up with was 'apprentice', but that didn't convey any of the subtler meanings that I was sure the word contained.

P'nad pointed to four of the slaves nearest him, apparently choosing them at random. The others began to move disconsolately back to their tents.

The Ladden with the wand held it out in front of him, a gesture that was fraught with ritual and superstition. I wondered if the wand, whatever it was, was actually functional. Perhaps it was merely a relic of a dead civilization, like this whole city, and was revered by the Ladden as something more than it actually was – or ever had been.

Any such thoughts were dispelled by what happened next. The Ladden twisted the two ends of the wand and it separated into two halves, each as long as the original and irregularly shaped, as though it had contained a fault line that followed a crazy path down its entire length, and the Ladden's twisting action had caused it to shatter cleanly along that fault line. P'nad held out his hand and the Ladden gave him one half of the wand which, I now noticed, was glowing faintly.

'You have until sunrise,' the Ladden said.

P'nad turned without a word and walked briskly out of the Ladden camp.

The other four slaves followed.

Mrs Catlin and I looked at one another.

'Go,' said the Ladden who held the remains of the wand. 'And never forget what you see.'

We turned to leave, and as we did so I caught the expressions on the faces of certain of the Ladden who had been most friendly to Mrs Catlin and me; they were hard to read, yet something in them, something utterly and completely alien, chilled me to the bone.

We caught up with P'nad in moments and I noticed that the faint glow from his fragment of the wand had increased slightly.

'Who ran?' I asked him. (My High Tongue was more fluent by this time, but I still found it difficult to put together lengthy sentences. I think some of the other slaves thought I was a bit dense, and had a habit of speaking more freely in front of me than they perhaps would have had they realized that my deficiencies with the spoken language did not extend to my understanding of it.)

'K'nen,' he replied curtly.

I was startled. K'nen was the red-headed young man with whom I had had more than one altercation since entering the Ladden camp. He had not struck me as the type to do something like this.

I couldn't help noticing how grim my companions looked; and why, I asked myself, had no Ladden accompanied us? Did they trust P'nad so implicitly to return with K'nen? Did they not think P'nad – or one of the others with us – might not follow K'nen's example once we were on his trail? And why was it that Mrs Catlin and I had been sent along on this manhunt? What was the 'lesson' we were supposed to learn?

I wanted to ask P'nad some of these questions, but my awkwardness with his language and the terrible expression on his dark countenance persuaded me to wait until this night was over before pursuing them.

We left the city by an exit I had never before used and struck out onto the open savannah beyond. The grassland was not as lush now as it had been when we first came to the city, yet another indication that the summer was drawing to a close. In the far distance I could make out the suggestion of mountains, their peaks reflecting the moonlight and hinting that they might be capped with snow. Between the mountains and the city were only some low foothills and then the vast expanse of open plain. There was no cover whatsoever, nowhere for a fleeing man to hide. It seemed foolish of K'nen to have come this way.

As we made our way through the long grass another thought came to me, one that offered a suggestion as to K'nen's intentions. This direction was the same one I had heard the Ladden speaking of when discussing their impending departure from the city for their winter home. Perhaps K'nen had come this way because it was territory that was known to him and was thus less likely to offer unpleasant surprises. Perhaps, even, his own country lay in this direction.

My deductions were entirely reasonable and logical. And wrong. Because I was as yet unaware of two very important facts. One of these was the true nature of the anklets worn by the Ladden slaves. The other was the fact that K'nen was – in earthly parlance – an Olympic-standard runner, and this plain provided the single exit from Hippom Ather that offered no obstacles to a running man.

We were perhaps a mile from the city when P'nad stopped and bent down to examine the ground at his feet. I heard him grunt wordlessly and then arise and walk on. The other slaves followed, none of them bothering to look at what it was that had caught P'nad's attention.

Mrs Catlin pushed past me and stooped down where P'nad had. I peered over her shoulder in the darkness.

She looked up at me.

'Blood,' she said.

77

We hurried to catch up with P'nad and the others.

Some yards further on there was more blood, and still more a little way beyond that. K'nen's trail through the grass was easier to read now: having lost its summer vitality, the grass did not now conceal his passage as it once would have, and even without the evidence of the blood – which I took for granted was K'nen's – it was plain to see that his path was becoming erratic, less true. In places he seemed to have fallen. The blood was thicker there.

We finally came upon his body a little over three miles from the city.

Mrs Catlin took one look at it and turned away, retching. That I was able to control myself better astonishes me even now, but I remembered what the Ladden had said when he sent us out on this hunt and I forced myself to examine K'nen's remains as closely and in as much detail as my stomach would allow.

His injuries, clearly, had begun in his leg, just above the anklet that marked him as a slave. It was as though the blood vessels had become enlarged, rupturing and bursting through the skin. The damage had spread upwards – slowly, I judged, since he had come almost two miles since the first of his blood had marked the trail – claiming his thigh and eventually spreading over his hip to his waist. From there it had climbed even further. The left side of his rib cage was a spider web of distended veins; the destruction stopped just below his left ear, at which point, I presumed, he had died. By the time the effect had reached his throat his left ankle must have been virtually eaten away since the anklet was hanging loosely on the exposed bone. The muscles in his calf appeared to have been partially cooked by the heating action of the thousands of bursting blood capillaries within them.

'Come,' said P'nad, 'we must hurry.'

'Why hurry?' I asked, startled.

He cast me a bitter look, his eyes blazing with a ferocity that his years of slavery had done nothing to diminish.

'At dawn,' he said, 'if we are not back at Hippom Ather, Hareg of the Ladden will activate his portion of the mutahiir. When that happens, we will share K'nen's fate.' He glanced at my left ankle, bare as it was of the anklet. 'Or does that not concern you?'

He stooped and picked up K'nen's body as though it was weightless. I wanted to say something, to deny the accusation in his tone, but before I could find the words a new element was suddenly introduced to the grim tableau.

One of the other slaves drew in a startled breath and gasped, 'A Mugatih!'

We all turned to look in the direction he was staring; only Mrs Catlin and I seemed not to have understood the word he'd used.

Thirty feet or so away from us, in the direction K'nen had been running, stood a man. Or, at least, I assumed it to be a man. His entire body was concealed beneath a voluminous, hooded robe; in the moonlight it appeared to be the colour of mercury, but from the way it reflected the light I guessed that its true colour was red. His face was lost in shadow, and his wide sleeves fell to below the tips of his fingers. Standing there, motionless but for the stirring of his robe in the light breeze, he might have materialized in that spot the instant before we had turned to look at him. Actually, I couldn't think of any other way that he could have got there. Somehow, looking at him, I couldn't bring myself to believe that he had been hiding in the knee-length grass all around us.

I sensed P'nad at my side.

'Come away,' he breathed. 'Do not interfere with the passing of a Mugatih.'

I nodded, sensing the fear in P'nad's voice even though he did well to hide it.

We all edged slowly away, the Mugatih not moving as we did so. It was some time before we felt ready to turn our backs on him, and even then it was not something we did easily. Without knowing who or what the Mugatih was, I was still able to feel the power of the man. Tentatively, I translated *Mugatih* as 'Magician'.

I don't know when the man vanished, but none of us saw him go. No one else seemed surprised by that, so I decided to keep silent.

'It will be light soon,' P'nad said, too casually.

I looked at him.

'How long?' I asked.

He shrugged.

'About a ji,' he said.

That was barely ninety minutes. It seemed like not much time.

'Then let's get a move on,' I said.

I was sweating; I had no desire to watch someone die the way K'nen had.

P'nad glanced at me, and a faint smile split his dark face.

'Yes,' he said, 'I think we should.'

He increased his pace to a jog, the weight of K'nen in his arms seeming not to slow him down. The rest of us struggled to keep up.

We reached the city within minutes of the dawn, and P'nad silently handed his half of the device he'd called a mutahiir back to the man known as Hareg. The Ladden was alone, and he said nothing as he fitted the two halves back together. He walked away without a word, and P'nad and the other slaves took K'nen's body back to their own tents.

Mrs Catlin and I kept in the background while the slaves prepared K'nen for a vinh funeral. There was an air of ritual to what they did that disturbed me: it indicated that they'd done this before – often.

The funeral itself was a brief and low-key affair. Everyone filed out of the city onto the plain. Mrs Catlin and I followed at a discreet distance. A shallow grave was dug. K'nen was cremated over it, his corpse supported by the mound of firewood and the ashes collapsing into the pit. They left it like that: no marker, just a hole in the ground filled with ash. In a couple of months it would be completely overgrown.

I looked around the plain as we made our way back to the city. How many other such graves were out here? I wondered. I recalled the feeling of antiquity that pervaded everything we had yet seen in Ragana-Se-Tor, and suppressed a shudder. This plain could be a single vast graveyard, and unless we were careful it could represent the only future that Mrs Catlin and I would have on this world.

Chapter 10

SLAVE

The Ladden decamped and left Hippom Ather a week later. Mrs Catlin and I went with them. In my case, I had no choice. Although, to be fair, I suppose Mrs Catlin had no more say in the matter than I did.

For two days, following the death of K'nen, we had been treated very coolly by both the Ladden and their slaves. We did not fit in their neatly ordered society, and both halves of the camp resented our 'celebrity' status.

Mrs Catlin had overcome the absence of raw materials for her artistic endeavours by the simple expedient of cutting small sections from her clothing and using them to make collages. This form of art was new to the Ladden and her popularity had increased proportionately. In direct proportion, however, her wardrobe diminished. She was already wearing her shirt halter-top style, and her jeans now only just reached her knees. I didn't like to enquire too closely about her underwear, but I had noticed small quantities of white lace appearing in some of her creations.

As the security of Mrs Catlin's position among the Ladden seemed to increase, my own went into a decline. I lacked her broad-based talents and, irritatingly from my point of view, excelled

81

at only those activities that the Ladden considered the province of slaves.

And thus it was that, on the morning of the third day following K'nen's death, as I assembled with the slaves for the allotting of our daily tasks, I found myself facing four very stocky-looking Ladden men; behind them was the Ladden I knew as Hareg, and in his hand was the crystalline wand that P'nad had called the mutahiir.

I took a step backward and found my way blocked by two more Ladden. I looked at Hareg, and at another Ladden behind him who held in his hands a greyish bar of what looked like clay. The sight of it sent a surge of irrational fear through me.

'No—' I said, and felt strong hands grasp me from behind.

I looked wildly around me, and saw P'nad and the other slaves standing to one side, studiously not looking at me. Any doubt as to what was about to happen vanished from my mind at the sight of them.

I heard Mrs Catlin's voice raised in concern from among the knot of Ladden behind Hareg.

'Shaw?' she called, an edge of panic in her voice. 'What's going on?'

The four men who had stood in front of me now closed in. Behind them, Hareg held up the mutahiir and said in a quiet voice that somehow carried over every other sound in the plaza, 'I am sorry, Shaw, but there are only two kinds of citizen in our camp. And, sadly, you will never make a Ladden.'

Two of the four in front of me reached for my left leg, and the fear that had all but paralysed me until that moment suddenly galvanized me into furious action. I lashed out with my right foot, taking the nearest of the Ladden in the throat. The look of astonishment on the faces of all those present would have been comical in any other circumstances, but at that moment all I could think of was to take advantage of their surprise.

I jerked free of the two behind me and drove both elbows backwards with all the force I could muster. I heard two gasps as the men doubled up in pain, and felt an evil satisfaction at the way I had disabled three of them so easily. It was a short-lived satisfaction, as in the next instant I was hit from all sides and borne heavily to the ground. I landed hard under a press of bodies and the breath was driven from my body. I was manhandled into a half-sitting position, my left leg held in a half-dozen powerful hands, while another grasped my hair and turned my head so that I could not look away from what was about to be done.

Hareg squatted next to my left leg, looking at me with a mixture of surprise and irritation.

'It is good you fight,' he said, much to my own surprise. 'Those who resist at first ultimately make the best slaves. P'nad resisted' – he glanced at the black figure standing to one side, but P'nad would not look at him – 'and now he commands our workforce. One day, you will take his place, I think.'

'I'll see you dead first,' I hissed.

Hareg laughed good-naturedly.

'Perhaps,' he said, 'but I think not.'

He gestured to the man behind him, the man holding the bar of grey, clay-like material. The man bent down and wrapped the bar around my ankle until the ends met. He pressed them together and they stuck, leaving the substance hanging loosely from my ankle. Hareg extended the mutahiir and touched it to the substance. I felt a burst of heat and suddenly the clay-like material was flowing like mercury. It shrank to fit my leg snugly, and then became as hard and as cold as steel. I stared at it in open-mouthed astonishment. I had known that the mutahiir was an artefact of an advanced technology, but until that moment I had not suspected how advanced: what it had just done was, I was convinced, beyond any earthly science.

'Now,' Hareg said quietly, 'you are shabo'on no longer. Now, you are one of us.'

He stood up and took several steps backwards. He gestured for the other Ladden to release me and they did so. I got slowly to my feet, my eyes fixed on the band around my ankle. Then I looked slowly up into Hareg's face. He waved the mutahiir in the direction of the anklet and pain like nothing I had ever known exploded in my leg. I collapsed in a gasping heap to the ground, convinced that Hareg had killed me. In a moment, the pain had gone, but not the memory of it.

I sat up slowly, wiping agonized tears from my eyes, and

realized that the group of Ladden around me was breaking up
and they were going about their business, as though nothing of
significance had occurred. Even Hareg was walking away without
a backward glance. I hugged my leg to my chest, still shaking from
the experience.

Someone threw her arms around me and I turned on her in an
instant, snarling like an animal. It was Mrs Catlin, but it took me
several seconds to realize it. And in the meantime I had grasped
her arms as though to tear them from their sockets. I released them
slowly, and she put them once again around my neck, holding me
tightly against her. I was too shattered from the experience of the
last few minutes to be properly startled by her behaviour, and in any
case it was precisely the kind of attention I needed right then.

Before either of us could get embarrassed by our behaviour
she pushed me gently away from her and looked guiltily at my
anklet.

'Shaw,' she said, 'I am truly sorry. This is my fault . . .'

'Stop taking all the credit,' I snapped. 'If I'd had any sense I would
have gotten us both out of here as soon as we saw what they did
to K'nen.'

'But we're trapped now,' she said, a note of despair in her voice.
'Even if we could find our way back to the cave . . .'

'Drop it,' I said. 'There must be a way to reverse the effect of that
mutahiir, and one way or another we'll find it.'

We had been speaking in English, but a voice behind me said,
in the High Tongue, 'There is no escape from the mutahiir.'

I looked round to see P'nad towering over me. For a moment I
thought he had understood what we had said, but I had long ago
established to my own satisfaction that no one in the Ladden camp
could speak any Earth language.

'You mentioned the mutahiir,' he said, as though reading my
mind, 'and the rest was not hard to guess.'

He glanced at Mrs Catlin.

'Mistress,' he said to her, using a Ladden term that implied
deference born out of social standing rather than personal respect,
'you should not be so concerned over the fate of a slave. It is
unseemly in a free woman.'

I felt Mrs Catlin bridle at my side and I cut off any reply she might have made by putting my hand firmly over hers.

'Let it be,' I said quietly in English. Then, in Ladden, 'P'nad is right, mistress. I'll be all right. You should let me get on with my work.'

She threw P'nad a glance that would certainly have killed a lesser man and then suddenly stood up and was gone.

'She has fire, that one,' P'nad said quietly, giving me a look that I failed entirely to understand.

'Come,' he said, offering me his hand. 'There is much to do.'

Preparations for leaving the city were well under way among the Ladden by the time they were ready for their slaves to begin the task of disassembling the city of tents. The care of their artistic tools and materials and products was something the Ladden undertook themselves, not trusting the source of their income to mere underlings. The actual transportation of their goods, of course, fell to us – and woe betide any slave who let harm befall his charge.

I found the dismantling of the city of tents to be both fascinating and frustrating. Seeing how the tents came apart reinforced yet again my opinion of the skill and craftsmanship of their Ladden designers, but I was so unfamiliar with the ages-old system that the slaves had evolved for the undertaking of this routine task that I spent most of my time simply getting in everyone's way. It was a state of affairs that was to no one's satisfaction.

The day dragged on relentlessly and it was past noon before we were ready to move out. Everyone – Ladden and slaves alike – ate a perfunctory meal before the march began, and in all that time I saw nothing of Mrs Catlin.

The march was hard work, but no more so than a typical day in Hippom Ather had been. Most of the heavy gear we hauled on large, two-wheeled carts, each of which took four slaves to pull, but some of the stuff we simply had to carry. The Ladden carried very little themselves, mostly just their few personal possessions and the more precious tools of their various crafts. Among the slaves a kind of rota seemed to exist, allowing each man or woman an occasional day with only a light burden. I was perversely pleased to note that the load I carried was easily as large as that carried by any other slave; it seemed as though all those days spent fetching water had helped add a little extra bulk to my frame.

It seems strange to me now, looking back, that it was on that day that I first remarked a curious anomaly in the composition of the Ladden camp – strange, because it was so obvious a thing that I should have noticed it much sooner. Perhaps it was just that this was the first time I'd seen the whole group assembled *en masse*. The anomaly was the fact that there were very few old people and no small children in the camp. One or two of the Ladden women were nursing babies, but where were the toddlers, the infants? I resolved to discuss it with Mrs Catlin as soon as I could.

The land we were marching through was unremarkable, being merely endless miles of open savannah. The 'trail' we followed seemed to exist only as a theoretical line between two distant points, since there was no visible road nor anything by which to navigate other than the often cloud-obscured sun.

We marched until just before sunset and then camped for the night. The whole group crowded into four tents, the largest four that we had brought. The mood, generally, was subdued.

After the evening meal, at which everyone, it seemed, consumed rather more wine than usual, most people were content to find a quiet spot in one of the tents and settle down for the night. It was a sensible enough idea, but I was feeling strangely restless and found myself walking some distance from the camp before I really knew what I was doing.

On the horizon behind us I could still see the towers of Hippom Ather, and the dense woodland beyond. We had come very little distance, really, yet already the time we had spent in the city seemed like a dream.

I glanced up at the stars, and not for the first time on this strange world I tried to spot familiar constellations. It was a wasted effort, of course, but the effort alone was relaxing.

I heard footsteps behind me, recognizing them instantly.

'It's a fine night,' Mrs Catlin said.

'It's turning cooler,' I replied.

'Not enough cloud cover,' Mrs Catlin observed.

'Do you have any idea where we're going?' I asked.

'Only vaguely,' she said. 'They call it Ytterol Ley which, not surprisingly, means Winter Home, although like all their expressions it means a dozen other things as well. As to where it's located, all I can gather is that it's beyond the mountains we saw when we followed K'nen's trail. We're paralleling his . . .'

'I know,' I snapped.

I hadn't meant to be brusque, but why did she have to be so damned analytical all the time? She talked about K'nen as though what had happened hadn't affected her, even though we both knew it had.

'You came out here to be alone,' she said stiffly. 'I'm sorry I disturbed you.'

I half-turned, but she was already walking away. For an instant I almost followed, but for the life of me I don't know what I would have said if I had.

Chapter 11

BATTLE

On the third day, a little before noon, we had to make an unscheduled stop. The reason for this was that, with no warning at all, we found ourselves in the middle of a snowstorm.

P'nad had two of the female slaves break open a large bundle on one of the two-wheeled carts and in moments they were handing out winter furs to everyone in the convoy. (This clothing, like the tents, furniture and cooking utensils, was the communal property of all the Ladden, and as with their normal garb the Ladden themselves tended to favour uninspired garments while their slaves were decked out in truly sumptuous, splendid outfits. The fur that was handed so casually to me would, on Earth, have fetched a price that might have run to five figures.)

While we were getting bundled up, I noticed P'nad standing off to one side and staring fixedly away into the distance. Something in his stance bothered me, so I walked over to stand alongside him.

I followed his gaze, which was directed into the heart of the storm whose leading edge we had blundered into. I could make out a line of low hills in the middle distance, their slopes dotted with what looked like trees. Nothing that I could see seemed worth a second look.

'Some storm, huh?' I said; P'nad hadn't looked at me – hadn't turned his head by a fraction of an inch from that straight-ahead stare – but I knew he was aware of me at his side.

'Most unusual,' he agreed. 'I cannot recall ever seeing snow this early in the winter months.'

I looked where he was looking. The swirling snow combined with the bad light to create strange, shadowy shapes in the midst of the storm, ever-changing shapes that occasionally hung on the very edge of visibility for long enough to seem like real objects moving through the snow.

'Shouldn't we get moving?' I asked. 'If we stand around too long we're all going to stiffen up . . .'

P'nad grasped my arm suddenly, his grip like a steel trap.

'Look there!' he hissed, his other arm pointing furiously into the storm.

I looked, and suddenly I saw it: a single shape, taller than a man and a little broader, moving towards us. It was almost a mile away and seemed to be moving rapidly.

'What is it?' I asked. I suddenly remembered the first night Mrs Catlin and I had spent on this world, and the 'predator' we had sensed but never seen.

'Bandits,' said P'nad. 'They would not normally attack a full caravan of the Ladden, but if this weather has been building across their lands for some time they may have been forced to desperate measures.'

'But I only see one . . .' I said, trying without success to outstare the storm.

'They ride in single file when attacking,' P'nad said.

He turned abruptly from me and raced back to the caravan. I followed, casting doubtful glances back over my shoulder as I went.

P'nad was barking orders to the other slaves before I had time to get to grips with this new development. Life among the Ladden – even as a slave – had been relatively peaceful; the idea that they needed to defend themselves against hostiles had never come up.

I had seen no weapons in the Ladden camp, but now they sprouted from bundles all up and down the line of the convoy.

It was a moment before I realized that only the slaves were arming themselves – fighting, it seemed, was something else that the Ladden considered beneath them. The weapons seemed to consist of longbows and pikes and not much else, although I did see a few knives.

I was standing amid the organized chaos of the convoy's flurry of activity when I found P'nad at my side once again, a pair of unstrung bows in one hand and a quiver full of arrows in the other.

'Can you handle a bow?' he asked.

'I . . . I . . . can use one,' I stammered.

He thrust one into my hands.

'Join the line,' he said.

I looked where he was pointing, and saw the slaves – men and women – lining up between the convoy and the oncoming bandits. They moved with practised speed and efficiency, those with long hair binding it back out of their eyes, some casting off their winter furs for greater freedom of movement, and each of them strapping on forearm and finger protectors. Many had already unsheathed their arrows and planted them point down in the earth at their feet; several had strung their bows and were testing them for pull.

Swallowing hard, I stumbled forward and joined the line. My hands were shaking as I took the leather protectors P'nad had given me and pulled them on, one over my left wrist and the other over the fingers of my right hand. I stuck my arrows into the ground in front of me and strung my bow – it was a powerful weapon, more so than the compound bows I'd used in archery practice with Mrs Catlin.

I looked nervously into the storm. The single shadowy figure was much closer, and I saw now why it had seemed so large and so fast – the bandit was mounted.

'Wait for my signal,' said P'nad – he was standing beside me, but I hadn't even seen him until he spoke.

'P'nad—' I said.

'Speak swiftly,' he said, fitting an arrow to his bow.

'P'nad, I . . . I've never had to kill anyone,' I said.

He cast me the briefest of glances.

'If you wish to wait with the Ladden—'

'No,' I said quickly, perhaps too quickly. Was that what I actually wanted? 'It's just . . .'

He peered into the storm, judging the distance. 'There is no time for doubt,' he said tersely. 'Stay or go – but decide.'

I swallowed uneasily, but held my place in the line.

P'nad abruptly turned to the line of slaves and yelled, 'Draw!'

Every bow sprouted an arrow, the strings drawn back to the full length of each arrow. I snatched a shaft from the earth in front of me and nocked it. The head, I saw, was a bodkin, armour-piercing. I wondered what that should tell me about the kind of people we were likely to encounter on this march.

I tried to find a target in the swirl of snow in front of me, but it was an almost impossible task. I wondered how much to compensate for the gusting wind, and tried to map the gusts in the patterns of snow.

'Loose!' P'nad yelled.

I shot my arrow into the storm along with the dozens of others – I hoped for our sakes that the others had taken a better aim than I had.

In the storm, the 'single' bandit suddenly exploded into a score of mounted figures, and their mounts – which I was desperately trying to convince myself were horses – suddenly broke into a gallop. The bandits let out bloodcurdling yells and a dozen crossbow bolts came hurtling out of their midst. One slammed into the earth not three feet in front of me, and I heard a gasp of pain as, somewhere to my right, one of the Ladden slaves was sent staggering backwards. I glanced towards him in time to see him go down with six inches of crossbow quarrel protruding from his forehead. I recognized him instantly; he was one of the few Orientals in the group, and was called – ridiculously enough – Chang.

'Rapid string!' P'nad yelled.

The speed with which the slaves nocked and loosed their arrows now became almost unbelievable, and given the weather conditions the number of hits they scored was nothing short of miraculous.

I pulled myself together with no little difficulty and tried to follow their example. I could barely manage half their rate of fire, and I don't think I actually planted an arrow in anything but the earth three hundred yards away, but at least I felt – and, I hope, looked – as though I was being useful.

A second volley of crossbow bolts landed among us, doing more damage than the first had, and then the bandits were right on top of us.

Their mounts were *not* horses, though they were as big as Clydesdales. Their mouths were dog-like, full of pointed teeth, and their eyes were red, and the muscles were all wrong. Later, I would spot other differences – claws instead of hooves, no mane and only a vestigial tail, fur instead of hair. At the time, there was simply too much to take in.

One of the bandits was coming right at me – perhaps I looked like an easier target than my fellow slaves; I certainly felt like one – and I saw that, crossbows aside, the bandits' principal weapon was a kind of sabre, long and slightly curved.

I drew an arrow to my cheek and let fly. It hadn't registered properly that the bandit was wearing some kind of helmet, but as the arrow sliced off it I realized that I had aimed too high and that there was no time for a second shaft. There was a blur of motion from my left and the bandit suddenly pitched sideways, blood fountaining from his neck. I felt P'nad's huge hands drag me to one side as the riderless mount thundered past, trampling my remaining arrows in the process.

'Th—thanks,' I gasped.

He didn't respond, and I looked down to see the feathered shaft of a crossbow bolt protruding from high in the right side of his chest. His face was clenched in a rictus of pain. I clutched at his arms as he crumpled to the ground at my feet.

'Leave me,' he gasped. 'Save—'

His head fell back, his eyes closed in agony.

I looked around me in despair, and saw that the battle had turned into a mêlée. We had lost at least four slaves, and the bandits had lost two of their number. There were upwards of a dozen walking wounded, some theirs, more – too many – ours. At my side, P'nad's arrows – the eight or nine that remained – were still sticking out of the earth. I grasped the nearest and fitted it to my bow. I drew careful aim on the nearest bandit and let fly. The shaft passed through his body and sailed away into the distance. He looked around in surprise, and slowly tumbled from the saddle. I strung a second arrow and wasted a precious few seconds deciding where best to put it. I spotted a bandit who seemed, for no reason that I could have put into words, to be directing the actions of those around him. I put the arrow through his head – he *hadn't* been wearing a helmet – and reached for a third. As the man sagged forward in his saddle the bandits on either side of him wheeled around to see where the arrow had come from. I nocked another shaft and let fly at the nearest of them, hoping to dissuade the others from charging me. I should say at this point that I am pretty good with a bow – although the one I was using at that moment was not as accurate as the kind I had trained with on Earth. But I had just scored three direct hits in a row – even if one of them had been deflected – and that kind of good fortune was doomed not to last. The shaft that I had just loosed missed its target by about a yard and before I could reach for another two of the bandits were charging right for me, uttering the most hideous war cries I had ever heard.

For the briefest of instants I felt myself freeze, paralysed by the realization that I was staring death in the face and that there was nothing I could do to avoid it. Then the mount of one of the bandits staggered, lurching to one side and knocking the second bandit's beast off its stride. The sudden disruption to the flow of events was like ice water in my face. I snatched up an arrow, drew it to the pile, and released it towards the man whose beast had not stumbled. I didn't try for a clever shot this time, but simply aimed dead centre and hoped that at this range and on a bow with this much pull I could depend on a fairly flat trajectory. It seemed my guess was a good one, because the shaft buried itself in the bandit's sternum, his makeshift body-armour absorbing enough momentum to trap the arrow in his body but not enough to keep it from punching clean through to his spine.

I started to reach for another arrow when, glancing round briefly to take stock of the battle, I realized that it was all but over.

The bandits had been out for loot, not open warfare, and the loss of over half their number had obviously convinced them of the futility of pressing the attack. To a volley of arrows from the

Ladden slaves the bedraggled remains of the raiding party went galloping off into the snow.

I sank back onto my heels, suddenly exhausted. I glanced down at where P'nad lay at my side. He was conscious, but clearly suffering very badly; the arrow, I guessed, was pressing against a nerve. Removing it would be a hideously dangerous operation. With the bandits in full retreat, some of the non-combatant slaves began to move among the wounded; I looked around for Mrs Catlin and only now saw, to my horror, that she had been in the line of archers, scarcely five places away from me. She seemed drained, worn out, but mercifully uninjured.

I came up with a start as I suddenly wondered what had happened to the bandit whose mount had stumbled. I could see the animal through the thickening gusts of snow, still thrashing about on the grass some yards away from me. From the same location I could hear curses that were in the High Tongue but with an accent I had never heard before, even among the multi-racial slaves.

I pushed myself to my feet and walked cautiously over to the downed animal. I saw in an instant what had caused it to stumble: it had put its right foreleg into a pothole and the limb was broken, the bone protruding through the fur.

Under the beast, his leg trapped by its barrel-like torso, was its erstwhile rider. He saw me as soon as I saw him and reached for the sabre that lay on the ground beside him. He saw the bow in my hand, and even though there was no arrow fitted to it he sank back with a fatalistic resignation that was a candid indication of the kind of justice he expected to meet at my hands. I felt vaguely sick, but knew that in the heat of the battle I had been prepared to kill him without hesitation.

One of the other slaves, a six-foot pikestaff in his hands, saw me standing over the trapped bandit and, evidently realizing I was unarmed, rushed to my side and raised the pike, the head aimed at the bandit's chest. To his credit, the bandit didn't flinch.

I shoved the pike aside, giving the slave a further impetus with my foot. He gave me a look that was a mix of confusion and anger and edged slowly away.

I looked down at the bandit. He was giving me the kind of stare that told me he was wondering what kind of sadistic torture I had in store for him that had made a pike through the heart seem too merciful.

I bent down and eased the weight of his mount off his leg. The animal snarled and snapped at me with its ferocious jaws but its pain was making it woozy and the attempted bite missed by at least a millimetre – I decided not to get close to one of those creatures if it was in full possession of its faculties.

The bandit got his leg free and sprang to his feet, backing away from me.

I studied him closely. His clothing was mostly leather, plates of iron sewn into it as a crude form of armour. It was trimmed with various sorts of fur and some of his accoutrements seemed more refined than the rest – he was, for instance, wearing tooled steel greaves. I guessed that the better items were ones taken on raids.

I looked down at the sabre that lay between us on the ground, half covered in snow. I sensed him shift uneasily, but I made no move towards the weapon and neither did he.

The sabre, I reflected, was a cavalry weapon – not a weapon carried by an infantryman who just happened to be on a horse, but a weapon specifically designed and shaped by a race of fighting men who considered cavalry to be the only armed force worth mentioning. And all the bandits had been so armed.

I looked slowly towards the wounded animal at my side, letting the bandit follow my gaze. His crossbow hung from the saddle, a quiver of bolts tucked under it. I reached over and unslung the bow, tossing it to the bandit.

I stepped back.

He looked at the bow in his hands, then at the animal writhing in pain in the snow. He met my gaze and his brow furrowed, a look in his eyes that suggested he did not find trust an easy concept.

Then, incredibly fast, he sprang forward, snatched a bolt from the quiver, and jerked the bow's cable back. He fixed the bolt in its groove and placed the point against the wounded animal's head. He muttered something I couldn't quite hear and pulled the trigger.

The animal stopped moving pretty soon and the bandit stepped back.

We stared at one another for several seconds and then he tossed me the bow. I tossed it back at him. The expression on his face was so comical I almost laughed out loud. Instead, and to hide the smile that I couldn't suppress, I bent over the dead animal's saddle and retrieved the quiver of arrows. I threw them to the bandit. He looked around, as though he didn't know what to do next.

I gestured into the storm, in the general direction his fellows had fled.

He pointed at his dead beast, as though no other mode of travel was conceivable.

I pointed at his feet.

He threw back his head and laughed a laugh that sent a shiver through me.

Then, with that same terrifying speed he had shown a moment before, he sprang upon the sabre that lay between us on the ground. The blade flashed up towards my throat and stopped before touching the skin. I could feel sweat streaking my body, but I stood stock-still while we gazed wordlessly into one another's eyes. The bandit grinned, and dropped the sabre at my feet.

Then, without a word being spoken, he turned and ran off into the storm.

I found that I was shaking.

Slowly, I bent down and retrieved the sabre. It was a fine weapon, beautifully made and lovingly kept. The blade was heavy enough to shear through armour, yet light enough to allow for delicate point work. That the bandit had, effectively, gifted it to me seemed astonishing.

Wearily, I turned and made my way back to the Ladden caravan.

At Mrs Catlin's direction some of the other slaves had erected a crude lean-to against one of the waggons, and P'nad had been laid out under its limited shelter. We piled furs around him while Mrs Catlin inspected the wound; I didn't like the look on her face.

I turned to one of the other slaves.

'Is there no one trained in medicine among the Ladden?' I demanded, already knowing the answer.

'They have no need of such things,' the slave said.

'He has need,' I snapped, pointing at P'nad.

'He is only a slave,' the slave said. 'They will regret the loss, but it will be replaced.'

'You're worse than they are,' I snarled.

He looked at me with genuine, and uncomprehending, hurt.

Behind us, a voice said, 'Will he live?'

I turned to see Hareg.

'If he does,' I said, 'it will be no thanks to you.'

'Sheathe your tongue, slave,' Hareg said with only slight irritation. 'P'nad will get what help we can give – he is a good slave and deserves that much.'

'But you have no doctors,' I observed acidly.

'Why should we have?' Hareg asked. 'The strong live, the weak die: it is the way. To aid the weak is to weaken the race. What point in that?'

'Thank you, Adolf Hitler,' I muttered in English. Then, 'What if he can be saved? He won't be able to work . . .'

'If P'nad is strong enough to survive this we will gladly support him during his convalescence,' Hareg said. 'He will return to us stronger for the experience. And it will, I think, have earned him the right to fatherhood – a rare privilege for a slave.'

I tried to keep the look of disgust out of my face.

'The "right" to father a slave race for you?' I said.

'Don't be absurd,' Hareg snapped, now genuinely angry. 'His child would have the same rights to earn its freedom as any child. What do you take us for? Barbarians?'

I turned away, too bewildered and angry to make any kind of reply – every time I thought I'd got a grip on this society it turned to quicksilver and ran out of my hands. I wondered if I'd ever understand the Ladden. Or their slaves.

Mrs Catlin said, 'I daren't remove the arrow. I think his lung is damaged. If I pull it out, he'll either bleed to death or drown in his own blood.'

Hareg said, 'Some of what you said I did not understand. What is "lun"?'

Mrs Catlin and I were both fairly comfortable with the High

Tongue by now, and when we needed a word that we didn't know the appropriate English word tended just to slip in without our conscious knowledge.

'Bellows in his chest,' I said; 'two bags for sucking in air when he breathes.' I wondered how advanced the study of anatomy was amongst the Ladden. For all I knew they might have thought their insides were no more differentiated than the trunk of a tree.

'Ah,' said Hareg, 'tchugai – if that is punctured he will die.'

On this world, I thought grimly, *you're probably right.*

'Only a Mugatih would have the skill to save him now,' Hareg went on matter-of-factly, 'and for a slave none would bother.'

'Suppose we could find one of these Mugatih,' I said. 'What would persuade him to help?'

Hareg laughed.

'Money,' he said.

I cringed; the word 'money' in the High Tongue seldom referred to the medium of exchange that is most commonly in use on Earth. It was, instead, a synonym for 'trade' or 'barter', but with the emphasis placed strongly on one of the parties involved having to meet the other's price rather than haggle. I deduced, from the fact that Hareg had chosen that particular word, that a Mugatih's price would be high – too high for the Ladden to waste it on a slave, even one as valuable as P'nad.

Mrs Catlin said, 'What chance have we of finding one of these Mugatihs?'

Hareg said, 'In five days we would have come upon a trading town; it is a place with its own Mugaraht.' He paused, then added, 'Mugatihs sometimes purchase our goods. For their private collections.'

'With what do they buy them?' Mrs Catlin asked.

I cursed softly; always the academic . . .

'With things like the mutahiir and the slave bands,' Hareg said. 'Sometimes with slaves. Sometimes with knowledge – the Mugatihs "know" things.'

I caught Mrs Catlin's eye and realized, ashamedly, that her interest had not been abstract but practical – what, she had been wondering, could we offer to these Mugatihs in exchange for P'nad's life? By learning what the Mugatihs had to offer she had been trying to work out what they might want in exchange.

'P'nad will not live five days,' she said quietly. 'If he is lucky, he might live three. But in this weather—'

'Then we get to the trading post in three,' I said.

'Through a blizzard?' Hareg asked, smiling condescendingly.

'Through, as you say, a blizzard,' I replied. 'Or is that beyond your abilities?'

Hareg laughed.

'I like you, slave,' he said. 'You have no conception of your place in the world. Among my people you will ever be a curiosity, a constant source of entertainment.' His expression turned cold as he said, 'In any other part of the world your attitude would spell instant death. I hope you appreciate our lenience.'

He turned and walked back towards his own people.

'Break camp,' he yelled. 'Prepare for forced march to Vraks'has. Slaves will obey the man Shaw until P'nad's recovery or the appointment of his replacement.'

I started to yell something that I might have regretted but Hareg obviously wasn't going to listen.

Looking at the slaves gathering around me I saw some unfriendly looks coming my way. I saw some relieved ones as well; perhaps, in their opinion, there could have been worse choices for someone to lead them.

We broke camp rapidly. I had a pretty fair idea of the various strengths and weaknesses of the slaves, as well as knowing which ones would require careful watching if we were going to make the kind of pace I knew we would need to make to save P'nad's life.

For three days Hareg and I drove our people to the limit of their endurance – and, I think, a little beyond.

I could only speculate on Hareg's reasons for pushing the Ladden so hard, and their own reasons for letting him. It may have been my own ego that let me believe he did it to test both my own resolve and the extent to which I was prepared to go to save P'nad. Or perhaps he actually cared enough about P'nad himself to want to save his life. Perhaps. After all, P'nad was an expensive investment for the Ladden and would not have been cheap to replace.

During the whole march Mrs Catlin hardly ever left P'nad's side. There was little enough she could do for him but with the aid of some of the Ladden – and a few of the slaves who seemed to know more about medicine than any of their masters – she managed to help him hang onto his life until someone more skilled than she was could be found actually to save it.

There was only a single incident of insurrection during the three days and I didn't get to find out about it until the day after it took place.

I hadn't made many friends among my fellow slaves, although I managed to get on well enough with most of them. But there was one young man with whom I felt a special camaraderie and his name was S'nam. He had been a friend of K'nen and had been with us on the night we fetched K'nen's body back. After that he and I – and, to a degree, he and Mrs Catlin – had spent much of our free time together. We had swapped life stories – not easy from my point of view, since most of what I wanted to say couldn't be expressed in the High Tongue – and had grown to regard each other as dependable. It was to S'nam that I owed the prompt putting down of the minor insurrection on the second day of our forced march.

It had happened, he told me the next morning, during our brief midday break. The weather had worsened on the first day of our march and then had seemingly passed us by during the same night. On the day of the 'uprising' it was bitingly cold and the ground was patchy with snow. But the sky was clear, the wind had dropped and the watery sun was a brilliant yellow disc forty-five degrees above the horizon, and, amazingly, everyone seemed to be in good spirits.

Everyone except a woman named Sharekt. Sharekt was, in earthly terms, about thirty years old and had had a long-term relationship with K'nen. According to S'nam it was Sharekt who had been responsible for K'nen's perpetually bad mood. She was, it seemed, something of a social climber (!) and had constantly pressed K'nen to oust P'nad as leader of the Ladden slaves. A combination of good sense and a genuine admiration for P'nad had kept K'nen from ever attempting such a move, and thereby he had guaranteed himself a constant thorn in his side. But like most men in such situations he was unwilling to remove the thorn, and his seeming vacillation only served to increase Sharekt's goading.

And now, with K'nen gone and P'nad crippled and an alien newcomer walking straight into the place that she had felt should, even if only by proxy, have been hers, Sharekt had apparently decided that enough was enough. Midway through the brief meal break she had begun sounding off about how every bad thing that had happened to the slaves in the past year had been as a direct result of my arrival – which would have been quite a feat given that I hadn't been among the Ladden for anything like that long. She had timed her speech well, however, and caught the slaves when their indignation was at its highest and their logic at its lowest. Had no one spoken up she might actually have succeeded in rousing the slaves into some kind of rebellion, but S'nam had spotted the danger immediately and, partly out of friendship for me but mostly, I suspect, out of loyalty to P'nad, he had acted to defuse the situation. And he did that by simply reminding everyone that P'nad was the best leader that they'd ever had and that not only was he not yet dead but that it was I who was most actively working to keep him alive.

It was a testimony to S'nam's quiet eloquence and P'nad's own popularity that Sharekt's rabble-rousing suddenly fell on deaf ears. She had, from all accounts, turned pretty nasty at that point, even going so far as to threaten S'nam with physical violence. I knew from what he had told me previously that S'nam came from a race who regarded violence by men against women as the lowest form of social disgrace, so Sharekt's threat was not something he would be likely to take lightly. Fortunately there were others in the group who also knew this, and Sharekt promptly found herself surrounded by three other women who were not gentle in their defence of S'nam. Sharekt, it transpired, was likely to spend the remainder of the journey under the equivalent of open arrest.

I decided against acknowledging the threat to my 'authority' that Sharekt might actually pose. Leaving aside the fact that the women in the slave group seemed eminently capable of dealing with her without my help, there was the far more salient point – from my perspective, at least – that any authority I did possess was likely to be of so fleeting a nature as not to be worth defending.

In the middle of the third morning following the attack by the bandits we sighted the market town known as Vraks'has. It had taken us less than seventy-two hours to reach it.

Chapter 12

CONSULTING THE MUGATIH

Vraks'has was not remotely like Hippom Ather. Its age, I guessed, could be measured in centuries rather than millennia, with many of the older buildings being composed almost entirely of wood. The newer buildings were stone, large blocks fitted together without the aid of cement. The roofs were a mix of slate and thatch, and so constructed as to suggest it must rain here quite regularly. I wondered at that; in all the time we had been at Hippom Ather the weather had been temperate, with less than a dozen light showers in several months. Since Hippom Ather was less than two hundred miles from Vraks'has I could only assume that the change in seasons must be quite extreme.

The level of technology that had built the market town (which, in the High Tongue, was the literal meaning of 'Vraks'has') was somewhat less than that which I would have expected from the Ladden themselves had they deigned to attempt anything so menial as construction work. In design and execution, however, the town was the antithesis of everything Ladden. It was certainly functional, and parts of it even bordered on the aesthetic, but the overall impression was one of squalor. It was a curious mix of Western frontier town and Dark Age hovel.

None of it inspired me to believe that anywhere within its confines would we find aid for P'nad.

Hareg led the caravan through the outskirts of the town where we attracted no more interest from passers-by than would a half-dozen trucks and vans passing through an English industrial town. That Hareg knew where he was going seemed obvious, and I wasn't about to question him at this moment, but I couldn't help voicing my misgivings to S'nam who was marching along beside me at the time.

'Oh, but the Mugatih doesn't live in Vraks'has,' he said. 'It's just the Mugaraht that's here.'

'But the Mugatih lives close by,' I ventured.

'As to that I couldn't say,' said S'nam. 'For all I know he may live on the other side of the world.'

I looked at S'nam and saw that he was being perfectly serious. Suddenly – and all too belatedly, if it was true – I wondered if this whole forced trek had not been some hideous practical joke by Hareg. What if he truly did want P'nad dead? But, no; if that were the case, why had the slaves gone along with him? Why hadn't they told me? Unless they too wished P'nad removed from office as their leader. Perhaps the death of K'nen had been blamed on P'nad. K'nen, I reminded myself, had been S'nam's friend. And now S'nam was, it seemed, my friend. Yet K'nen had disliked me from the moment we met. I looked at S'nam and wondered at his motivations.

Hareg halted the column on the edge of a large open space in the middle of the town. Like Hippom Ather, Vraks'has was constructed around a central plaza, but here the purpose of the plaza was more obvious than it had been in the ancient city – it was the market place. And about a third of it was filled with brightly coloured tents and awnings, some already assembled and others still being erected. There was a sense of bustle and activity, of purpose, that was so much more vibrant and alive than the rest of the town that I could scarcely credit it to the same race of people.

And, of course, that was the point: they were not a single race, but many. And Vraks'has itself existed only to service them, to provide lodgings and casual labour and amusements for those who could not find such things in the market place. Seen from this new perspective the town took on its true colours; it was drab today because we had arrived early. The market was not due to open for business for three days, on the day after we had been due originally to arrive.

The Ladden convoy broke up without a word from anyone and its various members – Ladden and slave alike – began setting up their own tents and stalls. As with the striking of the camp at Hippom Ather the whole procedure smacked of years of experience and a routine that had become so much a part of life that its execution was entirely devoid of the necessity for conscious thought or direction. Not for the first time I pondered the antiquity of the Ladden race; surely they had not been living this lifestyle for as long as cities like Hippom Ather had been standing deserted by their original builders?

As I stood about watching the Ladden convoy convert itself into a small encampment I was approached by Hareg. He looked oddly nervous.

'Come with me,' he said.

I followed him across the market square.

'Where are we going?' I asked.

'Where do you think?' he demanded.

Given what S'nam had said earlier I decided to say nothing; I'd let Hareg have enough rope and then see how high I could hang him.

We skirted the market square and headed into what I could only describe as the uptown quarter of Vraks'has. Here all the buildings were stone and the quality of the construction had a somewhat 'prettier' look, as though the architects had expected to have to live here themselves and thus had had a vested interest in how the place would look.

We emerged from a narrow street between two long, low buildings and into a second plaza, much bigger than the market place, bigger even than the one at Hippom Ather. This one must have been at least five hundred yards across, and unlike either of those other two places this one was occupied by a central structure that surprised me considerably.

It was a building, but one totally unlike any other I had seen on this world. It was circular, about two storeys high, and at least a hundred yards in diameter. What was surprising about it, however, was the fact that it appeared to be built from red brick. It had no windows at all, and only a single door that was no bigger than the average house door. The circular outer wall was topped with a ring of rounded, grey stone, and behind it was the suggestion of the shallow curve of a domed roof. The outer wall had been buttressed in places, but whether these were structural or simply affectations on the part of the builder was difficult to tell.

As we approached the small door to the building I noticed with surprise how quiet the streets around this building seemed to be. I didn't like the idea of getting chatty with Hareg but there was no one else to ask and I was even less well disposed towards going into that strangely intimidating edifice in total ignorance of its significance.

'Why are there so few people in this part of town?' I asked.

Hareg looked at me as though I were a simpleton.

'The Mugaraht,' he said, and from his tone of voice I guessed that any further enquiry would be regarded as deliberate obtuseness on my part.

I said, as casually as I could, 'I suppose they aren't as popular here as they are where I come from.'

Hareg turned on me with a look of fury.

'Do you mock me?' he demanded. 'Do you mock my people?'

I started to reply, totally baffled by his attitude, when he cut me off.

'You forget your place, Shaw,' he hissed. 'Don't make me remind you of it.'

I felt my own anger rise to match his, but before I could find a suitable response he had turned and was striding away from me towards the Mugaraht. Fuming, I hurried to catch up. I almost ran into Hareg as he abruptly stopped and wheeled to face me again. The look on his face had changed, and somehow this new expression worried me far more than his previous anger had. He was looking at me now as though I was truly an alien – which, of course, I was, but both Mrs Catlin and I had been very careful to disguise that fact.

'There *are* Mugarahts in your country,' he said, his tone of voice making the statement hover on the edge of being a question.

'Of course,' I said; I still didn't know what a Mugaraht actually was, but from the look Hareg was giving me I had no intention of saying anything he might not be willing – or able – to believe.

He looked at me intently for several seconds, then turned away with a muttered curse. Together we entered the Mugaraht.

Inside, the building revealed itself to be a series of nested circles – which, after Hippom Ather, shouldn't have surprised me; but it did. This building, I was sure, was of human construction, and there was no reason for it to follow the architectural pattern of that ancient city.

Inside the single entrance we found ourselves in a narrow, circular corridor that followed the circumference of the building and that descended, ramp-like, to either side. Overhead, the ceiling was two storeys away; the building's outer walls were simply a shell, with whatever mysteries it contained being located somewhere below ground.

We descended the left-hand ramp, eventually coming to a point that I guessed to be a further two storeys below ground and diametrically opposite the entrance. The ramp levelled off at this point before ascending again some yards further along. In the wall on our right, the wall giving access to the inner part of the building, was a second door. It was the first such door we had come to since passing through the outer one.

We passed through this door and found ourselves in a second corridor, identical to the first.

'How many of these corridors are there?' I asked.

'Five,' said Hareg.

'All going down?' I asked.

'All going down,' said Hareg.

'Why?' I asked.

I got *that* look again; I was asking questions no grown man should need to ask on this world – possibly questions no child would even have to ask.

Hareg seemed in the mood to humour me, though I couldn't have guessed why.

'For defence,' he said, 'and for meditation.' I thought he was going to leave it at that, but he added, 'When one is going to consult a Mugatih one should have sufficient time to collect one's thoughts, don't you think?'

'Of course,' I said. I thought quickly, then said, 'I guess I can understand that part, but I can't imagine a Mugaraht needing defence. Who would attack it?'

I'd meant that I couldn't imagine anyone having a *reason* to attack a Mugaraht, but Hareg misunderstood.

'No sane man would dare,' he said. 'But in times past fanatics have made the attempt. They have failed, of course, but sometimes they have done great harm before being stopped.'

We came to the next door just as a man stepped through it and into our corridor. I felt my fists clench at sight of the man – he was a bandit, like the ones we had fought several days earlier.

Hareg and the bandit looked hard at one another, then exchanged curt greetings before the bandit turned and walked off down the corridor away from us. I relaxed, but this unexpected encounter made me appreciate the power of this Mugaraht over the people here.

We traversed the remaining corridors without incident and finally emerged into the central part of the building, which was a single large chamber over seventy yards in diameter and twelve storeys deep.

The chamber was dominated – and almost filled – by a single object, and in attempting to describe it I find myself confronted by the sheer inadequacy of language.

It was beautiful. That was the first thought to strike me, and the one that has remained with me ever since.

It was a crystal – or rather, it was a mountain carved from crystal. Except that everything about it denied the charge that it was a *made* thing. It had that wild, untamed look that only nature can produce. Somehow, in some unfathomable way, this structure had *grown* here.

Light seemed to be trapped inside it. It didn't glow, or shine; it just seemed to eat light. And, once trapped, that light shattered into a multitude of colours and patterns, all in constant motion within the elaborate form of the thing.

The thing – I stopped myself: *this* was the Mugaraht. I don't know why I should have been so utterly certain of that fact, but I was.

The Mugaraht was so vast it almost filled the whole chamber. There was a circular floor space around it of perhaps ten yards radius, and its irregularly shaped tip fell short of the ceiling by a couple of yards. There was a very definite suggestion that the building had been built *around* it, rather than the Mugaraht somehow having been grown inside the building.

When I finally looked away from the impressive object I began to notice other features in the chamber. Around the edge of the structure, standing perhaps six yards away from it, were what looked like lecterns of some sort, their slightly concave surfaces inlaid with rectangles of a greenish, glass-like substance.

Hareg made for one of these lecterns, and I noticed that several of the others were occupied by men or women, sometimes singly, sometimes in small groups, standing next to them and doing something on the smooth surfaces that I couldn't quite make out.

I stood behind Hareg as he positioned himself behind the lectern, facing the crystal structure in the centre of the chamber, and picked up an object I had not noticed before that had been resting in a small groove in the base of the lectern. The object was a kind of stylus, and with it Hareg made a series of marks on the green surface laid into the lectern. I was surprised to see a glowing line appear where the stylus touched the surface, and with a start I realized that Hareg had written something. It was the first writing I had seen since joining the Ladden, and I marvelled at the fact that I had never wondered about the written form of the High Tongue before this. Then again, I reflected wryly, I hadn't exactly been short of things to keep me occupied.

Like a bolt from the blue the meaning of Mugaraht suddenly hit me. Library! This was a library! I looked at the crystal object with a sudden surge of realization; I had known when first I saw it that there had been something vaguely familiar about it, and now I knew what it was – it was made of the same stuff as the mutahiir. Was it possible that this huge object was some kind of data storage system, a crystalline computer? If so, then the knowledge stored in it could reach back to before the fall

111

of civilization on Shushuan, and might truly be of use in saving P'nad's life.

Hareg's marks had vanished from the surface as soon as he had finished writing them, and were now being replaced by other, different signs.

'What are you doing?' I asked, my voice an unintentional whisper. If my guess was right, I already knew what he was doing.

'I am asking for the assistance of a Mugatih versed in medicine,' said Hareg. He looked at me. 'Is that not why we are here?'

'Mugatih', I now assumed, meant 'Librarian'. I remembered the quasi-mystic figure who had stood on the open plain on the night of K'nen's death and I suppressed a shudder. If the knowledge in this library had become steeped in myth and lore then getting at it could be a hazardous task, to say the least.

I returned Hareg's look with a blank stare; if he was planning anything underhand I had no intention of letting him know I was on to him.

'And what is the reply?' I asked.

Hareg studied the writing.

'We are to await a decision,' he said. He touched the surface with the stylus and the writing faded. He wrote something briefly and then it too vanished. The surface remained blank.

Hareg said, not looking at me, 'If the price the Librarian asks is beyond what I consider to be P'nad's worth you will be indebted to me for life. Do you understand?'

I did, but I said nothing.

'As will the woman,' said Hareg.

I clenched my fists, but I refused to be drawn.

Hareg grinned.

'You bargain well,' he said, a bit too inscrutably for me to believe it was intended as a compliment.

The surface before us lit up with more writing and Hareg said, 'The offer is accepted. Librarian Sonder will be here directly.'

'Do you know this Sonder?' I asked.

'I have met him,' said Hareg. 'He is quite well known in these parts.'

'What is he like?' I asked.

112

Hareg shrugged.

'He is a Librarian,' he said. He glanced towards the crystal structure in the centre of the chamber. 'He is here,' he said.

I followed his gaze and found myself struggling to understand what I was seeing. The figure of a man seemed to be stepping out of the solid crystal, as though he were no more substantial than one of the many rays of light that passed through the object. I almost went cross-eyed trying to make sense of what I was seeing, and then suddenly my mind seemed to make one of those lateral deductions that the human brain is occasionally prone to and I realized what was happening. Looking at the crystal structure I had assumed it to be a solid cone, but it was not. Because of the play of light upon its surface, and the nature of the substance itself that made it difficult to focus on, it had appeared to me that its outer surface was relatively flat, when in fact it did not have a single outer surface at all. It was, instead, a maze of crystal stalagmites, growing together as they climbed so that the upper part of the cone truly was a fused mass, but the lower part was nothing more than a collection of bizarrely-shaped columns. Even with this realization, it was impossible to force the eye to see it as it truly was: as soon as the man had emerged from within the complex structure that made up the cone's base I was once again confronted with a perfectly solid surface, and no amount of rationalization could convince my eyes or my brain otherwise.

I looked away from the thing before the frustration could drive me crazy – and found myself face to face with the Librarian.

He was no taller than I, but managed somehow to look it. His hair was long and ash-blond, beginning to turn to grey; his eyes were blue and betrayed a chilling intelligence. In earthly terms, I would have judged him to be about fifty years of age. His single visible garment was a white robe that reached the floor and whose broad sleeves covered his hands. The only adornment on the robe was a vertical column of gold embroidery that ran from just below his left shoulder to the hem of the garment at his feet. The embroidery looked vaguely like writing, but fancifully done. I doubted that I could have read it without difficulty even had I not been illiterate in the writings of this world.

The Librarian – Sonder – regarded me for several moments and then turned to Hareg.

'Hareg of the Ladden,' he said, and I noted that his accent was not that of the Ladden. I hadn't expected that it would be, since Sonder was clearly not of Hareg's race, but what did surprise me was that I recognized the accent: it was the same as S'nam's.

'Sonder-jin,' said Hareg, bowing.

'One of your people is ill?' Sonder said; he showed not the slightest concern.

'An injury,' said Hareg. 'An arrow sustained during a battle with bandits.'

Sonder raised an eyebrow about a millimetre; I took it as a gesture of surprise – the Ladden, as he was no doubt aware, do not do their own fighting.

'What is the identity of this injured person?' he asked.

Hareg actually swallowed before answering.

'He is named P'nad,' he said.

Sonder's expression briefly registered surprise, and something more – amusement? It was like trying to read the expression on a block of granite.

'A slave?' he said.

'Our chief slave,' said Hareg, and I almost laughed; a chief slave was no less a slave than the slave of a slave.

'And for this Chief Slave,' said Sonder with heavy sarcasm, 'you are willing to pay for my services?'

'We are,' said Hareg.

'No, no,' said Sonder, dismissing Hareg's reply out of hand. '*You* are willing to pay?'

He looked pointedly at Hareg, and I saw the Ladden tremble slightly.

I said, 'I will pay.'

Sonder paused briefly before looking at me – it was the most effective put-down I'd ever seen, and I felt about an inch tall as his gaze met mine.

'You have nothing with which to pay,' he said.

'I have myself,' I told him.

'No,' said Sonder, 'you have nothing. The "self" of which you

114

speak belongs to this man' – he indicated Hareg – 'and is not yours to give.'

I felt crushed by what he had said. In the Ladden camp it had been possible to cling to the notion that I was a slave only in the eyes of a backward race of egotistical nomads, and that in my own heart I was still free. But this man represented established authority in this place, and the sudden knowledge that to him – and therefore to the society he represented – I was nothing more than property brought me back to the realities of my situation with a bitter sense of futility.

'I will give him gladly,' said Hareg, and in that instant my resentment towards him turned into hatred. 'And in our camp there is a woman – of the same race as this slave – who is skilled at many arts and crafts. We had taken her as one of our own, but for your services she will be a small price to pay.'

'Very small,' said Sonder dryly. 'Some might say insulting.'

Hareg looked as though he might be sick at any moment.

Sonder said, 'But we will settle later. First, let us save the life of this . . . slave.'

Hareg almost threw himself at Sonder's feet, in the process casting me a look of such venom I almost laughed out loud – if I had lost something today, Hareg had probably lost a great deal more, or at least was soon to do so.

Chapter 13

GOODBYES

We followed Sonder out of the Library, taking the ramps back to the single entrance/exit at street level opposite to those we had taken on the way down. I tried to discern some hidden significance in this but decided that it was probably simply due to ancient tradition.

The streets of the market town were busier when we left the Library than they had been before we went in, but we made easy progress through them. This was due to the fact that everyone we passed gave Sonder a very wide berth; most of them fell to one knee at sight of him, averting their eyes; some – slaves, mostly – fell prostrate until he had passed them by. There was little of reverence in any of the expressions we saw on the faces of the townspeople, and much of fear.

We reached the Ladden camp to find that it was now fully erected and that P'nad was being tended by Mrs Catlin in what would be the general slave quarters. Some of the other slaves were hanging around the area of the large tent, but at sight of the Librarian they quickly scattered.

At the entrance to the tent Sonder turned to Hareg and said, 'Remain here.' To me he said, 'Come with me.' Seeing Hareg's sudden flash of annoyance Sonder said easily, 'You did say this slave was my property.'

As far as I could recall Hareg had never actually said that – after all, P'nad had yet to be saved. It seemed as though Hareg did not wish to dispute the point, however, and I followed the Librarian into the tent.

P'nad was almost unrecognizable. His skin was ashen, and his former mighty frame seemed wasted away. I could hardly believe he had survived this long, and didn't know whether to credit Mrs Catlin with this miracle or to attribute it to P'nad's own tremendous stamina.

Mrs Catlin looked up as we entered; she was bathing P'nad's wound, the shaft of the arrow still protruding from it. She gave the Librarian the most perfunctory of visual examinations before returning to her task.

Sonder crouched down beside P'nad and waved Mrs Catlin aside. She glared at him but said nothing.

The Librarian poked P'nad's shoulder and the injured slave groaned feebly. He seemed only semi-conscious, feverish. Sonder grunted at the response.

'He will live,' he stated.

'Simply because you say so?' Mrs Catlin asked acidly.

'I know my talents, slave,' Sonder replied emotionlessly. 'The man is beyond your aid, but not mine.'

'I am not a slave!' Mrs Catlin said.

'You are,' said Sonder. 'You and the boy are my payment.'

Mrs Catlin glared at me briefly and I nodded.

'He is not a boy,' she said softly, and anyone who had ever heard Mrs Catlin say anything softly would have known just how furious she was at that moment. 'And neither of us are property.'

'You are mistaken,' said Sonder. 'Now leave while I earn my payment.'

'I will not—' Mrs Catlin began.

Sonder pointed at her and with a concussion of sound and force she was flung across the tent. I leaped to her side, scarcely able to believe what had happened. Sonder carried no visible weapons, and his hand as he had pointed it at her had been naked of any mechanism – how had he done what he had? Surely he did not possess some magical power? Or perhaps some psychic ability? The possibilities terrified me. We now belonged to this . . . man.

I helped a shaken Mrs Catlin to her feet. She was winded, but seemed unhurt.

Sonder looked at us with that irritatingly level gaze of his.

'You are my property,' he told us. 'Being the slave of a Librarian is not necessarily an unpleasant existence, but it can be so if you wish it.' He looked down at P'nad as though we were not even there any longer. 'Go,' he said distantly. 'And await me at the Library entrance.'

I could feel Mrs Catlin's body grow rigid in my arms but before she could speak I half-dragged and half-carried her out of the tent.

She threw off my grasp as soon as we were in the open air. I readied myself for an explosion of temper but, to my amazement, she turned away from me without so much as a sarcastic comment and sat down on a bench beside the tent. She seemed totally washed out, drained of all life and energy. And somehow I knew it had nothing to do with what the Librarian had said and done.

I sat down beside her.

'He will save P'nad,' I said.

She nodded, and from her expression I knew I had guessed right about what was bothering her.

I started to say something when I realized that we were not alone. I looked up to see Hareg standing over us. Behind him were a couple of the Ladden who had assisted him in putting the slave band on my leg. Hareg held the mutahiir in his hand and, glancing past him, I saw that one of the men held a long strip of the grey substance that, once in place, became the slave band.

'You're not wasting any time,' I said.

Mrs Catlin gave me a puzzled look. Then she looked at Hareg and the others and the light of realization dawned in her eyes.

'Isn't this a little premature?' she snapped. 'For all you know P'nad may yet die.'

'That no longer concerns you,' Hareg said. 'Whether he lives or dies you will be a slave; either the Librarian's – or mine.'

All the hate I had felt for Hareg in the Library suddenly returned, and springing to my feet I punched him in his smug face, more than moderately hard. He fell back, blood pouring out of his mouth, and with an inarticulate cry of rage he pointed the mutahiir at me. It flared with rainbow light and instantly my left leg felt as though I had plunged it into a blast furnace. I went down in an instant, howling in pain, and felt my grip on consciousness desert me.

I came to only minutes later, but at the time it felt as though I had spent an eternity in a fiery hell. I clutched at my leg, expecting to find a charred stump, but found instead a perfectly normal and healthy limb. I looked around, still dazed, and realized that Mrs Catlin had been kneeling beside me and cradling my head in her lap. Her left ankle now bore the badge of a slave.

'How do you feel?' she asked. I tried to tell myself she hadn't been crying, but didn't entirely succeed.

'OK,' I said. 'You?'

'A little humiliated, but unhurt,' she said. A look of utter malice briefly crossed her face and she said, 'Thank you for hitting Hareg. It didn't exactly help the situation, but it made it a little less intolerable.' She smiled weakly. 'Not a very civilized response, I'm afraid.'

'But a very human one,' I told her, grinning.

I meant it kindly – I wanted to let her know that despite some of the things I had accused her of in the past, I knew that deep down she had just the same feelings that I had. Unfortunately, she didn't take it that way.

'I *am* human, Shaw,' she snapped, shoving me away and standing up. 'Even if you do find that hard to believe.'

She stormed off before I could reply, and I cursed myself for every kind of fool, even though I hadn't – from my point of view – done anything wrong.

I had been sitting on the hard ground for several minutes when I suddenly remembered Sonder's parting words to Mrs Catlin and me as we left the tent. We were to wait for him at the Library!

I jumped up and raced after Mrs Catlin, only to find myself intercepted and stopped by a group of the Ladden slaves, led by S'nam.

'Shaw,' he said, by way of greeting. 'We hear P'nad will live.'

'I think so,' I said, wondering what Sonder would do if we weren't at the Library when he arrived there. That he had something like the mutahiir seemed inevitable.

'And,' went on S'nam, ignorant of the need for haste, 'that you are now the property of a Librarian. You and the woman Linna.'

'We were payment for P'nad, yes,' I said.

'We will miss you,' said S'nam.

I felt the haste drain out of me as I realized, belatedly, that S'nam and the others had come to say goodbye. I hadn't exactly made friends among the slaves – we were a little too alien for that – but I liked S'nam, and I liked a lot of his companions. I liked P'nad in a perverse kind of way, and I'd liked poor Chang who had died during the raid by the bandits. The idea that I might never see any of these people again was a surprisingly painful one.

'I will miss you too, S'nam,' I said. 'I will miss you all.'

'The Librarian has not yet left the camp,' said S'nam, revealing that he had known of my need for haste all along. 'He confers with Hazeg over his payment – sadly, you and the woman are not very valuable and a Librarian's services are not cheap. Also, the Librarian will want your khiri from the mutahiir.'

I still didn't like the idea of delaying our departure, but what S'nam had just said intrigued me.

'I've never heard that word before,' I told him. 'What is *khiri?*'

'Each slave band has its own khiri within the mutahiir,' said S'nam. 'The khiri tells the mutahiir which slave band to activate if a slave is to be punished. Every time a new slave band is fitted a new khiri is added to the mutahiir.'

'Is a slave band ever reused?' I asked.

'Never,' said S'nam. 'When set to kill, a slave band destroys itself as well as its victim.'

'Destroys how?' I asked. K'nen's slave band had been intact.

'Becomes simply metal,' said S'nam.

'Suppose a slave band were removed before death,' I said. 'Would it be reused then?'

'A slave band cannot be removed,' said S'nam. 'To do so would kill its wearer.'

121

I'd been afraid of that, but until now I hadn't actually broached the subject.

It occurred to me that some of Mrs Catlin's academic obsessions had rubbed off on me: S'nam had come here to say goodbye, and all I could do was to quiz him on a subject that he could hardly have found pleasant. But there was one more thing I had to know.

'When K'nen ran,' I said, 'how did he expect to get away?'

S'nam's face clouded with the memory, but he said, 'The mutahiir has a limited range. When a slave is found to have escaped, his khiri is set to kill and left that way. If he escapes the range of the mutahiir before it is set to kill he must forever remain out of its range or it will kill him should he again enter its range. It is an . . . efficient way to control slaves. The lands over which the Ladden roam are extensive.'

'It remains set to kill *forever*?' I said.

'If the slave dies, his khiri in the mutahiir dissolves,' said S'nam.

'The range,' I said, thinking this the most important point; 'do you know how far it is?'

'Less than one day's walk for a strong man,' said S'nam.

I knew what would be considered 'strong' by the slaves of the Ladden; that gave the mutahiir a range of perhaps twenty-five miles. How could K'nen have thought he could escape?

'S'nam,' I said, 'I talk too much. Will you forgive me? And accept my hand as a mark of friendship?'

S'nam took my proffered hand in the way of his people – by clasping my wrist just behind the thumb. I returned the gesture. The other slaves crowded round and we all shook hands, or clasped arms or did whatever was the custom in their home lands.

'The woman Linna is with the slave women,' said S'nam. 'I think they were fond of her – the gods know why!'

I laughed at his expression; S'nam had been on the receiving end of Mrs Catlin's wrath more than once, though he had never – to my mind – done anything to deserve it.

I left S'nam and the others and went in search of Mrs Catlin. When I found her I got something of a surprise. She was standing outside one of the smaller slave tents and was flanked by three of the other female slaves. And she was dressed as one of them. Gone were the tattered remains of her checked shirt and jeans and in their place was the layered, asymmetric skirt and chiton of a Ladden slave woman. And the quality of the material was the finest I had ever seen. Her whole appearance was now pure Vinh; her skin was as tanned as that of a Ladden, and her hair was now much longer than she had ever worn it on Earth. Its reddish tint was also more pronounced, giving it a lustrous sheen that its previous style had not even hinted at.

Looking at her, I wondered at my own appearance – the Ladden have no mirrors, and the only reflection I had seen of myself lately had been in the distorted surface of a lake.

Mrs Catlin was shivering slightly – there was still a fair bit of snow on the ground – but she made no attempt at pulling on her furs.

I walked up to her and, realizing how I was staring, found myself tongue-tied. She seemed no less embarrassed, and the giggles of the slave women didn't help much.

'You look . . . nice,' I said.

And we both broke up, probably as much from nervous tension as from the actual humour of the situation. But it felt good to laugh, even if the laughter was strained. The slave women only saw the laughter, of course, and joined in with open good humour. I think they had never understood the relationship between Mrs Catlin and me, and in that we had something in common. But I think they ascribed a degree of intimacy to our relationship that did not exist, and found our public reticence highly amusing.

Pulling myself together, I said, 'We must hurry. If we are not at the Library when Sonder arrives we could be in trouble.'

Mrs Catlin nodded, and I saw that despite her personal antipathy to Sonder she was not so foolish as to underestimate his power over us.

'Shaw-jin——?' said one of the women.

'Just "Shaw",' I said. 'You owe me no titles.'

'Shaw-jin,' she repeated, coyly not meeting my gaze, 'we have a gift for you.'

I was surprised, to say the least, and more so when I saw a bundle being passed from inside the tent. It appeared to be a rug, rolled into a tube. The woman took the tube and handed it to me.

'You have earned this by your every word and deed since the day P'nad was struck down,' the woman said, using a very formalized grammatical structure that I usually associated with Ladden poetry. 'We wish that you should have it, both to remember us by and to bring you the fortune you have brought to us.' She glanced sidelong at Mrs Catlin and added what was normally a ritual phrase but which she imbued with a wealth of meaning: 'May your offspring honour your name.'

Mrs Catlin blushed from head to toe, which was a slightly less astonishing sight than the contents of the bundle: it was the sabre I had been given by the bandit.

'Librarians, like Ladden,' said the woman, 'are not averse to letting others fight for them. And as they cannot be harmed by material weapons they do not fear to have their slaves go armed.'

I wondered at the remark about Librarian invulnerability, but conscious of how much time had already gone by I decided to let that mystery wait for another day.

'Will you get into trouble for this?' I asked; slaves were not permitted to own property, so this sabre was not theirs to give.

The woman shook her head.

'Few of the Ladden pay much attention to our weapons,' she said. 'They are not likely to miss one blade.'

I didn't know if that was true, but I decided not to press it – there might come a day when I would be glad of the weapon.

I said, as formally as I could, 'The accepting of a gift honours the giver.'

It wasn't even remotely a Vinh saying, but it was one that translated exactly into the High Tongue.

Saying our final farewells, Mrs Catlin and I walked out of the Ladden camp and headed for the Library.

'I'll miss the Ladden,' Mrs Catlin said as we walked. There was an uncharacteristic wistfulness in her voice; it wasn't like my former teacher to be sentimental. It was true that the Ladden had provided us with shelter for a time, and that they had taught us enough to survive on their world, but the negative aspects of our time with them far outweighed the positive, to my way of thinking. Strangely enough, though, I found myself agreeing with her.

'We may see them again,' I told her. 'The Librarians, from what I've heard, use the same trade routes as the Ladden.'

Mrs Catlin glanced at me. 'That isn't what I meant,' she said.

I decided that she was in the mood to be enigmatic but that I wasn't in the mood to indulge her. I thought for a moment she was going to elaborate, but then we emerged from the alley leading to the Library and I saw with dismay that Sonder was already there. He was standing to one side of the small doorway, and I was not in the least reassured by the fact that there was no trace of impatience on his face.

'I think we're in trouble,' I said.

'Shaw,' Mrs Catlin said pensively, 'there are a lot of variables at play in this situation, and we don't have a clue what most of them are. Don't do anything precipitate until we're more sure of our standing.'

'We're slaves!' I snorted. 'How much more sure do you need to get?'

She shot me a look that had more threat potential than anything even Sonder could have managed, so I shut up.

Sonder greeted us with what might almost have been a smile and said, 'You are late. If ever you are late again the penalty will be painful. I now control your slave bands, and unlike the barbarian Ladden I need no mutahiir to activate them.'

'We apologize for our tardiness, master,' Mrs Catlin said.

'Do not,' said Sonder. 'Your thoughts, feelings, opinions – lives – are without value. Simply serve as you are required to serve. And the title "master" is inappropriate – you are not my vassals, you are my property. Should it be necessary for you to address me you will simply refer to me as Librarian – is that clear?'

'Yes, Librarian,' we said in unison. I felt sick, and I had a pretty good idea Mrs Catlin did too. I tried to match her diplomacy, but I don't think I succeeded.

'Now,' said Sonder with a very businesslike tone in his voice, 'the barbarian Hareg tells me you are not native to this continent. Please say something in your native tongue.'

I started to reply but Mrs Catlin cut me off.

'Je le ferai, Shaw,' she snapped, using her most school-teacherish voice. I caught the implicit warning and looked sheepishly at her. Sonder almost laughed.

'Say more,' he commanded.

In French, Mrs Catlin said, 'This is our native tongue, which we call French. Our home is a land called France, on a distant continent. Is this information of value, Librarian?'

Sonder looked at me.

'Speak,' he said.

'If this is some kind of test,' I said in French, 'I'd be curious to know if we've passed.'

Sonder nodded to himself, but I had the distinct impression that he hadn't understood a word we'd said.

He pointed to the sabre that I was now carrying openly – I hadn't wanted him to think I was concealing it.

'You may carry that weapon for however long you are in my service,' he said. 'You will, however, refrain from using it unless I so direct.'

He turned and began to walk away, circling the Library building. Not knowing what else to do, Mrs Catlin and I followed.

Chapter 14

PREPARATIONS

I shouldn't have been surprised to discover that Sonder lived in a palace, but I was.

It was a stone-built affair on five storeys, and stood in its own grounds on the far side of the Library. It was very imposing, but only in a relative sense; there was nothing about it to suggest the advanced technology that was responsible for the Library.

Sonder's staff numbered hundreds – all slaves. He had kitchen slaves, stable slaves, household slaves, body slaves, garden slaves – and so many armed slaves that I wondered if he had plans to start a war with somebody.

He left us in the care of some kind of overseer – himself a slave – and returned to the Library. Over the next twenty days we saw him perhaps five times, and seldom for more than a few minutes at a time.

Life with Sonder, as we quickly came to discover, was completely unlike life with the Ladden. To the Ladden we had been people, albeit – in my case – enslaved; and the subsistence-level existence had made every day a full one, with little time for self-indulgence or the intensive study that both Mrs Catlin and I had needed in order to pass for natives of this world. To Sonder, however, we were, as he had said, no more than property. We were assigned specific duties, to be performed at specific times, but beyond that he had no interest in us. It was as though to the Ladden we had been general-purpose tools to be used in a variety of ways for a multitude of tasks, but to Sonder we were specialist instruments designed only for a handful of predetermined purposes, and when we were not engaged in these specific tasks he had no further use for us. It was a change in lifestyle that required a very conscious shifting of mental gears to accommodate.

For Mrs Catlin, whose duties were vaguely secretarial in nature, it was an ideal opportunity to expand her knowledge of this world. And, in our long periods of inactivity, to play the role of teacher. It was my task, during these times, to be the ever-attentive student.

My own duties with Sonder placed me in his barracks. Given the number of men-at-arms he already owned I couldn't see any reason why I should be singled out for special attention – but I was. His orders, apparently, were that I should be outfitted as his personal bodyguard, and that I should he equipped for a very long journey. (I had heard mutterings in his household about this journey, but nothing that could be construed as more than idle gossip.) The elderly overseer who was assigned the task of getting me outfitted had looked at me with ill-concealed scepticism – for which I could hardly blame him – and then dragged me off to another part of town in an attempt to fulfil his mission.

This part of Vraks'has was one I had not seen before and was something of a surprise. I had thought that the only trading in the town took place in the market, but this proved not to be the case. There was a small collection of businesses, all situated on a single street, that had permanent residence in the town. They were a diverse lot, but seemed to deal principally in perishable and semi-perishable goods. This, on reflection, was sensible enough – the town needed servicing, after all, and its inhabitants could hardly survive from one market to the next without food and essential supplies.

At the end of the street was the largest building in the row and its wares, if they could be dignified by such a title, were of the semi-perishable variety: slaves.

In addition to its human merchandise, the shop also supplied all the accoutrements that a slave-owner might need, such as chains and collars and the like, as well as a varied assortment of liveries. I noticed the assorted types of shackles on view and wondered at their necessity, given the rather efficient ankle band with its multiplicity of functions.

My guide led me to the clothing section of the store where an assistant with the most superior manner I had ever seen eventually deigned to notice us.

'This is a new slave for the Librarian Sonder,' said my guide, indicating me.

The assistant barely glanced at me, which irritated me a bit, especially as I was carrying the bandit sabre at the time.

'Ladden?' the assistant asked; he might have been naming a type of disease.

'A former slave of the Ladden,' said my guide. 'By birth he is a barbarian.'

The assistant sniffed. 'And what would you call the Ladden?' he asked dismissively.

My guide shrugged. 'Nevertheless,' he said, 'my master wishes him out-fitted as a bodyguard. We are to make a journey to the Great Plains and fighting men may be necessary.'

The assistant actually managed to look interested at that.

'Ktikbat, eh?' he said, which was a new word to me. 'Then he'll want something that can stop an arrow at long range but still leave him free to wield that piece of cutlery he's grasping so fiercely. As it happens, I have the very thing in stock.'

He moved deeper into the store and my guide followed. Fuming, I did likewise.

The outfit he eventually strapped me into was not unlike the regalia the bandits had worn, except that its principal colours were a mix of green and brown, done in random patterns, presumably for camouflage. The main element was a sleeveless tunic that came down to mid-thigh and which was composed of layered, toughened leather. It was sewn with dull plates of beaten iron that might indeed have turned aside an arrow at long range, although I wouldn't have liked to stake my life on it. In addition to the tunic were woollen leggings, a long-sleeved woollen shirt to wear under the tunic, calf-length leather boots, and a broad belt covered with straps and buckles for carrying a variety of weapons and pouches. I found a suitable buckle and fastened the scabbard of the sabre to it.

'Armour?' asked my guide of the assistant.

'Mounted or infantry?' asked the assistant.

'Mounted,' said my guide.

I didn't like the sound of that; the only riding I'd ever done had been on motorcycles.

The assistant produced a teardrop-shaped shield made of iron-bound wood and an almost full-faced helmet with a narrow, Y-shaped opening for the eyes, nose and mouth. It had a chin strap and felt very uncomfortable.

I had noticed, against one wall of the store, a collection of weapons, among them a longbow.

'What about a bow?' I ventured.

'A what?' asked the assistant; he seemed genuinely taken aback.

'A bow,' I said. 'Like that one.'

My guide grabbed me by the arm and dragged me roughly to one side.

'Do you seek to shame my master?' he hissed.

'No,' I said, snatching my arm away. 'But I thought the idea was to protect him. And I gather the ones I'll be protecting him from will have bows and arrows. Doesn't it make sense for us to do the same?'

'The bow,' said my guide, 'is a peasant's weapon. As my master's property you are a reflection of his status. If you carry a bow, that makes you a peasant, and that makes my master a peasant. If you suggest such a thing again I shall have you flogged.'

I looked at the little man and found no trace of fear of me in his eyes. I decided that if he hadn't been so obviously satisfied to be a slave I might have liked him – well, a little anyway. Instead, I simply shrugged and turned away. If these people wanted to add another kind of senseless bigotry to their canon I wasn't about to protest it. Although I would have felt more comfortable with that longbow at my side.

We left the store without making any kind of payment or signing any kind of promissory note, and I wondered idly if the assistant would try to rip Sonder off. Probably not, I decided.

The level of activity in Sonder's palace increased noticeably over the next few days, and I guessed that our impending journey was drawing closer. On the subject of where the journey would take us I had only one word for a clue: Ktikbat. Mrs Catlin, as part of her duties, had considerable access to the Library's store of data, and had found the word listed in the geography section. Ktikbat, it transpired, was a wilderness that lay to the west of Ragana-Se-Tor and which filled the whole of the interior of the Thek continent. It was not impassable – nor, for that matter was it an endless plain, despite being so called – but neither was it a journey to be undertaken lightly. I began to understand why Sonder's preparations had taken so long.

Like Mrs Catlin and me, Sonder's other slaves all had very specific duties, and the business of preparing for the journey left the two of us with very little to do. Consequently, Mrs Catlin sat me down and together we began the task of learning the written form of the High Tongue.

This we did with a device given to her by Sonder. It was a miniature version of the lecterns in the Library, a rectangle of a dark green, glass-like substance embedded in dark wood. Like the Library lecterns this tablet came equipped with a stylus.

I told Mrs Catlin about what had happened in the Library and my conviction that the crystalline Mugaraht was some kind of supercomputer.

'A computer?' she asked sceptically.

'Well, maybe that's not the best word to describe it,' I agreed. 'If I'm right, then compared to that thing an earthly computer would be like an abacus. But what would *you* call a data storage and retrieval facility?'

We were speaking in English, since the High Tongue did not contain the words for the concepts we were discussing. And I, for one, was glad of the practice – my native tongue was rapidly coming to seem like a second language to me.

Mrs Catlin doodled on the surface of the block with its stylus.

'If that crystal in the Library building is the, uh, mainframe,' she said, 'then this is just a terminal.'

She doodled some more, pensively.

'But why is the whole thing so shrouded in ritual and secrecy?' she said. 'These people have – or had – a technology that makes twentieth-century Earth seem like the Middle Ages. But for some reason the bulk of the population either doesn't share the knowledge or, at some time in the past, lost it. And only the Librarians have it now.'

'You think there was some kind of catastrophe,' I ventured, 'like a war – a big one – that shattered their civilization, blasted it back to the Stone Age, but somehow the Librarians, or their ancestors, retained what they knew and have kept it to themselves ever since?'

'It's a possibility,' Mrs Catlin agreed, 'but I don't like it. We've seen no evidence of the kind of carnage such a thing would leave, which would suggest it happened a long time ago – a long, *long* time ago. I can't believe civilization wouldn't have risen higher than it has in that much time.'

'Unless the Librarians have deliberately been keeping the rest of the population in ignorance,' I said.

She looked at me.

'The Librarians are powerful,' I said. 'They seem to walk through this land like gods. Why would they give up that kind of power?'

'That's disgusting,' Mrs Catlin said.

I laughed without humour; sometimes Mrs Catlin was disturbingly human – she couldn't imagine the kind of brutal, self-serving mentality I was describing.

I tapped the face of the 'terminal'.

'They really were pretty advanced, weren't they?' I said.

She held the device up to the light coming through one of the building's high windows. The glass-like substance was translucent with the light behind it, and showed no kind of mechanism buried within it. I'd been toying with the idea that it was some kind of resin, and that its 'works' were encased in it.

'I believe this device to have no individual components,' Mrs Catlin said.

'Perhaps in the case—' I ventured.

'No, I don't think so,' said Mrs Catlin. 'This is simply a wooden frame surrounding a quartz-like crystal—'

'Just like that overgrown chandelier in the Library building,' I said.

'Somehow,' Mrs Catlin muttered, 'the people who designed this thing knew how to encode the actual works *into* the crystal itself.'

She peered into the block, squinting against the light.

'You don't really expect to be able to figure it out, do you?' I asked; surely not even Mrs Catlin's intellectual arrogance went that far.

'Of course not,' she said dismissively. 'But it is possible to learn from simply making the effort. Or is that a lesson you've forgotten?'

I said nothing; rising to Mrs Catlin's bait was no longer as perversely satisfying as it had been on Earth. I think I was learning to appreciate how much I needed her in this environment – though I wondered if the need was mutual.

She studied the object for a few moments more, then said, 'Let's get on with the lesson, shall we?'

She took up the stylus and touched it to the screen in a particular way. A picture appeared, drawn in green light inside the block. It was the depiction of an animal that the Ladden had called a *hap*, a rodent-like creature that was not generally thought worth eating, although in times of poor hunting hap traps were quite successful in supplementing the camp's meat ration. Next to the picture were two symbols, drawn in a simplified fashion.

'This is going to be hard,' I muttered.

Mrs Catlin frowned.

'This first symbol,' she said, 'is either "h" or "ha". In which case the second—'

'Is either "ap" or "p",' I said impatiently.

Mrs Catlin gave me a look.

'I believe the second symbol is "ap",' she said, which was the opposite of what I had been going to say and so was almost certainly right.

'We need some writing materials,' I said.

'This will stimulate your memory capacity,' she told me.

'Overload it, more likely,' I muttered.

She touched the stylus to the screen again and the picture vanished to be replaced by that of a small domesticated bird called a *hiv*. There were two symbols beside the picture and the first was the same as that which had appeared first beside the picture of the hap.

'Score one for you,' I said dryly.

Mrs Catlin granted me a sarcastic smile before changing the image yet again.

We went on like that throughout the afternoon and long into the evening; the designer of the writing lesson had been very clever, and clearly had allowed for the fact that those learning from it would have no guidance from someone who had already mastered the art. Which is not to say that we did not have problems; some of the pictures depicted creatures that we had never encountered and of whose names we were completely ignorant, a factor that would not have had to have been allowed for with a native of Shushuan.

Mrs Catlin eventually called an end to the lesson, although as usual she couldn't resist giving me some 'homework'. During the short break we had taken for the evening meal she had obtained a writing tablet from one of the household slaves and a piece of hard chalk. She gave me these at the end of the evening and told me to write out as many characters as I could remember before going to sleep. I almost hit her over the head with the slate, but decided against it – whatever her motivations, it would do me no harm to learn the language as quickly as possible. Life in the household of a Librarian would, after all, almost certainly be ruled by the written word.

Several days later, and scarcely an hour after sun-up, Sonder's retinue assembled outside his palace for its intended journey. The efficiency of his slaves made even the Ladden pale by comparison. The entire train consisted of less than twenty people. Excluding Sonder himself, his party was composed solely of slaves, and other than Mrs Catlin and one middle-aged cook they were all men. I was the Librarian's nominal bodyguard, but he had three beefy-looking individuals along who were armed and armoured and who never strayed far from his side. None of the three wore a sword, but all had daggers and each carried a long-handled halberd or pike. They looked as though they were probably experts with them and I had no intention of putting it to the test. The remainder of the party were household and stable slaves.

My earlier trepidation at the discovery that we would be 'riding' turned out to be well founded. Sonder 'rode' in a covered waggon, one of the three that we would be taking. These were drawn by two of the animals that had been used as mounts by the bandits, and Mrs Catlin and I were expected to use two similar creatures as saddle mounts. Mrs Catlin disguised her unease at straddling the back of one of these ferocious creatures and sprang to the saddle as though she'd been riding them all her life, thus earning a few respectful glances from the other slaves. I tried to match her and my animal promptly tried to bite my arm off. I leaped out of the way and ended up in a very undignified heap in the dust. Some of the slaves smothered their laughter; the three armed slaves didn't try. I decided to save my revenge for another day – when I could get them one at a time and without those eight-foot pikes.

I made a second try at the creature, and when it snapped at me this time I gave it a sound slap across the snout. It looked at me with what, in an intelligent creature, might have been astonishment. I heard mutterings from the slaves, and grasping the animal's unfamiliar harness firmly I hurled myself into the saddle. The beast trembled with either rage or anticipation, but a sharp jerk on the reins seemed to quieten it and with some difficulty I coaxed it into line beside Mrs Catlin and her mount.

'Impressive,' she said, 'if a little foolhardy.'

'I was improvising,' I said. 'I've never liked horses.'

'These are not—' she began pedantically.

'I know, I know!' I said. 'Whatever they are, I like them even *less* than horses!'

'Gryllups,' she said.

I looked at her.

'They are called gryllups,' she told me.

'Fascinating,' I said. 'Absolutely fascinating.'

The caravan moved out, and we left Vraks'has, the Library and the Ladden behind.

Chapter 15

THE KTIKBAT

Several days' ride from the market town we came upon a dense belt of forest that stretched across our path, from north to south, for as far as the eye could see. There was clearly no going around it, so we began the slow and torturous task of hacking our way through it. There was a trail, barely visible, that had been left by previous travellers, and this speeded our journey somewhat. Even so it was a matter of more than four days' trek, in a more or less straight line, before we emerged on the other side. The view that met our eyes when we did so was totally unlike any we had yet seen on this world. We were standing on the edge of a vast open plain, almost unnaturally level and flat, that seemed to defy the boundaries of the very horizon. This late in the year, the hardy vegetation that normally covered the impressive expanse of emptiness was reduced to a little scrub grass and the occasional skeletal bush, and all of it the same uniform dun colour. I needed no native guide to tell me that I was looking upon the fearsome Plains of Ktikbat.

If Sonder was intimidated by the sight of that Plain, or the daunting prospect of attempting to cross it, he gave no sign. In fact, he did not even pause at the forest's edge, but headed unhesitatingly out onto the tableland beyond.

We, his servants, slaves and property, could only follow.

The journey across the Ktikbat was an epic adventure by any standards. At any other time of year, and with so small a retinue, even a Librarian would have been foolish to attempt it, for the savage, almost aboriginal natives of the Plain take no prisoners save for those they intend to kill by slow and ingenious torture. The roving bands of outlaws and bandits whom the natives seem to tolerate upon their lands have no authorities to check their raids upon passing caravans, or their profitable trade in stolen merchandise with those few travellers rich enough to be able to afford it – and powerful enough to be able to avoid joining them. But Sonder's journey would strike through the heart of the Plains in the depth of winter, when the native tribes, all of them nomadic by nature, would be in the warmer climes to the far south, and the outlaws and bandits either holed up in the fortress city of Xud, its location an open secret upon the Plains yet an impenetrable one beyond them, or passing the time until spring in the less inhospitable regions around Vraks'has and the more eastern parts of Ragana-Se-Tor.

But the first leg of our journey, one of several weeks' duration, was made during the relatively mild weather of late autumn. And it was a trying time for all of us.

Native tribesmen, usually in groups of no more than ten or a dozen, and always young warriors, harried us relentlessly during the mornings, vanishing completely – and unnervingly – during the afternoons, only to return to fill our nights with the sounds of drums and weird war cries, and with strange and mysterious noises that were more sensed than heard. By the end of the third night of such activity everyone in Sonder's camp was ready to fly off the handle.

Bandit raids served as punctuation marks to the activities of the tribesmen. And whereas the attacks by the native Ktikbati were always swift and brief – and usually relatively bloodless – the bandit attacks were prolonged, brutal, and always bloody. Most of the blood was bandit blood, but enough of it was ours for us to feel worried – if things were this bad now, after only a few handfuls of days, what would they be like months from now? A war of attrition was one we could not hope to win.

It was therefore a tremendous relief for us to sight, on the distant horizon, the high walls of a fortified encampment. Sonder had given no hint that a brief respite from his journey was in the offing, but that the walls ahead of us were our immediate destination seemed obvious.

We were attacked on the very doorstep of the Fort, a small but very determined group of natives appearing from out of nowhere and attempting to halt our passage. We fought them off as best we could, but in the end it took a concerted effort from the inhabitants of the fort to drive them away. Wearily, the rest of us followed our new hosts back into their tiny city.

They called it Fort Chtect, and we stayed there for four days. It was a breather that we were all glad of, but I couldn't make myself believe that this was why Sonder had decided to take it.

The Fort was one of many that were scattered across the Ktikbat, although for Mrs Catlin and me this was the first we'd heard of them. They were usually multinational in nature, since no one nation had ever claimed or tamed any part of the Plains. Largely self-contained, the Fort truly was a miniature city. It was a simple square in gross design, with high double stone walls, the inner wall higher than the outer and the space between a veritable maze of assorted death-traps. There was only one large entrance, although a second, much smaller entrance did exist for use in emergency, and if an invading force should ever have breached the main gate it would have found a virtually impregnable secondary gate set in the inner wall which – I was reliably informed – had, in this city, never been compromised. The inner and outer gates were never opened simultaneously, a defensive ploy that could be nerve-racking for anyone seeking asylum, but which had ensured the Fort's continued existence for many generations.

The time that we spent at Fort Chtect saw an unexpected but welcome friendship spring up between the men-at-arms in Sonder's party and myself. I think that this was partly a natural reaction to having shared so many skirmishes together before reaching the Fort, but it was also born of a growing and genuine mutual respect for each other's skills at arms. It began, as such things so often do, on an ill note, with one of the pike bearers, goaded by his fellows, challenging me to a 'friendly' contest. I accepted warily, and was severely trounced by him in short order. My lack of animosity, which was perhaps less genuine than I allowed him to believe, impressed him, and he spent the rest of a lazy afternoon in teaching me the finer points of duelling with a pike or halberd. His colleagues, who at first had offered good-natured insults at my skill – or lack thereof – eventually joined him and together we passed the hours until sunset, at which time we got very, very, very drunk. I swore to myself later that never again would I touch the foul brew that they had brought from Vraks'has with them. As with all such vows, it was heartfelt and short-lived.

The night before we were due to leave the Fort Mrs Catlin came to see me in the billet I was sharing with the other men in our caravan. She endured their whistles and catcalls with a lofty disdain and I joined her on the veranda outside the building.

'Someone should teach your friends some civilized manners,' she observed acidly.

I gave her a dark look and said, 'You were glad enough of their help on the trail.'

Seeing that, as ever, she was more than ready for a fight, I quickly added, 'But maybe a little twentieth-century diplomacy wouldn't do them any harm. What did you want to tell me?'

Visibly unimpressed by my rather obvious ploy, she said, 'I know where we're going.'

This was good news – or at least, I hoped it was.

'Where?' I asked.

'A place called the Vohung Kingdoms,' she said. 'That's a mis-nomer, but it's what they're called. There is only one Kingdom, and it's divided into thirteen smaller states, each ruled by a prince or duke or baron depending upon its size and importance. The Vohung were originally three brothers, and each ruled a third of the Kingdoms, hence the name. That was long ago, of course, and today no living descendant of their line survives. But the name persists, as does the notion that each state is a Kingdom in its own right, even though—'

'Where is this place?' I asked; left unchecked, Mrs Catlin wouldn't pause for breath until she'd given me the entire history of the planet.

She raised one eyebrow in mild reproof at my interruption and said, 'On the other side of the Ktikbat. If you regard Ragana-Se-Tor as the easternmost point on the Thek continent, then the Kingdoms are the westernmost.'

'Are they friendly, these Kingdoms?' I asked.

'They aren't hostile to strangers, if that's what you mean,' Mrs Catlin said. 'But they are warlike. I think we will have to keep our wits about us.'

I nodded. After my time with Sonder's men-at-arms I didn't feel too much trepidation at meeting any race who valued a strong right arm. I just wondered how they felt about slaves.

We left Fort Chtect the next morning. It was a fine, clear day, with barely a hint of snow in the air; but there was already a breeze blowing in from the north, and I had seen once before how quickly the weather could change on this world.

We actually went three days before the weather broke. When it did, it did so with a ferocity that would have been fearsome enough to behold from a distance; being actually *in* it was terrifying.

We kept moving, Sonder's almost supernatural powers creating a pocket of relative safety through which we travelled. Without him, without his protection and his unerring sense of direction, we would surely have perished.

The weather brought with it one piece of good fortune: the raids by natives and bandits ceased. Somehow, I felt as though the trade had been a poor one.

Our journey now took on a vaguely nightmarish quality. We moved through a narrow corridor of calm in the heart of a white maelstrom, and but for the evidence of the footprints we left briefly behind us we might as well have been standing still. I think we were all startled when we came upon another fort, so convincing had been the illusion that our forward progress had ceased.

This fort – Haljhar'aj by name – was different from Chtect in a great many ways. For one thing it was built of wood, and for another its inhabitants were a racial mix that included native Ktikbati. I'd had no idea that the tribesmen were on friendly terms with any of the fortress encampments, and expressed my surprise to my fellow men-at-arms.

'They are Kabaro,' said one, a fellow who had spent some time on the Plains before entering Sonder's service. 'Theirs is a tribe of Ktikbati who are despised by their own kind. They were glad of the appearance of the Forts, since for the first time in their history they found men who were willing to be their allies.'

'Why are they despised?' I asked.

This seemed to me to be worth knowing.

'Who can say?' the man shrugged. 'They are a primitive, superstitious race. Their reasons for anything are seldom comprehensible to a civilized mind.'

We stayed at Haljhar'aj for only one night. After that, we did not sight another human habitation for many weeks, and by the time we did the worst of the weather had finally passed us by.

It came as a surprise to me – and, I think, to Mrs Catlin, though seemingly not to anyone else in our party – when we finally came into sight of our next brief stopover, for it was very clearly not a fortified encampment. It was, rather, a simple, stone-built town: a nearby quarry was still being worked as the settlement expanded. I would later discover that this region of the Plains was avoided by the Ktikbati tribesmen, with the exception of the tribe known as the Kabaro, and that as a consequence several towns like this one had sprung into being. Their reason for being here was something I was due to discover on the morning of the very next day but that I was oblivious to at the moment of our arrival due to a thick blanket of fog that lay across our path.

The inhabitants of the town, which was called Iskjdar South, were of no race I had seen previously, and were, I suspected, the result of interbreeding between the Kabaro and various other Vinh races. They tended to be tall, dark-haired and dark-eyed, dusky-skinned individuals, passionate in nature when roused but otherwise taciturn and self-absorbed. They were also, according to popular belief, the foremost breeders and handlers of gryllup in the known world. It was this latter characteristic, as I would soon learn, that was responsible for their presence in Iskjdar and all other such towns of the Ktikbat.

Sonder was made welcome at a large hostelry in the town, though whether that was due to his being known there, or his status as a Librarian, or simply the fact that he was a traveller arriving at 'low season', it was impossible to tell. The social set-up in Iskjdar was difficult to work out; everyone we met was equally deferential towards us, and seemed to mark no distinction between Sonder himself and his lowliest follower. Also, we were all quartered in the same part of the inn, and we each had individual rooms, albeit rather small and spartanly furnished ones, which could actually be locked from the inside.

We were given little time to enjoy this new-found luxury, however, since Sonder stayed in the town for only a single night. Although it was not, it must be said, a night entirely free of incident.

Following a communal evening meal in the main hall of the hostel I spent a tiresome hour in what was now a regular pastime, that of reviewing with Mrs Catlin my studies in the Vinh language and culture. I was now reasonably proficient with the written language, or at least as much so as could have been expected given the nature of my studies and the limited time I had had to spend on them.

Mrs Catlin, of course, was less than satisfied. It seemed that these days there was little or nothing I could do to please her, and the more I tried the more difficult she became. Quite why I was trying at all remained a puzzle to me.

Suffice it to say that I left her company that night in an all too familiar black mood and anticipated remaining in it until the next morning.

I was setting aside my weapons and other accoutrements in my room when there was a knock at my door.

'It's open,' I called.

I fully expected to see Mrs Catlin standing there, waiting to proffer a long overdue apology – which shows what an optimist I could be at times. Instead, to my surprise, I found myself facing Sonder's personal cook. She was the only other woman in our party, and had spoken not a dozen words to me in all the time we had been on the road. She was a very attractive woman who, in Earth terms, might have been forty years old. Her hair was a corn-golden blonde just starting to turn to grey, and her face, though undeniably that of a mature woman, was clear and unlined. Her eyes, I noted now, though not for the first time, were a strikingly pale blue.

And, standing in the open doorway to my room, she appeared to be both nervous and, beneath it, genuinely afraid.

I took a step towards her, at the last instant recalling her name and saving myself the embarrassment of having to admit I had forgotten it.

'Maritt,' I said, 'what's wrong? You look like you've seen a ghost.'

She stepped into the room, looking around nervously.

'I am afraid, Shaw,' she said. 'Tomorrow Sonder takes us across the feyrvahne, and . . . I do not . . .'

She seemed close to tears. I had no idea what a 'feyrvahne' was, but obviously the prospect of facing it terrified her.

I crossed the room and put my hands on her shoulders, wondering what comfort I could offer when I didn't even understand the cause of her fear. She threw herself into my arms and clung to me for dear life.

'Shaw,' she whispered, shaking, 'I . . . I do not wish to be alone tonight.'

She looked up at me.

'Do not send me away,' she said. 'I . . . will do anything—'

'Stop that!' I said, quickly pulling her into my arms again; one more look from those startlingly clear eyes and she wouldn't have to ask me twice. But the fear she felt was obviously real, and I wasn't yet so desperate for female company that I would take advantage of her under such circumstances.

'You . . . you will not send me away?' she asked.

'No,' I said. 'If it's what you want, you can stay here tonight.'

She sniffed and said, 'Thank you.'

She eased herself out of my arms and said, 'Are you not afraid?'

I shrugged. 'I don't know what a feyrvahne is,' I said. 'Uh, will we have to fight it?'

Maritt laughed throatily, and I tried to recite the alphabet

144

backwards to keep my mind from pursuing some very unworthy thoughts.

'You are very strange, Shaw,' she said. 'Where do you come from that you have never heard of the feyrvahnen?'

'A long way away,' I said dryly. 'A *very* long way away.'

'Tell me,' she urged.

I hesitated, then decided that, if nothing else, talking to Maritt would help keep my mind from other considerations.

'Let's sit down,' I said. 'This could be a long story.'

Sometime before the dawn, with my throat growing hoarse, I realized that Maritt was asleep. We were sitting on the narrow bed, her head in my lap. It had felt good to talk, to tell someone about what had happened to me, even if she probably hadn't understood most of it. I drifted off to sleep feeling better than I had in weeks.

I woke up the next morning to find Maritt leaning over me and smiling.

'Hallo,' she said.

'Hallo,' I replied, feeling momentarily disorientated.

'You tell a fine story,' she said, 'but one built more on your imaginings than on your experiences, I think.'

I made a noncommittal sound and started to get up.

'You still scared?' I asked.

'Not so much today,' she replied. 'In the light of day, few things seem as fearsome.'

That was a relief. I would probably have enough to do today without having to worry about Maritt as well.

We made ourselves presentable and set off for the main hall. Directly outside the door to my room we ran into Mrs Catlin.

For the briefest of instants I offered her a smile of greeting, but at the look in her eyes the smile died on my lips. For no reason that I could see, she was looking at me with mute fury. I took a half-step forward, wondering what could possibly have angered her so much, but before I could utter a single word she had spun on her heel and marched rapidly away. I stared after her, dumbfounded.

Maritt put her hand on my arm.

'I did not intend this,' she said.

I didn't know what she was talking about.

'Intend what?' I asked.

She looked searchingly into my face. Then she smiled, rather sadly it seemed.

'Go to her,' she said. 'Apologize. Even—' she added, seeing that I was about to interrupt, 'even though you do not know why.'

She reached up and kissed me briefly. Then she turned and walked away.

Any attempt at an apology was delayed by the necessities of making ready for Sonder's departure. All in all, I couldn't really say that I was disappointed.

Mrs Catlin avoided me fairly effectively during the hours that followed, largely by the simple expedient of staying in Sonder's presence – ostensibly to tend to his Library equipment – at a time when my duties kept me busy elsewhere.

We headed north out of the town, and I was surprised to note that we did so on foot. A team of native bearers, about thirty in all, carried the assorted contents of our three waggons, and we, the armed members of the Librarian's entourage, were required to bear our own equipment on our backs. I seemed to be the only one who didn't understand the necessities for this arrangement, and not wishing to appear foolish I did not query it.

At the northernmost edge of the town we came upon the feyrvahne, and once again the world of the Vinh reminded me that it had an infinite capacity to startle me.

If the Plains of Ktikbat gave the impression of an infinite flatness, then what I was seeing now took the illusion and expanded it to the point where illusion and reality became indistinguishable.

Ahead of us, defying the horizon that I *knew* couldn't be more than a day's slow march away, was a geometrically flat plane. It was black, shiny, a glassy surface that might have been rock after exposure to tremendous heat and pressure, and it went on, and on, and on, and on. It stretched from east to west, its edge so straight and sharp that I doubted the most accurate of surveying equipment could have detected any curvature, and ahead of us, to the north, it filled the landscape for what looked like a hundred miles. The air above it was sharp and clear, so much so that I could discern, at the very limits of vision, on the far side of the blackness, the irregular line of a row of buildings. Iskjdar North? It seemed probable.

I sensed someone at my side. It was Vennin, the man-at-arms who had taught me to fight with a halberd. He was looking across the black expanse, his eyes squinting at the impossibly distant horizon.

He grunted. 'Not too bad,' he said. 'We should be across it before nightfall.'

I looked at him.

'I've seen feyrvahnen,' he said, with the air of one repeating a travellers' tale, 'that it took nearly three days to cross. Can you imagine sleeping out on one of those things?' He shuddered.

I knew I was inviting scorn by asking, but I had to know. 'Why can't we ride across?' I asked. On a gryllup, it should have taken only five or six hours.

Vennin looked at me, but he didn't laugh. I silently thanked him for that.

'Animals will not step onto a feyrvahne,' he said. He didn't add, 'As everyone knows,' but his eyes said it.

Now I began to understand the purpose of this twin town. Some kind of reciprocal trading agreement must exist on either side of the feyrvahne; we left our beasts with the stables on this side, were given a receipt of some kind, and handed that receipt to the head of the stables on the other side, where presumably we would acquire fresh animals. It was a sensible arrangement, but not one that could have sprung up over night. I recalled the mixed-race appearance of the people of Iskjdar South, and wondered at the antiquity of this set-up. Was there nothing on this continent that was *new*? Nothing that was a modern innovation? Was everything shrouded in generations of tradition and ritual?

Before we set foot on the feyrvahne – I asked Vennin if his people had a name for it, since the word was clearly not a Ktikbati one, nor even remotely Thekkish, and wished I hadn't; the name he used translated into English as Death Zone – Sonder had us all don additional footwear; this was in the form of clogs with thick wooden soles. It seemed foolish to me, and made our progress even slower than it would otherwise have been – not to say noisier – but no one else questioned it so I kept my mouth shut.

We clomped off across the feyrvahne with our bearers following, and it was like stepping off the edge of the world and into limbo. The sound of our noisy footfalls echoed away into the distance, preternaturally clear and loud, as did every single other noise we made. Yet no other sound came to our ears; not the cry of a bird, the whisper of the wind, nor the bustle of the town we had left behind. And although the sky over Iskjdar was cloudy, and the ground still white with snow, the Death Zone was roofed over with pure cobalt blue, and its surface was as dry as dessicated bone.

Our journey seemed to take place outside of normal time, and it was impossible to know how long we had been walking when Sonder called a brief halt. I accepted a drink from a water bag and, seeing that everyone else had already drunk, I set the animal-skin container down at my side. We stood upon the empty blackness for several minutes, taking what rest we could, and were about to move off again when Vennin suddenly cursed and snatched the bag up. I wondered what had startled him, but his only concern seemed to be with the bag's underside. He looked at me sharply, then sighed as he realized that I hadn't the faintest idea of what was bothering him.

'Look,' he said, showing me the bag.

Where it had been in contact with the feyrvahne the cured animal hide was perfectly smooth, its surface bearing the appearance of having been worn away. I stared at it stupidly; then, slowly, understanding came to me. I looked down at the clogs I was wearing; I raised one foot and examined the sole of the shoe; it was not as it had been when I had first put it on. Its original surface, roughened and unmachined, had been replaced with one that was almost perfectly smooth. I looked at Vennin, who now seemed to have satisfied himself that the water bag was still watertight. He smiled grimly. 'Death' – he said – 'Zone.' Then walked off, casting the bag to one of the bearers.

I crouched down, holding my hand palm down an inch or so above the black surface. It gave off no heat. I lowered my hand until it was almost touching the surface, but could feel nothing. Puzzled,

I straightened up. If not heat, then what? Entropy? Some kind of accelerated ageing process? Certainly it could not be abrasion – the surface was smoother than glass. Yet we did not slip while walking on it. I tried sliding one clog over the surface, and found the exercise quite difficult. The resistance was about what you would expect from tarmac, but what was causing it?

My experimentation was curtailed by the continuance of our march, but I resolved to discuss it with Mrs Catlin as soon as I could – or, more to the point, as soon as she would let me.

We reached Iskjdar North just before sunset; from the pace of our march that placed it at some twenty-five miles from Iskjdar South, which was still visible across the expanse of the feyrvahne. At ground level, that was impossible. The twin towns should have been shielded from one another by the curvature of the planet.

Iskjdar North was different from its sister town. Its construction was primarily wooden, with brick chimneys and red-tiled roofs. The forest from which the wood came could be made out along the western edge of the feyrvahne, perhaps five miles away. The town was slowly spreading in that direction.

That night, after supper, I finally managed to corner Mrs Catlin when Sonder wasn't around. She looked at me with a stare that would have shamed a glacier.

'I'm sorry,' I said. I should have left it at that, but instead I added, 'Whatever it is I've done, I'm sorry.'

She smiled sarcastically.

'You're apologizing without even knowing what you've done,' she said. 'Do you know how big a fool that makes you?'

'I don't care how big a fool I am,' I said, 'the apology is genuine.'

'How can it be?' she demanded. 'How can—?'

'Please,' I protested, 'don't analyse me! Accept the apology or reject it, but spare me the enlightened insight!'

She seemed on the point of saying something, then snapped, 'Couldn't you at least have picked someone your own age?'

Stunned, I realized what it was that was bothering her. I still couldn't work out why, however – even if it had been true. I suppose I could just have told her the truth of the situation, but by this point I was probably as annoyed with her as she was with me.

So instead I just said, 'Like who? Who else is there?'

Her eyes blazed like lasers, and I flinched, actually expecting to be cut down where I stood.

'Apology accepted,' she said tersely. 'Now get out of my sight.'

I didn't need a written invitation for that, nor did I intend to make the first move at patching things up between us again. If she wanted to harbour stupid prejudices then that was her affair, and the next time an apology was called for it wouldn't be me doing the answering.

The remainder of our journey, another seventy days or so, was largely a replay in reverse of the first half. The weather on the north side of the feyrvahne was less extreme than it had been on the south side, and even though the landscape remained buried beneath its blanket of snow for several more weeks we no longer needed Sonder to protect us from the elements.

The raids by bandits did not resume during this time, but we did run into large numbers of hostile natives. One particular battle was especially bloody, so much so in fact that even Sonder had to involve himself in the caravan's defence. He had climbed down from his waggon, a look of total unconcern on his face, and strode calmly towards a charging line of Ktikbati gryllups. Arrows flashed past him, not one striking home, as he gestured in an arcane manner at the ground in front of him. A veritable tidal wave of rock and dirt had reared up before him, swamping the advancing tribesmen. Only one of the mounted Ktikbati survived, his gryllup leaping through a cleft in the wall of dirt and immediately attempting to trample the Librarian into the ground. The animal had seemed to strike Sonder full in the chest, but it might as well have charged the side of a mountain for all the effect it had on him. Stunned, the animal had collapsed at Sonder's feet, trapping its rider beneath its body. Calmly, the Librarian had reached down and, with a movement that was more caress than blow, had stoved in the creature's chest. It died instantly, heart and lungs transfixed by its own shattered ribs. Then, with no more concern than he had shown all along, Sonder brushed his hand across the Ktikbati tribesman's neck and virtually decapitated the man.

Those of us watching, which was all of us since we no longer had anyone left to fight, had given our master a very wide berth as he went back to his waggon.

It is with genuine sadness that I must record the death of Vennin during this encounter. I could not claim with any sincerity that the man had been my friend, and in all probability he was a merciless cut-throat, but we had been companions together in the face of common enemies and such a bond is not lightly dismissed. His fellow pike-bearers mourned his passing, in typical Vinh style, by getting falling-down drunk, and I feel no shame in confessing that I joined them wholeheartedly. Sonder turned a blind eye to our grim ceremony, and Mrs Catlin refrained from uttering the words of condemnation that I am certain were in her mind.

On the subject of Mrs Catlin, it seemed as though a permanent wedge had now been driven between us. Throughout the whole of this second leg of the journey she spoke scarcely a dozen words to me, and our evening lessons seemed to have become a thing of the past. In some ways this pleased me, but for the most part I felt oddly bereft. I had lost something that had been a constant in my life for almost as long as I could remember, and I would have given anything to have had it back. Anything, that is, except the one thing she seemed to want, which was that I – yet again – should make the first move. Well, this time the first move was up to her. If overtures of peace were in the offing, I would gladly accept them, but I was damned if I'd be the one to voice them.

The days grew slightly longer as our journey turned westward once more, and the weather 'improved' from bad to just plain miserable. Snow gave way to constant rain, and the endless vistas around us were swathed in fog, so that sometimes it would seem as though we travelled on and on for days without ever leaving the same spot. It was a soul-destroying time, and even Sonder seemed more detached and aloof than usual, so that no one dared approach him except on the most important of business. The hunting was poor, and the Plains provided little in the way of nourishment, so that within six or seven weeks of leaving Iskjdar North we were down to the dregs of our preserved supplies; even the water was beginning to taste foul, and our individual moods were no better. More than once I found myself getting into stupid fights with one or other of the surviving men-at-arms, though no one was so reckless as to let things escalate to the point where Sonder would have had to get involved.

When the weather began genuinely to improve, even if only a little, it lifted our spirits considerably, although it continued to be punctuated by unexpected freezing rain showers, and we knew that the true transition to spring was still weeks away. Nevertheless, the promise of warmer climes was there, and we clung to it with grim desperation.

The changeable weather dragged on for several more weeks, the rain showers growing fewer in number and less severe in nature, and then, finally, one day in early spring, with the Plains slowly beginning to regain something of their colour, we sighted an unbroken line of green on the horizon. It was the eastern borderland of the Thek continent's most western Kingdoms – and our ultimate destination.

Chapter 16

INTO THE KINGDOMS

The sight of the lush countryside of the lands that, according to Mrs Catlin, were known as the Vohung Kingdoms, was sheer paradise after the dismal expanses of the Ktikbat. Much of our delight stemmed only from the effects of the change in the weather, since I knew from my studies that in summer the Plains were as beautiful in their own way as any part of the planet. But as the rolling green hills of the country known as Arndorul hove into view ahead of us I felt like letting out a mighty cheer. The knowledge that what awaited us in the lands of the Vohung was not likely to be any more pleasant than the life we had already been leading did nothing to dampen my spirits. Nor, I think, those of Mrs Catlin; for although she had continued to avoid me, I had not been oblivious to the miserable time she had been having lately. Few of the other slaves were inclined to be friendly towards her – her standing with Sonder guaranteed that – and the Librarian himself treated her with no more regard than he would a footstool. If I was feeling lonely without her to talk to, then she must have felt like a positive pariah.

With the change in scenery came a stepping-up of the small caravan's pace. Part of this was due to our improved spirits, but mostly it was a sudden mood of impatience that seemed to possess

Sonder. We didn't know if it was some unguessable schedule that spurred him on so relentlessly, or merely a natural (human? Sonder? It seemed unlikely) desire to see an end to his long journey, but whichever it was, we underlings had no choice but to comply with his wishes.

As the weather continued to improve and the land around us burst into colour, we all abandoned our thick clothing and winter furs and donned lighter garments. I packed away my leather armour in favour of a cotton tunic bearing the typically asymmetric pattern that denoted Librarian status – or, in my case, indicated that I was the property of a Librarian. The design was undeniably a form of writing, but it was not the script with which I had become more and more familiar over the past months. During the earlier part of our journey Mrs Catlin had offered the opinion that it was a form of ancient Thekkish, a long-dead language that the Librarians continued to use in much the same way that certain schools of learning on Earth continue to use classical Latin. As comparisons go, however, this falls somewhat short of the mark: according to Mrs Catlin the Thekkish language was far more than a scholarly lingua franca, or even an intellectual conceit. It was, in fact, a means of preserving knowledge that cannot be expressed in the High Tongue. Although this was largely guesswork on her part – confirmed to a degree by Sonder's refusal to discuss the subject – it made a deal of sense. The High Tongue, for all its sophistication in expressing nuances of mood and feeling, was a primitive language where technology and science were concerned. All of its words for the devices that had survived from past civilizations or whose invention can be attributed to the Librarians were idiomatically descriptive in nature, referring to function rather than form. The word 'mutahiir', for example, translates literally as 'punishment stick'. If the concept of television had existed on Shushuan I am certain the High Tongue would have called it 'picture box' or some such. Saddled with a language like the High Tongue, I couldn't imagine the Vinh people ever reinventing technology for themselves. Which was yet another bit of evidence to support the notion that the Librarians were deliberately keeping their fellow citizens in a needlessly primitive state.

As to what the symbols on the clothing of the Librarians and their slaves denoted, I was completely in the dark. I compared the various differences in design from person to person, but could make out nothing of significance in either the similarities or differences. Perhaps, I was half-ready to concede, they were merely fanciful reworkings of ancient symbols whose meanings the garment makers had never known.

We crossed Arndorul in little more than a week, and although we were keeping up a brutal pace we found little of which to complain. Food was now plentiful, in the form of fruit and wild root-vegetables as well as a variety of sizes of game. The spring rains were pleasantly refreshing when they came and the water we collected from the abundant streams and rivers of this Kingdom had a clear, sparkling quality that made it a pleasure to drink. All in all, our eight-day trek was a welcome holiday after all those weeks on the windswept Plains.

We encountered only a handful of people on our journey, and all in the form of armed patrols. Sonder had purposely avoided Arndorul's towns and cities – we could have crossed the Kingdom in half the time had we travelled in a straight line – since he had no desire to be waylaid by even the most trivial of distractions. The patrols that we did meet questioned us in the most perfunctory fashion, clearly familiar with the power and authority of Librarians and not inclined to risk offending one. They were not quite as deferential towards Sonder as the people at Vraks'has had been, however, and although they were not insolent as such, they seemed to regard the Librarian as a power to be tolerated rather than feared. I found this more than a little interesting, but had neither the time nor the opportunity to investigate it.

As for the patrols themselves, they were a startling sight when first I saw them, since they were quite unlike anything I had yet seen in my travels.

That the men in them were soldiers was instantly apparent. They wore hauberks, but of silver scalemail rather than chain, over cotton shirts and leggings that were uniformly reddish-brown in colour. Most wore helmets, conical and open-faced but with a pronounced and ornamented nasal and occasionally bearing a

155

chainmail neck-protector. All wore swords, metre-long hacking weapons with thick blades and weighted pommels for counterbalance, and either carried or had strapped to their saddles teardrop shields of the same design as the one I had carried at the start of our journey; these, however, were banded with steel rather than iron. The gryllups that these soldiers rode were as different from ours as I could imagine within the confines of a single species. Their coats were longer and the fur silkier, and their coloration was more striking – all the gryllups I had seen before reaching Arndorul had been brown or tan, but here they came in black, white, piebald, and even russet – but the most obvious difference was one of temperament. While not exactly tame – the notion of a 'tame' gryllup was ludicrous – they were certainly more tractable than their eastern counterparts. I wondered how much of this was attributable to genetics and how much to a different method of training.

Costume and gryllups aside, the most noticeable thing about the soldiers was their hair, which was long and blond. There were exceptions, of course, as there are in all racial types, but the blue-eyed, blond-haired image was the one that cropped up most regularly and seemed to be the norm. After all those months spent with the Ladden and then on the open trail crossing the Plains the sight of so many fair-skinned, light-haired people was quite startling. What was more surprising still were the frequent glances that they seemed to be giving me, as though somehow they thought at first that they recognized me and then were disappointed at being mistaken. The idea was, of course, ridiculous.

The transition from Arndorul to the country we were seeking, Benza, was not merely uneventful but completely undetectable. It was only a chance remark from another slave that brought the fact to my notice. There had been no visible frontier, and the landscape had not, so far as I could see, altered in any way. I don't know what I had been expecting – a river, perhaps, or at least a fence – and the reality was vaguely disappointing. What had all those Arndorulian patrols been for if the border with their nearest neighbour was totally undefended?

We encountered our first Benzans on the second day after

entering their Kingdom. They differed from their eastern neighbours in only a few particulars: their cotton garments were a true red rather than reddish-brown and their hauberks had a bluish tinge, as though the steel had been manufactured by a slightly different process. Also, the men carried light spears, javelins really, and had two or three more in special sheaths at the sides of their saddles. Racially, the Benzans seemed to be of the same parent race as the Arndorulians: I assumed this race was the Vohung people from whom this collection of Kingdoms was descended.

The leader of the Benzan patrol greeted Sonder and informed him that he had been expected and that a ceremony was being readied in the city of Benza itself. This seemed to me to be the most improbable thing I had ever heard, and I wondered if the man might have a little Ladden blood in him – that anyone could have anticipated our arrival so precisely after all the months we had been travelling was, frankly, unbelievable. More likely, I said to myself, the man had sent a messenger on a swift gryllup back to Benza to inform its ruler of our impending arrival, giving him enough time to prepare the aforementioned ceremony and thus give the impression that we had arrived precisely on schedule as expected. I silently congratulated the Benzan soldier for his diplomatic talents and his inventiveness.

Sonder did nothing to dispute the man's fantastic claim and, earlier than was our usual habit, we made camp for the night. I gathered, from that, that we would sight the city of Benza sometime during the next day and that Sonder was graciously giving its ruler adequate time to make a proper job of his 'planned' ceremony. It was a gesture I could not have predicted from anything I had yet seen in the Librarian's character, and it made me wonder what these Benzans could possibly possess that Sonder would want and would feel he could not simply take. That he was merely being polite did not occour to me for an instant.

The camp that night was very jolly. The Benzan patrol, numbering thirteen men in all, was eager for travellers' tales, and we were eager for other faces and voices than those of our little group. Much wine was consumed – the word for 'wine' here, I noted, was 'suki', not 'sukoki', and the wine itself was a little less civilized than the drink favoured by the Ladden – and tall tales grew Brobdingagian in the frequent retellings.

Yet again I found myself the centre of some attention, and although I was clearly marked as a slave the Benzan soldiers seemed to regard me instead as a brother-in-arms. The bandit sabre fascinated them, though a few claimed to have seen its like before, and although I was loath to give it up I allowed it to be passed around and inspected. It was, I had come to realize, a superb weapon. The blade was extremely flexible, yet strong enough to chop through a thick wooden shield or, if the necessity arose, the bones of an arm or leg. It was a light weapon, compared to the swords worn by the Vohung soldiers, but not an effete one. The guard was similar to that of an earthly sabre, though offering protection to more of the hand than would the guard of a duelling sabre. The hilt was hard wood around a flat steel core, bound with dark red leather and pinned together with dowels. The pommel was very small, little more than a flat circular plate, since the blade was perfectly balanced. I think the pommel's only purpose was to allow for a backhanded clubbing action without the risk of inflicting damage to the guard.

The soldiers asked many questions about the weapon – how I had come by it, how often I had had to use it, how effective it had been against a variety of similar and dissimilar weapons – and I tried to answer them as truthfully as I could, at the same time not being afraid to add the kind of embellishments that seemed to be the norm with such stories. It may be that I was a little the worse for the wine we were consuming, or that I was just having too much of a good time being treated like a human being again, but somehow or other I found myself roped into a 'friendly' round of duelling.

For safety's sake I was kitted out in a spare hauberk, though how much good it would do if anyone got carried away was debatable. I borrowed one of the soldiers' heavy swords, since I was curious to see how it compared with the sabre, and before I knew it I was facing off against my first opponent. He was even more drunk than I was, and came at me in a weaving line that made me seasick just to watch. I parried his attack and prodded him in the chest with my blade. He fell on his backside to riotous laughter from his colleagues, two of whom dragged him to his feet. He was grinning inanely, but his second attack was more studied, and his feet seemed to be back under his control. He did a feint to my hip and, as I lowered my guard, flicked his point up to my neck. It was a relatively straightforward sabre trick and I didn't fall for it; I parried and slapped him on the sword-arm with the flat of my blade; in combat, that would have left him at my mercy. A round of applause greeted the move and the soldier looked at me closely for a moment, possibly wondering if I was playing with him. He grinned again and we squared off for another point. His attack this time was complex, and although in competition I could have beaten him easily I had to remind myself that this was supposed to be a real duel, even if only for points and not kills, and that the concept of 'right of way' was meaningless – to get a point, I had to hit him without letting him hit me. I did what I hoped would be the unexpected, and instead of parrying as I had in the last two attacks I dropped back a pace, drew him forward, and then batted his blade aside with all my strength. To my amazement the weapon flew from his hand and narrowly missed spearing one of his colleagues. I recovered my composure and tapped him lightly in the chest with my point. After a moment of startled silence the group of onlookers burst into applause and cheers, and my former opponent laughed loudest of all and clapped me to his breast, knocking the breath out of me. The other soldiers crowded around us, and the group gradually re-formed with two other duellists taking centre stage.

The impromptu contest seemed to go on for hours, long after darkness had fallen and the camp had set out burning torches to augment the moonlight. I fenced with most of the soldiers at one time or another, and although I didn't win all the exchanges I think it's fair to say I won the majority. It was all very good-natured, and as the evening wore on it grew increasingly more anarchic as more and more wine was consumed. Sonder's other slaves, particularly his two surviving men-at-arms, joined in the activities, and I was surprised at how proficient some of them were. I had known that they could fight, but until now I hadn't realized that they possessed technical skills in swordplay, the kind of skills that can only be learned by hours of practice. Mrs Catlin, whom I knew to be an excellent fencer, joined in a little, but I noticed that she did not perform to her full potential and that she avoided all attempts at getting her drunk. She seemed unduly troubled, wary, as though expecting trouble of some kind. If things had been a little less strained between us I might have asked why, but I didn't think she would appreciate the intrusion, so I let it pass.

Things had passed the point of anarchy and were descending into slapstick when I decided to call it a night. I fully expected to have the mother of all hangovers the next day and saw no reason to add exhaustion to my problems. I was making my way back to the slave tent when I was surrounded by laughing and jostling bodies and manoeuvred back towards the duelling, which actually seemed to be over. I tried to explain that I was tired and needed to get to my bed but the soldiers shushed me and muttered something about the contest not being over yet.

In the clearing where the duelling had been taking place I saw one man standing with his back to me. He was leaning casually on his sheathed sword, and somehow I knew that he was aware of precisely where I was standing and the fact that I was staring at him. I recognized him instantly, even from behind: it was the officer who was in charge of the patrol, he of the prodigious powers of diplomacy, not to say invention. I realized that I had not seen him take part in any of the duelling and for a moment I attributed this to his sense of his rank and a desire to remain apart from the horseplay of his men. The moment passed, and somehow I knew that however plausible such an explanation might seem it was not the correct one.

One of my new-found escorts said thickly, 'We been keeping score, friend, and you won more fights than anybody. You get to fight the champ.'

The officer turned slowly to face me; his face was set like stone. I'd heard the expression 'a sobering experience' many times in the past, but until that moment I hadn't fully appreciated what it meant. As I stared into those ice-blue eyes that regarded me so emotionlessly I felt every trace of alcohol being driven from my system.

'He's your, uh, champ?' I asked of my inebriated companion.

'Best in the cavalry,' he replied proudly, slapping me on the back and nearly falling over backwards. I steadied him. 'Won the King's Trophy three seasons running.'

The officer watched impassively as I was herded to the opposite side of the clearing from him. I straightened my mail shirt and tried to look impressive. I don't think I succeeded.

The officer's lieutenant weaved a little unsteadily between us. Obviously someone had decided that this bout needed a referee.

'Best of five points,' he said, and staggered back. As a Master of Ceremonies he left something to be desired.

The officer unsheathed his sword and cast the scabbard aside. I realized that I was unarmed – I had handed my borrowed weapon back to its owner about an hour ago. A pair of rather small hands pressed a weapon into mine. I looked into Mrs Catlin's eyes.

'Be careful,' she said.

I looked down to see that it was my sabre she had handed me.

I unsheathed it, handed her the scabbard, and stepped away from her.

The officer said, 'My name is Tor Taskus.'

'David Shaw,' I introduced myself.

We saluted one another and fell into our preferred on-guard positions. I knew that he'd had the whole evening to watch my technique and that I hadn't the faintest idea of what he might do, so rather than risk an attack I hung back and waited to see how he would start.

What he did was to launch the most astonishingly fast attack I had ever seen. His blade came at me, it seemed, in a dozen places at once, and only my reflexes held him at bay. I was fencing purely on instinct – there was no time to plan – and he drove me back pace after pace until I was certain he meant to force me all the way to the Ktikbat. I could feel myself starting to sweat from the exertion, and so far there hadn't been time for a single riposte. I increased the speed of my retreat, creating an opening between us and thus a break in his attack, and then sprang forward with an assault of my own. He parried me with ridiculous ease and slapped the flat of his blade down on my right shoulder. I felt the bones creak under the impact, and my knees almost gave way beneath me.

'Point to the Captain!' yelled our referee. The cheers were deafening.

We returned to our starting place and came on guard once again. This time I didn't wait for his attack, but pressed one of my own. I'd learned from my mistake, however, and didn't try to match his speed or ferocity. Instead I relied on techniques that Mrs Catlin had taught me, in her own irritating fashion, and which I knew to be unfamiliar to these people. Tor Taskus, however, proved himself to be a very quick study, and although I came close to scoring on several occasions he always managed to fend me off at the last instant. For the space of a dozen seconds that felt like an eternity we stood and traded parry-riposte, parry-riposte, until my arm felt like it was holding up a steel girder. And the end, when it came, was so swift that it took me several seconds of mental replay to realize what had happened. What had happened was that Tor Taskus's parry had been off by a fraction of a second and my body had responded before my brain had even registered the fact. I had turned his blade aside and scored a hit on the outside of his shoulder, the edge of my blade opening the sleeve of his under-tunic but missing the skin beneath.

We both stepped back, and the Captain fingered his shirt carefully, opening up the cut so that everyone could see that the hit had been clean. It was a magnanimous gesture in front of his own men and I didn't know who most of the cheers were for.

'Point to the Librarian's man!' called the referee, using what seemed to me an odd choice of phrase: it was as though he had deliberately avoided using the word 'slave' but had so worded his pronouncement that everyone would know the avoidance had been deliberate. I wondered if it was a veiled insult, aimed at the Librarian. Since Sonder was not within earshot that seemed unlikely.

We returned to our starting points and began again.

Tor Taskus took the third point in seconds, feinting to my head and then almost hurling himself to the ground to score a low cut across my abdomen. His point actually shaved some of the scales from my armour, giving me a new sense of respect for both the weapon and its wielder.

If Tor Taskus took the next point he would have won, and I confess I was loath to give him a three-to-one victory in front of his own men. Consequently I tried a trick that had won me points against Mrs Catlin on several occasions, but never more than once in any given session. As soon as we had come on guard I lunged: no feint, no defence, no fancy bladework, just a single thrust with all the strength, speed and ferocity I could manage. I had once bent a foil at right angles on Mrs Catlin's sternum with this trick, and against Tor Taskus I achieved a similarly spectacular result. My point took him squarely in the solar plexus, and even though I pulled the hit at the last instant the impact knocked him flying from his feet.

The silence from the onlookers was not a little frightening. Then someone started a very slow handclap and someone else began stamping his feet and then the whole place was in an uproar. I didn't know whether to feel relieved or intimidated.

The Captain picked himself up and examined his chest. A row of scales in his armour was dented where the blade had skidded across them, and I would have bet a fair amount of money that the skin underneath was black and blue.

He regarded me evenly as the referee called out, 'Point to the Librarian's man. Two points each. Deciding point.'

As we stepped back to our places Mrs Catlin rushed forward and, to my astonishment, threw her arms around my neck. There were raucous cheers from the soldiers, and with her voice masked by them she whispered in my ear, 'Forget the sabre; remember the foil.' Then she stepped back and, grinning at the assembled soldiers and slaves, she called out 'For luck!' and hurried off the field of play.

I squared off against Tor Taskus for the last time and wondered what she had meant. I gazed into the eyes of the Benzan Captain and saw a determination there that made me feel very uneasy; how much, I asked myself, did winning this match mean to him? Probably a great deal, I decided, which made him doubly dangerous.

We assayed a couple of careful passes, all fairly text-book stuff, before falling warily back from one another.

What had Mrs Catlin meant? I knew she had always criticized

my work with foil and épée, saying that slashing moves should be reserved for sabre fencing, but the weapons we were using now *were* sabres, or at least were analogous to that particular weapon.

Tor Taskus came at me, and I parried again and again as I stepped back away from him, keeping an even distance between us. He broke off his attack, edging further away. I advanced, and he lunged again, his blade all over my defence but, so far, failing to pierce it.

We separated again, and I wondered what he was waiting for. He had seen everything I had to offer, and I didn't doubt his ability to defeat me. I had only taken the two points from him that I had by virtue of doing the unexpected, but my repertoire was pretty much exhausted now.

Without warning he changed his attack from my high ground, where most of his attacks had been directed, to my low guard. With a sinking heart I realized that this was a skill he had been keeping in reserve, and only some ferocious slashing and blocking kept his blade away from me. He stepped back a pace, then attacked again on the same beat, obviously hoping to catch me off guard.

The sabre is, of course, primarily a slashing weapon, its target area everything above the waist. The foil, by contrast, is a point-oriented weapon, where only a stabbing hit counts. The épée is a heavier version of the foil, though the legitimate target areas are different for the two weapons. In foil and épée work, the ideal is to keep one's point always on target with the opponent, all of the defensive work being done with wrist and finger movement of the root of the blade. It is a weapon for fine detail work, not gross movement. My style of fencing had always made me favour the sabre, since my own movements are naturally rather vague and expansive.

As Tor Taskus drove me back I thought perhaps I was beginning to understand what Mrs Catlin had been trying to tell me. I back-pedalled rapidly, defeating the Captain's attack by simply outdistancing it. He paused, obviously curious – did he think I was afraid? I hoped so; it might make him careless.

I extended my blade at him, my arm straight and at shoulder height. Then I gave him the grin that had occasionally so disconcerted Mrs Catlin that I had been able to steal points from

her that she should have won. Tor Taskus bridled at what he
clearly thought was an insulting expression and rushed me, his
attack directed at my sword arm. I parried and backed off, parried
and backed off, not with sweeping gestures but with the carefully
controlled minimalist movements I had learned from the épée. My
opponent clearly couldn't understand what I was doing, nor why it
was working, and he made the most minute relaxation of his guard,
hesitating as he tried to gather his tactics. I sprang forward, the point
of my blade a blur as it whirred around in tiny circles in front of him,
and as he parried I took the edge of his blade on mine and executed
a manoeuvre that the Americans so graphically call the corkscrew.
Tor Taskus's blade was flung aside and he was wide open before
me. At which point my forward foot slipped on the grass and I fell
flat on my face in front of him.

I rolled over onto my back, overcome with helpless fits of
laughter. It may not have been the most appropriate reaction, nor
the one best suited to making me any new friends, but at the time
it was the only one I could summon up. The whole thing was just
too absurd for words – probably the best move of my life, and I'd
followed it up with a world-class bellyflop.

I felt something poke me in the ribs, and opened my eyes to see
Tor Taskus jabbing me with his sword. I tried to muster a properly
crestfallen expression and only succeeded in getting another attack
of the giggles.

'You are dead,' Tor Taskus said, adding, presumably in the hope
of curbing my amusement, '—slave.'

I struggled to find my feet, barely able to control myself, and
gasped, 'Then how come I feel so good?'

I could tell that his temper was on a hair-trigger and tried harder
to get myself together. Smothering a grin I said, 'Please accept my
congratulations. Your victory was well earned.'

His scowl deepened. 'Do you mock me?' he demanded.

'Not at all,' I replied, the last of the laughter finally fading. 'I
had my chance and I didn't make enough of it. You deserved
to win.'

'The victory would have been yours had you not slipped,' Tor
Taskus said, which I thought was a fair evaluation of the situation,

but was also very gracious of him under the circumstances. 'I took advantage of your misfortune. Let us play the point again.'

'No,' I said, and when he began to protest I went on, 'If I hadn't slipped, I might have won; because I did slip, you had the chance to win and took it. In other words, the winner was decided by a freak occurrence, an act of the gods if you like, and in the real world such things happen all the time. In an ideal world I would have won – but in an ideal world I wouldn't be a slave, would I?'

He looked puzzled, and I couldn't blame him – the effects of the drink were starting to catch up with me again.

'Shall we call it a draw?' I suggested.

Tor Taskus glanced around at his men.

'For today,' he said, 'such an outcome would please me.'

He held out his hand and I took it, to yet another round of cheers and applause from the soldiers and slaves around us.

'Perhaps another day,' Tor Taskus said, 'we may look forward to a rematch.'

He smiled broadly, and I guessed that this outcome genuinely did please him – had he lost in front of his men it would not have done their morale any good. But to have defeated me would have risked annoying the Librarian who was my owner, particularly since I was his personal bodyguard. I began to understand why the Captain had seemed so grim both before and during our duel, and why he now looked so relieved.

'That,' I told him, 'is something I will look forward to.'

We parted, and once again I made my way back to my tent. I had taken not five paces when I heard footsteps behind me.

'I couldn't quite follow the philosophical parts of that conversation,' Mrs Catlin said, 'but the rest of it seemed to go OK.'

I looked at her and saw that she was smiling.

'The philosophy of the bottle,' I told her, and her smile broadened into a grin.

'I think you're due an apology, Shaw,' she said. 'You haven't deserved the way I've been treating you. I'm sorry.'

I didn't know what to say. An apology from Mrs Catlin was an event in itself, but the genuine humility in her voice was almost embarrassing. She didn't owe me anything; everything I had that was of any value I owed to her. It occurred to me I'd never told her that. I was about to try and find the words when she said, 'Good night, Shaw,' turned, and walked quickly away.

Chapter 17

BENZA

The next morning we broke camp early and began the last leg of our journey to the city of Benza. As expected, I had a head that felt like the inside of a football stadium.

Hangover apart, it was a fine day, and I couldn't help but feel a sense of optimism about what lay ahead. Had I known what did lie ahead I might have felt differently.

Tor Taskus rode alongside me beside Sonder's waggon, and talked animatedly about the celebrations that awaited us. I just hoped my head would be able to stand it all.

Mrs Catlin did not ride beside Sonder's waggon, in a break with her usual habit, but rode alongside the second waggon in the caravan, which at that moment was being driven by Maritt. I felt a little unease at the fact that Mrs Catlin and Maritt were engaged in some kind of conversation, but since they both seemed to be in good spirits I assumed I had nothing to worry about on that score. All the same, it was an unsettling development.

The country around us underwent a subtle change as our journey progressed. The rolling hills that we had been traversing ever since entering the Kingdoms began to give way to a more rocky landscape, reminiscent of parts of the Yorkshire Dales. The rocks were white and, on Earth, I would have said they were carboniferous limestone. Certainly the patterns of the formations suggested the cumulative effects of erosion and glaciation, and the overgrown appearance of many of the larger outcroppings hinted at considerable age. I even saw, scattered about, the huge boulders known as erratics, great masses of stone that had been carried in the bowels of glaciers and deposited at random about the countryside as the ice melted. The similarities to my own former home were so striking that I felt a wave of melancholic nostalgia come over me, the first attack of true homesickness I had felt since arriving on this world. I found myself thinking about my father. By now, I realized, he would have been long since buried, our few relatives having grieved briefly and moved on to other things. Some, no doubt, would have wondered at my own fate, and in the depths of various police filing systems my name would no doubt be stored as a witness to his death, perhaps even as a suspect in an unsolved possible murder. What, I wondered, had been the verdict of the inevitable coroner's court?

My attention was brought back to the present by Tor Taskus repeating the same question several times. The homesickness left me as quickly as it had come, the sheer exigencies of my current situation allowing no time for such self-indulgence.

'I'm sorry, Tor,' I said, 'I was just remembering my own country – it's very much like Benza. What were you asking me?'

'I was asking if you would teach me the unorthodox style of swordplay you used last night,' he said. 'But now I am more intrigued by what you have just said. Where *is* your own country, Shaw?'

'A long way away,' I said wearily, 'a very, very long way away.'

'Further than the Plains of Ktikbat?' asked Tor Taskus.

I laughed.

'Much further,' I said.

'Further than Ragnar-Se-Tor?' he asked, using the local corruption of Ragana-Se-Tor. I knew that the Ladden territories were regarded as the end of the world by many people in the Kingdoms.

'Further than Ragana-Se-Tor,' I said.

He whistled.

'That is far,' he said. He grinned. 'Now, will you promise to teach me your barbarous fighting tricks?'

'Only if you will teach me yours,' I replied.

'Agreed!' he enthused.

I anticipated some interesting sessions with Tor Taskus, and just hoped Sonder would grant me the time to make the most of them.

We took a short break at noon for a simple meal and to water the gryllups. This we did in an idyllic little spot beside a silver stream whose banks were lined with the Vohung equivalent of weeping willows. The sense of peace and tranquillity was positively Elysian.

Mrs Catlin joined me on the bank of the stream.

'I could settle down here,' I told her. 'Build a log cabin just over there, raise vegetables, maybe breed a few gryllups to sell in Benza once or twice a year, and spend an awfully long time growing old gracefully.'

'You're too young for such dreams,' she said. 'You should be thinking of adventures in faraway places.'

I laughed at the sheer irony of such a statement after all that we'd been through. It was a half-hearted laugh, because I didn't quite know how to take what she'd said. Her reaction to it wasn't what I would have expected.

'You're a young man, Shaw,' she snapped. 'You should be having a young man's dreams, not a septuagenarian's pipe dreams.'

She stomped off in seeming anger, and once again I was left feeling somehow responsible. Normally I would have let her go, hoping that she would calm down on her own, but I'd had my fill of her strange moods over the past months and I was feeling a bit reckless. I ran after her, grabbed her arm and spun her around.

'What's wrong with you?' I demanded. 'And if it's something I've done then for the gods' sakes tell me what it is!'

She looked at me in surprise.

'"For the gods' sakes"?' she repeated. 'My, my, we have gone native, haven't we?'

'Yes,' I said angrily, '*we* have – how could *we* not?'

I saw the muscles work along the sides of her jaw, as though she was physically restraining herself from saying something. And then, to my astonishment, I saw huge tears well in her eyes.

'What the hell—?' I muttered in English.

She tried to turn away, but I caught her arms and, before I had time to realize what I was doing, I pulled her to me and put my arms around her. She pressed her face to my chest and I could feel her shake as she wept.

'What's wrong?' I asked as gently as I could – I was actually still angry with her, and this intimacy was . . . disturbing.

'Shaw,' she said quietly, 'have I ruined your life by bringing you here?'

'Don't be idiotic,' I said. Self-pity? From Mrs Catlin?

'But you're a slave—' she sobbed.

'So are you,' I laughed. 'And as I recall, the decision to stay here rather than go home while we had the chance was a mutual one.'

'I know, but—'

'Enough,' I said.

I pushed her away; holding her like this was putting some very odd thoughts into my head.

'Let's get back to the others,' I said, smiling to take some of the abruptness out of my tone. 'We can't be more than a few hours from Benza now.'

She nodded, wiped her face with her hands, and went ahead of me back to the waggons.

And so we came to the 'city' of Benza.

We sat on our gryllups on the top of a gently rolling hill and gazed down into the valley where Benza stood, and all I could find to think was, 'Where's the city?'

I glanced at Tor, my face carefully devoid of expression – I did not want to offend him.

'Benza?' I asked.

He beamed.

'Not so ancient as Ymii,' he said, pride in his voice, 'nor as big as Garvik, nor as rich as Carmalt, but home of the greatest fighting men in the Kingdoms. And the land of my birth.'

I looked down into the valley and felt a black despair. Without consciously knowing it, I had been pinning all my hopes for my

172

and Mrs Catlin's future on Benza, and all those hopes now seemed dashed.

The 'city' of Benza consisted of a large stone fortress surrounded by a high-walled enclosure, itself surrounded by perhaps five or six hundred single-storey dwellings of stone, wood and thatch. And nothing else. If it numbered three thousand inhabitants I would have been surprised. The 'town' of Vraks'has had been almost as big.

Mrs Catlin edged up alongside me. She caught my eye and said quietly, in French, 'It may not be as bad as it looks.'

'It couldn't be,' I replied gloomily. I shook myself; if I wasn't careful I was going to give in to the despair I was feeling.

'What do you make of it?' I asked.

'Low level of technology,' she replied, 'certainly not up to Ladden standards, but the design looks good. We're not dealing with idiots.'

'That's a relief,' I said dryly.

Mrs Catlin smiled and I actually managed to return it.

'It's similar to a Norman fortress,' she said, peering intently at the various parts of the city. 'That square keep is pure eleventh century, and the design of the palisade is what's known as "motte-and-bailey"—'

'I thought they were wooden,' I said – I did remember *something* from my history lessons.

'Originally, yes,' she said, 'but later the more permanent ones were replaced with stone, and the original design carried over.' She frowned. 'It doesn't add up, though. You don't build a motte-and-bailey in a valley, you build it on a hill – "motte" meant "mound". It's as though . . . No, that doesn't make sense.'

'Go on,' I said.

'Well, it's as though they copied the design from an earlier civilization,' she said, 'but didn't realize *why* it was designed the way it was. As though they just *liked* the design, rather than needed it or understood it.'

'But they *are* warlike,' I said, 'so surely they'd grasp the concepts of fortified defences. Unless . . .' It was my turn to hesitate; were we making assumptions that had no basis in fact?

I turned to Tor and switched back to the High Tongue.

'It's some city, my friend,' I said – and in its own way it was; my own disappointment was no reflection on Tor's people, but merely on my own expectations. 'Tell me, when the Vohung Kingdoms make war, how are the cities defended?'

Tor looked at me. 'The cities?' he said. 'Why, by men, of course.'

'But what about, uh, siege machines?' I said, struggling for the right words.

'What a strange expression,' said Tor. 'What does it mean?'

'Um, nothing, forget it,' I said. I turned to Mrs Catlin; she had followed the exchange without comment.

'They make war by manpower alone,' she said in French. 'Maybe their cities are merely fortifications from which to launch their attacks, not defensive structures as we understand the term.'

'Which is why they've built Benza in a valley, perhaps,' I said. 'Look at the path of the river – the city's virtually standing on it.'

'Shaw, how is this possible?' Mrs Catlin asked. 'Is their society so deficient in its thinking that they can't build war machines, yet can manufacture steel swords? It makes no sense.'

'We're missing a vital piece of the puzzle,' I said. 'And until we get it we're going to stay confused.'

Tor put his hand on my arm.

'Does something trouble you, Shaw?' he asked.

'We were just discussing your city,' Mrs Catlin said. 'It reminds us of similar structures in our own land. When did—?'

'Woman, be silent!' Tor snapped. 'When I wish your opinion I shall ask for it!'

Mrs Catlin's eyes widened and I could tell she was about to give Tor the verbal equivalent of a flogging. Which seemed to me like not a terribly good idea.

'I apologize for the woman, Tor,' I said quickly, ignoring Mrs Catlin's look of astonished disbelief. 'In our land women have the same freedom to speak as do men.'

'Even slave women?' Tor asked, not much impressed.

'We have no slaves,' I said.

Tor looked at me sharply.

'There are slaves everywhere,' he stated. 'It is the law of nature.'

'Our . . . slaves,' I said carefully, 'are not called slaves, and thus the institution of slavery has become . . . vague. The dividing line between master and slave is not so clear-cut as in your country.'

Tor grunted. 'That is bad,' he said. 'A slave must know its place, just as a master must know his. Otherwise, there is no civilization. There is only anarchy.'

His words seemed to come from more than mere philosophical belief; I sensed that the time Tor spoke of had once existed in his culture and that the memory of it was still strong in his people. It didn't give me much confidence in the fate that was in store for Mrs Catlin and myself.

'What about me, Tor?' I asked. 'I'm a slave, aren't I?'

'You are a born warrior, my friend,' said Tor, 'and that means more to my people than your man-made status. In the Kingdoms, and especially in Benza, a man's heart is what counts the most. For one with enough heart, anything is possible.'

I felt the first hint of optimism since sighting the city. So far I had taken it for granted that I would be expected to wear the anklet of a slave forever – even though I intended to do everything possible to get it removed – but here was the first suggestion that it was possible to change my social status *within* the laws of the land.

'But enough of such things,' said Tor, just when I was about to question him further. 'Here comes the parade!'

If my estimation of the size of the population of Benza had been accurate then the entire city was turning out to meet us. A procession like a vast, multicoloured snake was wending its way up the shallow side of the valley towards us. At its head was the retinue of what I took to be the Duke, a large, powerfully built though slightly portly man in robes of blue and purple and ornamental armour, his helmet fashioned like a crown.*

---

* Having adopted the English word 'kingdom' as the nearest logical translation of the High Tongue expression for the Vohung lands, I have continued the analogy where the royalty and nobility of the Vohung are concerned. Translations are not exact; in his writings, Shaw used transliterations of the actual High Tongue names, but I considered that the use of such would probably be confusing to earthly readers, and would add nothing to the flavour of his narrative. Should anyone take exception to this bit of editorializing, the fault lies entirely with me and not with Shaw. PW

Flanking him were a hundred soldiers, their scalemail burnished and glittering in the sunlight, ceremonial cloaks slung about their shoulders. Tor told me that the first fifty men in the column all aspired to the title of Captain, which I knew to be a rank of great importance in the armies of the Kingdoms – there was an old saying that an army without Captains might have a head to plan and hands to fight and feet to march but would have no heart to win. From what I'd seen of Tor Taskus I could well believe it. Riding beside the Duke were two men whose power in Benza would be second only to his. One was his Warlord, and the other his First Councillor. Both men wore cloaks of simple brown cloth, but the Warlord wore full battle armour under his and the Councillor was decked out in all his palace finery.

After the Duke's retinue came the general populace, a brightly dressed and apparently cheerful collection of farmers, artisans and craftsmen. It was difficult to tell from this distance, but I couldn't make out anyone who looked like he or she might be a slave. I decided not to push my luck by asking about it.

What I did find to ask about was the seeming absence of court members – nobles and suchlike. The answer startled me.

'They are there,' said Tor, pointing, 'behind the king.'

I looked.

'The Captains?' I asked.

'Of course,' said Tor.

The old saying suddenly made a lot of sense: the Captains were not merely soldiers, they really were the heart of Benza, its nobility and its aristocracy. I had not thought that the social set-up in the Kingdoms was feudal, but now I began to wonder.

As the procession drew closer I heard a voice that hadn't spoken ten words in my hearing in the last few weeks.

'Shaw,' said the Librarian, 'I will ride the gryllup you have been using. You will remain in my waggon. You are to speak to no one until I tell you.'

I caught Tor's angry look (I think he had been intending to present me to the Duke, or maybe to the Warlord) but I knew better than to argue with Sonder. Biting down on my own anger – I'd been counting on Tor's backing to help establish my position in Benza

– I dismounted and climbed into the back of the waggon. As Sonder mounted the gryllup I heard him say, 'Catlin, you will wait in the second waggon. You, too, will speak to no one until I send for you.'

I had to smile at that – two rebukes in one morning was something of a record for Mrs Catlin, especially since neither of them had come from me.

I saw very little of the festivities after that. No one was about to risk crossing the Librarian in order to have the pleasure of my company, or to bring me any of the food from the many vendors who were working the parade. I knew we were in the city when the sound of the waggon wheels told me we were driving over flagstones, but I saw nothing of the interior of Benza except for a six-inch-wide strip that was visible through the half-open flap at the back of the waggon. What little I did see was somewhat reassuring; the design of the city might have been medieval, but its execution displayed a high degree of craftsmanship, second only, perhaps, to that of the Ladden. The few doors that I saw all looked well made and skilfully mounted, and a few windows that passed my narrow field of view actually seemed to have glass in them, albeit rather thick and grainy glass. In addition, and contrary to what I had originally thought, the buildings of the city were not drystone constructions but had been made by the cementing together of regularly shaped if rather large grey and brown stone blocks.

Sonder's waggons were detached from the main part of the parade as soon as we had passed through the main gatehouse in the outer city wall, which I could now see was actually a double wall and not a monstrously thick single one as I had at first thought. The twin walls – I dug into my memory of lessons in medieval history: *curtain walls* – the curtain walls each had a catwalk on their inner sides, the one on the inner wall being machicolated where it overlooked the space between the walls. I pondered this for a time, then realized that it was a defensive measure against the possibility of the space between the walls being taken by an enemy force. From the relative safety of the inner wall, missiles could be rained down upon the invaders without placing the city's defenders at further risk. The outer wall, of course, was crenellated to permit long-range defence by archers. I wondered why the outer wall was not also machicolated.

The area just beyond the gate house, in the larger of the two *wards* that surrounded the castle, was given over to livestock pens. And it was here that I was to pass a considerable period of time while I awaited Sonder's pleasure.

At sundown I was fed on bread, fruit and water by a tight-lipped individual who would not be drawn into any kind of conversation, no matter how innocuous. Clearly, Sonder had given instructions that I was to remain incommunicado until he sent for me.

The next day saw me stiff and cramped from my confinement; it also saw me still confined at nightfall. This, I decided, was treatment of a distinctly cruel and unusual nature, even for Sonder.

Day followed day relentlessly, and I was beginning to think I would go mad if I did not get out of that damned, wretched waggon soon. I lost track of time, but I am sure I was kept cooped up thus for the better part of two weeks, a steady diet of bread, water and fruit doing absolutely nothing for my mental state – or my digestive one.

When Tor Taskus finally appeared at the rear flap of the waggon I almost didn't know him. From the look on his face when he saw me I guessed that he had a momentary lack of recognition also, then his startled expression settled into one of anger and he said, 'Come, my friend; you are to be released into my custody until the Librarian has need of you.'

I tried to speak, but it was impossible – I think I had almost forgotten how. Two weeks may not seem like much time to be kept a prisoner, but when that imprisonment amounts to nothing less than solitary confinement it becomes equivalent to two months, two years, two decades – left alone with your thoughts, time becomes purely subjective. And the thoughts I had been left alone with had been of the blackest kind.

I accepted his assistance in getting out of the waggon – I had little choice; my legs were useless – and when the world had ceased spinning around me I croaked, 'Mrs Catlin? Where is she? What has—?'

'The woman was released days ago,' Tor said, walking me with agonizing slowness around the yard in which the waggon stood. 'I have protested this treatment of you so loudly that the Duke himself intervened on your behalf with the Librarian. It seems,' he said, almost snarling, 'that the Librarian had forgotten about you, so concerned is he with other matters.'

I felt like I was walking on the points of spears, but what Tor had just said shot through the pain and straight to my brain.

'Other matters?' I said.

Was I finally to discover the reason for Sonder's being here? For the purpose of his trek across the Ktikbat?

'Later, my friend,' said Tor.

I gripped his arm.

'Now, Tor,' I said, '—please. This is important.'

He sighed and said, 'We have heard in the Kingdom of the things called Libraries, yet there have never been such things here. Your Librarian proposes to establish one. And he is petitioning the Duke for the site of this edifice to be in the lands of Benza.'

I stopped in my tracks and felt cold sweat bathing my body. If that was truly Sonder's stated intention, then it was an out-and-out lie. No new Libraries had been built in millennia; the method had died with their mysterious creators. And all attempts at transplanting Libraries from one location to another had resulted in their destruction. All of this Mrs Catlin had uncovered from her studies, and I had no reason to doubt the truth of her findings. Which meant that Sonder was deliberately hiding the reason for his being in Benza. But why?

Chapter 18

NIGHTMARE

I spent the next few days getting on Tor's nerves – and the nerves of everyone else I came into contact with. The reason was simple enough: I wanted to know what was happening to Mrs Catlin, who had not been seen since her release from her waggon. It was not that I was especially concerned over her safety – I *knew* she was safe; yes, OK, I *was* worried about her – but what I really wanted was to talk to her about what I had learned concerning Sonder. I was sure she would have some significant information concerning him by now, something that would point to his real reason for being in Benza. In the end, and cursing women from one side of the known world to the other, Tor undertook to find out what the Librarian was doing with her. What he was doing, it transpired, was putting her through the equivalent of postgraduate studies in Librarianship. Not that he intended to make a Librarian of her, of course – he wasn't letting her anywhere near the vast fund of knowledge his self-obsessed caste was privy to – but apparently there was a worldwide dearth of quality slaves for routine Library work. I'm sure it irritated my former teacher immensely to realize that she was being schooled in the duties of a glorified clerk, but knowing her as well as I did I suspected she would be learning a lot more than Sonder intended – or realized.

Once I knew that Mrs Catlin was safe, and that she was, in all probability, spending her time profitably in both our interests, I was able to settle down and make something of the opportunity Sonder had handed me by putting me in Tor's care. My slave status seemed to be completely ignored by everyone in Benza, other slaves included, and after a time I almost came to forget it myself.

The people of Benza were probably the friendliest I had ever met, and the time I spent with them was one of the happiest I had ever known. Her warriors, reputedly the finest in the world, were the epitome of the chivalric tradition, courteous and gentlemanly, never abusing their lofty status in the Vohung social hierarchy. They spent their days in training and maintaining their weapons and equipment, or in patrols of Benza's borders that usually lasted for several weeks and that every soldier was expected to make at least once a year, Captains included. Their evenings were spent in drinking and feasting, the Captains frequenting the banquet halls of the castle and the lesser soldiery her inns and taverns, of which she seemed to have an inordinate number. Entertainment was a hit-and-miss affair, relying primarily on troupes of travelling players or circuses, or on the talents of the Captains themselves. Many of them proved to be marvellous singers and musicians, and I learned dozens of songs and parts of a couple of epic poems during my evenings with them. I even, to my own astonishment, learned to play one of their musical instruments, a stringed device that I thought probably resembled a lute, although when I say I learned to play it I may be doing myself more credit than I actually deserve. My colleagues were kind enough not to belittle my efforts, however, and I was more than happy to bow to their superior judgement.

If the people of Benza had one fault – other than the fact that they kept slaves, but that is a larger issue for another day – it might have been a tendency towards being generous with the truth, particularly where their fighting men were concerned. Given that Benza was the second-smallest Kingdom in Vohung, the idea that she had produced the world's greatest soldiers seemed, to me, far-fetched.

I could not deny the fact that something had kept the Kingdom from being overrun by its neighbours, but I suspected that political and strategic considerations had more to do with her security than did military might.

All doubts aside, I could not help but agree that the soldiers of Benza were a formidable bunch. I trained with Tor and the other Captains for several weeks and learned no end of new tricks and techniques. The fencing skills that I was able to pass on to them they adopted with remarkable swiftness, mastering in a matter of hours moves in which it had taken me weeks to become proficient.

As time wore on, the balmy spring weather gave way to summer, and the training sessions took on an increasingly leisurely pace. The Captains seemed content to spend most of their time in gaming and afternoon-long siestas, and I found myself growing increasingly restless. The good life had been nice for a while, but with so much time on my hands I found my thoughts turning again and again to the problems that still lay before me. It was with a mixture of relief and apathy, then, that I greeted what looked like being simply one more diversion.

'I am to lead a patrol,' said Tor as he met me in the main courtyard of the city. 'I would like you to come with me.'

The idea was attractive; for all its diversions, Benza was coming to resemble a prison, and I would welcome the chance to get out into the countryside for a while. But would it be possible? Mindful of the deadly band around my ankle, I decided to ask Sonder for his permission.

I found him in the 'library' of the keep, a *real* library with heavily bound books and scrolls, tended over by a small group of scribes. Sonder had set up a lectern in the library, presumably connected by some etheric circuit to his own Library, and he was working at this with a slave woman when I found him. This, I presumed, was window-dressing for his pretence at establishing a new Library in Benza. Silently, and grudgingly, I congratulated him; I wouldn't have thought play-acting was a natural part of his repertoire.

I was slightly startled to realize that the woman with him was Mrs Catlin, and that I had almost not recognized her. She was tanned even darker than when we had been with the Ladden, and her hair had grown considerably. I realized that this last was an illusion: not actually having seen her for months I had recalled her in memory as I had most known her, with her appearance fixed in my mind as I had known it on Earth. Her hair, though certainly longer than when I had last seen her, had in fact been growing unchecked since first we arrived on this world. It now reached to her waist, and was thicker and richer than I would once have believed possible.

Sonder acknowledged my presence and I put my case to him. To my surprise he offered no objection whatsoever.

'But be advised,' he said, 'that should the patrol return without you – living or dead – this woman will pay the price for your desertion.'

Mrs Catlin looked from Sonder to me and back again.

'Her death will be slow,' Sonder told me matter-of-factly, 'and painful beyond your tiny imaginings.'

I met Mrs Catlin's gaze and saw something that rather surprised me: she trusted me. And it was such an unquestioning trust that I felt a little unnerved by it.

'I shall return, Librarian,' I said simply.

He waved me away and I went, suddenly very eager to be outside in the warm fresh air.

Tor's patrol left the next morning: four Captains, thirty men-at-arms, and me. It was an unusual combination, and I said so to Tor.

'There are murmurs of unrest on the western border,' said Tor. 'It is probably nothing – we have never gone to war against Kolhos, as far as I can recall – but one must observe the forms. It would not do for the court of Duke Zanek to think it could raid our lands unchecked.'

Kolhos, I gathered, was the Kingdom immediately to the west of Benza, and Zanek, I supposed, her ruler. Border raids were pretty much a way of life in the Kingdoms, and no one would consider them an act of war. They were more in the nature of tests of strength, each Kingdom pressing its neighbours just enough to provoke a response but not so much that the response was too painful to bear. It seemed a little childish to me – not to say dangerous – but according to Tor it had been going on for generations so I guessed the Vohungs had got it pretty much down to a fine art. It was a rare event, I gathered, for border patrols to return with dead to bury, although not so rare for them to return with a number of walking wounded.

'How long a patrol will this be?' I asked; I wasn't sure how patient Sonder would be if the entire patrol failed to return in good time. For that matter, I didn't know how long the Librarian planned to stay in Benza. It seemed to me that he had done very little in the time we had been there, other than to instruct Mrs Catlin and discuss various esoteric subjects with the city's scribes.

'Several weeks at most,' said Tor. 'We will scout the most likely areas for raids but our primary duty will be merely to put on a show of force.' He grinned. 'It is too hot at this time of year for serious fighting.'

I had already noted that the Captains on our patrol were dressed in silks rather than armour. Even the men-at-arms, made up of a combination of civilian militia, or *fyrd*, and professional soldiers, had abandoned their usual leather regalia in favour of lighter cotton tunics or sleeveless vests. The impression of a group of schoolchildren setting out for an adventure was once again reinforced in my mind, dispelling any notion I might have had that this patrol was likely to encounter anything overtly dangerous.

The days passed uneventfully as we made our way first to the borderland adjoining Kolhos and then along the valleys and hillsides that constituted the border itself. We passed through several villages on our patrol, all peopled largely by peasants: the men were stocky individuals, generally fair-haired and broad-shouldered, their hair cropped short unlike their fellows who lived in the city; the women, those few I caught glimpses of, looked similar to the men, except that their hair was generally a little longer. None of them seemed particularly fearful of our patrol, although they were respectful, and I guessed that any downtrodden appearance they might have had was due simply to the hardships of the life of a primitive farmer and not to any overt oppression by their masters. What interested me most about the peasants we saw was the proliferation of longbows among them, a weapon for which I had a long-standing affection and of which I had seen nothing in the Kingdoms until this moment. I asked Tor about it as we continued our patrol.

'It is a peasant weapon,' he said simply, 'and not suitable for a professional soldier.'

'Why?' I asked. I had heard this argument before, and I was beginning to get a little sick of it.

'It is unmanly,' Tor replied. 'What honour is there in striking an enemy down from a great distance? That is not the way a warrior behaves.'

'Then the bow is never used as a weapon of war?' I asked – I was deliberately pushing Tor now, trying to see just how deep this stupid prejudice went.

'In time of real war,' he said, almost snapping at me, 'peasant archers are drafted into the fyrd. But such wars are rare. The bow is not really a weapon, merely a hunting tool that lends itself to certain types of military strategy.'

I laughed out loud, much to Tor's annoyance, and that of some of the other Captains. I realized Tor was not the only one who was growing irritated at my questions.

'My apologies for laughing,' I said – not very convincingly, I'm afraid. 'But what you are telling me . . .'

A hand grasped my sleeve, pulling me around in the saddle to face one of the other Captains.

'You are a guest, and Tor Taskus's friend,' the Captain said through clenched teeth, 'but I find you insulting and I will have satisfaction.'

'I meant no insult,' I said, trying to remain calm despite the man's grip on my arm. 'If I have offended you, I apologize. Now, please release my arm.'

The man leaned towards me. I wondered if he was going to attack me there and then, but instead he suddenly jerked spasmodically in the saddle, eyes wide with apparent surprise, and fell limply forward across the neck of his mount. An arrow shaft protruded from his back. My astonishment barely had time to register before my gryllup let out a pained howl and reared up, hurling me from the saddle as the beast pitched onto its side and lay writhing on the grass. I was stunned for a moment, aware vaguely of shouts and cries all around me, some human and some animal. Then three arrows thudded into the grass beside me and I came to my senses with a jolt. The patrol was under attack! It was an ambush, and one the like of which Tor and his fellows would never have expected. This was no show of strength, but an all-out attempt at massacring the patrol. From what I had seen and heard over the past months, such an attack as this made absolutely no sense.

All of these thoughts flashed through my brain in an instant, and as they did so I was already trying to find cover from the unseen archers who had killed my gryllup and, from the looks of things, almost half of my companions. Men and beasts were milling about in sheer confusion, arrow shafts raining into them from both sides of the trail. Bodies were falling constantly to the bloodied grass to be trampled by those around them still on their feet.

I felt the bulk of a gryllup bump into me and then a powerful hand had grasped me by the arm and I was being hauled into the air. It was Tor Taskus, his shield unslung and bristling with broken arrows, his silk tunic ripped and splattered with blood.

There was no time to talk, and barely time to think; I gained the saddle behind Tor and with a ferocious kick he sent the gryllup forward along the trail. Arrows flashed past our heads, but we were only two men and the majority of the bowmen were concentrating their attack on our helpless companions. I risked a glance back, and felt my heart sink: not a man was left standing, yet still arrows rained into the patrol, thudding into bodies where they lay heaped one upon another.

Branches whipped our faces as the trail narrowed and Tor kept the gryllup as close to its edge as he could. To my disbelieving astonishment I realized that the whole ambush had lasted less than a minute.

'Tor!' I yelled. 'Where are we going?'

He made no reply, and I wondered if he actually knew where we were heading or if he simply wanted to put as much distance between us and our attackers as possible. Yet I wasn't prepared to believe that Tor was afraid, or even that this was a case of discretion being the better part of valour; it seemed to me that, knowing how familiar my friend was with this part of his kingdom, he would have some specific destination in mind.

We rode as fast as the overloaded gryllup could go until nightfall, and then only slackened our pace as much as was necessary for safety. I had seen no sign of pursuit, but I did not doubt that it was there. The sheer scale of the attack on the patrol convinced me that our assailants, whoever they had been, had been determined to kill each and every one of us. They would not be likely to let Tor and me get away.

At sometime around midnight, with a full moon to illuminate the scene, we came upon a peasant village. Or rather, we came upon what was left of it.

'By the Thirteen Gods,' whispered Tor.

The village was a smouldering ruin, its dirt streets littered with dead. Its livestock pens were broken open and empty, its grain stores had been raided and then destroyed. The smell of burned thatch and charred flesh hung heavy in the air.

Our gryllup chose that moment to let out a wail of protest and collapse beneath us. We tumbled from its back and came quickly to our feet, naked swords in our hands. We had both taken the creature's collapse to be the result of an arrow wound, but the truth was rather more prosaic: the animal had collapsed from sheer exhaustion.

Tor sheathed his blade and moved slowly into the remains of the village. I followed, but I kept my sword drawn – I was stunned by what I was seeing, and although I expected no attack (this destruction was hours old) I needed the reassurance of the cold steel in my hand.

The village produced no surprises; it was all just as it had appeared at that first glimpse. It also gave no answers; why had it been sacked so brutally, and by whom? It made no sense.

'It is war,' Tor said quietly.

'Undeclared?' I asked; such, I knew, was contrary to every code of conduct that existed in the Kingdoms. But then, so was the extent of this destruction.

A thought struck me.

'Tor,' I said, 'do the Kingdoms ever make war on other nations?'

He looked at me, a faraway expression on his face.

'Not since the old times,' he said.

I cursed silently; the more I learned of the history of this bizarre world the more I realized how little I knew.

'Tor,' I said, trying to be patient, 'what are the "old times"?'

He seemed to come back from whatever reverie he'd been lost in. He half-smiled as he said, 'Before the time of the Librarians. How is it you do not know these things, my friend?'

'My, uh, country,' I said, 'is very . . . isolated. We know little of the rest of the world.' I added, smiling at the half-truth of the statement, 'It was to learn of the world that my companion and I left our own land. Please, Tor, I need to know more. How long have the Libraries existed?'

'They would have us believe they have always existed,' Tor replied, 'but any fool can plainly see that this is not so. The Libraries were created by the mythical Y'nys in the mists of Creation's first morning, and are all that remain of that long-dead race. The empires of Man have teemed across the face of the world in a thousand guises since those days, and only in recent times have the Libraries come to be used again. But many generations before the first Librarian appeared the Great Wars had ceased to be possible. Now, each land makes war only upon its own neighbours, and then only rarely.'

I realized that when Tor spoke of 'war' he was referring to the all-out subjugation of one land by another, and not to the perpetual internecine battles that were the normal way of life in the Kingdoms and in most of the other lands of this world. From what Mrs Catlin and I had learned in our time with Sonder I knew that a reasonably reliable figure for the period of time Tor was speaking of was probably between one thousand and twelve hundred years. His people had made no advancement in either military or social terms in all that time. And there was no evidence that any outside agency had prevented them from doing so. I couldn't understand it.

'Why did the old wars stop?' I asked. 'What changed?'

'It is not recorded in our history,' said Tor, 'although certain legends speak of it. There had been a time when the gods walked our world, directing all that we did, making of our lives a golden age. But then the gods fell to warring, and all that they had built fell into ruin. Without their fabulous powers to assist us, we could not undertake the kinds of campaigns necessary to make war over great distances, since the minds of men are not as those of the gods and are unable to deal with such colossal concepts. Thus, we now make war only in and around our own countries, where the scale of battle is not beyond our human imaginings.'

I turned away; what Tor said he obviously believed, but the implications terrified me. His people were conditioned from birth – through social custom and nursery fairy tales – to a totally parochial view of the world and themselves. But beyond the confines of the Kingdoms, in lands further away than Tor could imagine but in reality only across the face of the continent, other peoples would not necessarily share his blinkered view, either of life in general or of warfare in particular. And unless I was missing some vital clue, I was convinced that it was one of those peoples who had decided to invade the Kingdoms. I didn't give much for Tor's race's chances.

'Come, my friend,' said Tor. 'We cannot remain here.'

I looked around me, seeing not this tiny village but the city of Benza, razed to the ground and its people slaughtered or enslaved. I'd come to love Benza, for all its primitive dwellings and slightly egotistical inhabitants. It was the first place on this planet where I'd been met with genuine friendship, and where I'd been accepted for myself. I faced the prospect of its destruction with a kind of despair I hadn't felt since I'd had to stand and watch my father kill himself. With a sudden flash of anger I swore to myself that I would do everything in my power to prevent it from happening, and that meant only one thing.

'Tor,' I said, 'one of us *must* get back to Benza. If we can enlist Sonder's aid the city might be saved.'

'The soldiers of Benza will save their city,' Tor said with a certainty that I felt boded ill for his city's future. 'But if the Librarian wishes, we will not reject his aid.'

'Good enough,' I said. 'Now tell me, how do we get to the city from here without being killed in the process?'

'We lead our pursuers to believe we are already dead,' Tor said.

He turned and marched back to his gryllup, which was beginning to stir but otherwise showed few signs of life. He encouraged the animal to its feet and led it slowly towards the remains of a building on the outskirts of the village, a gutted shell whose original purpose was now unguessable. The building looked more than a little unsafe.

'Quickly, Shaw,' he called to me, 'pick up the body of a man and follow me – and be sure to leave a trail.'

I shuddered as I approached the nearest male corpse, a man in early middle age with a dozen arrows in his lower body and legs, and hoisted him to my shoulder. His eyes, open and sightless, stared at me as I bore him towards where Tor was standing.

'Place him here,' Tor directed, pointing to the entrance of the building. I did so, and Tor arranged the man so that his right arm was sticking over the threshold but the rest of him was 'inside' the tottering building. Then he drew his own short sword and placed it in the man's hand.

'Move through the building and out at the rear,' Tor told me. 'Take the beast with you.'

Puzzled, I led the gryllup out of the building through what had once been its back wall. Tor looked about him carefully, as though measuring the dimensions of the remaining parts of the building. Then, drawing his long-sword, he delivered a blow to one of the remaining uprights of the framework, and leaped back as the whole lot came down with a brittle crunch and a cloud of white ash. He staggered back to where I was waiting, and as the dust settled we looked at the result of his handiwork. There was hardly anything left standing now, just a great mound of charred rubble. I could just make out, protruding from the far side of the debris, a human hand, and the silvery blade of a short sword.

'It seems,' Tor said, 'that we entered the remains of this building and that it collapsed upon us.'

'You think this will fool them?' I asked.

'If it does,' said Tor, 'we will have earned the right to die defending Benza. If it does not, we are dead anyway.'

'Putting it like that,' I said, 'I guess we have nothing to lose.'

We edged away from the building, covering our tracks until we were clear of the village in order to maintain the illusion of our deaths. Once in open country again Tor led his tired beast by the head, giving it what little rest he dared.

'We will not head directly for Benza,' he told me. 'If the subterfuge in the village does not fool our pursuers then perhaps this next diversion will. We will circle to the south and enter the city from that direction, which is the least-populated region of the Kingdom. We will lose perhaps one day by doing so, but will improve our chances of arriving at all. I believe the risk to be acceptable.'

He glanced at me, and I could see that he wanted my approval. He loved his city at least as much as I did, probably – undoubtedly – a great deal more.

'I agree,' I said.

Chapter 19

I MAKE AN ENEMY

We were at the furthest point south on Tor's mental map of our route when we encountered the madman. He was walking seemingly aimlessly northward, apparently totally unaware of his surroundings. His clothing was unidentifiable, a collection of rags and tatters that were rigid with mud and dirt and blood. There was a hideous wound in his scalp that would undoubtedly kill him eventually, and to which we attributed his unbalanced state of mind.

He walked directly past us, and I think Tor would have been content to let him go his way, but his appearance at that moment concerned me, especially given his condition. It occurred to me that he might have run into the same ambushers that we had.

Tor cursed at the delay, but at my urging he turned the gryllup after the man and quickly overtook him.

'Ho, fellow!' he called. 'Where are you from?'

The man kept walking, and it was difficult to tell whether he had heard Tor and was ignoring him or had actually not heard him.

'These are the lands of Benza, stranger,' Tor called, a hint of a threat in his tone. 'Where are you from?'

The man stopped and turned to us with a twitch that shook his whole body.

'Benza?' he shrieked. 'Benza, you say?'

Foam flecked his lips and his eyes were wild, but his body was so exhausted only his face betrayed his manic state of mind.

'Then I've made it after all!' he cried, and fell to laughing and crying in alternate brief and horribly violent bouts.

'We'll get nothing from this lunatic,' said Tor.

'Lunatic?' the man yelped. 'Lunatic, is it? Aye, and you'd be mad too, seen you what I seen!'

'What have you seen?' I asked.

'I'll not tell,' he hissed. 'I'll never tell! I'll take it to the grave – aye, and beyond, too! Wings? Wings, were they? Hah! Shadows, more like, shadows of death, more like. Aye, Death's shadow over the lands of the Kings!'

'What are you saying, fool?' Tor demanded. 'If you've seen something that threatens the Kingdoms . . .'

'Threatens? Threatens?' the man squawked. 'Dooms them! Like my poor Sjaadok. Poor . . . poor . . .'

He began to weep once more, but the sound was different now, less manic. It was the weeping of a man facing utter despair, but not that of a lunatic.

'What's Sjaadok?' I whispered to Tor.

'A city in Kolhos,' Tor replied, now clearly concerned. 'It lies to the south, beyond the Vorx river, and is surrounded by treacherous marshes and woodlands full of wild beasts. It is more impregnable even than the capital itself. If it has fallen . . .'

'Fallen, fallen,' the man wept, looking up at us now with eyes that were horribly sane. 'The wings, the wings of Death, the giant lalantha, spewing out death, raining down on my poor Sjaadok . . .'

'What's a lalantha?' I asked Tor.

He gestured with his hands, clearly as frustrated by the gaps in my vocabulary as I was.

'An insect,' he said, 'with brightly-coloured wings, such as you have seen in the gardens of the keep . . .'

'Butterfly!' I said. Then, 'A giant butterfly? Spewing out death?'

Tor shrugged. 'He is mad,' he said simply.

As though to confirm this the man began shrieking and wailing again, and tried to take a bite out of our gryllup's left front leg. The animal head-butted him out of the way, and he railed at it ferociously, mouthing such obscenities as I had never imagined could issue from the lips of a human being.

'Come,' said Tor to me, 'we can learn no more from this creature.'

And so we rode away from the man, but neither Tor nor I could dismiss what he had said from our minds. I noticed that we missed our regular meal break that afternoon and pressed on instead towards the north and Benza.

Our eventual arrival two days later was something of an anti-climax. The city was utterly peaceful, and nothing we had encountered on our journey there, other than the dubious information furnished by the lunatic, had in any way confirmed the fears we had entertained on the night we had found the burned-out village.

'I must see the Duke immediately,' Tor told me as we rode through the city's outer gatehouse. 'Will you be available if I need you to speak?'

'Of course,' I told him. 'I need only report to Sonder that I'm back in Benza and then I'll wait for you in the main hall of the castle.'

Tor nodded and we parted company.

There was a lot going through my mind as I approached the library in the upper part of the castle, not least how I could convince Sonder to help the city. I still had no idea of why he was here, nor of the political motivations of his people. How would he regard the fall of Benza? Or even the fall of the whole of the Vohung Kingdoms? This was not his country, and as powerful as he undoubtedly was it would not be a venture free from personal risk to undertake its defence.

Preoccupied as I was, I was unprepared for the sight that greeted me as I entered the large room that housed most of the library. Here it was that Sonder had set up his lectern, and it was beside this lectern that a ferocious argument was taking place, between a broad-shouldered, armed and armoured Captain, and a half-naked slave woman. The woman was Mrs Catlin, and her state of undress was purely relative; she was wearing her Ladden slave costume, presumably because the climate was too warm for anything heavier at this time of year. The women of Benza, whether free or slave, tended to be a little more conservative in their dress, and I think Mrs Catlin rather enjoyed the fact that her appearance set her apart from them.

I didn't know the Captain personally, but I'd seen him around the city and knew that he was generally regarded as a man not to cross.

'For the last time, you intellectual pygmy,' Mrs Catlin was saying as I entered, 'I have no intention of yielding to any of your advances, so take your inflated male ego and get out of my sight.'

I winced at her tone, wondering if either of them knew how much trouble they were flirting with.

'Woman,' I heard the Captain snarl, 'you may be the property of the Librarian, but you are in Benza now and subject to her laws and customs. And if I want a slave to do my bidding, whether for an hour or for the rest of her miserable life, she will obey me.'

'Not this slave,' Mrs Catlin said icily.

The Captain's hand shot out and grabbed her by the scruff of the neck, shaking her like a rag doll. She twisted her head and sank her teeth into his wrist, so hard that I almost thought I could hear them grinding on his bones. He let out a yelp of pain, snatching back his hand. Mrs Catlin grinned at him, blood on her teeth and lips. She seemed very pleased with herself. The Captain flung a backhanded slap at her, not holding back at all. She crashed through the lectern, sending it to the floor with a sound like breaking glass, and tumbled over it to lie motionless on the stone flags.

I let out a cry of the purest rage I had ever felt, my sword out of its scabbard long before I had time to think about what I was doing. The Captain whirled around, drawing his own blade, and as soon as he saw me let out a short, barking laugh.

'Get out of here, boy,' he snapped. 'This is man's work.'

'Then you had better leave,' I snarled back, 'because you will never be a man.'

His face went dark with rage, but he held himself in check.

'I will not offend our guest by destroying his slave boy,' he said heavily, 'but let one more such remark escape your lips and I will see to it that you will beg for your death.'

'Only a coward strikes a woman,' I said softly, seething inside but trying not to let my anger make me too reckless. 'I call you coward.'

The Captain's face contorted and with a war cry that he obviously intended should paralyse me with fear he sprang towards me. I met his attack with a defence that was every bit as ferocious, and then switched to an all-out attack that sent him staggering back across the chamber. Out of the corner of my eye I could see Mrs Catlin beginning to stir, but her movements were so laboured and slow that it was more distressing than reassuring to witness. I could hardly believe the fury that was driving me on, or the extent to which I wanted to hurt the man before me. I think he sensed something of the demon that was in me, because he abruptly fell back and pointed his blade to the floor, a universal signal for a pause in hostilities. I copied the gesture, shaking with emotion.

'You have proved your courage, man,' he said, his voice not steady, 'and your skill. But do not further risk your life for some bitch of a slave. Come, let us . . .'

My point sprang up.

'Defend yourself, you scum,' I yelled.

His blade only just parried mine, but so powerful was my attack that he had no opportunity to counter-attack. He backed away from me, defending wildly, and I broke through his guard long enough to cut a slice out of his right sleeve, taking a piece of the arm with it. He redoubled his efforts, and I hacked a chunk out of his right thigh. He limped back, blood trailing him across the stones, and I pressed him harder still. I feinted to his injured arm, avoiding his weak parry to open the seam in the side of his mail shirt, exposing his chest. In another moment I had drawn blood in three places on the exposed flesh, and then as he sought to protect that area I gave him a three-inch gash across his cheek to remind him to keep his guard up.

I stepped back, lowering my point.

'Had enough?' I asked, mockingly.

His eyes were bloodshot, his teeth so tightly clenched he must have been loosening them in their sockets. Without a word he rushed me, and with a ferocious parry I sent his sword clattering across the floor. My point flashed up to his throat, and for an instant I almost finished him. But by then it would have been murder, and as furious as I was I wasn't quite prepared to go that far.

'Get out of my sight,' I snarled.

He backed away, circling the room towards the door without turning his back on me. As he passed his sword he hesitated, but I snapped, 'Leave it!' and with a look of hate he fled the room.

'Was that really necessary?' Mrs Catlin asked.

I turned to face her. She was standing beside the overturned lectern, swaying unsteadily; her face was bloody, one side already swelling.

'I thought so,' I said, although I was now beginning to wonder.

'Seemed a bit childish to me,' she observed.

She looked down at the lectern.

'Sonder will be angry about this,' she said.

'Well, bloody good for bloody Sonder!' I shouted.

'Really, Shaw,' Mrs Catlin said, 'there's no need to raise your voice.'

'And that's another thing,' I said, more angry now than I had been with the Captain. 'My name isn't "Shaw", it's David. You're not my teacher any more, so either call me by my name or don't talk to me at all.'

'I have a name too, Sh— I have a name, too,' she said, still studying the lectern as though it was the most important thing in the world. 'And as you say, I'm not exactly your teacher any longer.'

'I don't know what you are,' I told her. 'Sometimes I think you're not even human.'

She looked up at me. If she'd had tears in her eyes I think I might have relented, but her eyes were dry and devoid of all expression.

'Don't you have any feelings about anything?' I demanded. 'Is this really all just some kind of intellectual game to you? Aren't you *involved* at all?'

She half-opened her mouth, as though to deny what I was saying, but whatever she had been going to say never got said.

198

At that precise moment another voice entered the discussion: Sonder's voice.

'What has occurred here?' he asked softly.

I looked round to see him approaching from the same doorway that the Captain had left by a few moments earlier.

'There has been an accident, Librarian,' Mrs Catlin said. 'The lectern has been damaged, I think.'

'Who is to blame?' asked Sonder.

'I am,' I said immediately, and promptly cursed myself for reflexes I couldn't control.

'You did this?' he asked me.

'He did not, Librarian,' Mrs Catlin said. 'A Captain of the Duke's guard is to blame.'

Sonder studied Mrs Catlin's face. He touched her cheek.

'And this?' he asked.

'That too, Librarian,' she said.

Sonder tutted.

He looked at me.

'Your gallantry would be a virtue in a free man,' he said. 'In a slave it is merely stupid.'

Yeah, I thought, *that's me: stupid. And showing no sign of ever growing out of it.*

'The lectern is no longer necessary to my plans,' Sonder said, showing a rare consideration for our opinions. 'But to inflict damage on my living property is unacceptable. This Captain will have to be punished.'

I hesitated, then said, 'He has been punished, Librarian.' Sonder looked at me. 'By another item of your living property,' I told him.

'In anticipation of my wishes?' Sonder asked.

It was a dangerous question; Sonder seemed to want Mrs Catlin around, but I had the distinct impression that I was starting to become superfluous.

'In defence of your property, Librarian,' I said, 'for which task you have told me I am responsible.'

He said nothing for a moment, then muttered, 'A slave with initiative is a mixed blessing, so the saying goes.' He looked at me. 'The Captain is not sufficiently punished to satisfy me. He is to be killed. Do it.'

I swallowed, trying to find an argument that Sonder would be able to accept for sparing the Captain's life. With a sinking sensation I realized that the best argument in the world would fall on deaf ears.

'You hesitate,' Sonder observed.

'No, Librarian,' I said, attempting to sound enthusiastic.

'You bluff better when you do not need to lie so directly,' he told me. 'Your hesitation is both natural and, to a point, acceptable. It ceases to be so when it causes you to question your orders, rather than simply to dislike them. I do not need your approval for the tasks I set you, but I *will* have your obedience.'

'Yes, Librarian,' I said, my throat suddenly very dry.

'Go, now,' he said. 'I believe the Captain called Taskus requires you.'

I hurried away from the Librarian, trying hard not to think about what I would do when he found out that I had not carried out his orders. As I passed the Captain's sword that still lay on the floor I stooped and picked it up; I had half a mind to return it to him along with a strong recommendation that he leave Benza as soon as possible, preferably never to return.

I found Tor in the central hall of the keep. He looked harassed.

'Where in the gods' names have you been?' he demanded. 'The Duke is waiting for you. And for all our sakes, Shaw, tell him all that you remember of the ambush and the burned village, especially the impression we had of the beginnings of an all-out war.'

'I take it you failed to convince him,' I said.

Tor shook his head dejectedly.

'No one has made real war here for generations,' he said. 'The Duke cannot believe anyone would risk their entire country simply for the sake of taking another's.'

We marched up the steps leading to the palace quarters at the top of the keep. Tor was not so distracted that he didn't notice the sword I was carrying.

'A Captain's sword?' he observed. 'Did someone promote you in my absence?'

'Not exactly,' I said, and related the events that had taken place in the library. I described the Captain in question to see if Tor knew him.

'He is called Hol Krexus,' Tor said. 'His family is an old one, but not a particularly wealthy one. He has a bad habit of simply taking what he wants, since he knows he cannot afford to buy most of the things he covets. Since he is possessed of a formidable sword arm and a temper to match he is seldom challenged for his thefts.' He gave me a wry grin and added, 'Though not seldom enough, it seems.'

'A bad man to have as an enemy,' I observed.

'The worst,' said Tor. 'But since you must now kill him he will not be an enemy for long.'

'I can't just kill him,' I protested. 'I'm not a murderer.'

'My friend,' Tor began, then paused for a moment. He seemed to consider his words, then said, 'But for that band you wear upon your ankle, you could be a Captain tomorrow. I would propose you myself, and a dozen others would fight for the honour of sponsoring you. But being a Captain means more than simply knowing how to fight. It means knowing how to obey the orders of your master. Even if you do not agree with those orders. Like it or not, Sonder is your master. You must do as he says.'

We were at the door to the Duke's audience chamber now, and I felt far from prepared for the task before me.

'Tor,' I said, 'no man can order you to do something you know to be wrong. The excuse, "I was only following orders" just won't do.'

'My friend,' said Tor, 'it is the only excuse that *will* do. A man must obey his master, or he is not a man. Without the law, there is no civilization. There is only chaos.'

'Better chaos,' I said, 'than the kind of law you're describing.'

Tor shook his head, obviously convinced I was some kind of anarchist and probably regretting some of the things he had said about me. Then he ushered me into the presence of the Duke.

The audience was about as bad as I'd expected. Duke Joshima was nobody's fool, but he just couldn't bring himself to believe what Tor and I were suggesting. In his place, I suppose I might have been sceptical, but it didn't help Tor or myself, nor did it bode well for Benza's future – if we were right.

The Duke was about to dismiss us when I suddenly remembered something. I caught Tor's eye and mouthed the word 'Sjaadok'. He looked puzzled for a moment, then suddenly turned to the Duke and said, 'Highness, have we heard anything of late from the city of Sjaadok?'

'Is this some new business, Captain?' the Duke asked. 'As you know the regular trade caravan from the west is due here in some five days, Sjaadok being its last stop before entering Benza.'

'By your leave, my liege,' Tor said, 'I believe Sjaadok to have been invaded as a precursor to the attack upon Benza. Let me take a small troop along the trade route to investigate. If we meet the trade caravan, then nothing has been lost. If we do not, then will you accept it as a sign that something is amiss?'

'What is the source of your suspicion?' the Duke asked.

Tor and I had agreed earlier that we would not mention the lunatic, since his ravings had made little sense and would only detract from our own credibility if repeated.

'I would rather not say, sire,' Tor said. 'The information was not obtained, uh, honourably. I would not involve Your Highness any more than necessary.'

'Hmmm,' Joshima said pointedly, clearly not much convinced. 'Oh, very well, Captain. But when you encounter the traders and all is well I shall expect to hear no more from you on this subject. Is that clear?'

'Yes, sire,' said Tor, his grin splitting his features from ear to ear.

We were promptly dismissed and Tor raced off to the Captain's quarters to rally some troops. Since I had lost all but the clothes I was standing up in during the ambush of the patrol I set off for the city armoury to acquire new scalemail and armour. It occurred to me that I might also seek out one of the taverns frequented by the city's soldiery, since I hadn't had a decent meal in days, nor anything to drink except water from a leather flask.

The visit to the armoury was relatively brief; Sonder had unlimited credit throughout the city, and the armourer had outfitted me before and knew my sizes by heart. He was a grizzled ex-soldier with only one leg and enough scars on his face and body to satisfy any ten Captains, all of whom were inordinately fond of their battle scars. In addition, he was reputed to know by heart the measurements of every soldier in the city and their personal preferences for weapons, shields and accessories. Since it was known he could neither read nor write, and had no apprentice to help him who could, I did not find the claim that hard to believe.

'What'll ye be doin' wi' that sticker, lad?' he asked me, indicating Hol Krexus's former Captain's sword.

'I hadn't really thought,' I confessed. 'What do ye, uh, I mean, you suggest?'

'Lookee 'ere, lad,' the armourer said, grasping the weapon and slipping it into a free scabbard. 'There's many a way for carryin' a blade, and none o' 'em's any the better than another. It's just what tastes yer. I seen that bendy thing ye likes' [I guessed he meant the bandit sabre I always carried] 'but ye wears it wrong. Lookee.'

He unslung my sabre, which I usually wore in Benzan style, the scabbard on a long strap that went diagonally across the chest.

'If ye's gonna wear a bandit's tackle,' the armourer said, removing the straps from the scabbard, 'ye's got ta wear it bandit style.'

He fitted a different strap to the scabbard and reslung it, so that the sword was over my left shoulder.

'Naybody in the Kingdoms wears a blade like that,' he told me, 'but it's how the bandits out east wears 'em.'

He slung the Captain's sword in the conventional style and fitted it for me.

'Now ye's got a choice of either,' he said, adding, 'Or both, if ye's in a real din.'

I studied myself in the armourer's full-length mirror. Even after all these months in the city I still found my own appearance startling. I hadn't looked in a mirror from the day we arrived on Shushuan till the first day I visited the Benzan armoury, and the sight of myself had been a real jolt. Kitted out in scalemail and the colours of Tor's family house, and with Tor standing beside me, we might have been brothers. My hair was not quite as long as his, nor anything like as fair – and it lacked the three narrow braids down the left side that were an unofficial mark of his rank – but in every other respect we were very much alike. I was perhaps most surprised at how my build had increased since leaving Earth. My active lifestyle had always encouraged a reasonably athletic physique, but from the time Mrs Catlin and I had arrived among the Ladden I had done more physical toil than ever before in my life, and my muscles had responded in the only way they could: by growing. Some of my victories in the battles we had fought crossing the Plains of Ktikbat no longer seemed quite so amazing to me.

Looking at myself now, however, I wasn't too impressed by what I saw.

'What ails ye, lad?' asked the armourer, obviously seeing my sour expression.

'Too many weapons,' I muttered; in addition to the swords, I was wearing the customary daggers, one in the belt and one on the outside of the right calf, and I looked, to my earthly eyes, like a man about to declare war on everyone he met.

'Ye can't have too many claws when ye live in the jungle, lad,' the armourer said, which was a slightly distorted version of an old warrior saying. 'But suit yesel'. I'll bill yon scabbard to yer master and ye can please yesel' what ye do wi' it.'

I smiled at the armourer's automatic assumption of a sale and decided I was now long overdue for that meal I had been promising myself.

Outside, the evening sun was almost below the distant tree line, and the sky was painted in all the colours of fire and blood. It was the kind of sunset I'd only ever dreamed about on Earth, a sunset such as I imagined might have been seen a hundred thousand years ago when the race of man was just beginning the long haul up the evolutionary ladder. It seemed to me that a sunset like that should be shared with someone, someone who could appreciate it as much as I could and who meant something to me. I'd never really had anyone like that, but until that moment it hadn't occurred to me that I might want someone like that. And now that it had occurred to me only a single face came into my mind, and I laughed out loud at the sheer absurdity of the thought.

I was still chuckling to myself as I made my way through the narrow streets leading to the tavern I'd had in mind for my meal. It was just beyond the outer ward of the castle, in one of the sections of the city popular with Captains and soldiers alike. The ale, I recalled, was particularly good, but tonight I was more interested in the food.

I noticed the two men standing at the far end of the alley as soon as I entered it, but preoccupied as I was with one thing and another I didn't give them much thought. It was only when they stepped away from the wall and began to walk slowly towards me that I realized their stance had been a little too casual, their positioning a little too conveniently strategic. I glanced warily over my shoulder, to find two other figures now blocking the alley behind me. All four of the men were unknown to me. They had the look of militiamen, reserve soldiers who only fought in time of war or, occasionally, when their regular trade was not doing well, took part in patrols or border raids. They were generally thought little of by professional soldiers, but the more far-sighted Captains appreciated their worth in a fight. Most militiamen wore no armour, only toughened leather tunics and occasionally gauntlets plated with iron or steel. Their weapons tended to be a mixed bag, but from the looks of it these four had been supplied by a professional armourer, whether just for tonight or on a regular basis I wasn't sure. Three of them wore swords, the fourth carried a war axe, single-headed but with a heavy spike behind the blade for balance and for inflicting damage on armour that might resist the curved edge. The three with swords probably had daggers as well; the axeman had a cavalry shield, rounded at the top and tapering to a point at the bottom, designed to allow for use on gryllupback. He was, of course, one of the two behind me. Had he been in front the sight of him, so heavily armed, might have put me on my guard in time to cut out of the alley before it could be blocked at both ends.

I decided to put as much room between my back and that axe as possible, and strode confidently towards the two swordsmen in front of me.

'Step aside,' I ordered.

Neither man moved.

So much for the easy option, I thought.

'I have no money,' I said, making out that I thought them to be thieves, which I did not for an instant believe. Four heavily-armed men in Benza's most soldier-frequented quarter? The chances of their staying alive for more than a week would have been minimal.

'They do not want your money, slave,' said a voice behind me, a voice that I recognized.

I half-turned, keeping the two swordsmen in my peripheral vision. Beyond the two men behind me stood a third, a Captain dressed in full field armour and carrying a flail: the steel ball on the end of its chain was spiked rather than smooth. The smooth ball has the advantage of not becoming tangled in its target quite so easily. The advantage of the spiked ball lies, of course, in the amount of damage it can inflict.

'You have something of mine, slave,' said Hol Krexus. 'I will have it back.'

Five-to-one odds seemed to me to be a bit unfair, especially considering the code of conduct Krexus would have had to have sworn to in becoming a Captain. The sensible move would have been to have handed over whatever it was he wanted and then flee with all possible haste. What he wanted, I supposed, was his Captain's sword. I knew something of what went into earning such a weapon, and the disgrace that attended its loss during battle. So Krexus would not be satisfied with merely getting the blade back; he would want my life along with it.

I unslung the blade slowly, removing it from the new scabbard. The two swordsmen shifted uneasily, but held their ground. They would be Krexus's own men, handpicked for their abilities and, I presumed, their discretion. They would not attack until he ordered it.

I held the blade out, the point towards the Captain where he stood beyond the two at my back.

'Come and get it,' I said softly, 'coward.'

And as soon as the words were out of my mouth I spun around to the two in front of me. The blade flashed through the air, half decapitating one man and catching the other a slash across the cheek. I turned instantly to the other two, drawing my dagger in the same movement. The men were already rushing me, the axeman in front, his terrible weapon raised to strike. Realizing that he had lost the element of surprise he let out a wild war cry and flung the head of his weapon at my skull. I deflected the blow with my sword, the weight of the impact almost breaking my wrist, and thrust with the dagger. He got his shield around in time, and the blade embedded itself in the wood. We stood locked together for the briefest of instants, my sword hilt under his axe head as he strove to bring it down on my face. The edge was like a razor, and the lower point of its crescent was closing on my right eye. The man was a mountain of muscle, taller than me, and I was wasting too much time with him. I twisted the blade of the sword so that it hooked under the axe head and let myself be pushed back. The axeman was off balance for only an instant, but it was long enough. I sidestepped and tugged on the axe head, and he went crashing past me into the swordsman whose cheek I had cut a moment before. From their curses I guessed that one or both of them had impaled himself on the other's weapon.

I sprang at the remaining swordsman, noting that Hol Krexus had so far held back from the fight. Obviously he wanted me injured, or worse, before risking his own life.

The swordsman defended himself for all of five seconds before taking my point through his right shoulder. Dropping his weapon, he sank to the floor of the alley, moaning.

Still Krexus held back, so I turned once more to the axeman. He was lying in the alley with his colleague's sword sticking out of his side, his body wrapped around the blade in a knot of pain. The swordsman looked at me, looked briefly at the axe where it lay at his feet, then turned and fled.

I turned to Hol Krexus. He didn't move.

'You want this?' I asked, brandishing the bloodstained blade.

He said nothing.

I took the weapon and, with all the strength I could muster, hammered the point into the wall at my side. The blade shattered into three pieces. I flung the hilt at Krexus's feet.

'Have it,' I said.

He looked at the stump of his sword and, with a cry of such

hatred as I'd never before heard, swung the flail over his head and charged me. My sabre left its scabbard with a flash of silver in the moonlight, the blade intercepting the chain of the flail. I leaped inside the ambit of the weapon and punched Krexus as hard as I could on the only part of his face left exposed by his helmet, the point of his jaw. His body spun around, his feet tangled up in one another, and he crashed to the ground and was still.

I untangled my blade from the chain of his weapon and cast the flail aside. Then I turned him over and checked that he was still alive. He was, but not likely to regain consciousness for some time.

Straightening up, I sheathed my sword and looked around at the litter of bodies in the alley. It seemed like a very high price to pay for three feet of steel.

I turned and headed towards the tavern that had been my original destination. Now, however, the ale seemed a more pressing need than any amount of food.

Chapter 20

DEPRESSION

Tor Taskus found me trying to put away a whole barrel of ale. I'd regained my appetite after the first few flagons and had devoured the largest meat pie the tavern had had on offer, along with the obligatory pile of assorted vegetables that were a staple of the diet of a Benzan soldier. Suitably fortified by this repast, I had returned to the ale with a vengeance, determined to get myself as close to comatose as my funds would allow.

Tor grabbed a tankard from the landlord and joined me.

'You've had a busy night, I hear,' he said.

I mumbled something that would have been scathingly witty had I known what it was.

'One dead, two wounded,' Tor mused, 'and one of them not likely to see the morning. And a Captain of the Duke's Guard left lying in the gutter like a sack of rotten vegetables.'

I had reported the fight in the alley to two members of the city guard who had been in the tavern when I arrived. I hadn't mentioned Hol Krexus's part in it; if he'd recovered and fled before the guards investigated I was prepared to let it go. If not, it was his problem.

'What will happen to him?' I asked Tor.

'If you make an official complaint he'll probably be executed,' Tor said. 'We take a dim view of Captains who bring the title into disrepute.'

'And if I say nothing?' I asked.

'His behaviour is already the subject of gossip,' said Tor. 'Joshima won't intervene without an official complaint, so it will be left to the council of the Captains. He'll probably be banished to one of the remote outposts and warned never to come near Benza again.' He took a long drink before continuing. 'He's not popular around here. Some Captain or other might decide this is a good excuse to challenge him to defend his honour on the field of battle. He would be unable to refuse such a challenge.'

Tor looked at me pointedly.

'I would not thank anyone for such an act,' I said, equally as pointedly.

Tor shrugged.

'You are a strange man, my friend,' he said, 'but I like you nonetheless. I think perhaps there is a little too much love in your heart for you ever to make a warrior.'

I raised my glass unsteadily.

'Amen to that,' I said.

I was buying trouble for myself with Sonder, I knew; and I owed that fool Krexus nothing. But I couldn't bring myself to be a party to cold-blooded assassination, whatever the cost. And even if I let Tor do what he was suggesting it would *still* be murder and, what was worse, the weapon would be our friendship.

'What's happening with your patrol?' I asked, deliberately changing the subject.

'We leave at dawn,' Tor said. 'You may accompany us if you wish.'

I intercepted a passing serving girl and swapped my empty flagon for a full one. She gave me a saucy wink and I gave it back with interest.

'Better not,' I said to Tor. 'I still need to speak to Sonder about helping us when the attack comes. Plus, this business with Krexus started over Mrs Catlin, and while he's at large in the city I don't think she should be left undefended.'

'I understand,' said Tor. 'Watch your back, my friend, and wish me luck.'

'May the Lord of Blood sup at your table,' quoth I, hoping the saying was the appropriate one.

Tor laughed heartily so I guessed it was.

He finished his drink and departed.

The serving girl sidled past again. On some level I was still thinking about that sunset, and the other thoughts it had prompted were combining with the ale to make me feel strangely depressed.

'More ale, Captain?' the girl asked.

She'd seen me often enough before to know I wasn't any more a Captain than she was, and although she meant it as a compliment it only served to remind me of my true status. This girl, who rated as low in the social hierarchy of Benza as any peasant in the fields, was as far above me as the Duke himself.

'No,' I said, standing up. 'No more ale.'

'There's a bed for you if you wish it, Captain,' she said, smiling invitingly.

'What I wish,' I said, an inexplicable anger building up inside me, 'is to go home.'

I walked unsteadily out of the inn; the cool evening air outside hit my senses like a hammer, and I swayed drunkenly in the moonlight, my hand groping for the stone door jamb. It found instead the shoulder of a man who was leaning against the wall. I began to proffer an apology for manhandling the unseen individual when a fist crashed into my face, sending me reeling backwards into the wall. Hands grasped my arms and the fist thudded into my belly; obviously the fist's owner was wearing gauntlets, otherwise he would have broken his knuckles on my hauberk. I was too drunk to feel much pain, but as the fist hit me again and again I felt my grip on consciousness weaken. My knees sagged, and the hands that had been supporting me released me and I sank to the ground. A foot slammed into my back and I fell to my face on the cold stone, and then my attackers kicked me soundly for several seconds. Finally one of them barked an order and the beating ceased. A hand grasped my hair and pulled my head back. For an instant I thought I was about to have my throat cut, and I struggled weakly to resist. A voice hissed in my ear, 'Can you hear me, slave? I have a message for you from my master. He advises you to be on your guard from now on, because his business with you is far from concluded.' He shook my head. 'Remember what I say, slave, because when next we meet my weapons will not be restricted to fists.' So saying, he struck me across the face one last time for good measure and dropped my head back to the stones.

Chapter 21

INVASION

The events of the next forty-eight hours are not pleasant for me to
recall. Even without the detrimental effects of the ale I had drunk
the beating would have taken some recovering from, but with the
two working together I was convinced I was upon my deathbed.
The worst of the feeling passed once I had put some fluid back
into my body, but I was destined to walk around like a puppeteer's
manikin for over a week.

I was found, shortly after the attack, by one of the night patrols,
and taken to Sonder's quarters in the keep. This would not have
been my own choice, but as the only practical alternative would
have been to have dumped me on Tor's doorstep I did not object
too strenuously – my friend the Captain had enough to worry about
at the moment.

And so I was left to the tender ministrations of Mrs Catlin. I do
not know how she initially received my unconscious body, but her
first words to me when I awoke were a curt, 'So, you're awake, are
you?' and were followed by several hours of surly silence. It seemed
I had succeeded in teaching my former teacher something after all:
I had taught her how to sulk. On top of all the other things I had
to feel bad about that seemed to me to be adding insult to injury.

I was able to get out of my 'sickbed' on the second day and was pleasantly surprised to find that I was no longer persona non grata with Mrs Catlin. In fact, she seemed almost pleased to see me back on my feet.

'There are things I have been learning,' she told me over breakfast, 'of which you should be aware.'

'Do tell,' I replied without much enthusiasm.

'Sonder is expecting a visitor,' she said. 'I gather it is the reason for his being here.'

I winced at Mrs Catlin's oh-so-perfect use of High Tongue formal grammar; in my time in Benza I had fallen into the habit of using the more idiomatic type of speech used by her soldiers, and by the population in general. I knew that Mrs Catlin would regard this as unacceptable, but I wasn't in the mood to pander to her ridiculous expectations of me.

'What visitor?' I asked.

'Another Librarian, I think,' she said. 'And someone else, not a Librarian, not even a scholar, which is unusual – Librarians tend to regard anyone who is not an academic as beneath their notice, or at the very least as being unworthy of their interest. But this visitor has Sonder practically excited – for Sonder, that is.'

I nodded; I'd never seen Sonder go any closer to excitement than the unintentional raising of an eyebrow over some unexpected event. The notion that he might be eager over an impending confrontation was so totally out of character that I found it genuinely worrying – as powerful as he was, what kind of personage could rouse him to such a degree?

'When is this visit due?' I asked.

'I'm not certain,' Mrs Catlin confessed. 'But soon, of that much I am sure. In fact, I think it may even be overdue.'

It occurred to me that Mrs Catlin probably knew nothing of what had happened to the patrol Tor and I had been on, and that Sonder's impending guest might not be unconnected with what Tor and I suspected was happening on Benza's borders. If there was a connection, and so far only the coincidental nature of these two unlikely events occurring at the same time led me to believe there might be, then my plan to enlist Sonder's aid in defence of the city seemed not only doomed to failure but might actually serve to precipitate the conflict. My mind began to conceive of all manner of plots and conspiracies, to tie up totally unrelated incidents that I had observed over the past months and to make of them some grand design to topple the city of Benza.

Which was, of course, ridiculous.

The Librarians, for all their seeming lack of political ambition, were the virtual masters of this world, even if their power in the Kingdoms was largely derived from reputation alone. What could they gain from mere mundane conquest?

Reluctantly, I told Mrs Catlin about the ambush, and about the burned village, and even about the lunatic, repeating such of his ravings as I could recall.

She listened in rapt attention, her face betraying an inner conflict of emotions that anyone who knew her less well than I might have mistaken for lack of interest, or even boredom.

While I related my tale I was conscious of the sounds of the city that drifted in through the open window of our quarters, and of a hubbub that I associated with market days or public holidays. Having lost track of the days due to recent events I paid no special heed to the sounds.

Mrs Catlin said nothing until my story was finished, then arose and paced the room in deep thought.

'You believe Sonder knows something of these attacks?' she asked.

'It's a possibility,' I said. 'And until we can be sure, one way or the other, I would hesitate to discuss them with him.'

She nodded, not speaking.

The noise through the window was becoming irritating; I wondered if some sort of procession was under way, or if a tournament was being staged.

'And the Duke did not believe what you and Tor told him?' Mrs Catlin asked.

'He believed our account,' I said, 'but not our conclusions.'

'The fool,' Mrs Catlin said.

'Not necessarily,' I told her, finding it strangely amusing that our usual roles in a discussion seemed to have been reversed. 'What we were suggesting hasn't happened here for generations. Why should he believe it was happening now?'

'Because of the evidence, damn it,' Mrs Catlin said. 'Twisting the data to fit your own personal theory is the worst kind of stupidity.'

I laughed, provoking first a frown and then a rueful smile from my former teacher.

Something in the noises outside was beginning to worry me; they were not the sounds of happy people. There was fear in them.

I arose and walked to the window. Mrs Catlin gave me a quizzical look and joined me.

'What's that?' she asked, pointing.

'Where?' I asked; she seemed to be indicating something outside the city.

'There – no, blast! The side of the tower is in the way.' She turned towards the door. 'Let's get up to the roof.'

I followed her, only to encounter a dozen or more crossbowmen racing up the narrow spiral staircase to the top of the keep.

'What's going on?' I demanded of one of them.

'The gods only know,' he grumbled, cursing as he struggled to pull on his mail hood.

We followed the men to the roof and rushed to the crenellated battlements that faced across the city and gave an uninterrupted view of the woodland and fields beyond.

My throat tightened, and I felt the sudden dig of Mrs Catlin's fingernails as she grasped my hand.

'Lalantha,' I whispered, 'a giant lalantha.'

There was little wonder the sight had driven a man insane, for the monstrous shape sailing over the tree tops towards us was an awesome thing to behold.

But it was not alive. Not a giant insect. Not anything from the realm of nature. It was artificial, man-made, a construct, of that I was certain, and it was men who controlled it, who swarmed all over it, and who had brought it *here*.

It was . . . an airship. That was my first thought. An airship, a vast, silvery envelope filled with a gas that was lighter than air. But

I dismissed the thought even before it was fully formed. That thing was solid, rigid, a defiance of every law of gravity and momentum that had ever been written.

It was . . . a butterfly. A central core, perhaps a hundred metres long and two or three metres thick, tapering to a point at either end, from which sprang four arches, located roughly centrally, each of which stood fifty or sixty feet at its apex. The arches were equally spaced around the central axis, two above and two below, each at ninety degrees to its neighbours, and were spanned by a billowing, multicoloured material that rippled in the breeze. But what most made it look like an insect were its 'legs'. Eight of them, perhaps more, trailing along beneath it, with large, round 'feet' at their ends. They were ropes, and the feet were blocks of stone. I couldn't fathom their purpose at all.

I shook my head, trying to keep the scale in proportion – that billowing material that seemed so like gossamer wings was actually canvas, and constituted four vast sails. Whatever supernatural force was holding that thing in the air, its motive power was nothing less prosaic than the wind.

I tried to convince myself yet again that the 'butterfly' was not made of the hard, metallic substance it appeared to be, that a closer inspection would reveal it to be something as light as silk, but yet again I failed. The dull grey substance of the central spar and its four 'wings' was undeniably metal, albeit a metal that had somehow learned how to defy gravity.

As my sense of awe gave way to a more scientific curiosity, I began to pay more attention to those aspects of the airship that were not so daunting. Around the space where the wings met the main body of the thing the more recognizable handiwork of man could be seen. A conventionally shaped and constructed hull had been erected around the metal joints, a wooden vessel on some four decks extending for about ninety feet, or just about the distance between the forward and aft mountings of the skeletal wings. The construction of this hull was so much in keeping with Vohung designs and technology, and so totally at odds with the monstrous thing to which it was attached, that I instantly reviewed my opinion of the men who commanded it.

This was no invasion by a technologically superior enemy, but just one more example of how this planet's chequered past kept returning to haunt its present.

The airship – or air*frame*, to be more accurate – was yet another leftover from some earlier civilization, like the Libraries of the Y'nys, or the High Tongue, or the architectural concepts that we kept encountering again and again in parts of the world that otherwise had nothing in common. And someone, someone probably native to the Vohung Kingdoms, had discovered this airframe and, without the slightest clue to its origins or workings, had commandeered it for his own purposes.

I remembered something else the lunatic had said: a giant lalantha *raining death*. The soldiers of Benza had no idea how to defend themselves from an airborne attack – they could barely understand the concept of a siege machine at all! If this was indeed an attack, then I had to prepare myself to witness slaughter on a scale I had never before imagined.

'Come on,' I snapped, grasping Mrs Catlin by the arm and propelling her back towards the stairway. 'We can't afford to be exposed like this.'

'But what can we *do?*' she moaned. 'Arrows won't do any good against *that!*'

'You won't do anything,' I told her, 'except find a place to hide. I'm going to try and join up with some of the Captains I know – if they'll have me.'

We reached my quarters and I pulled on my mail shirt and sword belt. My mind was racing frantically in search of some viable defence against an attack from the air when the most potent weapon we possessed was the bolt of a crossbow. Then any plans I might have made were shattered by the arrival of Sonder.

'You will both remain in this room until I summon you,' he said.

I was holding my sabre, and I felt my fingers flex around the hilt.

'Librarian,' I said slowly, 'if you will permit it, I have certain duties to perform about the city.'

'I do not permit it,' he said.

218

I took a step forward. Sonder waved his arm at me and my whole body was consumed in fire. I collapsed to the floor of the chamber, writhing in agony, and realized that he had activated the slave band. I gaped through tear-blinded eyes at my ankle, fully expecting to see the flesh blistering from the bone, but other than a slight redness the skin seemed undamaged. And yet the blazing agony continued to pound through my body, drawing an animal howl from my throat. Distantly, through the thunder of blood in my ears, I heard Mrs Catlin's high-pitched scream, and realized that her band too had been activated.

The pain stopped as instantly as it had begun, and I writhed on the stone floor in the numbing aftershock.

'Do not leave this room until I summon you,' Sonder's voice said from the doorway.

I rolled onto my side, trying to push myself to my feet. I heard the door close and the rasp of the lock being turned. I almost laughed; if Sonder felt he had to lock us in after that display of punishment he clearly credited us with more courage than I at that moment possessed.

Mrs Catlin moaned from where she lay some feet away from me, and it took me a moment to realize she was calling my name. I crawled painfully towards her and pulled her into my arms. She shivered uncontrollably, and I'm not ashamed to admit that I did too. I had the slight advantage – if such it could be called – of having felt the power of the slave band before. Mrs Catlin, of course, had not.

The shakes receded slowly and Mrs Caltin eased herself out of my grasp, leaning back against the stone wall and wiping sweat from her eyes.

'That was—' she began, and obviously realized that no words could ever describe it.

'Poor K'nen,' I whispered, hardly able to conceive of how much pain he must have been in when he died.

Mrs Catlin nodded, then suddenly sat bolt upright, her eyes wide with some kind of shock. I wondered, for a brief moment, if she had had a heart attack, but then she spun to face me and grasped my arms in a grip like steel.

219

'*Poor K'nen,*' she said again, and I realized I was missing something. She waited, then said, 'Would you ever run, Shaw? Knowing the consequences?'

'No!' I replied, shrinking from her at the very suggestion.

'You're no coward, Shaw,' she said intensely, 'so why wouldn't you run?'

'Because it would be hopeless,' I protested. 'There'd be no chance of—' I paused, suddenly seeing it. 'There'd be no chance of escape,' I said slowly. 'Unless—'

'Unless we've been lied to,' Mrs Catlin said. 'S'nam told you the slave band could not be removed without killing the wearer. And K'nen *couldn't* have hoped to get beyond the range of the mutahiir before his escape was noticed and the band was activated. So—'

'So there is a way to remove the band safely,' I said, 'and K'nen thought he knew what it was.'

'But something went wrong,' Mrs Catlin speculated. 'He either failed in his attempt or—'

'Or he was supposed to meet someone who could remove it and they never showed up!' I said.

'Or,' Mrs Catlin said, 'they showed up too late.'

I looked at her, and a memory of that night came back to me.

'The Librarian,' I said.

The Librarian we'd seen on the trail, just beyond where we'd found K'nen's body.

'It's a possibility,' she said.

We stared at each other in silence for a long time. Suddenly everything seemed to have changed. Suddenly there was real hope for freedom. And yet in reality nothing had changed. In reality we were just guessing. Perhaps K'nen had been an incurable optimist who really *had* thought he could outrun the mutahiir. Or perhaps he'd had an accomplice in the Ladden camp who had been supposed to cover his escape and had either failed or had actually betrayed him.

As quickly as it had come the brief elation faded, to be replaced by an even deeper and darker despair. Not for the first time in recent days I truly longed to go home.

We spent the rest of the day in gloomy silence. Beyond our

small room we heard a constant bustle of activity, but nothing that sounded like actual fighting. The frustration of not knowing what was happening wore on our already tortured nerves, and the few words we spoke to one another were terse and abrupt.

The first break in the monotony came just before sundown. The door to our room was unlocked and we sprang to our feet, expecting to see Sonder. Instead, it was a serving girl with a tray of food.

'What's happening?' I demanded.

She looked at me, in her eyes fear that she was trying to hide.

'I know not, Lord,' she whispered. 'But I have heard the common soldiers speak of a vast army approaching from the south. I fear for my poor city.'

The south: Tor Taskus! I grieved silently for my friend, doubting I would ever see him again.

'What of the airship?' Mrs Catlin asked.

'It hangs over the city, Lady,' the girl said. 'I know no more.'

Something in her manner suggested that she *did* know more; and why was she treating us like visiting nobility? We were slaves, and the servant class in Benza was usually scathing in its contempt for slaves, and not slow to show it. While it was true that I had been treated like a free man ever since Tor had 'adopted' me, this girl was surely under no illusions as to our true status. The best we should have been able to expect from her was cool indifference.

She left and I voiced my thoughts to Mrs Catlin.

'I see the hand of Sonder in this,' she said, sitting down to the meal the girl had left.

I stared at her in disbelief. 'How can you eat?' I demanded.

'How can you not?' she snapped.

I fumed silently, cursing her for the way she was always right. Starving myself would do no one any good, especially if we were going to be incarcerated here for any length of time.

I sat down opposite her and forced myself to eat.

Chapter 22

BARGAINING

Neither one of us got much sleep that night. The chamber had been Mrs Catlin's, and was built for only one person, which meant one of us had to sleep on the floor. We argued for a ridiculously long time over who should have the bed, finding the most convoluted reasons imaginable for why either one of us should need a better night's sleep than the other. In a twist that was probably typical of every argument we'd ever had each of us insisted on yielding the bed to the other, both determined that no matter what happened the other one would sleep comfortably. Normally, our sense of humour would have come to our rescue in a case like this, but this time we remained resolutely true to our sworn intent and thus did not get to sleep until after midnight.

(If it is of any interest to anyone, *I* got the bed – winning an argument with Mrs Catlin is not something I have ever been able to accomplish.)

Had that ridiculous dispute been an isolated incident I do not think I would have placed much significance in it, but sadly it merely set the tone for the long stretch of days that we remained locked in the room together. And if I was to relate to you some of the things we argued about I think I should die of shame at the telling. I recall one particularly vitriolic exchange on the subject of the stonework of the walls of our chamber, an argument that almost had us coming to blows yet the actual content of which I cannot now even remember. I kept telling myself, during the lulls in our verbal battles, that we were just reacting to our imprisonment and that once we were set free we would laugh about it all, assuming that our eventual fate left us any time for laughter. Yet a nagging voice that lodged in my head and which would not leave me alone kept telling me that there was more to it than just the pressure of the circumstances; there was a major confrontation brewing between Mrs Catlin and myself, a turning point in our relationship that had been building quietly for many months. And this constant bickering was our way both of putting off the inevitable and of fencing around it, trying – without really understanding what it was we were doing – to come up with a resolution that we could both live with.

We were fed twice a day during our imprisonment, not always by the same girl but always by someone who showed us the same kind of deference. And as the days wore on, that deference seemed to change subtly, to become what I could only interpret as fear.

As to the events in the city we learned very little. There was indeed an army marching through Benza, an army such as the Kingdoms had not seen since the beginnings of their history. The intent of the army – whether the conquest of Benza or merely the transit of it on the way to some other destination – remained unknown. What was known was that the commander of the army was on board the airship that hung over the city. No one knew who this man was nor from where he came, but the Duke and a group of Captains had gone aboard the vessel to speak with him and had returned to a relieved court after several hours, apparently unmolested and in good spirits. The nature of their discourse with the commander of the airship had not been revealed.

I made repeated enquiries about Sonder's whereabouts, but it seemed no one had seen him since the day the ship arrived. This seemed to me to confirm my worst fears about the Librarian. I had no doubt whatsoever that he had somehow been secreted aboard the airship to confer with its occupants, occupants who had been known to him long before we arrived in Benza – perhaps before we even left Vraks'has.

The days turned to weeks, and all we could learn from the various servants who brought us our food was that the Duke was now going aboard the airship regularly for lengthy talks with its master, and that numerous members of the court had accompanied him, as had the highest-ranking Captains in the city. The army that was moving inexorably through Benza's southern quarter was clearly in no hurry, but equally as clear now was the fact that it was heading directly for the city. Even if its intent was peaceful, which was a possibility I could not bring myself to accept, its very presence in the Kingdoms was a danger to the peace of Vohung.

When the message finally came to us that Sonder commanded our presence aboard the airship I think that neither Mrs Catlin nor I was surprised.

While the servant who had brought the message stood and waited in impatient silence, I pulled on my mail tunic and slung my sabre over my shoulder. Mrs Catlin pulled a poncho-like garment on over her brief Ladden outfit and, casting nervous glances at one another, we allowed ourselves to be led from the room.

The airship was now moored above the outer ward of the castle, several lines securing it to the double curtain wall. It swayed gently in the light breeze, its sails furled but the seemingly weightless mass of the thing presenting a large cross-section for the wind to catch. A collection of rope ladders dangled from open hatchways in the belly of the wooden part of the ship, along with the weighted ropes I had observed earlier, trailing over the top of the curtain wall as armed sentries marched to and fro beside them.

Now that I could see the ship more closely I picked out many details that I had missed earlier. Two vast sailboards at the rear of the wooden hull were clearly for steering, but the four mainsails could also be used for this purpose to some extent since I saw now that they were not fitted to the vessel's 'wings' as I had first thought but were on slender masts that paralleled the trailing curve of the wings, allowing the sails to be adjusted to some degree during flight.

The hull of the ship was as crudely made as I had initially thought, but its gross design betrayed more understanding of the

225

construction of ocean-going sailing ships than I had originally realized. We had not seen an ocean since our arrival on this planet, nor a river that was navigable by large ships, so I had no idea of the naval capabilities of either the Vohung or any of the other races we had met on our travels.

Mrs Catlin and I were led to the top of the curtain wall, and I was irritated to note that whenever we passed anyone along the way they would invariably whisper to one another and point at us, as though they had been expecting our arrival and regarded it as a source of some excitement. This, to me, seemed absurd.

We reached the foot of one of the rope ladders and our guide turned us over to a Benzan soldier. The man was a lieutenant in the city guard, and although I had known him quite well during my time with Tor he now treated me like a total stranger. And, once again, there was that look of veiled fear in his eyes as he regarded us.

'Remove your hauberk,' he told me.

I hesitated; scalemail may have been a poor defence against an airship full of warriors, but it was comforting.

'You may keep your weapon,' he said, possibly reading my mind, 'but do not permit it to touch the metal of the ship. The mail shirt would kill you were you to wear it . . . up there.' He gestured with his thumb, not looking up at the vessel.

I removed the tunic and handed it to him, adjusting the strap on the sword to wear it Vohung style. I wondered about what he had said; if the metal of the airship was not some miraculous substance that could defy gravity, then its ability to float in the air could be the result of some kind of manipulation of electro-magnetic fields, which would make it a sensible precaution not to be wearing a suit of armour on board. But if the armour would be dangerous, why not the sword? Clearly the danger was not that the armour would act as a 'lightning rod', but possibly that it would generate a field of its own, effectively cooking anyone inside it. The sword, I reasoned, would probably develop a degree of static charge, but not enough to worry about – unless I let it touch the metal of the ship, in which case it would probably electrocute me.

I shook my head; I was applying layman's physics to something that was a thousand years ahead of anything I had ever seen; any conclusions I came to were automatically suspect.

I took hold of the rope ladder and peered up into the square of darkness in the ship's hull to which it led.

'Wait,' said the lieutenant, placing a hand on my arm. His hand trembled slightly.

He put his other hand to his mouth and called into the air, 'Two to come aboard!'

A face appeared at the open hatch. There was nothing exceptional about it, but then again what had I been expecting? Fur and horns?

'Come aboard,' the owner of the face called.

I began to climb. I felt the ladder sway and knew that Mrs Catlin was close behind me.

We reached the vessel without incident and stood in what appeared to be its forward hold, waiting for our eyes to accommodate to the semi-darkness. The hold was stacked with supplies – dried fruit, salted meat, vegetables – and was less than half full. I filed that fact away for future reference.

'Follow me,' said our new guide.

I studied the man as we went aft. He was darker than the average Vohung, and his rather short hair was black. He didn't have the cast of a Ladden, nor of a native Ktikbati, but he was clearly not from any of the Kingdoms. His mode of dress emphasized this, since he wore nothing more than a cotton loin cloth and an assortment of leather straps and belts that were fitted with a multitude of buckles and snap-rings. Some of the buckles were so placed as to suggest they might carry weapons, although all he wore at the moment was a dagger, but many of them were obviously designed for fastening to the ship's rigging.

The man led us up the whole length of the hold and then up a ladder to the second deck. This was clearly a crew deck of some description, but we passed through it immediately and I had no time for a lengthy inspection. The next deck was an assortment of compartments, including what looked like an armoury and a workshop. We were led to the stern section of this deck where our guide told us to halt outside a particularly stout-looking door.

He rapped on the door, said, 'Enter when you are called,' and then marched briskly away.

We were kept waiting for only a few moments before a voice called out, 'Enter,' and with a glance at one another Mrs Catlin and I reached simultaneously for the door handle. She smothered a nervous giggle and allowed me to open the door for her.

The chamber beyond was clearly the captain's cabin. There was a large table with charts and measuring instruments, an even larger four-poster bed with curtains round it, a collection of chests of various sizes and designs, a smaller table to one side with dining chairs around it, a wooden cabinet with a huge padlock, and a single upholstered chair that might have been a throne. Seated on this chair was a man I had not seen before, but I instantly knew him to be the captain of this vessel, and thus, presumably, commander of the army that was marching on Benza. He was an unremarkable man, though clearly not of Vohung origin, and was dressed simply enough in a rust-coloured silk tunic. He was unarmed. His skin was deeply tanned, but beneath, the tan seemed as light as my own. His hair, which was rather short, was fair but not blond. His eyes were blue. And there was something else, something I couldn't identify, that somehow I found familiar.

Apart from this man there were two others in the room when we entered. One, not to my surprise, was Sonder. The other appeared to be a Librarian also, except that the robe he wore was red, whereas Sonder habitually wore white. This man was standing at one of the cabin's windows and had his back to us as we entered so I couldn't see his face. He was tall and appeared gaunt beneath his robe; either his head was shaved or he was prematurely bald since his stance was that of a young man in the prime of life.

'So,' said the ship's captain, 'these are our comrade's young guests. Come in, come in! And they are from where, Sonder?'

'Allegedly from a place called France, Droxus,' said Sonder.

'Ah, la belle France!' said the man named Droxus. 'Mes enfants, j'aime de faire votre connaissance.'

To say that I was amazed by what he had just said would be an understatement. I think Mrs Catlin was no less astonished, but she managed to find the presence of mind to say, also in French,

'A countryman! But how did you come here? And . . . are you in command here?'

Droxus half-turned towards the Librarian at the far side of the room. 'Her accent is good,' he observed in the High Tongue, 'but she is not French.'

Mrs Catlin seemed taken aback, but said, with feined indignation, 'Sir, I am as French as you are!'

Droxus laughed.

'My dear,' he said in English, 'I already know that.'

'I . . . I do not speak English,' Mrs Catlin said in French.

'You speak it,' said Droxus. 'And unless you admit to it instantly, I shall have Sonder destroy your friend here.'

Sonder half-raised his hand towards me, and Mrs Catlin said, 'I speak English!'

Droxus smiled.

'You are English?' he asked.

Sonder had not lowered his hand.

'Yes, we are English!' Mrs Catlin said.

'Yet you chose to conceal that fact,' said Droxus. 'Why was that?'

'I don't know,' Mrs Catlin said.

Sonder's fingers twitched; I felt sweat soaking my tunic, could taste it on my lips.

'Truly, I don't know!' Mrs Catlin said. 'It just seemed sensible to hide the fact – we knew nothing about Sonder, about his intentions or his powers; I wanted to reveal as little about ourselves as possible.'

Droxus nodded slowly; personally I had always thought Mrs Catlin's little subterfuge had had more to do with our own morale than with any tactical advantage it might have given us over Sonder – it had been good to think that we were fooling him, that we were retaining some kind of control over our lives, even if, deep down, we had known that we were fooling only ourselves. Droxus, however, seemed satisfied with Mrs Catlin's explanation.

He nodded at Sonder and the Librarian lowered his hand. I felt the muscles in my body slowly unclench; I could taste blood in my mouth and realized I had bitten through my cheek.

229

I swallowed, feeling a bitter hatred for the Librarian build up inside me.

'Now that wasn't so bad, was it?' Droxus said cheerily. 'And now that there are no secrets between us we can discuss your future.'

'Do we have one?' I asked, barely able to keep the anger out of my voice.

'Of course!' Droxus enthused. 'A very bright one, if you're sensible.'

'We would welcome any kind of future,' Mrs Catlin said, 'that did not include slavery.'

'Quite right, my dear,' said Droxus. Switching back to the High Tongue he said to Sonder, 'My Lord Librarian, I think it is time for phase two of our little plan.'

Sonder nodded. He gestured at me, and I cursed myself for the way I instinctively shrank from him. To my astonishment I heard a tiny metallic click from my anklet and, as I gazed at it in disbelief, the slave band parted and fell from my leg.

'Freedom!' laughed Droxus. 'Isn't it wonderful?'

I looked at Mrs Catlin and realized that there were tears in my eyes. I brushed them away, but I couldn't wipe the smile from my lips, nor did I want to.

'And now for that talk,' said Droxus.

I looked at him sharply, my smile fading.

'What about Mrs Catlin?' I demanded.

Her slave band was still in place.

'What indeed?' said Droxus. 'She is, to borrow an earthly phrase, insurance. Lord Sonder tells me you are a formidable swordsman and, shall we say, a tad impetuous. He has observed your fondness for the woman, and tells me you will do nothing to endanger her. Thus, she remains our, uh, hostage for your good behaviour.' He smiled benignly.

I felt my hands clenching into fists; I wanted to smash that idiotic smirk off his face, but we both knew that I couldn't. Mrs Catlin put her hand over one of mine and said softly, 'Don't worry, Shaw, I know I can rely on you.'

I think she said it to reassure me, but after the miserable time we'd had together over the past weeks it only made me even more angry.

'You rely on me too much,' I told her, and at the look that passed through her eyes I instantly wished I had not. Of all the feelings I'd ever seen on her face this was the first time I'd ever seen her truly hurt.

'Now, now, children, no squabbling,' said Droxus.

Mrs Catlin looked away from me, and I knew that there was nothing I could do to take back what I had just said.

Droxus arose and walked over to me, taking me by the arm and leading me towards the door of the cabin.

'Let's take a walk, my boy,' he said. 'I need to explain a few things, and there's no need for us to have an audience.'

He led me out of the room and up a ladder to the open top deck of the vessel. We were on a catwalk that circled the main deck but that was some six feet above it, a slender handrail the only thing between us and the long drop to the ground below. I followed Droxus to the sterncastle, where a man stood on guard by the vessel's large steering wheel. It was like being on an ancient sailing ship, or at least the Hollywood version of one. I almost expected to see Errol Flynn and Basil Rathbone come charging on deck locked in one of their constant duels.

I turned to Droxus, leaning back on the handrail with a casual disregard for the drop beyond that was purest bluff.

'Who are you, Droxus?' I asked in English.

'Captain of this vessel,' he replied in the same language.

'Who *were* you?' I asked.

He laughed.

'Does it matter?' he asked. 'What counts is who I am now – and what I can offer you.'

'I have what I wanted,' I said. 'I'm free.'

'The woman is not,' he said.

'That's her problem,' I said, hoping the lie sounded more convincing to Droxus than it did to me. From the laugh it provoked I guessed not.

'I don't blame you for trying to protect her,' he said. 'She is quite beautiful.'

231

I wasn't accustomed to thinking of Mrs Catlin in those terms, but I realized that to someone who had never seen her on Earth and was now looking at her for the first time the word 'beautiful' was not entirely out of place. The mousy appearance she had seemed to cultivate during her time as my teacher had long since been replaced by something rather more feral, something more in keeping with the life we had led since coming to this planet. Seeing her through Droxus's eyes like this was a little startling to me; I think it was the first time I had actually had the chance to view her objectively since we had first met. In fact, thinking about it, I realized that the way she looked now was more like the way she had looked when I had first seen her, on that very first day when she had played the piano so incredibly in the empty school hall.

'Never mind her,' I said, finding the thoughts disquieting, 'let's get down to business.'

Droxus nodded, stroking his chin pensively.

'This planet,' he said, 'is very, very old. I'm sorry to spout clichés, but mighty civilizations have risen, thrived, and perished on this world a hundred times. Bits of some of them survive, but most of them have disappeared entirely. And the thing is, Shaw, they will never rise again.'

I looked at him, not sure what he was driving at.

'Civilization's had it with this world,' he said. 'Evolution, intelligence, mutation – they've all had their day, and it's over. These people are just marking time before becoming extinct so that some other species can have a go.'

'But they're not that primitive,' I said. 'You can see developments in their architecture, in their social set-up . . .'

Droxus shook his head.

'They've been stuck at the same level of development for over three thousand years,' he said. 'They haven't had a single original thought in untold generations. They are a dead race, Shaw – they just don't know it yet.'

I must have appeared sceptical.

'Look at their idea of warfare,' he said, and I must have betrayed my thoughts in my expression. 'So,' he muttered, 'you *have* seen it. You're no fool, Shaw, you know that what I'm saying is true.' He leaned over the guard rail at my side and studied the city below. 'Do you know,' he said, 'that in some parts of this continent, places where there are still functioning Library machines, the locals have outlawed the profession of Librarian? No? They claim that the Old Knowledge, as they so picturesquely call it, is offensive to the gods. Can you believe it? Knowledge is offensive! No wonder they're dying out.'

'There were times on Earth when the same philosophy was held,' I said. 'We got past it.'

'But we were still growing,' Droxus said animatedly. 'These people stopped growing generations ago.' He looked at me. 'All except the Librarians,' he added meaningfully.

'They want to control the world,' I suggested.

'To get this sorry race moving again!' Droxus exclaimed. 'And they've got the knowledge to do it. All they lacked was a bit of originality in coming up with a plan.'

'Ah,' I said. 'Now I see where you fit in.'

'Sure,' he said. 'I saw what they were up to and suggested how they should do it.' He gestured around him. 'I designed this,' he said proudly. 'They'd had the airframe for over a century and couldn't think what to do with it. They didn't invent it, of course, they just found it – it was half-buried in the side of a mountain, a leftover from an earlier civilization. Even the Y'nys' knowledge can't tell them how it works, and the Y'nys are the oldest recorded race on the planet. They weren't even human, they're that old.'

I scratched my chin. I was beginning to see what Droxus's 'plan' must have been; I wondered if he was mad, or just unspeakably evil.

'So let me get this straight,' I said. 'You found out that the Librarians wanted to take over the world but that they didn't know how to do it. So you suggested a war – a really big one, the kind they've forgotten how to wage on this planet. And to guarantee victory you had them build this ship in order to attack their targets from the air – a kind of attack for which no city on this planet would have any kind of defence. Am I doing OK so far?'

'You're close,' Droxus said. 'We used the airship to defeat the first few cities, but after that we used the manpower from those cities to build ourselves an army. Now we have so many men in the field we hardly need the airship at all. We just march up to each new city and overwhelm it.'

'How did you get the beaten cities to back you up?' I asked – this seemed to me most unlikely, knowing what I did of Vohung honour.

'Did you notice the holding pens in the upper hold?' he asked.

I recalled what had looked like a crewdeck on the second level, but there had been no time to explore the deck in detail.

'No,' I said.

I had an uneasy feeling about what was coming next.

'We've got over a hundred hostages in them,' Droxus said. 'Dukes, Barons, royal families, Warlords, Captains – some random women and children from the families of middle-ranking Captains – all held under sentence of death if their cities fail to obey us. And you know the truly crazy part? These prisoners told their people to fight us anyway, and by doing so played right into our hands. Their people now regard them as heroes, and will do anything to get them back. And since all we're asking them to do is invade the lands of their enemies they're happy to go along.'

I listened to Droxus's words and tried to find some hint of remorse in the man, some semblance of a conscience.

'What happens,' I asked, 'when you give these people back their rulers? Do you expect them to just leave you in charge?'

Droxus laughed.

'I've saved the best for last,' he said. 'The Librarians have a device that can affect the mind of anyone who's put inside it. It's not brainwashing exactly, more a kind of advanced hypnosis. It can only make you do something you have a natural predisposition towards doing to begin with. And since they're mostly military people we've got for hostages they all have an inbuilt penchant for conquest. All we're going to do is give their natural tendency to follow the strongest leader a little nudge in our direction. Then we send them home and they act as our voice in their own cities. It's priceless, don't you think?'

'Priceless,' I said, for the first time faced with the very real possibility that Droxus and his Librarian friends could actually pull this off. I looked at him closely. For all his big talk and his constant use of 'us' and 'we' I was coming to the conclusion that the man was little more than a flunky, a slave in all but name. Librarians, I knew, were the most egocentric species on this planet, regarding all other humans as vassals or property. I wondered if Droxus, too, knew this, and if the knowledge kept him awake at night. I hoped so.

'What happens after you've gained control in the Kingdoms?' I asked. 'Will you move on to the rest of the continent?'

'Not immediately,' Droxus said. 'We'll want to consolidate our victory first, make sure we've got a firm foothold in this part of the world. But, yes, we will go on from here; taking Benza was a big step in the plan, since Benzan warriors are a match for any force that the Kingdoms could ever hope to send against us.'

'Really?' I said. 'I always thought that was just a myth.'

'Not at all!' said Droxus. 'One Benzan Captain is worth ten from any other country.'

It seemed to me that this could not possibly be true, but I said nothing. If Droxus wished to believe it, it was in Benza's best interests that I let him.

'OK, Droxus,' I said, 'I've listened to all you've had to say and while I can't claim to go along with most of it I can see why you're doing what you're doing, and why you think it's the right thing to do. But what am I doing standing out here and listening to it? What possible use can I be to you?'

I consider it a personal victory that I managed to say most of that without throwing up; Droxus, however, seemed not to notice my sour expression.

'Until you met me,' he said, 'did you think you were the only Earth people to come to Shushuan?'

That didn't exactly answer my question, but it did echo a nagging doubt that had been burrowing away in my mind for some time.

'Not the only ones,' I said, 'but I did think we'd be few and far between.'

'Far between is right,' Droxus said, 'but not few. The rift, or whatever you want to call it, that allows you to cross from our world to this one follows a series of lines through the crust of our Earth and the crust of this planet. The lines are laid down by magnetic and gravitational fields in the two planets, and they can be changed or even destroyed by earthquakes or by heavy solar activity or even, occasionally, by exceptional weather conditions – electrical storms, that kind of thing. At irregular intervals, when our planet and this one come into some kind of conjunction, the lines match up and the rift opens. When that happens, hundreds of points of contact in both worlds become active. And very rarely does a point of contact fail to attract someone.'

'Attract—?' I said.

'The energy that creates the rift activates some kind of homing instinct in people,' Droxus said. 'Long ago, the people of this world had the instinct, but that's just one of the things they've lost over the centuries. Our people still possess it, but it's stronger in some than in others. The point is, Shaw, when you crossed over you were probably only one of hundreds – maybe even thousands. And all those people are wandering about out there somewhere, sources of alien knowledge that could throw a spanner into the works of the Librarians' plans. Because if I could do so much alone to help them, think how much more hundreds of humans could do if they decided to oppose them.'

'But that's sheer paranoia!' I laughed. 'Most of those people – if they're even out there – will be struggling just to survive. This planet isn't exactly a picnic, you know!'

'You're here,' Droxus said simply.

'As a slave!' I said.

'What did Sonder ask you when he bought you?' Droxus asked. 'What was the first thing he asked you?'

I suddenly knew what he was getting at.

'Where we came from,' I said quietly.

'Sonder, like every Librarian on this planet,' said Droxus, 'has been looking for people like you ever since they discovered me. They've been told by the Chief Librarian to buy any slaves who were not natives of any known race and get them safely to the nearest Library.'

'But Sonder brought us here,' I said.

'Across the Ktikbat,' Droxus confirmed, adding, '—on foot. Despite the fact that there's a simpler, shorter route – provided you're a Librarian, that is. But the Kahmar feyrvahne lies across the only trade route that crosses the southern Ktikbat, and for some reason the rift seems to favour feyrvahnen – maybe that's why the death zones are as they are, though no one knows for certain, not even the Librarians. But Sonder knew that there was a good chance of picking up more of our people in the towns around the feyrvahne, so he came that way. I gather he was a trifle miffed at not finding anyone.' He chuckled to himself, no doubt perversely pleased that Sonder had had a wasted journey. 'Anyway,' he went on, 'Sonder came to Benza because he was due to rendezvous with the Chief Librarian here. We wanted to see if what we were planning could actually work.'

'Why didn't you just have us all killed?' I asked – from what I'd seen of Droxus this seemed like the kind of thing he would have done.

'I would have,' he said, 'but the Librarians have a very specific way of looking at things. They virtually worship knowledge, and killing people like us would be akin to book-burning in their eyes. As dangerous as you and the others out there might be, the Librarians would rather have you alive to pick your brains than simply exterminate you. As I said, it wouldn't have been my choice, but I suppose for your sake it's just as well.'

'You still haven't told me why I'm here,' I said.

'To join us, of course,' said Droxus. 'Or more to the point, to join me. With our intelligence we could be running this planet in less than a decade. The Librarians have the upper hand now, but at heart they're as degenerate as all the others on this planet. They can't last forever, and who do you think will be best placed to take over from them?'

I paced about a bit on the sterncastle, wondering how far I could push a bluff with this lunatic.

'What if I say yes?' I asked. 'What happens then?'

'We take Benza,' Droxus said, 'and then sail south for the Chief Librarian's home city. We put our hostages under the mind device and come back to the Kingdoms to reinstate the hostages in their cities. Then we take the remaining cities in the Kingdoms.'

'What kind of time scale are we talking about?' I asked.

'We'll take Benza in a matter of days,' Droxus told me. 'The journey south will take about three weeks, wind permitting, so we should be back in the Kingdoms again by late autumn. We may have to sit out the winter in one of the countries we've already taken and then finish off the conquest of Vohung in the spring. By next winter every city in the Kingdoms will be under our control.'

'If I agree to help you,' I said, 'what would you expect me to do exactly?'

Droxus laughed. 'Keep out of my way, mostly,' he said. 'The plan for this campaign is set now, but when it's over we'll have to devise a new one for the next war. That's when I'll need you. Until then, just sit back and enjoy the show. What could be easier?'

'What about Mrs Catlin?' I asked.

'She can join the hostages,' he said. 'And please understand, Shaw, I am not a fool. I know that you do not share my vision for this world, but I'm willing to put that down to a foolish sentimentality on your part. So long as you play fair by me, I'll play fair by you.'

I closed my eyes briefly, trying to think of a better way of doing things, but short of a suicidal attack on Droxus himself – which would change nothing – I couldn't think of a single thing.

'Grant me one concession, Droxus,' I said, 'and I'll join you.'

'I'll consider any request,' Droxus said.

'Take Mrs Catlin's slave band off,' I said.

He studied me closely but I kept my face carefully neutral.

I said, 'If this is to be a deal between you and me, not involving the Librarians, then I can't leave her life in their hands. Put her in with the hostages, but take that damned shackle off her ankle.'

'A deal between you and me,' Droxus mused. 'I like that, Shaw – it speaks well for our future together. I will allow your request, but I will require something in return.'

I'd expected as much, but if I could ensure Mrs Catlin's safety where Sonder was concerned it would be worth almost any price.

'Name it,' I said.

'For the duration of your stay on my ship,' he said, 'your weapons will be locked in my armoury.'

It seemed a small price to pay, but spoke volumes for how little

Droxus really trusted me. I needed to keep in mind that, however twisted he was, he was nobody's fool.

'Agreed,' I said.

He held out his hand, and I took it as convincingly as I could. I felt as though I were bathing in maggots. Whatever else, I made myself a silent promise that Droxus would never live to see his megalomaniac dreams come to fruition.

Chapter 23

DEFIANCE

The next day saw the effective military defeat of Benza.

It began simply enough, with yet another visit by the Duke and his armed retinue to the airship. I had been informed by Droxus that these numerous talks were ostensibly about forming trade links between Benza and the more far-flung corners of the Kingdoms. The airship, of course, was the perfect tool for making such trade possible. It could cover in days distances that land-based caravans could not traverse in weeks. Although Duke Joshima was not, I gathered, entirely convinced of Droxus's good intentions he was sensible enough to keep the talks going, presumably realizing that if open hostilities were declared he was going to have a battle on his hands that he couldn't hope to win.

No sooner had he come on board than he and his party were surrounded by crossbowmen; outnumbered three to one and having not a missile weapon among them, the Benzan Captains, at the urging of the Duke, laid down their weapons. Had they not, a bloodbath would have ensued, and I gave silent thanks for Joshima's good sense.

As soon as the Duke and his people had been searched for concealed weapons they were herded below decks to the holding pens. I had tried to keep out of sight during the capture, but one of the Captains saw me and the look in his eyes told me I would have a hard time explaining my part in this – if ever such an opportunity presented itself.

With the decks cleared, Droxus turned to his master-at-arms and said, 'Break out the muskets.'

I looked at Droxus in speechless amazement.

'There are surprises within surprises,' he said cryptically.

Thirty of Droxus's crew lined up against the port guard rail on the main deck, and in their hands were what I could see quite clearly were muskets. I watched as the men loaded them: they were muzzle-loaders, with flints for firing the powder. They had priming charges, formed into pellets, for primary ignition.

'Not my invention,' Droxus confessed, 'despite what you may think. The musket was reinvented here over five hundred years ago. It was banned in the Vohung Kingdoms as "unmanly, ungodly, and lacking in honour". It's been in widespread use in the southern part of the continent for centuries, but even there it's regarded as a subsidiary weapon, much like the bow is regarded up here. Do you know,' he mused, 'the flintlock replaced the match-lock over eighty years ago, and it's still regarded as a modern innovation. And if you try to talk to their designers about breech-loading they look at you as though you're some kind of heretic. Honestly, these people!'

He shook his head, apparently in wonder at the strength of the ignorance of these poor savages.

What followed could have been worse, but not much. Droxus took a speaking tube, a primitive megaphone, to the railing of the sterncastle and addressed the city below. He informed them that their Duke and his entire retinue were now his prisoners and that the city was to be turned over to him without delay. The response, which took some minutes to come, was predictable enough. Whoever was in charge of the city in the Duke's absence – the Warlord, I assumed, since he had not come aboard the airship – ordered archers out onto the curtain wall and sent wave after wave of fire-arrows sailing onto the airship's deck. Droxus seemed unperturbed, and while fire-control teams doused the flames his musket bearers opened fire on the archers. The effect was not what

I had hoped, but judging from Droxus's expression it was what he had expected. Rather than fleeing in terror from the airship's superior firepower the city's defenders seemed to regard the use of muskets as a challenge to their bravery. Wave after wave of longbowmen and crossbowmen poured onto the curtain wall and were mercilessly cut down. Droxus could have ordered the airship raised, thus making any attempt at resistance totally futile, but he did not do so. Firing in three rotating teams, the musketmen kept up a steady volley of death into the helpless ranks of the Benzan soldiers. There was, of course, no defence against the ball of a musket; scalemail was blasted apart at these distances, and cavalry shields reduced to matchwood. The piles of bodies on the wall and in the middle ward began to grow to appalling proportions.

(An aside, something that seemed important in an as yet undefined way: I observed the effect upon the muskets of the airframe around them. With each shot, a discharge of electricity followed the ball from the weapon's barrel, an unfocused static charge that combined with the musket's natural discharge of smoke to form an almost fluorescent cloud. I noted the gauntlets worn by the musketmen: thick and stiff-seeming, they were padded with heavy rubber insulation.)

Dismissing these thoughts, I raced to Droxus's side on the sterncastle.

'You could stop this!' I cried. 'It's not necessary!'

Droxus smiled condescendingly, like an adult to a naive child.

'Of course it is necessary,' he said. 'When my army reaches the walls I do not want them to have to contend with archers.'

'But you said the army wouldn't be needed,' I protested. 'You said—'

'I say a lot of things,' Droxus said blandly. 'You shouldn't necessarily believe them all.'

I considered hurling him from the ship and into the arms of Benza's decimated defending force. Without the fear of the slave band to hold me back I had only my concern for the safety of Mrs Catlin to keep me from destroying the man. What did one life matter compared to what was going on all around me? The logic that killing Droxus would be a meaningless act – he was, I remained convinced,

243

no more than a puppet leader – was not what caused me to stay my hand. The simple truth was, I could not bring myself to perform any act that would result in Mrs Catlin's life being placed in jeopardy.

I returned to the railing and watched as more and more archers were cut down. Yard-long arrows carved from the beautiful rim-wood trees of Benza's forests filled the air around me, as did the shorter, darker bolts of iron-hard sardwood quarrels, but the damage they did was minimal. The musketmen were protected behind carefully placed shields, and could pick off their targets with relative impunity. I think Droxus's men had taken only three minor casualties in the attack, and only one of those had had to leave his post because of his injury. I sank to my knees beside the railing and almost wished for a stray arrow to strike me dead.

The carnage went on for more than an hour, and left the ranks of Benza's archers depleted by almost half. The only positive aspect to the 'battle' had been that none of her Captains or her professional soldiers had been killed, though how much good they would do in any future engagements was debatable.

When the ceasefire had gone unbroken for a half-hour or so Droxus returned with his megaphone to the railing. He began, in a voice that allowed for no debate, to dictate surrender terms. He made passing reference to the army that was now within one day's march of the city, an army which he claimed numbered in excess of one hundred thousand men. I myself doubted this figure, but even if the true number was a mere half of that claimed by Droxus it would still have been the largest body of fighting men ever to have been assembled in the Kingdoms within living memory. The mere thought of such an army would have crushed the spirit of the average Benzan soldier, used as they were to thinking in terms of battles between, at the very most, hundreds of combatants.

Droxus's chief demand was for additional hostages. The families of the city's Captains were to be rounded up on the curtain wall within the hour, and from them random selections would be taken. The chief Captains were then to come aboard the airship, disarmed and virtually naked, to receive their orders from their new rulers. Failure to observe any of Droxus's demands, he informed the city, would result in retribution too terrible to contemplate. And to convince everyone of this, he said, he had arranged a small demonstration.

I watched helplessly as, from the armoury, a dozen kegs of gunpowder were brought on deck. Each keg was fitted with a fuse, and at Droxus's command each fuse was lit and the kegs hurled overboard. The explosions rocked the airship on its mooring lines, and I raced to the guard rail to witness the extent of the damage. Only two or three of the makeshift bombs had hit anything of any real importance, but the sight of the middle ward littered with blast craters was silent testimony to the damage Droxus could inflict on the whole city if he so chose. I could make out a few of the faces of Benza's citizens, ashen as they gazed fearfully from their homes at the destruction all around them. To fight on against an enemy such as this would be unthinkable, even for so proud a race as theirs.

The surrender came quickly, much more quickly than even I would have thought possible. It was barely the middle of the afternoon before Droxus had his new intake of hostages, and less than an hour after that when a score of the city's Captains stood on the main deck of the airship, their eyes filled with hate, as Droxus himself stood on the sterncastle above them.

I kept out of sight, filled with an irrational sense of shame at remaining free while the city that had adopted me, the city I had grown to love, was deprived of its liberty by this power-mad lunatic.

I could make out only a few of the faces of the assembled Captains, but those that I could see surprised me somewhat. They were not the faces of the city's highest-ranking Captains, but those of her rank-and-file soldiers. I edged around the side of the mooring capstan that concealed me from their view and tried to pick out other faces. For the most part they seemed to be ordinary soldiers; Captains all, yet not those closest to the Duke and his advisers.

As they stood on the lower deck, ringed by bowmen and other warriors, their manner did not seem quite what I would have expected. There was a charged sensation in the air, as of violence about to erupt. That Droxus's men were aware of it was obvious; equally as obvious was the fact that Droxus himself had no sense of the menace all around him.

He began to address the men, telling them of his expectations, of how they would be absorbed into his fighting force, and as he did so I observed the men closely. They were each in motion, moving in some subtle way, either shuffling their feet or flexing their hands or tensing and untensing the muscles in their backs and legs and arms. And not one was looking at Droxus, or appeared to hear a word he was saying.

I reached instinctively for my sabre, but it was safely locked away in Droxus's armoury.

When the inevitable violence began it did so with such speed and such devastating force that the whole ship seemed to ring with it. As though they had rehearsed it for months ahead of time, the Benzan soldiers exploded into action. With a shattering war cry on every pair of lips, the mass of warriors erupted outward, each man hurling himself at the nearest of his enemies with such speed that to have blinked would have been to miss it. Three of the Captains died in the attack, not at the hands of the men they were individually attacking, but by stray arrows loosed by panic-stricken archers. In an instant the first charge was over, and suddenly there were crippled and dying bodies all over the deck, the bodies of Droxus's men, and the Benzan soldiers were now armed with knives and bows taken from their erstwhile captors; as one man they swarmed over the main deck towards the sterncastle.

Droxus, with more alacrity than I would have credited to him, fled the sterncastle and reached the safety of the lower decks. I wondered if his plans had ever suffered such an upset as this before, and if he had a contingency plan in place to deal with it. If he did, the men of Benza would need all the help they could get.

I turned and fled for the nearest hatchway. I ran headlong into a dozen or more of Droxus's musketmen, and the sight of them made me fear for the group of brave warriors on the main deck.

They swarmed past me with barely a glance in my direction, and I heard the crackle of firearms as they reached the deck. It was followed by a medley of screams, and a musketman staggered past me, bristling with arrows, to fall headlong from the ship to the ground far below.

I raced down into the upper hold and made my way swiftly to

where Droxus had said the prisoners were being held. This was a part of the ship with which I was unfamiliar, and I wasted precious seconds racing up and down dead-end passageways before suddenly blundering into what was clearly the ship's brig. The cells were mostly open-plan, half a dozen of them on either side of the broad hold, stinking, straw-filled cages of iron-hard sardwood in which the prisoners were penned like cattle, men, women and children mixed indiscriminately in each cell. An open space between the two rows served the twin functions of broad passageway and meagre accommodation for a handful of jailers. Fortunately for my plans only a single jailer was present at the moment, a bulky-looking individual carrying a wooden stave and with a coiled whip hanging from his belt. He was sitting sideways-on to me as I made my precipitous arrival and eating a bowl of stew. He looked up as I crashed into the passageway and sprang to his feet.

'You can't come this way,' he barked, obviously unsure of either my status or what the significance was of all the noise from the upper decks. 'Only Lord Droxus and the Librarians are allowed down here.'

I sprang forward and struck the man with all my strength across his jaw. He fell backwards, glassy-eyed, and sank senseless to the deck.

The prisoners on both sides of me were now crowding the bars of their cells, calling out to me and cheering. I snatched a bunch of keys from the jailer's belt and ran to the nearest cell. The man standing closest to the door pounded me on the shoulder as I wrestled with the lock, laughing a deep-throated laugh that those around him echoed with enthusiasm.

'I don't know who you are, boy,' he said to me, 'but by the gods I'll grant you a commission in the army of Kolhos if you want it. And a room full of gold if you don't!'

From the far side of the hold a voice that I recognized called out, 'Save your gold, Zanek! That lad is one of mine! And as soon as he lets me out I'll beg his forgiveness that I didn't listen to him sooner. And that we all misjudged him when first we saw him on the deck of this vessel!'

The voice was that of the Duke of Benza, and the relief I felt at what he had said amazed me by its intensity. I just wished that Tor had survived to hear his ruler admit how right we had been.

I got the cell door open at last and was almost engulfed in the tide of bodies that poured forth.

'Quickly,' I said, extricating myself from their ecstatic grasp, 'the battle is hardly started, let alone won. We have to get to the armoury.'

There were nods of agreement all round, and the knot of men scattered to allow me to finish releasing their fellow captives. I caught a brief glimpse of Mrs Catlin in one of the cells but there was no time to do more than exchange the briefest of greetings. The sight of her, safe and well, and with the slave band gone from her ankle, filled me with optimism.

'The armoury is this way,' I yelled, and the hundred-plus band of nobles and warriors followed me out of the hold, leaving the women and children huddled together in the passageway between the cells.

We reached the armoury without incident and found it locked. The door was stout, but with a dozen bodies pounding at it with relentless fury it proved to be not stout enough. In moments we were through it, and the armoury was ours for the taking.

I was disappointed to find no muskets in the armoury, but regarded this as a minor setback – after all, none of the men with me would have known how to use one.

We armed ourselves with swords and daggers, and those few who had some knowledge of archery took up what crossbows there were and as many quarrels as they could carry. I still had no idea of how many men Droxus had in his crew, but I was convinced we outnumbered them. I took a few more minutes to arm myself than was absolutely necessary because I had been looking for one very particular weapon, and with my own sabre in my hand again I felt ready to take on anything Droxus had to offer.

We were racing for the upper deck when suddenly the passageway we were in tilted over at forty-five degrees and then shuddered violently, its further end rising up steeply and tumbling us back the way we had come.

'Someone's cut the mooring lines!' I yelled. 'The ship's drifting!'

The implications that this had for our escape did not need voicing: if the ship rose higher than the reach of its ladders we would be at the mercy of its crew to get us home.

We scrambled up the tilted passage and burst onto the main deck. A pitched battle was already in progress, Droxus's men having abandoned their muskets and resorted to close-quarters weapons. They outnumbered the small party of Benzan warriors by almost ten to one, but the battle was far from one-sided. I began, at last, to believe the 'myth' of Benzan superiority in the arts of war.

Uttering the war cry of the city, and with a half-dozen other war cries echoing all around me, I charged for the nearest of Droxus's men.

The ensuing mêlée was an insanity of screams and cries and the crashing of steel on steel and the dull, heavy sound of swords striking the bodies of foemen. I scarcely had time to think between each engagement, and the fighting itself was a blur of motion, as bodies blundered into one another with scant regard for friend or foe. The niceties of fencing tactics counted for nothing in this brawl, where quick wits and a powerful sword arm were all that could keep a man alive. And it was in the brief glimpses that I got of the Benzan warriors during the battle that I came to understand the reason for their fame. While not noticeably better than their fellow warriors in the use of arms, and certainly possessing no stronger physiques, the superiority of the Benzan fighting men lay entirely in their psychology. The sheer unbridled ferocity of their attack was no mere battlefield tactic, but the controlled unleashing of something that most men – civilized or not – would rather not face, particularly within themselves. The men of Benza had not merely found their own inner demons, their primeval bestial selves, but had conquered those demons and harnessed them to their will. And now, when such totally selfless aggression was needed, they were able to release it, to the cost of their enemies. I had heard of such things in human history before, in the tales of the Viking berserkers, or in the house carls of the Dark Ages who won their battles through sheer hard fighting, but never before had I envisioned just what such a style of fighting would be like to witness – and to be a part of.

But still the men of Benza made up only a small part of our fighting force, and while the warriors of the other cities were formidable enough in their own right the men of Droxus's crew were beginning to hold their own against us. A small contingent of his archers had gained the high ground of the forecastle and were virtually at liberty to pick our men off, only the closely packed bodies of the archers' own crewmates in our midst affording us any protection.

It seemed to me that the battle had raged for hours, with not a man on either side escaping some kind of wound or injury, and each of us looking like an attendant in some madman's abattoir, when I sensed a subtle change in the tide of fighting. It was barely noticeable, almost a subliminal thing, but I was not the only one to feel it. Droxus's men, who had been holding out against us for many long minutes, suddenly seemed to falter. There was no one thing that could be said to give evidence of this, but the sense of it rushed across the crowded deck like a tidal wave. In its wake went up a mighty roar from the throats of those of us who had felt it and the fighting suddenly intensified to an unimaginable degree. Droxus's men staggered under the renewed onslaught, and not a man on that deck did not sense victory looming for the former captives. Even the constant rocking and tilting of the deck as the ship drifted aimlessly could not undermine our renewed optimism, even though until then it had been one of the largest factors in our enemies' favour, since such footing was as familiar to them as the solid ground would have been to us.

I was caught up in a wedge of Benzan warriors, a small group that had hacked and fought its way towards the sterncastle from where we could gain access to the ship's crew quarters, when the whole ship echoed to a sound that was like cannon fire. I had seen no heavy artillery on the vessel, and nothing to suggest that Droxus had such weapons at his disposal, so I couldn't begin to imagine what had caused the sound. When it struck again an instant later I realized, too late, that I *had* heard the sound before, although in a much reduced form. When it came the second time it was accompanied by a wave of concussive force that swept everyone before it, brushing men aside as though they were straws in the teeth of a hurricane. My body was flung to the bloodstained deck, my sword dashed from my hand, and the sheer pressure of the force blast seemed to suck the air from my lungs.

All around me, stunned and gasping, the men of the two opposing groups lay piled up on the deck, some having landed on fallen weapons and now having to watch helplessly as their blood drained away. Some had been close to the railings when the blast struck and I could still hear their screams as they tumbled to the ground, which was now who knew how far below.

I forced my head up, and gazed at the scarlet-robed figure standing on the sterncastle, his arms upraised but no readable expression on his face. It was the so-called Head Librarian, Sonder's superior whom I had glimpsed briefly in Droxus's cabin a day or so before. I had seen this power of the Librarians, this ability to hurl 'thunderbolts' like some god from Greek legend, but only used to subdue a single individual. I had never imagined that it could be used on a scale such as this.

Behind the Librarian, fear etched on their faces, were Droxus and a handful of his men; they all hung back from the Librarian, obviously unwilling to trust to the good intentions of anyone so powerful.

The Librarian said, without turning his head, 'Separate your men from the prisoners.'

Shaking, Droxus waved his small retinue forward. The men gave the Librarian a wide berth as they hurried to the main deck.

Many of the combatants on both sides were beginning to recover, and I wondered how this would affect the Librarian's plans. I soon found out.

One of the warriors close to me sprang to his feet, his sword raised to strike one of the newcomers, the war cry of his city on his lips, when the Librarian pointed at him. Something like chain lightning leaped from the Librarian's body and hit the sword of the warrior, vaporizing it and blasting the man to ashes. White-hot metal rain splattered the deck, some of it hitting those closest to the fallen warrior and sizzling on their flesh, and it was with dismay that I felt the skin of my left arm blister under the contact of some of those burning droplets. I gazed in mute fury and a fair measure of terror at

251

the Librarian, fighting an irrational conviction that what he had done was some kind of sorcery. If I once let myself believe such I knew I would have surrendered my intellect to primitive superstition.

No one moved to resist as Droxus's men were first separated from the rest of us and then, once those men had sufficiently recovered their senses, were ordered to disarm their captives and herd them below decks.

The battle had cost us almost half of our number, and when the wounds the rest of us had sustained had taken their eventual toll I suspected the count of dead would be higher still. And, worst of all, it had gained us nothing. We had decimated Droxus's men, but the ship itself was undamaged and its commanders unscathed. If it represented any kind of setback to the Librarians' plans it would be of the very smallest kind.

By the time we reached the holding cells I was feeling weak and wretched from a half-dozen wounds that, until then, I had not even noticed. My arm where the molten metal had hit it ached to the bone, and if Droxus had ordered my execution at that moment I don't think I would have cared.

Chapter 24

HAND OF THE GODS

We all passed that night in the blackest depression I had ever known. The sense of utter helplessness was like a miasma surrounding us, an almost tangible shroud of gloom. Had we been marched out on deck for any reason I think half of us would have thrown ourselves over the side.

Our cells, which had been some two-thirds full before the uprising, were now half-empty. We had all been crowded into the pens on one side of the hold, the women and children herded into them indiscriminately with us. Mrs Catlin was not in my cell, but was in the adjacent one. We found a corner at the rear of the pens and sat together, the wooden bars of the cage separating us.

'The losses were heavy,' she said quietly.

I looked around, trying to work out who was missing. I could see the Duke of Benza, the man I had taken to be the Duke of Kolhos, and a handful of Captains whose faces I knew. Of the group of Benzan soldiers who had led the attack I could see no trace.

'Too heavy,' I muttered.

Mrs Catlin removed her poncho and began tearing it into strips.

253

'Put your arm through the bars,' she said.

I looked down at myself; both arms looked like something off a butcher's slab.

'Which one?' I asked, and from somewhere I managed to drag up a smile.

Mrs Catlin brushed tears out of her eyes and said, 'Either one, you idiot.' Her voice shook, and it occurred to me that I could easily have been one of the dead, and that that thought was probably uppermost in her mind.

I put my arm through the bars and took hold of her hand. She looked up at me, weeping openly now, and I pulled her up to the bars and hugged her through them, stroking her hair as she sobbed against me.

'I want to go home, Shaw,' she wept in English. 'I've had enough of this. I just want to go home.'

'We will,' I told her, 'just as soon as we can. I promise.'

She pulled back from me and wiped her eyes.

'You shouldn't make promises you can't keep,' she said.

'I don't,' I said.

She took my arm and began to bandage it with the strips torn from her poncho.

'Then how do you propose to do it?' she asked.

'I have a plan,' I told her, grinning.

She looked up at me.

'I'd like to hear it,' she said.

'It has three parts,' I said.

'Ah,' she said.

'In the first part,' I said, 'we escape from this airship. In the second, we help Benza to defeat the army of the Librarians. And finally, we get the people of Benza to show their gratitude to us by organizing a caravan for us back to the Ladden country. Then we just wait for the worlds to come back into phase again and simply walk home.'

'I like the last part best,' Mrs Catlin said. 'The middle part I'm not so keen on, and although I approve of the first part I'm not sure how we could bring it about.'

'Well, since I thought of the plan,' I said, 'I thought perhaps you could work out that part. After all, I can't be expected to do all the thinking.'

She pulled me towards the bars of the cage and leaned closer to me.

'If I didn't know better, Shaw,' she said quietly, 'I would think that that was an attempt at humour.'

'Did it make you laugh?' I asked.

'Not noticeably,' she replied.

'Ah,' I said.

She smiled and said, 'But I appreciate the effort.'

She leaned through the bars and kissed me lightly on the lips. Then she turned and settled down with her back to the rear wall of the cell.

I looked at her speechlessly, but she refused to meet my gaze. A thousand questions and as many expletives flooded my mind, but for once I couldn't find the words to express any of them. I settled back beside her, each of us leaning into the bars that separated us. Feeling extremely strange, I put my arm through the bars and took her hand in mine. She said nothing, but her fingers closed around mine and she pulled my hand gently into her lap.

I must have fallen asleep, because the next thing I knew I was being shaken awake by one of my cellmates. My arm, which was still slotted through the bars of the cage, had gone numb, and Mrs Catlin was nowhere in sight.

'Quickly, my friend,' the man in front of me was saying, 'we must speak with you.'

The 'we' to whom he referred appeared to be the entire complement of our cell. Everyone was squatting or sitting around me and making me feel very uncomfortable with the intensity of their stares.

I extricated my arm from between the bars and rubbed it slowly to restore the circulation.

'What about?' I asked the man in front of me.

'Escape,' he said simply.

I put my head back to the wall and wondered if this nightmare would ever end.

255

'How?' I demanded.

'The crew of this vessel is barely sufficient now to operate it,' he said. 'We have listened to the talk of our jailers and learned that we are sailing south, back to the land from which these people have come. There will never be a better time to make our bid for freedom.'

'I say again,' I grumbled, '"How?"'

'It hinges on you, my friend,' he said.

'I might have guessed it would,' I muttered.

'You and this Droxus creature are from the same land, are you not?' the man asked.

'It's not something I'm proud of,' I told him.

'But he respects your counsel,' the man said.

'He said he did,' I agreed, 'until I helped all of you to try to escape.'

'If you go to him,' said the man, 'and tell him we wish now only to aid him, he will believe you.'

'You can't know that!' I cried.

I could see desperation in the man's eyes, and in the eyes of the others around me. They were clutching at straws, and praying to their gods for a favourable outcome.

'I do not think he will listen to me,' I said; I had no desire to be a part of another bloodbath.

'Will you not even try?' asked a man elsewhere in the group.

'If there was any hope of success—' I began.

'Soon,' said the main spokesman of the group, 'we will pass over the Asmina Valley. That will be the time when we will have the best chance of success.'

There were mutters of agreement.

'What is the Asmina Valley?' I asked.

He looked at me in astonishment.

'The home of the gods,' he said.

I put my head in my hands and tried not to groan out loud.

'No man has set foot in the Valley in a thousand generations,' said the man. 'Beyond it lie the Lost Kingdoms, the Vohung lands that were severed from us when the gods awoke and denied Man access to the Valley. When this ship passes over the Valley the gods will smite it from the air. Better to take our chances in the Trial of the Thirteen than—'

'Wait!' I said, my head reeling. The man was contradicting himself with every breath, but half of what he was saying was stuff I had never even heard before so I was not about to try and debate it with him. One point, however, seemed too glaringly obvious to ignore. 'If the gods will not allow this ship to pass over their Valley,' I demanded, 'then how did it reach the Kingdoms in the first place?'

The man looked at me as though I were a child.

'The winds always blow from the north into the Valley,' he said simply, 'so obviously they must have sailed around it when they journeyed from the south.'

Faced with logic like that there was little I could say. Although, to my irritation, I found a certain kind of validity in his claim. But I was not yet ready to stake my life on the strength of his religious beliefs.

'I will speak to Droxus,' I said, adding quickly, '—if I can. But I make no promises.'

Since I doubted that Droxus would have anything to do with me from now on this seemed like a safe enough offer to make.

And, of course, I shared the desire to escape that my cellmates had displayed; I just preferred to place my trust in our own abilities and not in the fickle nature of Vohung's gods.

The group broke up with a sense of optimism that I did not share. I looked into the next cage to try and spot Mrs Catlin, and became increasingly concerned when I could not find her. I called out to one of the other women in the pen and she came over to me. I asked her what had happened to Mrs Catlin, and her answer filled me with foreboding.

'She has been taken to the Librarians,' she told me.

'When?' I demanded.

'Some time since,' the woman replied, not very helpfully. 'She did not go easily.'

'What does that mean?' I asked.

The woman grinned. 'She fought like a wild thing,' she said. 'It took three of them to drag her out.'

I cursed silently. Had I been so tired that I had slept through something like that?

'Don't fear for her, boy,' the woman said. 'They were careful not to hurt her too much.'

I sank to the floor and ran my fingers through my hair, finding dried blood from a wound I hadn't even known I had. I wondered just how much blood I'd lost in the last twenty-four hours, and what kind of account I would be able to give of myself if another fight broke out.

I arose and paced the cell, feeling like a caged beast. I couldn't imagine Droxus having any use for Mrs Catlin, but Sonder had seemed almost fond of her – certainly he had devoted a lot of time to training her – so perhaps this was an attempt at gaining her co-operation, much as they had tried to gain mine. If so, I wished Mrs Catlin more success at double-crossing them than I'd had.

She was returned to her cell about an hour later, and any thought of her having been interviewed by Sonder was instantly banished from my mind. She could barely stand when they dragged her in, and her face and arms were bruised as though she had been beaten. I couldn't imagine a Librarian having to resort to such crude tactics, not with all the power they had at their disposal. I called out to her as she was left on the floor of her cell, but she wouldn't even look at me. Instead, she dragged herself slowly into the furthest corner of her cage and curled up into a tight ball, her head buried in her knees.

I called out to the woman to whom I had spoken earlier, and she came over to me.

'Look after her,' I said, '—please.'

'Don't worry, lad,' the woman said. 'We'll take good care of her.'

She went over to Mrs Catlin, signalling to several other women to join her. They formed a little group around Mrs Catlin and although I couldn't hear what was said I knew she was in good hands.

I sat down in what I was now coming to think of as my corner of the cell and racked my brains for some explanation for this treatment of someone who couldn't possibly be a threat to anyone on the ship. I knew Droxus was an amoral monster, willing to throw an entire continent into all-out war simply to secure his own future, but I'd seen nothing in his character to suggest he might be a woman-beater as well ... The phrase lodged in my mind; woman-beater. Why did it seem to have some special significance?

I put my head against the wall and once again sleep claimed me.

I was awoken this time by something rather less abrupt than the previous occasion. In fact it was several minutes before I came to full wakefulness and realized what had disturbed me. I opened my eyes to find Mrs Catlin reaching through the bars of our cage to shake me gently by the arm.

'You've slept for most of a day,' she said without preamble. 'I saved you some food.'

I sat up, rubbing my eyes. She passed some bread and a small pan of cold stew through the bars.

'Thank you,' I said.

She hadn't met my eyes once.

'How are you feeling?' I asked.

'Bruised,' she said, 'and a bit sorry for myself. It was Hol Krexus.'

I stopped with the bread halfway to my lips.

'On the ship?' I demanded.

She nodded.

'He's joined up with Droxus,' she told me. 'A small group of warriors came with him, mostly confederates of his from the town his family comes from. They came aboard after the escape attempt, about fifteen of them in all, and agreed to help recruit more followers to Droxus's army from the outlying towns and villages in Benza. I gather Krexus expects to be given control of one of the cities in the north in repayment for his treachery.'

I put my hand through the bars and took her by the shoulders. She winced.

'He did this to you?' I asked.

She took a very deep breath and looked at me for the first time.

'He did,' she said. 'And more—'

'I'll kill him with my bare hands,' I told her.

259

Quietly, she asked, 'Why?'

'Why?' I repeated, dumbfounded. 'Why do you think?'

She half-smiled.

'It's not what I think that counts,' she said. 'If you're going to kill someone, you'll need a better reason than revenge. Or at least, you will if you're going to do it in my name.'

'Sometimes,' I said, very wearily, 'I do not understand you.'

'Only sometimes?' she said, and her eyes sparkled.

'Mrs Catlin—' I said, trying to find the words for thoughts that, so far, had not even had words when I thought them inside my own head.

'Eat,' she urged. 'You need your strength.'

My appetite was gone, but I ate mechanically, knowing she was right.

She reached through the bars and stroked my hair, wincing as she found the matted blood in it.

'It's OK,' I said. 'It looks worse than it is.'

I finished the stew and we sat in silence, leaning against the bars.

'Mrs Catlin—' I said.

'Yes, Shaw?' she said.

'Is this—?' I began. No; that was too stupid.

'What?' she asked.

'I mean,' I tried again, 'are we—?' No! That was going to sound even more ridiculous.

'What?' she asked.

'I don't know,' I muttered. Gods, I was no good at this.

But what had I got to go on? One kiss and a lifetime of arguments? Hardly convincing evidence for the absurd thoughts I was thinking now.

'Did I ever tell you about Mr Catlin?' she asked.

I was a little taken aback.

'No,' I said.

'He was a nice man,' she told me. 'We met on a Sunday afternoon, at a craft fair, I think. It was love at first sight. We were married a month later. Six months after that we filed for divorce. It wasn't anyone's fault, it just didn't work out.'

She nudged me through the bars and I turned to look into her eyes. I didn't really want to know about her ex-husband, and I think it showed on my face.

'He was a nice man,' she repeated, 'but it didn't work out. We didn't *know* each other. And by the time we did it was too late.'

I looked at her, only half understanding what she was driving at.

'Love isn't about fireworks and poetry,' she said. 'What Kevin and I felt—'

'Kevin!' I laughed.

'Don't, Shaw,' she said. 'What we felt wasn't love – it was just being *in love*. And it didn't – couldn't – last.'

'That's very deep,' I observed, more sarcastically than I intended. 'But what's it supposed to mean?'

She clenched her teeth, but to my surprise she got a hold of her anger and said slowly, 'What I'm trying to tell you is that you *can't* have serious feelings for someone – certainly not love – without knowing them first.' She actually blushed as she said, 'I think you and I know one another better than any two people who ever lived – don't you?'

'Probably,' I said, though for some reason it came out angrily. 'But, Mrs Catlin – I've never even been "in love"; I don't know how it's supposed to feel. And the only person I can ever remember *loving* blew his brains out in front of me.'

We looked into one another's eyes for several moments, and I knew that whatever barriers had been coming down between us were all going back up again. I didn't want it – and I know she didn't – but I didn't know how to stop it.

The wooden bars between us seemed to be shaking, and I thought at first it was the two of us who were trembling, but then the deck began to shake and I realized that the effect was spreading throughout the whole ship.

'Is it a storm?' Mrs Catlin asked.

'You tell me,' I replied, drawing back from the bars.

A hand grasped my shoulder and pulled me around. It was the self-appointed leader of our escape committee, and there was a wild look in his eyes that I didn't like.

'We are over the Valley,' he said. 'The Hand of the Gods has touched this vessel. We must be ready to act. The gods must see that we are not allied to the heretics who control this ship.'

'Whatever you say, friend,' I replied, not prepared to risk the man's response if I denied his faith – or pointed out the fairly obvious fact that we couldn't possibly be over the Valley yet, not in so short a space of time.

The ship shuddered again, more violently this time. If we were running into seriously heavy weather I hoped Droxus's design specs had allowed for it – most of this ship looked like it was designed by a process of trial and error, and while I couldn't deny the ingenuity that had gone into much of it there was an equal amount that looked about as airworthy as a paper dart.

'Shaw,' Mrs Catlin said, 'look at the far wall.'

She had spoken in English, so I guessed she didn't want to panic our fellow prisoners. As casually as I could, I looked in the direction she had indicated.

The wall was, in fact, the outer hull of the ship, and in the dimly-lit confines of the hold it appeared to be glowing with a faint, almost phosphorescent light.

'What do you make of it?' she asked.

I shrugged.

'Some kind of St Elmo's Fire?' I suggested.

'Surely it's too localized,' she replied. 'And doesn't that usually affect exterior surfaces, like masts and rigging?'

It was perversely satisfying to me every time I found a subject on which Mrs Catlin was not an authority, but for once I passed up the chance to tease her about it.

'It's spreading,' I said. 'And we aren't the only one's who've seen it.'

Panic began to spread through the hold as the patch of brilliance expanded, people crowding the furthest corners of their cells to get away from the unearthly effect.

'The fire of the gods,' my omnipresent colleague breathed. 'We are marked for destruction.'

He made the sign of Gazig, the Lord of Blood, Benza's dark God of War. If he was invoking deities I thought he had made a pretty poor choice, given our circumstances. From what little I had read I knew that Gazig had scant compassion where prisoners of war were concerned. Feeling more than a little foolish, I caught myself making the sign of Azira, the Bright Lady of Mercy, who was supposed to intervene between mortals and other gods whenever they came into conflict.

The ship suddenly lurched to one side, a great ringing sound echoing through it.

'That's no storm,' I gasped, picking myself up. 'We hit something.'

A cry rang through the ship, a cry born of no human throat. It was the war cry of some monstrous animal, and it froze the blood of every man and woman who heard it.

'Bright Lady protect us,' whispered my companion, who had obviously seen my sign of a moment ago and realized the error of his ways.

'Shaw, the wall!' Mrs Catlin gasped.

The phosphorescence had suddenly grown tentacles of light that were snaking around the inner surface of the hull in writhing, undulating patterns. The original patch of light vanished, and each tentacle took on an independent life of its own. They flashed over the deck and up and down the bars of our cages, and where they passed a startled captive they flickered briefly over a foot or an ankle before scurrying on.

I had the distinct and disturbing impression that they were looking for something.

One of the tentacles slithered over Mrs Catlin's feet and, instead of moving on, flowed quickly up her body and enveloped her.

I yelled her name in belated warning, and she looked at me in surprise; she had not even been aware of what had happened. Then she glanced down at herself and seemed to see the light that covered her for the first time.

'Are . . . you all right?' I asked.

'Fine,' she replied, moving her hands this way and that to watch the way the light played over them. 'It doesn't hurt – it doesn't feel like it's there.' She touched her hands together, evidently expecting to see sparks fly, but nothing happened. 'What do you suppose it means?'

I shrugged, and one of the tentacles touched my own foot and suddenly I too was bathed in light. I fought down an urge to cry out, because Mrs Catlin had been perfectly correct; the phenomenon was entirely devoid of any sensation.

'We seem to have been singled out,' Mrs Catlin said.

I looked around the hold and realized that she was correct. No one else in the cells had been illuminated by the strange lights, but it seemed as though everyone had been touched by them.

We had not heard the strange cry again, but the ship shook repeatedly with minor impacts, and I wondered what was going on out on deck.

There was a sudden commotion in the companionway leading to the upper levels of the hold and then a detachment of armed men raced into the brig. They looked around briefly, then flung open the doors to the cells containing Mrs Catlin and me. Some of our cellmates made a tentative break for freedom, but the events of the last few minutes had unnerved them and the guards soon subdued them.

Then Mrs Catlin and I were grasped in strong yet oddly fearful hands and dragged up to the top deck.

The sight that met our eyes was one for which neither of us could have been prepared, either by our past experiences on this planet or by any of the superstitious mouthings of our fellow prisoners.

The airship had been boarded, but not by any human enemy. Looming over the deck, its vast, black wings spread to their fullest extent, was a monstrous bird. It had something of the aspect of a crow, but magnified to impossible proportions. It dwarfed the wooden part of the airship, and its wingspan was almost greater than the length of the metal airframe. Its black eyes, expressionless and yet somehow betraying an avian fury that dwarfed any similar human emotion, stared down at us from either side of its scimitar-like beak. One of its talons was closed around the aft section of the main spar of the airframe – that had been the clanging sound we had heard – and the other was sunk into the wood of the sterncastle, much of which was now crushed.

I became aware of the presence of others around me. I looked down from that terrifying creature that held us in its claws and saw the two Librarians and Droxus standing before me. Droxus was glowing like Mrs Catlin and me.

'I knew it!' Droxus exclaimed. 'Those lights were looking for Earth people!'

It seemed a logical deduction, but right now I was more concerned with how Droxus intended to deal with our more tangible intruder. I wondered why the Librarians had not acted to repel the attack, and with a sinking sensation I realized the truth – they had attempted it, and had failed. Our chances for survival now seemed slim indeed.

'Shaw,' Mrs Catlin said at my side, 'that thing cannot possibly be alive.'

I looked at her and saw that she was staring up with what I thought of as her 'teacher's face' at the giant bird. She was totally unafraid, and entirely fascinated by what she was seeing.

'Why not?' I demanded, wishing I had half her courage – or maybe a little of her irritating detachment.

'It's too big,' she said simply. 'It couldn't possibly fly, not like a real bird. Its own weight would break its bones, and its muscles would have to have the power output of a nuclear reactor. And that leaves aside the question of the tensile strength of its tendons . . .'

'So what are you saying?' I demanded. 'That it's an illusion, or something?'

'I don't know,' she confessed. 'All I do know is that it cannot possibly be what it appears to be.'

The Librarians, who had listened to our exchange with obvious interest, exchanged glances that seemed to indicate some kind of new-found understanding. They turned to face the bird and raised their arms. Pyrotechnics leaped from the Librarians, like the lightning effect I had seen them use before but less violent now, and more like the tendrils of light that had flooded the hold. The bird squawked, and flapped its wings. Everyone on deck, the Librarians included, were dashed from their feet, and with a savage snap of its beak the bird snatched up Sonder and cut him cleanly in two. His legs flew over the side, and the bird swallowed his upper half in a single gulp.

I stared in horror at the mighty creature, hardly able to comprehend what it had done. That Sonder was suddenly gone seemed to me incomprehensible. My hatred of him vied within me with irrational sympathy, and yet both were swamped by a numbness at the sheer enormity of what I had just witnessed. The bird – or whatever it truly was – had been immune to the attack of the Librarians. And Sonder's own defensive screen, which I had seen deflect everything from arrows to a charging Ktikbati gryllup with equal ease, had given this creature not a moment's pause. I knew, in that instant, that Mrs Catlin was right – the thing could not be a living being. But what was it? And how could we possibly fight it?

Droxus grabbed my arm, his face white under the lights that still played over it.

'Do something!' he pleaded.

I laughed in his face, enjoying a brief pleasure at his cowardice.

Then the deck shook and something hard and unyielding struck me across the shoulders. I heard Mrs Catlin's scream of fear, and felt myself yanked with bone-jarring force into the air. I tried to twist around in the unbreakable grip that held me, but it was impossible. The deck of the airship vanished from beneath me, dwindling away into the distance with impossible rapidity. A moment later I was engulfed in clouds, and from above me I heard a great avian cry of victory. And I knew that the iron hand that held me was the claw of the giant bird.

Chapter 25

THE VALLEY

Once I had realized the extent of my predicament I was surprised at how little fear I felt. To be sure my adrenalin level was high, but that was as much from the exhilaration of the bird's flight as from actual terror. I think a little of Mrs Catlin's intellectual detachment must have infected me, because all I kept thinking was, 'It *chose* me.' The bird had had no shortage of targets on the deck, and from what it had done to Sonder I knew that it was more than capable of killing if it so chose. But instead it had picked me up and carried me off. And, as I quickly established, it had picked me up relatively carefully; I was unhurt, and although its grip was unbreakable, it was not unnecessarily tight. There was a method to its actions, but what was its purpose?

We flew above the clouds for about an hour, and then the bird swooped down and broke through them once more. The sight that met my eyes as it did so was breathtaking. The logical impossibility of what I was seeing was swept from my mind, because this, I knew, was the so-called Asmina Valley. But the 'Valley' was over a hundred miles wide and stretched for unguessable hundreds of miles in either direction below me. It was bordered by twin mountain ranges, one of which was slightly closer to us than the other, and either of which would have presented a formidable obstacle to anyone on foot. It did not surprise me that the home of this world's gods had become a place shrouded in mystery and superstition.

The reality, as it met my astonished eyes, was spectacular in its primordial beauty. The land of Asmina was a vast, seemingly tropical, jungle. The lush green foliage of trees that I had seen nowhere else on the continent was interspersed with the blooms of flora whose dazzling colours covered the entire spectrum, and at times seemed even to exceed it. Even from this altitude I could smell the richness of the vegetation, and occasionally hear the weird and unearthly cries of its animal inhabitants. On a world as old as this one the discovery of this valley was the most amazing find imaginable. It suggested to me that Droxus's fatalistic prediction of this world's impending end could not possibly be true. Here, in this sheltered nursery, the story of creation was beginning again.

The bird flew on for mile after mile, the jungle broken only occasionally by rocky outcroppings or broad silver rivers. One such ended in a mighty waterfall, the thunderous sound of which reached even to the height at which I was flying. The lake into which it emptied itself was many miles across, and reminded me, on a much larger scale, of the place at which Mrs Catlin and I had first had our introduction to the Ladden. Had we arrived there via a waterfall such as this, however, all our hosts would have found would have been our shattered corpses.

After several hours of flying, and with my body growing close to exhaustion, I was snapped awake by the sight of the one thing I had not expected to see in this prehistoric landscape.

It was a road.

I struggled to apply some sense of scale to what I was seeing; if I was judging the size of the trees beside the road correctly then the broad, almost white surface was probably sixty feet or more across, and extended in an unbroken straight line for as far as I could see. There was no sign of any human habitation either beside the road or anywhere else for that matter, but there was no way for that ribbon of white to be anything but man-made.

The bird suddenly began to lose altitude, to descend in great spirals towards the road itself. That we had arrived at some pre-determined destination seemed obvious, but it filled me with little in the way of optimism. If I was expected to walk the length of that road then whoever or whatever was waiting for me at its end was due for a long wait.

The bird hit the road with its free claw, its wings flailing in the warm, humid air to break its fall. Even so, the landing left me bruised and breathless. The bird dropped me to the road and took off again with a thunder of flapping wings, dust rising from the surface of the road in great, choking clouds. I staggered back, shielding my eyes and coughing dryly as the dust filled my mouth and nose. It was some minutes after the bird's departure before I could see again, and a while after that before the soreness in my throat eased at all.

I stared around me in a state of slowly increasing despair. The road was a featureless expanse of greyish white that stretched to infinity on either side of me, and the jungle that bordered it presented an even less inspiring spectacle. The air, now that the dust had settled, was filled with midges and other flying insects. I had no doubt that some of them would be injurious to human life, and that it was only a matter of time before something against which my body had no defence decided to take a bite out of me.

I sat down in the road and put my head in my hands. There was no way of knowing which way to go, or even if there was any point in going either way. Perhaps the sense of purpose I had attributed to the bird had come only from my own desperation. Or perhaps my cellmate in the ship had been right, and this was some cosmic jest on the part of his gods.

I stood up and walked to the edge of the road. Whatever the outcome, sitting and moping was not going to get me anywhere.

The road was a mighty wall raised above the level of the surrounding jungle, a two-metre-thick, seemingly solid expanse of stone that must have taken generations to build. The stone was weathered from centuries of use, the join between adjacent blocks filled with dust so that, at a glance, it appeared to be one unbroken mass of rock. I traced the outline of one typical block: it was six feet square, and seemed to extend down through the full height of the road.

While I was making my explorations I came across an engraving in the face of one stone block. I brushed dust aside and found, to my surprise and delight, a milestone. The script was unreadable, although I recognized it as an ancient form of the High Tongue that was still used by the Librarians, but what was quite clear in its general meaning if not in its specific message was the arrow at the end of the brief legend. The arrow was pointing to my right, and had a number attached to it that had three figures in it. Like all human arithmetic, the system of counting on this planet was calculated from base ten, and although the system of notation used was not quite analogous to our Arabic system it was close enough to let me know that I had at least a hundred units to walk – and at most something in excess of nine hundred. Of course, I didn't know what units the road was measured in, which was rather less helpful. The standard unit in the Kingdoms was the *torbik*, equal to fifteen hundred 'paces', and was thus something under a mile, but the torbik was not an old system of measuring and, in any case, was not in use in some other parts of the Thek continent.

Feeling that somewhere Fate must be rubbing its hands and having a good chuckle at my expense I got to my feet and set off in the direction indicated by the arrow.

I had no food, no water and no protection from the oppressive heat or the humidity. I was beset by insects, and not a little aware of numerous rustlings and snortings in the underbrush at my side. My chances for survival seemed slim indeed, but even I was surprised when, barely two hours later, with the world spinning around me, I sank senseless to the hard surface beneath me.

Chapter 26

TRAVELLING COMPANIONS

I could feel a hand behind my neck, raising my head, and moisture against my lips. I remember thinking, *Good old Mrs Catlin; she's found me at last.* I opened my eyes and saw a woman in dazzlingly bright armour standing over me. Someone else, another woman I thought, was trying to force water down my throat, but I couldn't find the strength to swallow.

'Bright Lady,' I croaked deliriously, and the water went down, some of it going the wrong way and producing a series of hacking coughs.

The woman in the armour moved slightly, and starbursts of light danced over her brightly polished surface. She wore a parabolic helm, rather like that of a samurai, I thought, that concealed her features, only the lower half of her face being visible. I sensed a strength in her, but her mouth also hinted at a gentleness that was at odds with her apparel.

'He will live?' she said; it was barely a question, almost a command.

'Yes, mistress,' said the woman at my side.

I transferred my attention to her. She was extremely pretty, with very long curly blonde hair. Her eyes were blue. She was dressed

271

in what appeared to be a white, waistcoat-like top and a rather short white skirt, with a thin but voluminous hooded white cloak thrown over her shoulders.

'Who are you?' I managed to gasp.

'My name is Ailette,' said the young woman at my side. 'I am the bonded servant of the Lady Celebe, of the order of the Knights of the Thirteen Gods.'

I glanced at the armoured woman before me, whom I took to be the Celebe referred to by the woman calling herself Ailette.

I looked back to the woman at my side.

'Ailette?' I repeated. 'Française?'

'Oui, m'sieur,' she said. 'Yes, I am French. Or, I was.'

I took another drink from the water flask she still held to my lips.

In French, I said, 'Does *she* know you are not of this world?'

The woman called Celebe said, 'I know everything about Ailette, monsieur, and that includes the native language we both share.'

I sat up slowly. Beyond Celebe's shining form I could see three gryllups, saddled and standing idly in the sun.

'If you are ready to travel,' Celebe said, 'we have a long way to go.'

With Ailette's help I got unsteadily to my feet.

'I have a lot of questions for your Thirteen Gods,' I said, hoping my tone didn't sound as blasphemous as I felt.

'You may ask anything you wish of my masters,' said Celebe, 'but any man who claims to know the will of the gods is a liar.'

She turned and walked towards the three gryllups and Ailette and I followed. Now that my vision was clearing a little, and my head felt rather less like a burst watermelon, I was able to get a better look at Celebe's amazing body armour. It covered her entirely, with the exception of that part of her face left visible by her helmet, and had no visible joints or seams. Where it bent at elbow or knee or wrist or at any other natural joint in the body beneath, it simply acted like human skin, shifting in shape and form without a crease or wrinkle in sight. And while I had originally thought it to be silver in colour and made of metal I now saw that it was composed of some translucent, glassy substance, its surface catching every stray bit of sunlight and reflecting it with its brightness multiplied tenfold. It seemed to me that Celebe must be unendurably hot inside that contraption, but she showed no sign of discomfort, and moved as freely in her armour as Ailette did in her own brief garments.

We mounted our gryllups and moved off in the direction I had been travelling.

We rode until sundown, at which time we made camp. The night air was cool but not unpleasant, and did at least see the departure of the thousands of insects that had plagued me during the day. Celebe left us for a time and wandered off into the jungle, so I helped Ailette gather wood from the side of the road to make a fire. She made no attempt to light it, but merely sat beside it and waited for Celebe's return. I was surprised to see, when the Lady Knight did come back, that she was carrying the body of a small mammal, something like a deer, slung over her shoulder. She dumped her kill at Ailette's feet and the young woman drew a sharp knife and began to skin and section the animal.

When the carcass had been divided Celebe helped Ailette set up a small spit over the fire and fitted some of the meat onto it. She then lit the fire. She did this by pointing at it. I could feel the heat that radiated from her hand, and watched in silence as flames sprang from the dry wood. Celebe lowered her hand and looked at me. I said nothing. She turned away, went over to a spot near to our tethered gryllups and sat down on the road surface with her back to us.

'I've seen that kind of trick before,' I said quietly to Ailette.

'My Lady's armour is a source of great power,' Ailette said, turning the spit slowly over the fire.

'When I saw such things before,' I said, 'it was Librarians who did it.'

'They have some understanding of the power,' Ailette said, 'but only here in the Valley is it truly understood.'

I pondered on the fact that Librarians always wore their voluminous robes, and that those robes could conceal anything – including body armour.

'Is it magic?' I asked Ailette, fearing her answer.

She laughed softly.

'Was it not an Earthman,' she said, 'who once observed that any advanced science must seem like magic to those who cannot understand it?'

'So it isn't magic,' I said, feeling a sense of relief that had been a long time in coming.

'Not magic,' said Ailette. 'But more potent than magic, because those who command it do so with more efficiency than any sorcerer could hope to achieve with his powers. Magic is unreliable, its practitioners often ignorant; science is always reliable, because its laws can be understood and applied. The inhabitants of this valley know more of science than the people of our world will discover in the next ten thousand years.'

I studied her face closely in the flickering light of the fire and saw that she meant what she said.

'What do they want with me?' I asked.

'I don't know,' she said.

'Does Celebe know?' I asked.

'My Lady knows many things,' Ailette said. 'But she tells me only what she wishes me to know.'

I had noted already that Ailette did not wear any form of slave band, but she clearly believed herself to be Celebe's slave. I wondered what had happened to place her in such a position.

'You wonder about how I came here,' she said, as though reading my mind, 'and why Celebe is my mistress.'

I nodded.

'Only through Celebe can I go home,' said Ailette, 'and to go home is all that I desire.'

'To France?' I asked.

'To Earth,' she said. 'To return to France would be nice, but just to go home to Earth – that would be enough.'

'Do you hate this world so much?' I asked.

She looked at me with an openness that was embarrassing, but I didn't look away. She reached down with her left hand and raised the hem of her skirt to reveal her hip. It bore the symbol which, in the common written form of the High Tongue, meant slave: it had been branded onto her.

'Yes,' she said quietly, 'I hate this world. I hate Celebe too, even

274

though she is of Earth. And I am thankful that no matter what happens, she is doomed to live out her life on this world, for she can never return to ours.'

I gave her a puzzled look. She lowered the hem of her skirt and said, 'Those who aspire to the armour of a Knight must abandon their humanity in order to achieve it. Celebe is human now only in her thoughts. And not so human there, I think.'

I didn't understand all that she was saying, but the power of her hate was almost tangible in the air between us. It reminded me of the way I had once felt about Sonder, and for the briefest of instants I almost grieved for the Librarian. The moment passed, and I turned my attention back to Ailette.

'Tell me how you came here,' I said.

She examined the meat she was cooking and said, 'Eat first. Then I will tell you.' She looked at me. 'And then,' she said, 'you will tell me how *you* came here.'

Chapter 27

AILETTE'S STORY

Ailette, it transpired, had arrived on Shushuan at the same time as Mrs Catlin and I, but in a different part of the Thek continent – probably, I surmised, in the lands to the far south of the Vohung Kingdoms.

Her life before coming to the planet of the Vinh had been a relatively normal one. Her parents, who had lived in a small town called Alençon, had sent her to a good school at which she had acquired a passably good education. She had, in fact, achieved sufficiently high grades to give her her pick of a number of universities.

She had been on a visit to one such university, along with three friends – two boys, Jacques and Poul, and a girl, Monique – when they had felt compelled to explore the crypt beneath the university's ancient chapel. They hadn't fully understood their motivations in doing this, but I immediately attributed it to the 'homing' instinct Droxus had mentioned when discussing the phenomenon of the rift. The crypt had been the location of one such rift, and the boy, Jacques, had led them through it without even realizing. He had wandered off and found a dark, unlit passage which, with childlike curiosity, they had elected to explore. Using only a pocket torch to light their way they progressed for a considerable distance down the passage that eventually gave access to a rough-hewn tunnel leading gradually downwards. Ailette and the other girl in the group had suggested turning back at this point, but their male companions, constantly urging one another on, had refused, and since Jacques had had the only torch the girls were left with no choice but to go along with them.

At some point, just as Mrs Catlin and I had, they had left behind our world and slipped into this one.

They had arrived on Shushuan in the middle of a small town that was nestled among a collection of low hills. The tunnel had ended abruptly at the foot of a timeworn, crudely built stone staircase, at the top of which they emerged, to their astonishment, into the back of a small temple or shrine. They could not know it at the time, but the temple was a holy place forbidden to all but a priest of the Thirteen Gods. Ailette's memory of the temple was vivid, and particularly so where one feature of it was concerned. Spanning its outward façade was a single massive arch, seemingly fashioned from solid silver. So striking was the appearance of this arch that they had stood and stared at it in open-mouthed amazement while a group of irate locals had surrounded and apprehended them. They were promptly dragged before some kind of local law officer and, although they did not know it at the time, were summarily sentenced to death for their 'crime'. They were then thrown into the town dungeon to await their fate.

According to Ailette – who was, after all, in a better position than I to comment on such things – the local priest had intervened on their behalf and had had their sentence commuted. This was not through some sense of mercy or a desire to see justice done, but rather a part of his own political manoeuvring within the community. He had, apparently, invoked some ancient religious law whereby the accused were allowed to undergo a test to determine their guilt or innocence; this test was traditionally accompanied by a major festival and a public holiday, neither of which were likely to reduce the priest's popularity with the locals, particularly since the temple was picking up the bill.

Two days later, Ailette and her companions were dragged from their cell and, amid a cheering and happy procession, herded out of town and into the surrounding meadowland. They had no idea of what was due to happen to them, but despite the gaiety around them they all shared a feeling of considerable unease. This feeling increased when they beheld their destination. It was a type of stone circle, not unlike Stonehenge though far smaller in scale, and one of the stones bore all the hallmarks of a sacrificial altar.

The four young students were taken not to the altar but to four upright stones diametrically opposite to the altar in the circle. They were placed in front of these stones, one to each monolith, and their hands bound above their heads to iron rings set in the rock. Ailette was placed second from the right in the line; she was flanked by Jacques and Poul, with Monique at the end of the line. The 'Boy-girl-boy-girl' placings did not seem accidental.

Then, to screams of protest from the two girls and furious curses from the young men, all four were stripped of their clothing. The clothing was taken to a small side altar and burned by the priest amid a lot of chanting and arm waving.

A woman then entered the stone circle, one who was entirely unlike anyone Ailette had yet seen in this place. She was a warrior, but – as Ailette learned later – one of a very special breed of warriors. She was, of course, Celebe, Knight of the Thirteen Gods. In her hands she carried a pair of muskets, and a couple of temple acolytes following behind her bore containers of gunpowder and shot.

She carried the muskets to the large altar and laid them down upon it, then stood back as the priest approached. He made several passes with his hands over the weapons and uttered some more of the sing-song chants that he had used over the burned clothing. Then he stepped forward towards the centre of the circle and the two acolytes, having deposited their containers beside the muskets, drew a large veil across the front of the altar, obscuring it and Celebe from view. Ailette heard sounds that she soon identified as being those of the two muskets being loaded. When the sounds ceased the acolytes moved the veil aside to reveal the muskets laid out once more upon the altar and Celebe standing calmly behind them.

The priest stepped up to the altar and studied the muskets,

chanting his prayers the whole time. After a moment's contemplation he reached out and placed his hands upon one of the muskets, as though blessing it. Then he stepped aside and Celebe picked up the musket the priest had touched.

Ailette and her friends exchanged worried glances with one another as the Knight of the Thirteen drew back the hammer of the weapon and placed a priming charge in its pan. She then raised the musket to her shoulder and aimed it squarely at the girl named Monique. The girl screamed, and the musket roared once, spitting fire and smoke. The heavy lead ball struck the girl in the chest, probably killing her instantly. She jerked spasmodically in her chains, her blood gushing from the wound, and then sagged limply against the stone, supported only by the ropes that bound her wrists to the ring above her head. The flow of blood slowed, then stopped.

Through eyes blurred by hysterical tears Ailette saw the Knight raise the second musket, prime it, and then for no apparent reason fire it into the earth at her feet.

The priest walked towards Monique's blood-drenched body as, behind him, the veil was once more drawn across the altar. The priest laid his hands on Monique's head and said a lengthy prayer over her. The watching townspeople, who had been almost silent throughout the ritual up to this point, muttered their own prayers along with him.

When he was finished he turned and the veil was removed from the altar. The two muskets were in place once more, and Celebe standing behind them. The priest approached the muskets and once again performed the blessing ceremony on one of them. Whether it was the same one he had blessed before Ailette did not know. He stepped aside, and the Knight picked up the musket.

Ailette was weeping uncontrollably by this point, but the young man, Jacques, was in a virtual paroxysm of terror – he was next in line beside Monique. He jerked and tore at his bonds, the ropes cutting into his wrists but refusing to yield. He screamed obscenities at Celebe, calling her every name he could lay his tongue to, and was still railing when, a moment later, she shot him through the heart.

Ailette felt his hot blood splash her face and neck and immediately threw up. Through the roaring sound that filled her ears she heard the report of the second musket as, just as she had before, the Knight discharged it into the ground. Ailette was still retching as the priest came and said his prayers over Jacques's crumpled form, and with a kind of fascinated horror she watched as the two acolytes drew the veil once more across the front of the altar. She heard, with an almost preternatural clarity, the individual sounds of the two muskets being loaded, the rasping of the metal ramrod in the barrel, the clink of the Knight's armour as it touched the weapons.

And then the veil was drawn back once again and the priest approached the muskets. Ailette heard someone whispering, over and over again, the single word 'Non'. It took several seconds for her to realize that it was she herself who was speaking. She cast a glance at Poul who stood on her right, and saw that he was virtually in a state of shock.

She turned her gaze back to Celebe and found herself staring down the black maw of the musket. She screamed, and saw the muzzle flash of the weapon as it went off. White-hot fire erupted in her chest, a thousand smaller fires blistering the skin of her breasts and throat and abdomen. She ground her teeth in agony and bit through her tongue, her mouth filling with the coppery taste of blood. She felt the air shudder in and out of her lungs, every breath sending new agony through her body.

And yet, incredibly, she did not die. The pain was excruciating, but the very fact of it proved to her that somehow she had survived.

Dimly, she became aware of people cheering, and of the priest laying his hands upon her head and blessing her. She gazed down at her chest, where a great patch of burned and reddened flesh marked what should have been the impact point of the projectile. Her body was peppered with numerous smaller spots of red, each one blistered and painful.

She lifted her head and watched as the Knight raised the second musket and fired it into the ground, and the result was sufficiently different from the previous two such actions that, very slowly, Ailette came to realize what had happened.

On each occasion, only one musket had been loaded with a live round, the other being packed with wadding and powder but no ball. Thus, the 'guilt' or 'innocence' of the accused was left in the hands of fate – or the gods – and communicated via the priest's random blessing of one of the muskets.

Ailette, clearly, had found favour in the eyes of the priest's deities.

The reloading ritual was carried out once more and Ailette turned to Poul to try to offer him some kind of hope. If he heard her words he gave no sign of it, and a moment later the harsh crack of the musket cut her short, and left Poul hanging limply from the iron ring above his head.

Already weak from her ordeal, and sick in spirit at the senseless murder of her friends, Ailette was scarcely aware of what occurred next. She was cut down from the stone and seated on an ornate form of palanquin, which the cheering and happy villagers bore on their shoulders back towards the small town. She passed out several times on the return journey, and when the procession finally reached the town square she found that her ordeal, far from being over, had scarcely begun.

In the square she was taken from the palanquin and placed in a wooden frame, rather like medieval stocks except that the bar closed around her waist and pinned her on her back. Then, as she watched in disbelief, a man who had the appearance of a blacksmith approached her with an iron rod in his hand, the end of which glowed bright red. She opened her mouth to cry out, but no sound emerged. She wept in silent agony as the blacksmith, smiling innocently the whole while, pressed the branding iron to the outer curve of her left hip. She smelled her own flesh as the iron seared it, and then the smith was walking away and everyone was cheering once again.

The stocks were unfastened and she was pulled to her feet. Her legs buckled but many hands were there to help her stand. Then she was led to the head of the square and, as the people around her began to dance and sing to the music of alien instruments, she was seated in a large, throne-like chair and food and drink placed upon a small table at her side. The priest leaned over her and, to her dismay, seemed to be fondling her. This seemed like the crowning indignity to all the horrors that had been visited upon her that day and she feebly struck his hands away. He smiled benignly and continued his ministrations, and she slowly grew aware that the pain of the wounds in her chest was easing. She looked down and saw that the priest had not been simply stroking her wounded flesh, he was applying some kind of ointment. She sank back in the deep chair and, though both hungry and thirsty, she ignored the food at her side and let her body slip into sleep.

She awoke several times throughout the afternoon, and was glad of the food that was provided. It was fairly simple stuff, breads and cheeses and some meat, and the frothy drink that accompanied it tasted like weak beer, with a slightly sweet aftertaste. It was all sufficiently prosaic to take her mind off the events that had preceded it. And the beer, as she quickly discovered, was not quite as innocent as it tasted.

As evening drew in, the party began to lose momentum, small groups retiring to the various randomly scattered buildings of the village, some to continue the festivities, others to begin to sleep them off. Ailette, who was by now thoroughly inebriated and a little morose because of it, looked around her for some guidance – these people seemed friendly enough at the moment, and the pain and suffering they had inflicted upon her did not appear to have been vindictive in any sense that she could understand, but she felt disinclined to risk their anger by some careless act or thoughtless gesture.

As she peered over the back of her chair at a small group of revellers who were hurrying past, she became aware of a presence in front of her, and even before turning she knew who it was.

Slowly, almost casually, she turned her gaze upon the stern countenance of the Knight of the Thirteen; she couldn't see the Knight's eyes behind the protective lenses in her helm, but she gazed into them as fearlessly as she could.

To her surprise, the Knight smiled. She stepped forward and fell to one knee beside Ailette's chair, staring at the young French girl

283

with a peculiar intensity, as though waiting for something and, by sheer force of will, trying to provoke Ailette to some unguessable reaction. Ailette returned the gaze with wide-eyed innocence, until finally the Knight's smile broadened and she said, with staggering simplicity, 'Comment ça va, ma petite?'

Ailette's eyes grew wide and the effects of the alcohol seemed to boil out of her system. She felt the white heat of the brand on her hip – the only wound the priest had refused to treat with his miraculous salve – and heard again the death screams of her friends, and a bitter and terrible fury built up inside her.

And then, with a wordless shriek of naked anger, she threw herself upon the Knight. The woman fended her off easily, keeping her at arm's length until Ailette's berserker fury exhausted itself, which did not take very long. Ailette sank to the ground and wept, burying her face in her hands.

Celebe kneeled at her side and put one arm around her. In French she whispered, 'It is a terrible thing you have seen today. A terrible thing. But you have lived through it. You have survived. You must be strong and go on surviving. I will show you how. I will show you how I have survived, and together we will work towards the day when we can both return to the land of our birth.'

Chapter 28

CONFUSION

'Of course,' Ailette said, 'Celebe knew she could never return to Earth, not after putting on the armour of a Knight of the Thirteen. But she had patrolled all the lands where the rift was known to appear and had 'saved' dozens of our people, so I expect she was just saying what she knew from experience would be most likely to get the best response from me. We left the village the next day and headed for Asmina. We picked up four other Earth people on the way, all previously recruited by Celebe and then left in a place of safety to await her return. After that we came across one more newcomer, a man from Russia who was wandering aimlessly within a day's march of the Valley and who was more dead than alive. He had no idea of where he was or how he had got here and since none of us could speak Russian and he knew only a half-dozen words and phrases of English, communication was a little difficult.

'We entered the Valley through a secret pass in the southern mountain range and then crossed that hideous desert to the city—'

'Desert—?' I asked.

She looked at me.

'What would you call it?' she asked.

'I don't know,' I replied. 'I haven't seen it.'

'Are you blind?' she asked, 'or just mad? Look around you.'

I did so.

'We're in a jungle,' I said.

She stared at me for a long time and then said, 'Describe it.'

Wondering what she was driving at, I did as she'd asked, putting in as much detail as I could recall from my flight as well as the things I had seen on the road. When I had finished Ailette looked out into the darkness, as though seeing things in a way she was not used to seeing them.

'Now,' she said, 'I will tell you what I see in this Valley. There is no jungle, there is scarcely a living thing anywhere to be seen, except some sparse desert grass and a few cactus bushes. The landscape is a flat, featureless wilderness of reddish sand, broken only by the occasional boulder or small rocky plateau. The sky is permanently cloudless, and this road that you described in so much detail is, to me, scarcely visible, a simple dirt track marked out by stones that indicate the most direct route to the city of Asmina.' She stared at me. 'No jungle, David Shaw. Nothing of what you see.'

I glanced nervously at Celebe, who was sitting motionless some yards away, as she had for hours. Was she listening to us? What was she thinking? I turned back to Ailette, a sudden sick feeling inside me making me ask, 'What did you cook for us earlier?'

She looked at me and her eyes slowly went wide.

'What do you think I cooked?' she asked.

'Some kind of deer,' I said. 'It . . . it looked like a small gazelle . . .'

She shook her head.

'A reptile,' she said. 'An iguana, perhaps—'

We stared at one another for a long time. In the distance, I heard the cry of a bird. I wondered what Ailette heard . . .

We broke camp early the next morning. I don't think either of us had slept much, and I was certain Celebe had remained awake the whole night. The mood between us was grim as we travelled along the road, a road that seemed to exist only in our minds. I wondered what it looked like to Celebe.

Ailette rode her gryllup alongside mine and said, 'You have not told me your story. I would like to hear it.'

I looked past her at the jungle foliage beyond the road's edge. A huge head, grey and leathery, broke through the branches and stared at me with black eyes. It tore leaves from a nearby tree and ate them noisily. Ailette gave no indication that she had seen the creature, or any creature, and with a shudder I turned away.

'It's not much of a story,' I said, 'not compared to yours. I came here with a teacher from my school—'

'You are a teacher?' she asked.

I laughed, and the genuine amusement I felt at such a suggestion made me forget where we were for a moment.

'A pupil,' I corrected her.

'University?' she asked.

'Grammar school,' I said.

'But you are too old,' she protested.

'I was just eighteen when we came here,' I said. 'I was in my last year.'

'Then you are only, what, twenty?' she asked. She seemed to find it hard to believe.

'I guess so,' I said. 'I've lost track of time a little since we came here. I expect Mrs Catlin could tell you the exact date on Earth at the moment, but—'

'Mrs Catlin?' Ailette said.

'The teacher I came with,' I said.

'Go back, David,' Ailette advised, 'back to the beginning. And tell me what brought you here.'

After Ailette's candid telling of events the night before I felt a certain duty to be no less frank, and to my surprise I found myself telling her things I had never thought to tell anyone. I told her about Mrs Catlin, and about my father, and about my mother's obsession with the rift that she had discovered but never dared to use. I told her about our time with the Ladden, and about P'nad, and I found myself wondering how he was faring, if Sonder's 'medicine' had truly saved him. It surprised me to realize how fond I had been of P'nad, and how genuinely I wanted to see him again. And S'nam, and a dozen others whom I had liked and whose omission from

287

this narrative has been prompted only by a lack of space. I told her about our time with Sonder, and his eventual death, and how little satisfaction it had given me despite my hatred of the way he had treated us. (I hoped she would take this not very subtle hint, but she showed no sign of it. Her feelings for Celebe were too deep and personal for any amount of reason to dispel them.) I told her about Benza, and about Tor Taskus whom I was convinced had perished when his tiny force of men had met the army of Droxus on the march to the city I had learned to love. Of all the people I had met on this planet I would miss Tor the most; meeting him had been like finding a long lost brother. I told her about our adventures on the airship, and about Hol Krexus; and finally about how Mrs Catlin and I had seemingly discovered a previously unsuspected side to our relationship, only to have it snatched from us before we could explore it, snatched from us largely by my own stupidity – the more I thought about that last conversation we had had the more convinced I became that the entire fault for it turning out so badly had been mine. She had been trying to say something important, and I had retreated behind my own childish obstinacy because I hadn't liked the way she had said it.

'What is this woman's name?' Ailette asked.

I realized I had said rather more about Mrs Catlin than I had perhaps intended.

'Mrs Catlin,' I replied; surely I had already told her that?

Ailette laughed.

'Her *given* name,' she prompted. 'Her first name.'

'It's, uh, Catherine – I think,' I said.

'You think!' laughed Ailette. 'How can you not know? What do you call her when you speak to her?'

'"Mrs Catlin," of course,' I said.

Ailette was in fits of laughter, the first genuine pleasure I had seen her display since we had met.

'What's funny?' I demanded, irritated yet also pleased to see her face lose its usual grim expression. It was a very pretty face, and didn't deserve to look so unhappy so much of the time.

'You, Englishman!' she laughed. 'You are so . . . so . . . English!'

I shifted in the saddle of the gryllup.

288

'Well, I *am* English,' I said.

I looked at her and she broke up again.

'I am sorry, David,' she said, 'but truly, can you not see the absurdity of the situation? Here you are, sharing every thought and feeling you have ever had with this woman whom you clearly love—'

'I do not!' I objected, instantly wishing I had found a less childish way to put it.

'David,' Ailette said, 'only a repressed Englishman would deny it! And you have spent years denying it. It is time, I think, for you to face the realities of your situation.'

I turned on her, more than a little angry now.

'The reality is,' I said, 'that she's my teacher. Even if what you said was true she'd just dismiss it as a schoolboy crush. And rightly so.'

'I think she would not,' Ailette said. 'Because you are not. Not for some years now. And she, I think, knows this.'

'How can you say that?' I demanded. 'You've never even met her.'

'I am French,' she said. 'I know these things.'

And that, I decided, deserved no reply.

We rode on in silence, until Ailette eventually said, 'I am sorry I made you angry, David. It was not my desire.'

'You didn't,' I said. 'I'm mad at me, not you. I don't know how I can have led you to believe something so obviously untrue.'

'And I do not know how you can have something in front of you for so long and not see it,' Ailette said.

Chapter 29

THE THIRTEEN

The journey to the city of Asmina took four days. This was another impossibility, since from the air I had had an uninterrupted view of the road on which we now travelled and it had stretched unbroken in both directions for hundreds of miles. Of course, what I had seen then was no more reliable than anything I had seen since.

I rode up alongside Celebe. The city was still a good hour away, and since the Knight of the Thirteen Gods had spoken barely ten words to me in our journey I felt like pushing my luck.

'You know that Ailette and I see two entirely different landscapes when we look around, don't you?' I said.

Celebe said nothing.

'And this city,' I pointed out, 'was not here when I first arrived in the Valley. Or if it was, it was camouflaged somehow.'

Celebe offered no comment.

'Since it's clear I can't trust my senses,' I said, 'why should I believe that either you or Ailette are real?'

Celebe turned to look at me. Her eyes were hidden behind their protective coverings, two vaguely triangular, ruby-red lenses set into her silvery helmet. All the expression on her face had to be conveyed by her mouth, and her mouth was smiling.

'If we are not real,' she said, 'then you are wandering through your own delirium. And nothing that I say will make any difference to you.'

Nice logic, I thought.

'But if I am real,' Celebe went on, 'then how do you know I am as I appear to you? Perhaps I am not human at all, but some monster who is feeding off your mortal soul, making you see things and feel things simply to satisfy my own inhuman hunger.'

'Non-human,' I corrected, hearing Mrs Catlin's voice as I did so. What was happening to her? I wondered. With me out of the way, Hol Krexus would have no one to stop him from abusing her further.

'But I am human,' Celebe said, 'or at least I was once.'

She glanced at me, an almost wistful expression playing about her lips.

'It was not an easy thing to give up,' she said, and although there was nostalgia in her tone there was no hint of regret, or of self-pity. 'But the choice was one of life or death, and like all living things I did not want to die.'

'I don't understand,' I said.

Ailette had ridden up alongside me. I think there were things about Celebe that she did not know; it pleased me that she wanted to hear them, since it suggested to me that her condemnation of Celebe might not be irrevocable, or at least not absolute.

'There are things you will learn in Asmina,' Celebe said, 'but there is one thing you should learn now, and it is this: what they will tell you will be the truth – they are incapable of falsehood, as they are of original thought or of understanding the entertainment that we refer to as "fiction" – but their view of reality, and thus of the truth, is not as our view. They have senses that we lack, and are deficient in certain areas where we perceive with great clarity. Their time sense is not as ours – it is not that they can foretell the future, but rather that their existence transcends what we think of as linear time; for them, there is no "present", only an endless existence that is rooted in no single time or place. They cannot communicate to us events that we have not yet experienced – events that, to us, are in the future – because they are incapable of understanding what we mean by the word "future". They have a tendency to take for granted concepts that our species will never even become aware of, and thus their words occasionally become meaningless. They are not malevolent, or at least not in the way that we understand the concept. But neither will they act out of good will or compassion. Their motives are unguessable, but their immediate aims are always simple. They will communicate their wishes to you and will then leave you to make your own decision. Once you have made it, any preconditions that they have agreed to will simply come to pass. Sometimes these will be retroactive – your agreement may trigger an event in your past, an event that would not have occurred had you, instead, declined. You may never know what the event was, or it may suddenly become clear to you that *this* was why such a strange and unlikely thing occurred when and how it did. You must not feel that this power of theirs in any way robs you of your free will – predestination is a term that only has meaning to a life form with our own limited perception of time.'

She reined in her gryllup and we did likewise. The city was now laid out ahead of us like a monstrous ziggurat, a single structure the size of a small county. It was all steps, and its looming façade was a single flight of stairs, a thousand yards wide and twenty storeys high. From a mile away they had looked puny compared to the side of the city itself, but I had been fooled by the scale of the thing.

'I was given a choice,' said Celebe. 'They do not want Earth people here. We are a pollutant to the natural flow of history on this planet. They would have wiped us out, but a bargain was struck: in exchange for my humanity they agreed that we should be spared and all who survived long enough to be brought here should be returned to Earth.' Sensing my question she said, 'They never told me. Perhaps they use the armour with which they replaced my flesh as a kind of lens through which they are able to see the world as I travel through it. Or perhaps, through the armour, they feel what I feel, sense what I sense. Perhaps they are using it to increase their fund of knowledge. Or perhaps I am merely a curiosity, an amusement. It really doesn't matter. I will live for centuries in this form, and see more of this world than anyone has since the last fall of civilization. Perhaps I shall even see the next great civilization

293

arise. Whatever my fate, at least I shall have saved some small number of our people and seen them safely back to Earth.'

'Celebe,' I said quietly, 'you keep saying "they". Who are they?'

She looked at me.

'The Thirteen Gods,' she replied.

The city was silent as we entered it. Not quiet, not hushed, but silent. Our feet made no sound on the stone steps as we ascended them, and when I tried to speak I found that my words made no sound in the still, warm air. It was unsettling, but I had seen too many strange things in the Asmina Valley to be unduly concerned by one more bizarre anomaly.

We climbed the stairs slowly in the oppressive atmosphere, and I could feel the blood beating in my temples from the exertion, the sweat coating my body beneath the ragged remains of my tunic.

At the summit of that mighty staircase there stood an open doorway. It was at least a hundred feet high and slightly more than that in width, its upright pillars tapering in towards the top. I was getting a little sick of the sheer size of the structures of this city, whose builders seemed to have been incapable of doing anything on a human scale.

We passed through the doorway into a dimly-lit chamber that could comfortably have housed a football stadium, yet whose walls were seamless slabs of stone and whose vaulted ceiling had no pillars to support its tremendous weight. The room was unadorned, and its only feature other than the door through which we had entered was a second door at its far side; this, however, was a shallow arch, barely thirty feet high at its apex but spanning the entire wall at its base. It reminded me a little of some of the structures I'd seen in Hippom Ather, the summer home of the Ladden. And that city, I reminded myself, had not been built by human beings.

We crossed the chamber and passed through the next door.

What followed was a journey that lasted for most of a day and that took us through architecture such as I had never dreamed of – nor would ever wish to see again. Much of it I have forgotten – some of it deliberately – and only fragments now remain in my memory. I recall a spiral staircase that climbed for hundreds of feet, the steps wide enough for us to mount them side by side yet so shallow that we climbed them four and five at a time. There was a long corridor with an arched roof so high above us I expected to see it dotted with clouds and that we spent over an hour traversing. In another place there was a ledge set into the side of a wall and within a few yards of its top; its base was lost in distance, a yawning chasm that seemed to pull at us as we passed it, and although the ledge was as broad as a six-lane highway we moved along it with our backs pressed tightly to the wall and our eyes screwed shut. Ailette's hand never left mine as we crossed that ledge, and I think even Celebe was daunted by it. After that came a seemingly endless succession of chambers, all of grotesque proportions, all totally devoid of decoration, ornamentation, or any apparent function – unless it was to cow us into an attitude of abject fear, and it came very close to doing that. Had any of us essayed that journey alone – even Celebe – I think we would have failed in the attempt.

We were all bone-weary and thoroughly dejected when we passed through what was to be the final doorway.

We emerged into a room of ample, but human, proportions that was not only well lit but that was furnished with an opulence that was both startling and immensely welcoming. The floor was richly carpeted and the wall hung with elaborate and beautiful tapestries. There were luxuriously upholstered couches around the walls and, in the centre of the floor, a dark-wood dining table. The latter was, to our joint astonishment, laden with food and decanters of wine.

I sank onto the nearest couch and stared around me at the room with a mixture of disbelief and delight. I was slightly anxious about where the fifty-foot-high doorway had gone, since on this side it was an open arch a modest seven feet high and no wider than the average doorway in any normal human dwelling, but I wasn't about to quibble over minor details.

'Food,' Ailette breathed.

I was no less hungry than she, but all that walking over mile after mile of solid stone had left me with the tiredest feet I had ever had.

'Wine,' I said pointedly.

295

Celebe picked up a decanter and inhaled the bouquet of the dark red fluid within.

'Ladden sukoki,' she said, adding, 'The best in the world.'

'I'll second that,' I agreed, remembering the beverage with considerable fondness.

Celebe poured three large measures and we each drank. It was as good as I remembered, and I felt a pleasant buzz begin in my head.

'Let's sample some of that food,' I said, pulling myself to my feet.

It was a veritable banquet. There was every type of vegetable I had ever seen on this planet, cooked in a dozen different ways; and joints of meat, and whole roast fowl, and smoked fish and an endless supply of wine in red and white and rosé and something sparkling that could easily have been champagne. And, needless to say, we all did justice to it.

(And in the back of my mind, a strange, nagging doubt: I had never before seen Celebe eat.)

We were all rolling drunk by the time we had finished. Celebe made her way unsteadily to a couch and collapsed upon it, and apparently was asleep in an instant.

Ailette leaned across the table to me and said, a bit thickly, 'You are drunk.'

I looked at both of her and couldn't find it in me to argue.

'So are you,' I observed.

'Not that drunk,' she said, looking at me coyly.

'I, myself,' I told her, 'am never that drunk.'

She slid off her chair with a total absence of grace and crawled under the table to where I was sitting. With a great deal of effort she pulled herself up and sat heavily on my lap.

'Prove it,' she said, breathless from her short trip.

I met her defiant stare with a determined one of my own and took hold of the single clasp that held together the front of her minuscule bodice.

'Just you dare,' she said warningly.

She leaned her face closer to mine and said again, but this time with a tremor of anticipation, 'Just you dare—'

I brushed my lips over hers and carefully pulled open the clasp. She kissed me heavily, pulling my hand inside the open front of her bodice.

'Shaw—' she whispered into my mouth.

But the voice wasn't hers. And I wasn't hearing it with my ears, I was hearing it in my mind.

I drew back, a sudden horror filling me, and leaped violently to my feet, hurling from me the thing that now looked like Mrs Catlin.

'What's wrong, David?' asked Ailette's voice, coming out of Mrs Catlin's lips. 'You want this, don't you?'

She let her bodice slip from her shoulders and stood up in front of me.

'You've always wanted this,' she said. 'Haven't you?'

She unclipped her brief skirt and eased it down over her hips, letting it fall to the floor at her feet.

Her features kept changing, one minute those of Ailette and the next those of Mrs Catlin.

She stepped out of her skirt and flowed into my arms, warm and naked and seemingly as human as I.

'I love you, Shaw,' Mrs Catlin's voice said. 'I always have.'

She kissed me, her hands pushing my tunic over my shoulders, the fingers trembling in their eagerness.

With a cry of rage and bitter frustration I flung the creature away, and this time it did not try to rise again. Instead, it lay on the thick carpet, half curled up, and regarded me.

'This is what you want,' said a voice that belonged to no one I had ever heard before. The face was Mrs Catlin's, but it had somehow lost its humanity. It was the face of something whose life was not corporeal, not flesh and blood. Its words were carried on the air, but there was no breath behind them.

'No,' I said. 'It is not.'

'You have been told that we cannot create the thing that you call fiction,' said the voice of one of Vohung's Gods. 'Thus, whatever you see comes from within you. We supply only the substance to make it real. The design is yours.'

I was sober now, and I wondered if I'd ever been drunk.

297

I closed my eyes, wiped my hand over my forehead – I was drenched in sweat.

I opened my eyes, and stood in the presence of the Thirteen. I instantly knew them all, and never doubted which of them had spoken to me a moment ago.

'My Lady of Light,' I said, not a little bitterly.

'Why are you giving to Us this seeing?' she asked. 'It is not in your culture. We would appear to you as would be comforting and familiar. This seeing causes you pain. It is not in your natures to seek pain.'

I didn't know what she was talking about, and I hadn't the strength to argue.

'What do you want with me?' I demanded.

'Nothing,' she said.

I looked at the figure that could only be Gazig, Benza's favoured god, the Lord of Blood. I felt as though he should speak at this point, but he maintained a grim and surly silence.

'He is not master of his destiny in this,' said another of the Thirteen. It was a moment before I realized he was talking about me. 'He has done that which is intrinsically his, and from which he cannot be separated. His path is as fixed as Ours, and each choice was made from the within which is not seen. We are as We are because of his path. The choice is made.'

'He is too weak,' said the creature that I took to be Gazig. 'They are all too weak. Even now his weakness shapes the Light to the within that is seen, and ignores the within that is not seen.'

I looked at the Bright Lady, and her features were those of Mrs Catlin. Why did she keep changing like that? Was it some kind of trap? or a test? I didn't understand any of it.

'You are wrong,' she said. 'He has shown his weakness, and knows it for a strength. He makes of This One a likeness, but not a substance. I say he has the strength of his path. He will choose it. And you will aid him.'

'I have,' said Gazig. 'But still I doubt.'

They all looked at me in silence for a moment, and I had the impression that I was being asked to make the choice of which Celebe had spoken when we had stood outside the city. But what was the choice? I didn't have the faintest idea of what I was being offered – if, in fact, I was being offered anything.

The Bright Lady smiled with Mrs Catlin's lips and said softly, 'This choice finds favour.'

And then, with no warning, an absolute blackness came down like a curtain, and with it utter oblivion.

Chapter 30

GARDEN

'I think he is coming around,' I heard a voice say.

I opened my eyes, and immediately closed them again against the glare of a noonday sun.

Two pairs of hands helped me to my feet, one pair hard and unyielding as though encased in armour.

I forced my eyes open again and stared around me in confusion. I appeared to be in some kind of huge garden, with lawns and trees and flowering shrubs and flower beds and a couple of dozen gardeners going quietly about their tasks.

I pulled away from the hands that had helped me up and looked at their owners. I was not surprised to find that my companions were Celebe and Ailette.

'What's been happening?' I asked. 'Where are we?'

It was Celebe who answered.

'We are in the Asmina Valley,' she said. 'This is its true appearance.'

I looked around again, trying very hard not to take anything for granted. The impression of a garden was not diminished by further observation. In fact, the more I saw of the landscape the more convinced I was that a garden was precisely what it was. There were small animals in the underbrush, things that I had seen in the land of the Ladden, that resembled rabbits and foxes and field mice. It was all very comforting after what had preceded it, and for that very reason I found myself doubting it.

'You faced the Thirteen,' Celebe said.

I nodded.

'And now you do not know what to believe and what to disbelieve,' she said.

'After what I've seen,' I told her, 'I don't know if I'll ever believe anything again.'

Ailette said, 'Tell us what you saw, David.'

I looked at her, suddenly ashamed of some of the things I had seen and done, the feeling not tempered at all by the knowledge that I had been manipulated into seeing and doing them.

'Weren't you there?' I asked.

'Only up until the moment you preceded us through the last portal,' Celebe said. 'It closed behind you and we were . . . brought – here. To wait for you.'

'That's not the way I remember it,' I said.

'The Thirteen can only appear to one individual at a time,' said Celebe. 'It is the way they are.'

'They are not,' I said, 'the Thirteen Gods. They are not gods at all.'

'Yet you saw them as the Thirteen,' said Celebe; it wasn't quite a question.

I looked at her. I was already forming my own opinion about who – or what – I had encountered in the city of Asmina. I wanted to hear Celebe's own account of her first meeting with them, and Ailette's, in order to confirm my suspicions.

'How did the "Thirteen" appear to you?' I asked the Knight.

She gave me a very cold stare, then said quietly, 'Like the senate of ancient Rome. A vast, marble amphitheatre that could have seated tens of thousands yet that was empty except for a few dozen men. I cannot recall the beginning of the interview, only that I was on trial for my life. Details have become sketchy in my memory, leaving only a sensation, a feeling. There was no mercy in those men, no vestige of humanity. Only when they thought I could be of use to them did they even consider letting me live.' She looked at me and something of her natural gentleness returned. 'You know the story already. I agreed to round up the Earth people on this planet and in return the, um, 'senate' agreed to let us live if we were prepared to go back to Earth. I, of course, cannot return.'

Ailette said, 'My experience was nothing like that.'

From her tone I gathered she felt some degree of sympathy for Celebe, and was perhaps beginning to re-evaluate her.

'I met only one person,' she said. 'He was a kindly old gentleman, not unlike my grandfather, and he said how very sorry he was for what had happened to me. He said I could go back to Earth as soon as Celebe had completed her mission, but that until then I should stay with her and act as her squire. He said I had a great part to play in her mission but he wouldn't say how. It seemed foolish to me at the time – it still does. I have done nothing but ride with Celebe since then.'

A thought occurred to me.

'Why had you come back to the Valley when we first met?' I asked.

'We had just returned some more of our people to the city,' said Celebe. 'The Thirteen communicated with me through my armour – I have not been brought before them since that first time; few see them more than once – and they directed me to the road on which we met. I was told to bring you to them.'

Ailette said, 'Tell us of your meeting, David.'

Reluctantly, and waiting for an angry response from Ailette over some aspects of it, I did so. Unlike Celebe I could recall every second of my experience; it has remained burned in my memory to this very day.

To my surprise, Ailette was not offended by the illusion of her that I had seen. Instead, she seemed to find some special significance in the parts of my narrative that, to me, had been the most mystifying. When I confessed my confusion, she actually laughed.

'So English!' she mocked, obviously highly amused.

'If you weren't so damned French,' I said, 'you might find the decency to be offended.'

303

'Because you find me attractive?' she laughed. 'Or because at the moment of truth you see instead your "Mrs Catlin"?'

'David, Ailette,' said Celebe, 'enough of this. We are faced with a difficult task, and I for one do not know how to proceed with it.'

'What task?' I asked.

'The Liberation of Benza,' said Celebe, 'and the destruction of the man Droxus and his army, and the liberation of your woman.'

'Those are my problems,' I said. 'How are you involved?'

'The Thirteen have agreed to help you, have they not?' said Celebe. 'Their help is always indirect, and seldom understood. But the fact that Ailette and I are here, and that you have been allowed to see the Valley as it truly is, indicates that we are a part of their help.' She sighed. 'Sadly, I do not know what they expect of me.'

I looked around the Valley some more, wondering if it all looked like this.

'Who are these people?' I asked Celebe, indicating the gardeners.

'The people of Asmina,' she said. 'Their entire race is devoted to the upkeep of the Valley. In return, the Thirteen protect them from all invasions and disasters. Even the weather here is regulated, allowing a perfect growing season each year and a winter that is both mild and, for want of a better word, picturesque.'

I seemed to see, in the distance, a structure of some kind. I asked Celebe what it was.

'It is a small town,' she said. 'All the towns here are built on the same architectural principle as the city, a single building like a giant, irregular pyramid. That town is where the other Earth people are being quartered until they are returned.'

'When will that be?' I asked.

'Not for many months,' said Celebe. 'The next rift will occur sometime next year. Only the Thirteen know when.'

I looked around, puzzled.

'But where is the city?' I asked.

It seemed to me it should be within sight; otherwise, how did we get here?

'It is in that direction,' said Celebe, pointing to the north-west. 'About four hundred miles away.'

'Four . . .? How long was I unconscious?' I demanded.

'Only for several hours,' said Celebe. 'There is a Library in the city, and another in that town. We thought it best that you awaken here in the open so we carried you here.'

'You carried me here from the city?' I asked, confused.

'From the town,' said Celebe.

I shook my head.

'How did we get to the town?' I asked.

'Through the Library,' said Celebe.

'Celebe,' I said, 'assume I know nothing – which isn't far from the truth – and tell me what Libraries have to do with this.'

'You did not know that the Libraries are connected?' Celebe asked.

'Connected?' I repeated, getting a little tired of feeling so foolish.

'I thought you had had experience of Libraries,' Celebe said, 'but perhaps I took too much for granted. All Libraries are connected by a network of, uh – David, the High Tongue does not have the words, and I do not speak English. What do you call a form of communication that is broadcast but is not "radio"? Not limited by the speed of light?'

'You call it science fiction,' I said.

I knew what she was talking about, and I didn't have the words either. But—

'Celebe, what does that have to do with our getting here?'

'The system can be used for more than simple communication,' Celebe said. 'It is also a transmitter for objects – and people.'

I stared at her.

'A matter transporter?' I said.

She nodded.

I was stunned, but – yes, it did make sense out of some of the things I'd heard said about Librarians. S'nam's comment – meaningless to me at the time – that Vraks'has's Librarian did not live in the town, yet was available at a moment's notice if he was needed, suddenly seemed not so far-fetched as I had supposed.

'And it's possible to go from *any* Library to *any* other?' I asked.

'Of course,' said Celebe.

I wondered how many other properties of the ancient Libraries

305

still functioned, and if the Librarians knew of all of them, or if they had perished with the ancient Y'nys race that had built them.

I looked around me once more, wondering if the Y'nys had made their last stand against encroaching barbarism in this valley, and if the so-called 'city' of Asmina was the last example of their incredible handiwork ever to be constructed. Or, perhaps, the first, and rather than being the last bastion, this valley had once been the seat of their power, the hub of their world-spanning empire.

'Can you use the transport function of the Libraries?' I asked Celebe.

'My armour allows me to interface with the built-in maps contained in each Library,' she replied. 'I can activate the transport facility for myself and for up to nine others, but there is a danger. The Libraries are very old, and not all of them still function correctly. If the receiving equipment in our destination Library is defective we would be lost forever, our atoms wasted to space.'

'A pleasant thought,' I said wryly. Why was it that every time I found something to my advantage on this planet it was like finding an apple with a worm in it?

'Even if we could use the system,' said Ailette, 'where would we go?'

I shook my head, suddenly very depressed.

'I don't know,' I confessed. 'It just seemed like too good a discovery not to have some practical application.'

Celebe said, 'It will be dark soon. Perhaps in the morning we will all be able to think more clearly.'

Chapter 31

RETURN TO VRAKS'HAS

It was impossible, in that country-sized garden, not to feel tranquil and safe. And so, despite my frustrations and worries, I found myself getting the best night's sleep I had had in months. The weariness that had dogged me ever since the battle on Droxus's ship was drained from me, to be replaced by a feeling of strength and vitality. The effect that this had on my optimism for the future, however misplaced any such optimism may have been, was unbounded.

In the first light of the new dawn I lay on the soft grass under the gnarled black trunk of a sard tree and contemplated the events of the past days.

Celebe had said that the Thirteen – or rather, the intelligence that had manifested itself to me as Vohung's gods – had a view of time that was not linear. I found myself wondering now what that would mean in terms of their involvement with my form of life, and with the events that currently occupied me. How would their perception differ from mine?

I had in my mind the image of a movie producer, faced with a partially completed storyboard laid out before him. Hundreds of pictures illustrating static moments from the story he was making. To the characters in the story the events would unfold in

307

a continuous sequence, with a recognizable beginning, middle, and end. But the producer would be able to look at the entire sequence as a whole, his eye flitting back and forth from future to present to past to future again in any manner he chose. And while the characters were limited in the knowledge they could possess at any given moment by their memory of past events, the producer had no such limitation. He would *know* that a particular event would bring its share of new knowledge and if he so chose he could reshuffle the cards so that the knowledge came to one of the characters sooner rather than later as had been originally intended – sooner, so that that knowledge might change a life forever.

I sat up slowly.

And if two people should meet on this day or that day, at such-and-such a place and time, when under different circumstances they might never have met at all, might not one of them learn from the other something of great importance, something that otherwise would never have been known? And if it was in the producer's mind to have this happen might he not engineer such a meeting? And if he did, would the characters themselves not simply think it an act of random fate, a chance meeting that brought them good fortune – if only they had the wit to see it for what it was?

I found myself recalling Ailette's comment of the previous afternoon, that her supposed 'great part' in Celebe's mission had so far amounted to doing nothing more than acting as her squire. Her exact words came into my mind; 'I have done nothing but ride with Celebe since then.' And as a consequence of that, she and I had met. And she had recounted to me, in great detail, the story of her arrival upon Shushuan. In great detail . . .

I stood up and looked around. Celebe was sitting cross-legged in the open, watching me. Ailette was asleep some yards distant. I crossed to Celebe and kneeled facing her.

'Among the Earth people,' I said, 'are there engineers, craftsmen?'

'It is possible,' said Celebe. 'Why do you ask?'

'I may have a plan.' I said. 'Yesterday I would have said it was impossible, but today I'm not so sure. Can I talk to them? The Earth people?'

'Of course,' said Celebe.

She stood up and walked towards the town. I followed her.

My brief optimism lasted until we found our first inhabitant. He was an elderly Asminan who was tending some shrubs that had been shaped into the likenesses of animals, and Celebe asked where the 'honoured guests of the Thirteen' were being housed.

'In the Great Hall, Lady Knight,' the gardener said, adding, 'But My Lady is too late if she wishes to speak with them. The Thirteen have seen fit to permit our visitors to return to their own lands.'

I think Celebe was even more stunned by this than I was. If nothing else it meant that the Thirteen had lied to her when they had said the rift would not reopen for months.

'Are you sure of this?' I asked the man.

He looked at me with a hint of disdain.

'I attended the leaving ceremony in their honour,' he informed me. 'They departed, one and all, immediately thereafter.'

So saying, the man turned and resumed his topiary.

I looked at Celebe, and she at me.

'I guess that about does it,' I said tiredly.

'Your plan—' she began.

'Rather depended on the help of a qualified engineer,' I said. 'And a carpenter. And half a dozen other professions.'

'Have we three not sufficient knowledge?' she asked. 'We are all reasonably well educated—'

'Shut up, Celebe,' I snapped. 'Or in another minute you'll have me half believing you.'

I turned and walked dejectedly back to where Ailette still slept.

Irritated in a dozen different ways I abruptly spun round to face Celebe and said, 'OK, so maybe I could design the thing. I know more about engineering than most motor mechanics, and I know enough about drivetrains to cope with the concepts. But who's going to build it?'

Celebe shrugged. 'Not knowing what "it" is,' she observed, 'I could not say.'

'Well, I could,' I said. 'Nobody, that's who.'

I turned and walked away again.

'Craftsmen,' I grumbled. 'That's all I needed. Just a few good people who know how to work with their hands—'

I stopped. A thought occurred to me. It was absurd, yet the whole plan was absurd.

Without turning around, I asked Celebe, 'Do you know the Library at Vraks'has?'

She said, 'I know its location. I have never actually been there.'

'You could take Ailette and me there?' I asked. 'Through the Library here?'

'If the one in Vraks'has functions,' she said.

I remembered Sonder.

'It functions.' I told her. 'Let's wake Ailette.'

Less than an hour later we were standing in the chamber that housed the town's Library. It was a simple room, accessible from the public corridor beyond it by any of four doors, and was nothing like the elaborate edifice at Vraks'has. Its construction, however, indicated a technology that the builders of the market town had never possessed. Like the city of Asmina, the town was constructed from seamless slabs of a marble-like substance, and although its scale was less grandiose, still it was a trifle larger than it actually needed to be.

Celebe approached one of the obligatory lecterns that ringed the Library device itself and wrote on its surface, not with the stylus provided but with the armoured tip of her index finger. Peering over her shoulder I read what she had written.

DIRECTORY

The word vanished to be replaced with the Library's response.

PLEASE SPECIFY EXACT SUBJECT

Celebe wrote TRAVEL and made a symbol after the word that was meaningless to me. Clearly it had some meaning to the Library, since the screen suddenly lit up with a complex series of lines and dots and symbols. It took me a moment to realize that I was looking at a map.

Celebe pointed and said to me. 'This is the Library we are in. I believe the town of Vraks'has is here.' She indicated another dot on the map. 'The Libraries are not identified by name, however – the towns and cities of the present world did not even exist when the Y'nys ruled – but from your description of your journey with the man Sonder I believe this to have been your starting point.'

She made a sign over the dot in question and the map vanished.

SPECIFY DEPARTURE TIME, said the lectern.

NOW, Celebe wrote.

'Wait here,' Celebe said. 'If the Library at the other end is faulty you will soon know – I shall not return.'

'I'll go first,' I said.

I didn't doubt that the Library was functional – I'd watched Sonder step out of it. But I wouldn't have put it past him to have worked out a means of booby-trapping it.

'You cannot,' said Celebe. 'The machine will not admit anyone who is not accompanied by someone . . . like me. It was a safety device to prevent unauthorized use of the system. The Y'nys were not human – this armour is made of the same substance that they were.'

'Then we go together,' I said.

'And risk dying together?' Celebe snapped.

'If this system isn't operational,' I said, 'no plan of mine is going to be worth a damn. We go together.'

'Fool,' Celebe said, but she didn't object any further.

I glanced at Ailette.

'You can wait here if you wish,' I said. 'There's no need for you to risk your life.'

'There is no risk,' said Ailette. 'You have found favour with the gods – I will be safe at your side.'

'The gods,' I told her, 'are fickle.'

But together the three of us advanced on the great crystalline structure of the Library.

For purely historical reasons, if nothing else, I would like to have recorded the experience of stepping through the Library. But it is, quite literally, an experience beyond words. Every adjective that can describe it conflicts with every other: it was an utterly paradoxical experience, and though not unpleasant in itself, is not one that it is comfortable – or advisable – to dwell upon. Celebe said that some humans went mad when they used the Libraries this way,

311

that somehow their brains emerged from the transition out of step with the rest of reality. Somehow, I found myself not surprised by such an idea.

We stepped out of the Library at Vraks'has and created an instant panic among the folk already there. As far as I knew, no one but the Librarians themselves had been seen to travel via the Libraries in this way since the time of the Y'nys themselves.

I stood and looked around the chamber in which we now found ourselves, feeling a sense of acute disbelief. I had never imagined that I would see this place again, and certainly not under circumstances such as these.

'What now, David?' Celebe asked.

'We find the Ladden,' I told her. I walked over to the nearest Lectern. 'But first I need you to check something for me.'

She joined me, Ailette following and gazing around like a tourist.

'What was the name of the town Ailette materialized in when she first came to Shushuan?' I asked.

'It is called Uhrgratz,' said Ailette. 'The country it is in is called Gaahak.'

'One of the Lost Kingdoms of the Vohung,' said Celebe. 'They settled the lands south of Asmina and then were cut off from their fellow Vohungs when the Valley was closed off to the outside world.'

'Asmina was once passable?' I asked. 'On foot?'

'Long ago,' Celebe confirmed. 'But the spread of the Vohung race was troublesome to the Thirteen and they decreed a limit to their expansion.' She studied the lectern. 'What do you wish to know?'

'Where the Library nearest to Uhrgratz is,' I said.

Celebe said, 'I know that already. It is two days on gryllupback from Uhrgratz, in the middle of a swamp. Its location is known to few, and cared about by less. There are no Librarians in the Lost Kingdoms, and the natives regard the relics of the Y'nys as little more than curiosities.'

'Do you think the travel facility is active in that Library?' I asked.

'I know it is,' said Celebe. 'I have used it.'

'Then we're still in with a chance,' I said. 'Come on; let's go and find the Ladden.'

We began to make our way up the concentric corridors of the Library building, but had barely traversed half the distance before we were intercepted by a group of armed men. I had not known the nature of the internal 'police' force of Vraks'has, but I had guessed it would have one. The four men facing us were all armed with short swords, and three of them carried pikestaffs. The fourth was obviously their officer, and probably the only one of the four with any professional soldiering experience. He was a grizzled individual · with a badly scarred face; his straggly beard had a white streak in it that followed the line of one of the worst of the scars.

He regarded the three of us with a mixture of wariness and irritation – I suspected we posed something of a mystery to him, and he struck me as a man not likely to appreciate mysteries.

'Who are you?' he demanded brusquely.

'I am David Shaw, a Captain from the city of Benza,' I lied. 'This is the Lady Celebe, a Knight of the Temple of the Thirteen Gods. The girl is her squire.'

He looked at us briefly, his eyes sparkling with something unwholesome as he examined Ailette's brief attire, then said to me, 'What were you doing to the Library?'

'Nothing of consequence,' I said. 'We merely sought information. Is not access to the Library free to all?'

'It is,' he snapped. 'Yet a number of witnesses claim to have seen you come out of the Library itself.'

'How would that be possible?' I asked.

'I have seen it done,' said the man, 'but only by Librarians. I do not think they would appreciate others using their equipment in that manner.'

'Do you know that they would not?' I asked.

I was gambling on the fear the people in these parts had of Librarians to get us through this. I could see that the man was in two minds, so I decided to push him a little harder.

'Is my friend Sonder, the Librarian, in town today?' I asked.

The man paled visibly.

'He has not been seen for over a year,' said the man. 'And no other

Librarian has been seen in these parts in all that time.' He hesitated, then said, 'We feared the Librarians had deserted Vraks'has.'

I smiled to myself. As feared as they were, the Librarians were too useful to the town for its people to wish them away.

'You have not been deserted,' I assured the man. 'Sonder has had much to occupy his time in recent months. But that is no longer the case.'

The man smiled, visibly relieved. I felt bad about deceiving him, but I couldn't afford to have the three of us detained while he waited for Sonder to return – especially since we knew that he never would.

'And now,' I said briskly, 'perhaps you can assist us. We are seeking the tribe of Ladden led by the man known as Hareg. Do you know of them?'

'Many Ladden come to Vraks'has,' said the man. 'You should make your enquiries in the market place.'

I thanked him, and he and his men gave us an escort to the doors of the Library building.

Outside, the sun was already past its zenith, and the day was warm and dry. Something seemed slightly amiss about the time of day, but I put it down to a mild disorientation following my journey through the Library.

As we walked off towards the market place Celebe said, 'It is barely autumn here. Surely the Ladden will be at the place you called their Summer Home.'

I nodded. 'Hippom Ather,' I said. 'But small trading parties come to Vraks'has regularly, to buy perishable goods and to trade artefacts. I'm hoping to recognize someone.'

'Why not simply go to Hippom Ather?' asked Ailette.

'For one thing,' I said, 'I don't know what kind of reception we'd – I'd – get. And for another, I'm not sure I could find the way. The landscape was hip-deep in snow when we came to Vraks'has, and the trail wasn't marked. Most of all, though, I want to find out if Hareg is still in charge and how P'nad is.'

I was counting on P'nad's support for what I had in mind, but I didn't even know for sure if he was still alive. For that matter, I didn't even know if *any* of the group I'd known still lived. The bandit attack we'd suffered on the road from Hippom Ather had shown me how dangerous such journeys could be. What if another such attack had killed so many of the Ladden that the group had been scattered, the slaves perhaps killed by the mutahiir or taken prisoner by other Ladden tribes or even by bandits? There were so many unknowns, so much that could have happened.

We reached the market and began to mingle. It was a smaller affair than the last one I had seen, but busy enough for all that. I found myself smiling foolishly as we passed stands bearing Ladden goods, a sense of nostalgia that was wholly inappropriate making me pause to examine first one artefact and then another. The stall keepers were not Ladden but natives of Vraks'has, and their wares might have changed hands several times since being first sold by their makers.

The smells and sounds of the market were having a similar effect on Ailette, who was clearly enjoying herself immensely.

'It is like the village where I grew up,' she told me. 'It is the first thing on this planet I have seen that reminds me of home.'

Celebe put her hand on my arm.

'There,' she said quietly, pointing.

I looked where she was pointing, and felt myself grow unnaturally still. Someone bumped into me, grumbling, but I ignored him. Celebe was tensing beside me, ready for anything, but as motionless as I was. Ailette was off somewhere to one side, debating animatedly with some vendor or other, and oblivious to what we had seen.

'Do you know him?' Celebe asked quietly.

He was walking through the crowd as though he owned the whole world, and wherever he walked men and women parted before him with muted gasps of surprise. The ripple of excitement swept through the market place ahead of him, so that an avenue opened up for him in the crowd.

'Yes,' I replied, 'I know him.'

He was tall, angular, his head shaven. Even without his Librarian's robes I would have known him anywhere.

'He was with Sonder on Droxus's ship,' I said. I cursed softly. 'How did he get here? The ship was heading south, and even if it hadn't been the journey from the Kingdoms to this side of the Ktikbat would have taken weeks – months!'

'It took us a single heartbeat,' Celebe said.

'But he's walking *into* town,' I pointed out. 'Is there another Library around here?'

Celebe was silent for a moment, then she said, 'The nearest one is ten days' ride from here. And I believe it to be inoperative.'

'Why is he here?' I asked of no one in particular. 'What could he possibly want?'

Ailette joined us. She saw the Librarian and looked enquiringly from Celebe to me.

'This changes little,' Celebe said at length. 'It is the ship that is our primary concern and – I presume – the reason for our coming here.'

I nodded, not taking my eyes off the Librarian. He was heading into town, presumably towards the Library itself.

'I don't like his being here,' I muttered, 'but you're right: it doesn't change what we have to do.'

We moved away from the crowd of people who still followed the Librarian. I was still distracted and when a voice suddenly called out, 'David Shaw!' I leaped as though shot.

The three of us turned as one towards the source of the voice, and I let out a cry of delight as I saw, forcing his way though the crowds towards us, the figure of S'nam.

There followed a good deal of hugging and laughing and disjointed telling of tales. Celebe and Ailette stood patiently to one side, and I think S'nam did not even realize they were with me.

'What of P'nad?' I asked excitedly.

'He lives and is well,' said S'nam. 'His recovery was swift and he is once again our leader. What of your woman, that firebrand? Is she with you?'

'She is a captive of my enemies,' I told him, 'and the chief reason for my return.'

I waved my companions forward and made hasty introductions.

'S'nam,' I said, 'look.'

I showed him my ankle, and the absence of the slave band.

316

'Praise the gods,' he whispered. 'I had heard tales that such a thing was possible, but I only half believed.'

'Believe,' I said. I gestured to Celebe. She pointed at S'nam's own slave band and there was a loud hiss from the alien metal as it suddenly became fluid. It tumbled from S'nam's leg like a wounded serpent, coiling and writhing at his feet. Celebe's ability to override the power of the mutahiir was not like Sonder's had been. In the parlance of earthly computer programming, Sonder's equipment carried a higher protocol than the mutahiir and simply cancelled out the command that had formed the slave band in the first place. Celebe, however, used her armour in the manner of a computer virus: she infected the control circuits of the slave band and destroyed them.

S'nam's face was drained of all expression, yet tears of relief and joy poured unnoticed from his eyes.

'Come on, my friend,' I said, knowing exactly how he felt, 'I think this calls for a drink.'

S'nam looked at me, his mouth working but no sound coming out. I laughed good-naturedly, and after an instant so did he. And then he was dragging me through the market and laughing like a madman, whooping and cheering and grabbing total strangers to shake them by the hand or, if they happened to be especially good-looking female total strangers, planting kisses on their startled lips.

'Your friend seems happy,' Ailette said, running to keep up.

'With good reason,' I laughed, trying to prise S'nam off a strikingly pretty slave girl who seemed quite happy to have him stay exactly where he was.

'We are attracting too much attention,' Celebe warned me.

I knew that she was right, and spotting a refreshment tent I steered S'nam towards it.

'Let's get some wine into him and try to quiet him down,' I said.

An hour later S'nam was happily getting stuck into his second bottle of wine and, his boisterous good humour somewhat toned down, imparting to the three of us the information that we needed.

317

Hareg, it transpired, was still spokesman for the Ladden tribe at Hippom Ather, but there was a degree of ill feeling towards him because of his selling of Mrs Catlin into slavery. As unlikely as I might have found it, Mrs Catlin had been quite popular among the Ladden, not least because they had recognized her as a fellow artist. They saw in Hareg's treatment of her a betrayal of the fundamental essence of what it meant to be a Ladden.

Other than these minor grumblings, however, little had changed. There had been no further escape attempts – the memory of K'nen, although more than a year old, was still fresh in the minds of the slaves – but eight new slaves had been bought to replace those killed by bandits. According to S'nam, the bandits had had a bad winter and had been harassing the trade caravans at increasingly regular intervals. The Ladden themselves were reluctant to make the journey to Vraks'has, and argued over who should command each expedition. S'nam was here now with a man called Balor; I couldn't place the name, but I expected I would recognize him if I saw him. Six other slaves were in the party, and two had sustained minor wounds in an attack that had occurred within a day's march of the town.

'We carry little that is of value to the bandits,' S'nam said. 'They are not traders, and Ladden slaves are worthless to them – as soon as we are taken the mutahiir is activated and we are killed. They raid our caravans only on the off chance that we may be carrying gold or supplies. If we put up a spirited enough defence they soon lose heart.'

He finished the bottle of wine.

'You are here to free us all,' he stated.

I nodded.

'But my mission goes beyond that,' I said. 'And it will require the aid of the Ladden themselves.'

'That will be hard,' said S'nam.

I thought him a master of the art of understatement.

'The Ladden who accompanied you here—' I said.

'Balor,' S'man said.

'He has the mutahiir?' I asked.

'He has half of it,' said S'nam.

I puzzled over this for a moment, then recalled the night on which we had retrieved K'nen's body. Hareg had given one half of the mutahiir to P'nad.

'He can activate the slave bands with it?' I asked.

'No,' said S'nam. 'That part remains with Hareg always. Balor's half can be used to signal to Hareg if a slave has escaped. If that happens, Hareg activates the mutahiir. The slave then dies.'

S'nam was beginning to grow incoherent, but what he said confused me. The kill range of the mutahiir was about twenty miles, yet Hippom Ather was the better part of a hundred and fifty miles from Vraks'has. I voiced my doubt to Celebe.

She said, 'The signal to kill is restricted to the part of the device kept by Hareg, which is a natural precaution. Its range is limited due to the nature of the device – from your description I deduce it to be a slave-control device given to overseers in ancient times, and the slave owners would not wish too much power in the hands of such men, who would very likely be slaves themselves. The communication range of the device, however, is limitless. And it is entirely feasible that the kill command could be relayed from the main part of the device to the slave band in question via the secondary part of the device. In effect, you then have two killing fields, each some twenty miles in radius, but theoretically as far apart as the poles of the planet.'

I shook S'nam, a sudden fear gripping me.

'S'nam,' I hissed intently, not wishing to be overheard, 'how discriminating would Balor's message be? Could he identify a single runaway, or—?'

S'nam shook his head drunkenly.

'One runaway,' he slurred, 'all bands activated. We all hostages for each other. Clever, huh?'

'Oh my God,' I said softly. Celebe looked at me. 'What if breaking S'nam's slave band sent an alarm to Hareg?' I asked. 'Have we killed the other slaves that came to Vraks'has with S'nam?'

Celebe considered this for a moment.

'It is possible,' she conceded.

I put my head in my hands. When was I going to learn to think before I acted? We shouldn't have freed anyone until the mutahiir was safely in my hands.

I got to my feet.

'Get up, S'nam,' I said.

He looked up at me, his eyes bleary but stupidly happy.

'Let's go and see how many friends you have left,' I said.

Chapter 32

STRUGGLE

We came to Balor's camp on the outskirts of the market place and found it seemingly deserted. There were three rather small tents set up, and the evening meal was cooking slowly over an open fire, but there seemed to be no one in attendance.

'That's it,' I muttered. 'They're all dead. I've killed them all.'

A man who could only have been Balor emerged from one of the tents and crossed to the cooking pot. He stirred it, tasted the contents, and pulled a face.

'Ch'tan!' he called.

I remembered the name well from my days with the Ladden.

To my surprise, another of the tents opened and Ch'tan emerged. I closed my eyes and said a silent prayer to the Bright Lady. Evidently the mutahiir was not quite so sophisticated as I had feared.

To S'nam I said, 'Where does Balor keep his part of the mutahiir?'

S'nam pondered this question for a moment before saying, 'Don't know.' He smiled broadly, evidently well pleased with his answer. I was feeling too relieved at not being a mass-murderer to be angry.

'Celebe,' I said, 'I'm open to suggestions on strategy.'

'It would appear simple enough,' she replied. 'You must over-power the Ladden male so that he cannot use his half of the mutahiir. Then we search for the device and, when we find it, destroy it. Then we free the other slaves.'

'Free the slaves last?' I asked.

'We were lucky with S'nam,' said Celebe. 'I would prefer not to risk seven lives on a device whose exact properties are not known to us.'

'I agree,' I said. I took a deep breath. 'Here goes,' I said.

I strode into the Ladden camp, smiling broadly in greeting.

'Balor!' I cried happily. 'How are you, old friend?'

Balor looked up in surprise and I threw a right hook to his jaw that should have floored him. He must have had the fastest reflexes in the world, because at the last possible instant he pulled his head back and my punch barely made contact. I may have mentioned previously that the Ladden do not make war, being content to let their slaves fight their battles for them. They are, however, an intensely physical people, and not averse to a little hand-to-hand combat now and then. Balor, apparently, was the quintessential Ladden in this respect, and an instant later he was all over me. We went down in a thrashing heap of arms and legs, and I was beginning to get seriously worried when I saw the silver-clad form of Celebe loom over us, and suddenly Balor was dangling by his neck from Celebe's right hand.

I was just picking myself up when I was hit from all sides by a host of bodies, and once again I was fighting desperately on the dusty ground. I couldn't think where Balor's reinforcements had come from, until it occurred to me that his slaves would hardly be likely to take my attack on him as a friendly act. I was being beaten up by the very people I had come here to liberate.

I was jerked roughly to my feet, my body pulled this way and that, when I heard a startled voice gasp, 'By the gods, it's Shaw!'

Everything went still around me, and I found myself peering into a face that I seemed to know. I dredged a name from my subconscious.

'O'apt,' I said.

'Shaw,' he repeated, his eyes now locked on my left ankle as though in utter disbelief.

From the edge of the camp I heard a drunken voice say, 'An' me. Look – look!'

S'nam was hopping into camp, his left leg extended in front of him to display his bare ankle. I heard gasps from all around me, and looked quickly around to find Balor, suddenly afraid that in all the confusion he might have found his way to the mutahiir. I needn't have worried, however. Celebe was standing like a statue amid all the activity, Balor's struggling form still held firmly by the throat in her outstretched hand, his toes barely touching the ground.

I looked from face to face around me, seeing hope and fear in equal proportions.

I smiled.

'O'apt,' I said to the man who stood at my side, 'find the mutahiir and bring it to me.' He looked at me dumbfounded, and I laughed as I said, 'It's time for some changes around here.'

Chapter 33

FREEDOM

The changes were slower in coming about than I had expected.

It seemed that the Vinh were as prone to the absurdities of bureaucracy as was my own race, although it tended to manifest itself in rather more violent ways. The freeing of slaves, for example, was a capital crime. Only the duly-appointed Slave Master for each region had the power legally to free slaves; the region in which Vraks'has was situated covered several thousand square miles and had only a single Slave Master. To add to the stupidity of the situation, *anyone* could make a slave *of* anyone else, provided it was done in the legally-approved manner. If a slave could show that his enslavement had been illegally performed then his freedom was automatically conferred upon him, and this could be done in any court of law regardless of whether or not the Slave Master was present. Since Hareg was legally entitled to enslave any member of his society who failed to measure up to Ladden standards of artistic creativity, that effectively meant that none of his slaves could be freed legally without the Slave Master's approval. Since my only reason for wishing to free them was a built-in abhorrence for the institution of slavery I was unlikely to get a favourable hearing. In practice, of course, only a slave's master could successfully expect

325

to petition for the freeing of one of his charges, usually as a reward for many years of service or some such hypocrisy.

So no sooner had Celebe removed the shackles from the seven slaves than we found ourselves confronted by a deputation of the town guard, led by the same scarred individual who had accosted us in the Library building. This time, however, he seemed less inclined to listen to what we had to say.

It seemed someone had overheard S'nam's celebrations in the refreshment tent and had reported Celebe and me for setting him free illegally. This being, as I said, a capital crime, our grizzled friend from the Library had come with back-up.

'You will all come with me,' he ordered.

We seemed seriously outnumbered, not even allowing for the fact that none of us was armed.

'David?' said Celebe.

'I'm open to suggestions,' I said.

Any further delays could seriously jeopardize our chances of success, not least because they might bring us face to face with the Librarian from Droxus's ship.

'I will hold them off,' said Celebe. 'There are gryllups corralled in the animal pens beyond that row of tents. Get enough for all of you, and one for me. We will be out of here before they know what is happening.'

Without waiting for a reply Celebe let out a blood-chilling war cry and flung herself against the lines of the city guard. Blue fire washed over her armour, striking sparks off any weapon that touched her and sending its wielder flying away with his hair smoking and his body jerking spasmodically.

I grabbed Ailette by the hand and raced off for the stabling yard that Celebe had indicated. The former slaves wasted no time in following me.

The tent we passed was a storage area for many types of wares, and my gaze lit upon a rack of long swords just inside the entrance.

'Keep going,' I yelled, and ducked into the tent.

I scooped up the whole rack of blades – over a dozen in all – and turned to race after my companions. I found my way blocked by two very large individuals, each of whom had a naked sword in his hand.

'Do you know,' asked one, 'what we do to thieves in Vraks'has?'

'Community service?' I ventured, and flung all but one of the blades at him.

I slashed his colleague across the chest with the point of the blade I'd hung onto and then charged past them, cursing at the luck that had handed me only one weapon when we needed as many as we could get.

My companions had already released the corralled gryllups when I reached them, sending the majority stomping and snorting into the surrounding tents to create as much confusion as possible. I leaped into the saddle of the beast they had saved for me and led them all at full gallop back towards Celebe.

If I'd had any worries about the Knight's ability to look after herself they were dispelled the instant I saw her. Her armour's pyrotechnics were enough to dissuade anyone from attacking her with metal weapons, and those few with the wit to try their luck with wooden implements soon found that it was resilient enough to withstand them too. And anyone who got within arm's length of her rapidly discovered that she was an expert at a particularly dirty style of in-fighting.

We ploughed through the milling bodies of her cursing attackers and, an instant later, with Celebe astride a sleek black gryllup, we all rode at full tilt for the open landscape beyond the town.

We had left Vraks'has a deal more precipitately than I had intended, and our journey to Hippom Ather was now hindered by the fact that we were unprovisioned and largely unarmed. That aside, we were all in boisterous good spirits as we rode our beasts at a steady canter towards the open plains. There had been no pursuit from the town, which did not surprise me greatly. Our companions had been Ladden slaves, and although the town guard had been eager enough to enforce the law within the confines of Vraks'has itself they had no incentive to pursue us beyond its borders. Should we ever attempt to return, however, I felt sure we would receive a warm reception.

Our journey was swift and uneventful, the occasional groups of bandits that we glimpsed giving us a wide berth. I put this down to Celebe's presence, and her display in the town – the town was as popular with the bandits as it was with the Ladden, and I did not doubt that word of us had spread among the former. I just hoped it had not yet reached the latter.

On the journey Celebe approached me on the subject of the Librarian we had seen in the town.

'I believe I have deduced his purpose in being there,' she said.

'Go on,' I urged.

'It may be that he learned, through his fellow Librarians, of our use of the travel system from Asmina to Vraks'has,' she speculated. 'This is entirely possible in itself, as I believe there is a system for monitoring such travel built into the Library network. Knowing that the system had not been used by any of his own Librarians, and aware that no one coming out of the Asmina Valley would do so merely as a tourist, he probably concluded that we were a threat to his own plans, even though he had no idea who we were or what we were doing.'

I nodded, mulling the thought over. If I was plotting the overthrow of a continent and found that that continent's gods had suddenly sent out a messenger on an unknown mission I think I would have wanted to investigate that mission a little. But how had the Librarian reached Vraks'has so quickly if not via the Library there?

'I think there's more to it,' I said. 'He was walking *into* Vraks'has – and we'd only arrived minutes earlier. How could he have been informed so quickly?'

Celebe opened her mouth to reply, then closed it again.

'You are right,' she said. 'I had not allowed for the time factor.'

'It's a puzzle,' I told her. 'And one that, much as I hate to say it, we'll have to leave for another day.'

Celebe, S'nam, O'apt and I debated long and hard the method we should use in approaching Hippom Ather. Every possibility had its merits, but unfortunately each one had as many drawbacks. I had left the half of the mutahiir that we had taken from Balor in

Celebe's charge, not daring to have her destroy it until we had its other half safely in our possession. And gaining the other half of that evil device was, I was convinced, of paramount importance in any plans we might make.

Celebe did not agree.

'If all the slaves are free,' she said, 'the mutahiir is nothing more than prettily coloured glass.'

I looked at her angrily, wondering how much of her humanity she had surrendered to that Y'nys armour whe was wearing.

'And if we miss so much as one slave,' I said, 'the Ladden will have us in their power.'

'One life—' Celebe began.

'One life!' I shouted, drawing curious glances from those of our travelling companions who were not privy to our discussion. In a more controlled tone of voice I said, 'I will not risk a single life simply for the sake of convenience. Any plan we make must be on those terms. Do I make myself clear?'

I couldn't see Celebe's eyes behind the crystalline lenses in her armour but I imagined they sparkled with annoyance at that moment.

'Perfectly clear,' she said.

S'nam said, 'Shaw, I do not dispute your will, but there is a way to ensure all the slaves are freed.'

I looked at him.

'And,' he added, 'I can think of no way to gain the mutahiir that is not fraught with risk.'

'Go on,' I said reluctantly.

'P'nad will know the location of every slave at any given moment,' S'nam said. 'If we contact him first, he can round them all up without arousing Hareg's suspicions. You know yourself that P'nad often does this to ensure that no one goes missing.'

What he said was true, and it annoyed me that I hadn't thought of it myself. I smiled ruefully at Celebe and said, 'It appears you were right after all. My apologies.'

She inclined her head, and I gathered the matter was forgotten. I wasn't sure how relieved that made me.

We decided that the fewer of us who actually confronted P'nad the less chance there was of something going awry. Consequently, S'nam, Celebe and I left our companions several hours' ride from Hippom Ather and headed into the city alone.

It was an eerie sensation for me, returning to this place after all that had happened since I was last here. I felt as though I had changed beyond all recognition from the boy I had been when I arrived here with Mrs Catlin. I felt that I had grown up, and wondered if that was why I was having such a hard time sorting out my feelings for my former teacher. I insisted on thinking of our relationship in the same terms that I had while on Earth, even though I knew, rationally, that that relationship had ended long ago. Perhaps even, I thought uneasily, before we had actually left Earth. It seemed to me, looking back, that for several years I had had feelings for Mrs Catlin that I had never been able to acknowledge. Part of that had been because of the social restrictions that our respective roles had imposed upon us, but a larger part was because we were both too defensive about our deeper feelings to ever let ourselves become friends. Or more than friends.

Riding cautiously through the outskirts of the city, I found my concentration disturbed by a deep-rooted concern for Mrs Catlin's safety; had the only threat to her been Droxus and the Librarian I think I might not have been so worried, but with Hol Krexus on the airship the situation took on a much darker complexion.

S'nam grabbed my arm and I reined in my gryllup hard, the beast snorting angrily at such rough treatment.

'In the gods' names, Shaw,' S'nam whispered, 'keep your mind on where you are!'

I realized the cause of his concern as soon as I saw where Celebe was looking, and where I should have been looking had I not had other thoughts on my mind.

A group of slaves was crossing an intersection less than a hundred yards from where we stood, and even at this distance I could make out the towering black figure of P'nad.

'I knew he'd be with the water bearers,' S'nam said, obviously pleased with himself. 'There are a half-dozen newcomers among them and P'nad always likes to break them in personally.' He glanced at me with a grin and I winced at the memory of my own time as a water bearer in the city. It had been the hardest physical labour I had ever known.

'Can you remember where the storage house was?' S'nam asked.

I looked around and realized that I was hopelessly lost.

'Sorry,' I said, 'I never did get the hang of navigating in this maze.'

'Follow me, then,' said S'nam.

We took a parallel course to that taken by the slaves we had seen and then cut across at right angles to intercept them. No sooner had we glimpsed the vast storage building than I knew exactly where I was, and felt confident that I could find my way unaided to the city square should it prove necessary.

'Is there a back entrance to this place?' I asked S'nam.

'Unfortunately not,' he replied. 'But there is a building in the next block that faces the front entrance and from where we can observe it unseen.'

'Let's go,' I said.

Moments later we were peering out of a large round window at the broad, shallow arch of the entrance to the storage building. We could just make out the forms of the slaves moving about within, gathering up their carrying vessels ready for the long march to the river which provided all the Ladden's fresh water.

We waited in silence as the slaves emerged one by one with their earthernware pots slung over their shoulders, the last to emerge being P'nad himself. He paused in the open doorway, giving the other slaves time to become strung out ahead of him, not putting too much pressure on the newcomers while their muscles got accustomed to their new tasks, and I realized that we'd never get a better chance than this.

'Now,' I said to Celebe. 'Do it now.'

P'nad turned to follow the other slaves and stopped in his tracks as a cloud of steam rose from his left ankle. There was a moment of unalloyed fear in his expression – clearly he believed Hareg had activated the mutahiir – and then his face was an almost comical mask of disbelief as the slave band fell with a clatter from his ankle.

'Stay here,' I said to Celebe and S'nam.

P'nad was staring at the slave band where it lay at his feet, and did not see me emerge from the building and walk across the street towards him.

'Hallo, P'nad,' I said quietly.

He sprang back from me as though shot, his face coated in sweat. Clearly he was having difficulty believing what was happening.

He looked at me for long seconds, no trace of recognition on his face, and then slowly his tensed muscles seemed to relax as it dawned on him who I was.

'Shaw?' he breathed, apparently doubting the evidence of his eyes.

'It's me,' I said.

He looked down at his ankle.

'No trick, then,' he said hoarsely. 'No trick. I thought—'

'It's no trick, P'nad,' I said. 'It's freedom. For all the Ladden slaves.'

He looked at me, and his usual stoicism seemed to return to him.

'There can be no freedom for us on this side of the Ktikbat,' he said. 'We are known to all. It would be death for any of us to be seen without our slave bands.'

'If you come with me,' I said, 'you can be free men.'

He gazed at me with evident scepticism.

'Where?' he asked.

'The Vohung Kingdoms,' I said.

'Across the Ktikbat?' he asked with a laugh of derision. 'What chance would a bunch of escaping slaves have out there? If the natives didn't get us the border patrols would.'

'There are . . . other ways to reach the Kingdoms,' I said. 'But I need more than your people for what I have in mind. I need the Ladden.'

'Then whatever you have in mind,' said P'nad, 'is doomed.'

'Perhaps,' I said. 'But with what is at stake, I have to try.' I paused, then said, 'I'd like your help.'

He smiled broadly. 'Shaw,' he said, 'I owe you my life. I have not forgotten that. Ask anything you wish of me, and it will be yours. But do not ask me to make promises for anyone else.'

'All I ask is your support,' I said.

'You have it,' said P'nad. 'Tell me – what is your plan?'

I began to outline the scheme S'nam and Celebe and I had put together for liberating the Ladden slaves, but I had scarcely got out ten words when P'nad stopped me.

'Shaw—' he began, then hesitated, then smiled and said, 'My friend, it is good to see you again.'

Chapter 34

ALLIES

The plan, much to my surprise, went off with scarcely a hitch. It was easy enough for P'nad to round up the other slaves, and once that was done Celebe had them all freed in a matter of moments. It was what came next that presented us with all the headaches.

I presented the former slaves with my plans for the future, including the necessity for the Ladden's co-operation, and although there was much consternation and a predictable amount of scepticism about the eventual outcome the vast majority were not merely willing but positively eager to accompany me. I think the idea of being truly free, even if it meant abandoning any hope of ever returning to their own lands, was so appealing to them that they were willing to risk anything to bring it about.

The Ladden, of course, had nothing to gain by aiding me, and if I had my way they would lose their workforce. In fact, they would lose their entire way of life, because without their slaves they would have to do themselves all the menial work that their lifestyle entailed, leaving little or no time in which to indulge their artistic pursuits. Of course, they could always get more slaves, but that would take time, and then the slaves would need training – and how many of the Ladden would have the knowledge that that would require? My guess would have been not many.

Riding my gryllup, and with Celebe and Ailette riding alongside me, I led the former slaves towards the Ladden camp in the main city square. I was not looking forward to the next part of the plan, but there was no sense in putting it off.

We were met by Hareg and a large deputation of his people. None of them looked particularly happy, and Hareg was carrying his part of the mutahiir. Beyond them, I could see the rest of the Ladden beginning to assemble slowly.

I reined in the gryllup a few yards ahead of Hareg and we regarded one another with ill-concealed distaste. I hadn't forgotten his treatment of Mrs Catlin and me, and clearly he hadn't forgotten what we had put him through over P'nad.

'What is the meaning of this?' he demanded. 'How dare you return here in this manner?'

'I return, Hareg,' I said, 'as a free man. And all these people behind me are now also free. And they are coming with me, away from you and your hedonistic little lifestyle.'

'I will see them all dead first,' Hareg snapped.

He raised the mutahiir; I think it was only intended as a threat, but it was what I had been waiting for.

'Celebe,' I said.

She gestured, and the mutahiir exploded in a cloud of crystal shards.

'And the rest,' I said.

She took the other half of the device from her saddlebag and tossed it into the air. It came down as a shower of multicoloured glass.

The stunned expressions on the faces of the Ladden were even more extreme than had been those of their slaves when we removed their anklets. The destruction of the mutahiir meant the end of something for which there was no substitute. It was not merely the freeing of one batch of slaves, but potentially the end of slavery itself.

Hareg seemed almost apoplectic.

'You have not the right to do this!' he cried.

I leaned forward in the saddle of the gryllup.

'Perhaps not,' I said quietly. 'But I have the will to do it, and I have the power to do it. And, right or wrong, I *am* doing it.'

I sat up straight and looked at the bemused faces of the Ladden.

'Your slaves are now free men and women,' I told them. 'And they are coming with me to the Vohung Kingdom known as Benza.'

'They will be enslaved again before they leave Ragana-Se-Tor!' someone shouted.

'No,' I said calmly, 'they will not.' I pointed at Celebe. 'This is a Knight of the Temple of the Thirteen Gods,' I said. 'She has access to the secret of instantaneous travel between Libraries, the secret supposedly known only to the Librarians themselves. With it, I will transport to Benza anyone who wishes to accompany me.' I looked at the Ladden pointedly. 'Anyone,' I repeated.

Hareg struck a pose in front of me and said, 'Why would the Ladden choose to follow a slave?'

'The city of Benza,' I said, speaking over his head, 'is besieged by the largest army that this world has seen for many generations. This army is led by a Librarian. And the conquest of the Vohung Kingdoms is only the first part of his plan. He will not rest until the whole of the Thek continent is under his domination. When that happens, what do you think will happen to you, and to your way of life?'

I heard gasps at the idea of a Librarian making war, and knew that it was in this part of the continent that such a concept could be grasped in its full import.

'This man,' I said, 'is my enemy. And he is your enemy too. I am giving you the chance today to do something about him, because if you fail to act today, you will have no tomorrow.'

Hareg shouted, 'He lies! The Librarians do not make war!'

'I speak the truth!' I called, the level of frightened chatter in the square rising. 'The Librarian Sonder, whom you all knew, was also involved in this plot. He was killed in the Valley of Asmina. I was there – I saw it!'

Asmina was known on this side of the Ktikbat, but its supernatural aspects were given little credence. The notion that a Librarian had been killed in such a place, however, would force the Ladden to rethink their views.

'We are not fighters,' one of the Ladden called. 'What can we do?'

Hareg said angrily, 'Do not listen to this slave! He is trying to destroy us!'

'No,' P'nad said, his deep voice stilling every other in the square. 'He is trying to save you.'

A dozen separate arguments had broken out among the Ladden, some of whom clearly had difficulty in believing me, but a few of whom, and they were growing in number, saw the truth of what I was saying. Or, at least, recognized the potential danger and wished to do something about it.

Celebe leaned closer to me and said, 'They are split. It is now between you and the one called Hareg. Whichever of you persuades them now will carry the argument.'

I looked down at Hareg, who was fuming silently and was obviously as desperate as I to come up with a decisive argument. I suddenly remembered something S'nam had said and an idea came to me.

'Which of you,' I called, 'remembers the woman who was with me when I lived among you?'

'Linna!' someone called, using the High Tongue corruption of Mrs Catlin's name by which she had been known in the camp.

'What has become of her?' another cried.

'She is a prisoner of the Librarian,' I said. 'Sold into slavery by Hareg, she is now a captive of your enemies. Was she not once accepted as a Ladden herself? Was she not as gifted an artist as any born Ladden?'

There were murmurs of assent at this, and visible dismay at Mrs Catlin's fate. I saw some black looks being cast in Hareg's direction.

'It is to save the woman Linna, as much as to liberate the city that I now call my own,' I said, 'that I come to you for aid.'

'What is it you want of us?' someone asked.

'Do not believe him!' Hareg yelled, but his tone now betrayed his desperation.

'Be silent, Hareg,' said one of the tribe's more elderly members. 'We would hear this man.'

I felt a wild elation at the man's tone: nothing Hareg said now could save him. Like all civilized societies, the Ladden respected their elders, and even though as a tribe they had no elected or hereditary offices other than Hareg's own, they were a closely-knit community, and tended to regard themselves as a single family. For Hareg to engage in an open dispute with a respected member of an older generation would be such a gross breach of etiquette that it would probably cost him his rank.

Visibly shaken, yet retaining enough good sense to keep his own counsel, Hareg took a step back and let the old man address me directly.

'What is your plan, David Shaw?' he asked me.

Resisting an urge to cheer, I leaned forward in the saddle and began to outline what I had in mind.

Chapter 35

THE JOURNEY BEGINS

Hearing myself actually describe the plan that I had been concocting since before leaving the Asmina Valley revealed just how many unknowns it contained, and how much it was depending upon their turning out favourably. Even if every aspect of the plan went well, there would probably be a high body count on both sides. The Ladden, of course, would not concern themselves with that aspect of the mission; I needed them for their talents as craftsmen, not as warriors.

The old man who had become de facto spokesman for his people listened to my outline in polite silence, but I could read in his expression that he had some serious misgivings.

'It seems to me,' he said, when I had reached the end of my impromptu briefing, 'that of all the factors that could bring your plans to ruin the most obvious is the one you must confront first: the structure you believe to exist in the town you call Uhrgratz. And you have only the description given to you by a frightened girl to lead you to believe it is the thing you need.'

I nodded and said, 'That is true. However, the first stage of my plan did not depend upon that structure, but upon gaining the co-operation of the Ladden. If I have succeeded in that, I will consider it a good omen for the future. Have I succeeded?'

The old man smiled.

'Perhaps,' he said. 'Let me discuss it with my people.' He looked around. 'The hour is late,' he said. 'We will speak of this again in the morning.'

Without another word he turned and walked back through his people; they all seemed to want to talk to him at once, but he ignored them. I looked at Hareg, who still stood at what had, until that moment, been the front of the crowd. His right hand twitched as though to grasp the mutahiir, and I think that if he'd had it there at that moment he would have killed everyone within range who was still wearing a slave band. Of course, no one was. His jaw twitching in mute fury, he turned and followed the other Ladden towards their tents.

The elderly Ladden, whose name was Nehrman, would speak with no one that night except Hareg, as I later learned. Clearly, he did not wish to usurp Hareg's position, and by conferring only with him he gave the Ladden's leader his implicit support. Had Hareg refused to do what his people wanted, however, I think Nehrman might have stood against him. As it turned out, he did not need to do so, and the following morning Hareg announced his intention to lead the Ladden people against the army of Droxus and his Librarian allies. To this end, Hareg proclaimed, he would follow the guidance of David Shaw, although the latter would have no direct authority over the Ladden people. As to the illegal manumission of the Ladden slaves, this was a matter that could not be debated until the more immediate threat of Droxus and his army had been settled. Until that time, and by his authority as leader of the Ladden, Hareg declared an amnesty for all and any slaves who chose to accept the authority of David Shaw over that of their rightful masters. The fact that they no longer wore a visible badge of their servitude, he pointed out, in no way affected their legal status.

I met P'nad's eyes at this last part of Hareg's proclamation and found a dark humour mirrored in them. Hareg may have fooled himself with his little speech, but no one else doubted the realities of the situation.

The rest of that day was spent in preparation for our journey. The Ladden did more work than I might have expected, but on reflection I realized that this was not actually so surprising. They were not a weakling race, nor a lazy one – if they had been they would never have survived all these generations. And, as I pointedly reminded myself, they were born nomads and were perhaps secretly a little excited at the prospect of travelling to new and unfamiliar lands.

My plans for the next stage of our mission had undergone numerous changes over the past few days, and although the basic outline remained unchanged there were some minor detail differences that had evolved from talks with Celebe. Her knowledge of the travel function of the Libraries was crucial to my plan, as was a detailed understanding of where the various Libraries were situated.

We spent that night on the open trail some ten miles from Hippom Ather, and the next day saw us up early and making good time on our journey to Vraks'has.

The one great worry on my mind at this point was the Librarian we had seen in Vraks'has on the day we arrived. Celebe's explanation for his presence was superficially plausible – certainly I hadn't come up with a better one – but I still wasn't convinced. The crowd that had seen him walk *into* the town had reacted as though they had never seen him before. I was certain that somehow he had transported himself to a point outside the town and that that day had marked his first entry to the town. For the life of me, I couldn't work out why he hadn't just used the Library. But no matter what Celebe said about its being the only one in the immediate vicinity I was certain her explanation was wrong.

We eventually made camp several hours' march from Vraks'has. With the Ladden as our travelling companions I had no doubt we could avoid trouble with the local authorities (although I intended for Celebe and I to enter town heavily disguised) but I was deeply concerned about the possibility of running into the Librarian. To do so would be to risk overturning all our plans, since I was convinced that our entire entourage would stand no chance against him. I knew that Celebe was itching to test her powers against those of a Librarian but I had no intention of letting her attempt anything so risky at this stage of the game. Without her my whole plan was purest fantasy, and it gave me no end of sleepless nights wondering how far I could trust her. I knew she was on my side, but she was a very headstrong woman and not always predictable. In a lot of ways, she was just like Mrs Catlin. And in a lot more – perhaps the ones that counted most – she was nothing like her.

I had a brief conference with Hareg and Nehrman and together we decided to send half a dozen of the Ladden on ahead to scout out the town and discover whether or not the Librarian was still in residence. I was glad of Nehrman's presence at these little meetings because without him I doubt Hareg and I would ever have been able to agree on a single decision. I don't know what was going through the mind of the Ladden's leader, but whenever I had to reach any kind of an accord with him I found myself unwittingly playing devil's advocate, and coming out with the most outrageous statements I had ever heard. It wasn't intentional, but I couldn't seem to stop myself. Fortunately Nehrman was much easier to talk to, and working through him Hareg and I managed to avoid actually coming to blows.

Our reconnaissance party returned after half a day and reported that the Librarian was widely believed to have left the town. They had visited the Library itself, ostensibly to clear up an esoteric point of slave law, and seen no trace of the man. I wasn't entirely happy to trust this negative intelligence but there seemed little alternative. With darkness drawing on, we broke camp and headed en masse for Vraks'has.

It was my hope that by arriving at night we would attract less attention, and amazingly enough the strategy was an unqualified success. The few patrols we met on the town's border and in its hushed streets took Hareg's authority for granted and simply waved us on.

We reached the Library building without incident and made our way through its nested hallways to the machine at its centre.

'Is your plan unchanged?' Celebe asked me as we all crowded around the crystalline structure.

'It is,' I said. 'Take the Ladden to Asmina, then take P'nad and his people and me to Gaahak.'

'What about me?' asked Ailette.

'You go to Asmina,' I told her.

'I want to go with you,' she said.

I'd expected this, but I saw no reason to risk her safety.

'You go where I say,' I told her, 'or you don't go anywhere. Is that clear?'

She glared at me angrily.

'Very clear,' she said.

I turned to Celebe.

'Let's get on with it,' I said.

In groups of nine, Celebe led first the Ladden and then P'nad's people through the Library. I sent P'nad through with the first of his men, hanging back myself until the last group. I had wanted the women in P'nad's group to go to Asmina with the Ladden but neither they nor he would hear of it. I felt like a hypocrite for insisting Ailette go with the Ladden, but P'nad knew his people best so the whole lot of them went to Gaahak.

Chapter 36

ALL OR NOTHING

There was a time differential between Vraks'has and the location of the Library machine in Gaahak. (Actually, strictly speaking, there were several – the two locations were over 3,500 miles apart.) This was a concept I could easily understand, but actually encountering it was seriously disorientating. It had been the dead of night when we left the market town; we emerged into a spectacular sunset that we had already seen once that day.

As confusing as the experience was for me it left P'nad's people dumbfounded.

I made my way through them to survey our immediate surroundings.

The Library was exposed to the air here, the remains of a drystone building that had once housed it now reduced to little more than a wall around it. Even when whole, the building would have closely encased the Library, since there was a clearance of only a few feet between the machine and the surviving stonework.

The landscape around the Library was unlike any I had yet seen on the Thek continent. Celebe had said this region was a marsh, and looking at it I could easily believe her. It was only the scale that had fooled me; I had been expecting something like the countryside in

347

Vohung, but this place was more like the Florida Everglades. Huge, branch-entangled, green-mould-covered trees obscured our view in every direction, and the air was full of the sounds of insects and birds. The Library stood on a patch of solid ground, one of many such that dotted our immediate vicinity, but where the ground ended and the swamp began was anybody's guess.

Celebe touched my arm and said, 'The way is not easy, but if you follow me exactly the swamp is passable.'

'How far?' I asked.

'We stand at its northern edge,' she said. 'Two hours' walk will see us out of it.'

I looked around. I couldn't imagine walking out of this place in two days, much less two hours.

'How big is this swamp?' I asked.

'That is hard to say,' Celebe replied. 'There are no accurate maps of this part of the world. Suffice it to say that if you landed in the middle of it, you would never walk out alive.'

'Charming thought,' I muttered. Then, 'OK, we'd better get a move on. You said it was two days' gryllup ride to Uhrgratz?'

She nodded yes.

'How long on foot?' I asked.

'With these people,' she said, 'three days at most.'

I almost smiled; if Celebe thought well of P'nad's group then they must be the most impressive bunch of people on the whole planet.

We organized ourselves into a human chain and followed our Lady Knight into the marsh.

The journey was a nightmare, with stinging insects and leeches the least of our worries. More than once we had to fend off attacks by underwater creatures, the majority of which we never even got to see, and I was thankful we were all well armed. Only one man strayed from the path that Celebe was following, and we spent almost an hour rescuing him from what Celebe assured us was a bottomless quagmire. The man did not stray again, and everyone was doubly careful about where they put their feet after that.

We eventually emerged into a wooded glade, different from the marsh only in that the ground underfoot was reassuringly solid. By this time it was fully dark and the larger moon was obscured by clouds, making any attempt at further progress inadvisable. P'nad took charge of his people and in very short order we were camped for the night.

Over a meal of bread, cheese and pressed meats P'nad and I discussed our plans for our arrival in Uhrgratz: this was one of the parts of my scheme that I didn't relish, but from what Celebe and Ailette had told me I could see no alternative to it. The people of the village were never going to simply permit us to do what we needed to do, so they would have to be subdued. By force. My only consolation lay in the fact that P'nad's people were all armed and fully trained in the arts of war. Against them, the unarmed and unskilled villagers would be able to put up little resistance. I was hoping the whole thing would go off bloodlessly, but I wasn't counting on it.

The tangled, jungle-like countryside gave way to more familiar territory the next day. We travelled along sloping hillsides from which protruded greyish-white limestone paving, and encountered no livestock more dangerous than the odd vol, a goat-like creature raised in some parts of the Kingdoms for milk, cheese and meat. These animals, however, appeared to be wild. Of human habitation we saw no trace.

'There is no centralized government here,' said Celebe. 'When these lands were cut off from Vohung they quickly degenerated into a primitive state. There are no cities in the Lost Kingdoms and few towns. In what were once five countries there are now only a few hundred villages and perhaps two dozen fortresses. The level of sophistication of these is comparable to our own Iron Age, perhaps not even that advanced in some places.'

'I don't understand,' I said. 'I thought Droxus's army came from down here. And what about the muskets you used when you first met Ailette? They weren't yours, they belonged to the village.'

If Celebe felt any guilt or remorse over that incident she showed no sign of it.

'Droxus's army was partially recruited from the fortified strong-holds in this region,' Celebe said, 'but the largest part of it came from lands even further south than this, lands never settled by the

Vohung. The muskets his men have came from the same place. As to how such weapons found their way into Gaahak I could not say, but they can be found playing a ceremonial role in many of the primitive temples in this region. The ceremony at which I officiated when I first met Ailette is a very old one; the use of muskets is merely a modern innovation. I believe the original ceremony involved the use of two poisonous reptiles, the poison sacs of one of which had been drained.'

We came upon the village of Uhrgratz entirely unannounced. The few farm workers we had passed in the fields around the village had not seen us, and there were no sentries posted on any of the approaches through the hills. With a sense of impending disaster, I gave P'nad the word to advance.

Our initial attack met slightly more resistance than I had expected, but not enough to make a difference. The former slaves of the Ladden, men and women both, were a formidable fighting force, and the largest and most troublesome of the villagers went down before them without a single weapon having to be used in anger. I wasn't sure where P'nad had learned unarmed combat, but I made a mental note never to tangle with him unless I had a sword in my hand. His companions were scarcely less deadly, and I found myself wincing every time one of the villagers made the mistake of attacking one of them. I saw one of the women in P'nad's group, a slender, graceful creature who stood all of five feet tall, get in the way of a giant of a man armed with a grain flail. She evaded his roundhouse attack with a dainty little sidestep and then kicked him between the legs so hard I'm sure I heard his pelvis crack. He thudded down onto his knees, his breath leaving his lungs with a high-pitched whistle, and the girl casually chopped a nerve in his neck before leaving his unconscious body in the dust.

The 'battle' was over in less than an hour, even allowing for the inevitable mopping-up of the more intelligent resistance. We rounded everyone up in the largest building in the village and barricaded it to prevent any escapes, then posted guards all around it. Finally, P'nad, Celebe, half a dozen others and I headed for the village temple.

The state of my nerves at this point was such that it was an effort for me to put one foot in front of the other. If I was wrong about this temple, if Ailette's description had been inaccurate, my whole plan would collapse like a house of cards. So much depended upon this one element that I hardly dared to contemplate being wrong. It would mean the end of Benza, perhaps of Vohung, and certainly the end of any hope I might have had of ever seeing Mrs Catlin again.

We emerged from between the haphazardly arranged huts of the village, and there before us stood the local Temple of the Thirteen Gods.

And my heart sank.

Every detail was as Ailette had described it, every detail except for the one that counted. There was no metal arch, merely a high wooden façade shaped like an arch.

How could she have been so wrong? And how could I have entrusted so much of the fate of my city and my friends to something so tenuous? I felt my knees begin to give way and struggled to stay upright. It was all over, but I couldn't let myself give in. The hopelessness of the situation was so intense that any hint of weakness now would be the end of me.

Celebe was saying something, and I had to force myself to listen to hear what it was.

'It is exactly as I remember,' she said. 'Come, Shaw, let us go inside.'

I looked at her.

'Inside?' I repeated, too stunned by what she had just said to think of anything else. She had known that Ailette had been wrong? She had known and said nothing?

'Inside,' she urged. 'Unless you can see through solid wood.'

I looked up at the wooden arch stupidly. My senses suddenly swam, as realization hit me. Ailette had emerged from *inside* the temple; she had seen that arch from *behind*.

I ran forward, scarcely daring to hope that I was right. The others didn't try to keep up, and I passed through the wooden façade alone. Beyond it, perhaps ten feet away, was the true entrance to the temple. I spun around, my head back, and stumbled backwards, gazing up at the reverse side of the façade. I fell over, laughing

351

with a wild and uncontrollable relief. Behind the wooden boards, its silver surface glinting dully in the strong sunlight, was an arch of metal.

The others joined me and stood looking up at the expanse of the arch above us.

'What now?' P'nad asked.

'Now,' I said, 'we start digging.' I looked at Celebe. 'And you will have to bring the Ladden,' I told her. 'It's time to build our own airship.'

Chapter 37

PLANNING AND DIGGING

For the first time in weeks I felt a true sense of purpose. All the guessing was over, and now it was time to get down to work. There would be many questions to address in the days ahead, and countless problems to solve. But the solutions would be practical solutions, and would be arrived at through the application of engineering principles that I could understand and whose underlying laws could be relied upon. Gone was the need to trust to fate, or luck, or the whims of the Thirteen Gods, and in its place a reliance upon my own skills and abilities, and the talents of the men and women around me.

Celebe arrived with the Ladden after five days, and by that time P'nad's people had torn down most of the temple and had begun to excavate the ground around the arch. If my calculations were correct they would have to dig down some twenty to twenty-five metres before hitting metal, and the sheer scale of the operation began to appear daunting. We were going to have to demolish the entire village in order to unearth the whole structure, and the only digging equipment we had was a collection of shovels and a lot of muscle. I had had P'nad arrange his people into shifts, so that we could work around the clock, and even so I could see this job taking weeks.

My only fear at this point was for how long Benza could hold out against its enemies. Without Droxus, the invading army would be leaderless, but had he left standing orders that did not require his presence to be carried out? And if so, what were they?

No sooner had Celebe brought the Ladden into the village than I took her on one side.

'How quickly could you get to Benza?' I asked her.

She showed no irritation at being handed another major task so quickly, but instead did a rapid mental calculation and said, 'If I can find a gryllup from somewhere, maybe twenty days.'

'I want you to go there,' I said. 'I need to know how much time we have.'

'You think the city still stands?' she asked.

'It has to,' I said.

She didn't reply, but I could tell what she was thinking: I was placing too much faith in the notion that the plans of the Thirteen coincided with my own.

'I will leave immediately,' she said. 'Allowing for difficulties, I should return in no more than fifty days.'

'By then,' I said, 'we should be well on the way to completion.'

Celebe hesitated, then said, 'I wish you luck.'

She turned and walked away without another word or a single backward glance.

I gave the Ladden time to set up their tents outside the village and then called them all together for our first major planning session. I already had a fairly fixed idea in mind, and thought I had worked out solutions for a lot of the problems that we were going to encounter. But when it came to craftsmanship I bowed my head to the superior talents of the Ladden, and it was those talents that I needed now.

The metal arch we were excavating was, I was convinced, one 'wing' of an airframe like the one Droxus's ship was built around. And with the Ladden's help I intended to build another, but one far superior to the sailing ship of our enemy.

Droxus's vessel was built for two main purposes: it was a troop carrier, and a primitive bomber. In aerial combat it would have all the manoeuvrability of a garbage scow.

My ship was going to capitalize on all the failings of Droxus's, and then go as many steps beyond that as time and resources would allow.

To begin with, it would not be a sailing ship. My original plan had been for a single propeller at the front of the vessel, but I had quickly dismissed this idea. Although preferable from an engineering purist's point of view it had too many practical drawbacks. I had eventually settled upon a twin rear-propeller design, with baffles and sailboards for steering.

Problems presented themselves with alarming facility. The propellers and their drive would have to be made from wood. Even if it had been possible to forge them from iron or steel there was no way the airframe's own pseudo-electromagnetic field would tolerate such large moving metal parts in its vicinity. And, while sard wood was reputedly as durable as steel, still it was wood, and had all the friction and heat-expansion problems of wood.

Then there was the matter of how to drive the propellers. The only feasible solution to that one was about five thousand years old, but was as valid today as it had been back then. Our vessel would be powered by oarsmen, but their oars would turn two driveshafts the size of tree trunks, and, if my calculations were correct, would give us a maximum airspeed in excess of twenty miles per hour.

Attempting to present all of this to the Ladden, who had never even heard of a propeller and who knew of the existence of Droxus's airship only through my own descriptions, was not an easy task. It was made worse by the fact that they, despite their relative ignorance, instantly identified problems that I had not thought of in weeks of planning.

The session went on right through the afternoon, broke up briefly for a dinner that was punctuated by a dozen or more separate and animated debates, and then reconvened and lost little of its momentum all through the night. It was just beginning to run out of steam with the first rays of the dawn.

I went back to my own tent among P'nad's group feeling tired but strangely elated. The Ladden had initially regarded my proposal with astonishment, but now they had adopted it as their own and I knew that if anyone could make it work they could.

Ailette was sitting outside the tent when I arrived, a small fire

355

burning in front of her and a cooking pot set over it. In the distance, I could hear the sound of digging. Someone was singing, an old slave song that I'd been hearing a lot lately. I felt like joining in.

'You had a good meeting,' Ailette said; it was not a question, and I guessed my feelings must have been showing on my face.

'Very good,' I said.

'You will build your airship,' she said.

'Yes,' I said, 'I believe so.'

'And free your city,' she said.

'Yes,' I said.

'And,' she said, 'be reunited with your Mrs Catlin.'

I smiled, finding the prospect more pleasing that I would ever have dreamed.

'Yes,' I said. I looked at her. 'And then we can all go home.'

I said it for her benefit, knowing how much it was what she wanted. For myself, the prospect of returning to Earth held little genuine pleasure. When Ailette called Benza 'my' city she spoke truly; if I had had to live out my life in the Kingdoms I would have done so with perfect contentment. I did not expect the Thirteen would give me that option.

'Have something to eat,' Ailette said.

I sat down beside her and took a bowl of Ladden zhurba from her. The scent of it brought back memories, and I found myself smiling as I recalled the first time Mrs Catlin had served it to me in Hippom Ather, when our status with our alien hosts had remained in doubt and our time there had been one great adventure.

I ate, surprised at how hungry I was.

One of the Ladden joined me, squatting down by the fire.

'What controls the height of the vessel in the air?' he asked me, accepting a bowl from Ailette with an absent nod of his head.

I laughed at his typically Ladden singlemindedness.

'How would I know?' I asked.

He frowned.

'When we've finished digging,' I said, 'perhaps we'll find out.'

He nodded and ate slowly and without enthusiasm. The dedication of his people when working on a project was miraculous to behold, and highly contagious. I found myself remembering things about Droxus's ship I had only been half-aware of.

'They lower weights on ropes,' I said.

He looked at me.

'When the ship comes in low,' I said, 'they lower stone weights on long ropes. It's part of what makes it look like a giant lalantha. But when it's in high-altitude flight, the weights are raised.'

We looked at each other. The discovery seemed important, perhaps even significant, but without more information it was impossible to be sure.

The young Ladden finished his breakfast in pensive silence and then stood up.

'What you did to our slaves,' he said matter-of-factly, 'was a great crime. But this project you have given us is the most exciting thing we have ever worked on.' He shrugged. 'Perhaps there is a price for everything,' he said.

He turned and walked away, leaving me wondering whether I'd just been rebuked or thanked.

The project advanced with predictable slowness over the next few days. The Ladden spent endless hours in technical debate, sometimes all together but more often in small groups. They built models of various parts of the assembly I had described to them, and drew thousands of sketches on wax tablets and chalk boards. They passed me from one group to another like a barely-tolerated schoolteacher in a class full of geniuses – they needed the specific technical knowledge I possessed, but in every other respect they regarded me as a Neanderthal. On the occasions when they didn't seem to need me I was only too happy to spend my time helping P'nad's group in their digging. While that task may not have been as intellectually challenging, it was at least easier to chart our progress, and to feel some sense of achievement.

As the days turned to weeks, however, I began to grow concerned. The Ladden had built hundreds, perhaps thousands, of models, some of them of the drivetrain I had described to them and some of the finished vessel. Of the latter, many were fanciful beyond words, and I wondered if the Ladden were allowing themselves to become overwhelmed by their own inventiveness. This project was supposed to be a purely practical one, but I got the impression they regarded it as being primarily a chance for them to exercise their artistic talents, and only coincidentally something that would have a tangible end product.

I hesitated to broach the subject directly, not wishing to give offence to a temperamental group of people whose help I desperately needed. Knowing that I would get little in the way of a fair hearing from Hareg, I waited until I had an opportunity to speak to Nehrman privately and then voiced my concerns over the length of time the project seemed to be taking.

'Is it not said,' he replied affably, 'that any product is only as good as its design? And that even the best execution of a flawed design will result in a product flawed ten times over? Have patience, David Shaw, and have confidence in my people. They are the world's finest artisans. Your vessel will be built, and it will work as you have asked to have it work. And,' he added, as though it was an afterthought, 'it will be completed to the schedule you have set us.'

I didn't doubt Nehrman's sincerity, but for several more days nothing of any great significance seemed to happen. In fact, the work the Ladden were doing seemed actually to slow down, as though they were losing their initial enthusiasm and, perhaps, were considering giving up on the project. I didn't sleep at all well during those few days.

Although these worries had the highest priority for me at that time, other things were happening in what little now remained of the village of Uhrgratz that also required my attention. First of all, the inhabitants of the village, who were still ostensibly our prisoners, demanded to see me. Actually, they demanded to see our leader, and although I felt uncomfortable at being pushed into such a role there was no one else in my group who could legitimately adopt such a title – certainly neither P'nad nor Hareg would have allowed each other to do so. And since Nehrman was, technically at least, subordinate to Hareg, that ruled him out for the job.

Feeling faintly ridiculous, I had the leader of the people of

Uhrgratz brought before me. His message from his people was short and direct, and slightly staggering.

'We wish to follow you,' he announced.

Ailette was with me, partly as window dressing – she was pretending to act as my secretary, or scribe – but also because I felt that if I was going to make any major decisions here today then I wanted a reliable second opinion.

'You do not even know what I am doing here,' I told the man.

'You are an emissary of the gods, are you not?' asked the man, with what appeared, were his assumption correct, to be an incautious lack of respect.

'You could put it that way,' I replied.

'We fear the gods,' the man said, much as one might have said 'We fear a little rain now and then'.

'That is wise,' I told him, without a trace of sarcasm.

'We wish to honour the will of the gods,' said the man. 'We wish to serve your quest.'

I was about to say something when Ailette caught my eye.

'You wish to comment?' I asked her in French.

'I was just noting his choice of phrase,' she replied. 'He wishes to "follow" you, but he wishes to "serve" your quest.'

I looked at the man, who obviously hadn't understood the exchange. He wasn't looking at Ailette but at me; he hadn't acknowledged Ailette's existence since being brought into our presence. It occurred to me that he may have recognized her, and was nervous of her new-found power over him, given his people's previous treatment of her.

'You are offering to follow me in my present mission,' I said to him, 'but no further. Do I understand you correctly?'

'Perfectly,' he replied. 'It is well known that the ways of the gods are beyond human understanding, but the tasks they set us are always specific. Since you are here – now – and bring with you one honoured by the gods, it is clear they favour your quest. We would aid you, thus gaining their blessing for our future acts.'

It took me a moment to realize that the one 'honoured by the gods' to whom he was referring was Ailette. His refusal to acknowledge her was not born out of embarrassment or fear but out of some bizarre kind of respect. She had survived at their hands because of the intervention of the gods – supposedly – and was now accorded some kind of special status in their eyes. I remembered her telling me that, after the ceremony in which she had witnessed the deaths of her friends and her own trial had taken place, she had been virtually ignored by everyone. I couldn't pretend to understand their behaviour, but at least it was consistent.

'What will you do,' I asked the man, 'when my, uh, quest is ended?'

'We will rebuild our village,' said the man.

His reply had contained no hint of irony or bitterness, and I saw no animosity towards me in his expression. I supposed that living in a world where the whim of the gods was a familiar reality would promote a different kind of attitude to disaster than the one I myself would have thought normal.

I glanced at Ailette for support but her face was expressionless. I think she had not forgotten – or forgiven – what the people of Uhrgratz had done to her.

I looked back to the man in front of me.

'I accept your offer of assistance,' I told him. 'And when my task is over, I will help you rebuild your village.'

If, I added silently to myself, *I am still alive.*

The second thing that happened was that we had a wedding. This, if anything, was even more startling than the announcement of the Uhrgratz leader. In Benza, and the Vohung Kingdoms generally, there is no analogue to our institution of marriage. Families are organized by House affiliation, and while contracts involving the exchange of young men and women between Houses are entered into quite freely by all involved these contracts do not involve the pairing of specific individuals but rather the 'adoption' by one House of a member or members of another House. In this way the blood lines of Houses are kept from becoming inbred and political amity is maintained by placing friendly agents in potentially rival camps. Had this system been in use only in the Kingdoms I might have been startled by it, but a similar set-up had existed in many places I had visited while in the employ of Sonder. The Ladden, by contrast, have an entirely open and rather casual approach to the concept of family ties. Their tribes are each self-contained families, with a single nominal speaker or patriarch such as Hareg; on the occasions when several tribes meet – which I was led to believe they did every four or five years – they exchange members with one another via some kind of lottery, the mechanics of which I never did understand. This process, I gathered, was centuries old and was entirely unquestioned, the 'losers' in the lottery going off to their new tribes without a word of complaint.

So it was with no little amazement that I was confronted with an invitation to the wedding of two of P'nad's people.

'The Ladden forbade marriage among their slaves,' P'nad told me. 'These two were enslaved together when very young, but had been betrothed to one another from birth by their parents. Being denied their brithright was a source of great distress to them, and one that they would now like to see set to rights.'

I resisted the urge to pursue any of the half-dozen implied contradictions in what P'nad had just said and settled instead for a purely practical observation.

'Their timing could have been better,' I said.

'They have lived a life of abstinence since being enslaved,' said P'nad, 'as their religion requires. Having been freed, and thus having nothing to stand in the way of their union, they are finding continued abstinence impossibly frustrating.' He smiled and added, 'You need not fear, Shaw; they will be wed during their rest period and will be back to work the next day. And their work will be all the better for their improved frame of mind.'

I smiled at P'nad's obvious manipulation of me and said, 'Who am I to stand in the way of true love?'

'You will officiate, then?' P'nad said.

I looked at him.

'By the laws of their land,' said P'nad, 'only an individual from one of two levels of social status may perform a wedding ceremony. Since a Priest of the Temple of Jandtz is not likely to be found within a thousand miles of here that leaves only the second option: the wedding may be performed. by the most senior member of their tribe, and that, my friend, is you.'

'Me?' I said.

'You,' P'nad said.

'Why me?' I asked. 'Why not you?'

'They have sworn their lives to me,' P'nad said, 'as I have to you. Thus, you are now their master.'

And that was how I came to perform my first, and probably my last, wedding. It was a joyous occasion, although a little improvised in many respects. Ailette agreed to play one of the official roles, and P'nad and two of the other former slaves had parts to play although I never quite worked out what they were. I was coached in my own part by the groom, who was the only one other than his bride who knew the ceremony – they were the only two members of their race currently in the group, although I gathered that in the past there had been others. The whole thing went off without a visible hitch, and the happy couple retired to their tent with tremendous haste and not the remotest hint of embarrassment. They had been with the Ladden, I gathered, for over six years, and had, as P'nad so delicately put it, practised total abstinence for all that time.

'I hope they've got the strength to dig tomorrow,' I muttered to P'nad as we shared a celebratory drink.

He laughed dryly. 'They will dig twice as hard tomorrow as they dug today,' he vowed.

Ailette said, 'I couldn't help noticing how alike they are. Is their race particularly distinctive, or am I missing something?'

'Their race is a derivative of S'nam's,' said P'nad, 'although separated from it geographically by many miles and culturally by many generations. But their resemblance to one another is simply due to their kinship.'

'Kinship?' said Ailette. 'You mean they are already related to one another?'

'Of course,' said P'nad. 'They are brother and sister. Did you not know?'

Ailette's eyebrows went up in horror.

'I did not!' she said, slamming down her drinking goblet. 'That's . . . that's . . . disgusting!'

She stood up and stomped off, leaving P'nad looking very confused and, I thought, a little angry.

'Our customs are not the same as yours,' I told him. 'The marriage of brother to sister is illegal in our culture – and considered by many to be immoral. I gather Ailette shares that view.'

'In my society,' said P'nad, 'the concept of marriage does not even exist. But I do not pass judgement on the customs of others.'

I shrugged. Had this been Earth I might have shared Ailette's reaction, but under the present circumstances I probably agreed with P'nad; I just hoped that if the newly-weds were thinking of starting a family together they were aware of the potential risks.

I was just beginning to despair of the Ladden ever putting their weeks of planning to any practical use when Hareg approached me while I was helping with the excavations.

'We need some of your labourers,' he announced.

It was unusual for Hareg to approach me directly, and I was instantly on my guard. He seldom passed up an opportunity to undermine my authority or to make me look foolish, and this unannounced demand seemed like a classic piece of political manoeuvring. Obviously Hareg expected me to refuse his request – the digging was, after all, a full-time job. And when I did so he would use that refusal as an excuse for delaying the construction work still further. I had no intention of letting him get in the way of the project, however.

'How many do you need?' I asked.

'Half,' he said.

I saw the looks of dismay on the faces of those of P'nad's people who were digging with me. But I had been keeping a careful tally of how much earth we had shifted each day and how long the rest of the excavation would take. We were well ahead of schedule, and Hareg's request was not remotely as crippling to us as he had probably intended.

'Half is too many,' I said, not enjoying playing his political games but recognizing the necessity. 'I can spare fifteen, no more.'

Hareg hesitated; fifteen was so close to half that to dispute the difference would have made him look petty.

'Send them to the Ladden at once,' he said. 'We will have to work them harder, but the responsibility for that lies with you.'

He walked off, and I grinned at his back. I said, loudly enough

363

for everyone to hear, 'The Ladden's idea of hard work is a day that includes less than eight rest periods.'

There was much laughter at that, and although Hareg must have heard it he showed no sign.

Chapter 38

BUILDING AND TRAINING

In the days that followed, the project seemed to race along. P'nad's people had already uncovered the main spar of the buried airframe and one of the horizontally laid wings. The other wing was more than half exposed, and even with a reduced work force we would soon be ready to start digging out the deepest portion of the frame, the second vertical wing.

I allocated Hareg's people a sizeable proportion of the newly converted population of Uhrgratz, since the work he needed labourers for was tree felling and the locals were skilled in such work. Also, they knew where the best trees of the types Hareg needed could be found.

The actual working of the wood was done by the Ladden themselves. Working with hand tools that, outwardly, appeared crude and primitive, and with no measuring instruments other than their own trained eyes and the occasional length of twine, they devoured the raw materials brought to them by their labourers like the components of a living factory, and in less than a day the finished product was already beginning to take shape. My respect for their talents grew by the hour, and any misgivings I might have had over the validity of their seemingly interminable planning were banished by the end of that first incredible day.

It was late in the afternoon of that same day that S'nam came to me while I was watching the Ladden work. The look on his face made me instantly wary, for it was clear the digging party had made an unexpected discovery.

'It may be nothing,' he said quickly, seeing my reaction, 'but you'd better take a look at it.'

We had struck the central spar two days earlier, and had been excavating along its length before actually uncovering it completely. This part of the task could be dangerous, because any metal tool, such as the blade of a shovel, touching the airframe could release a charge of electricity of sufficient potency to kill or maim the tool's wielder.

When I reached the dig site I found that a large area of the central part of the spar, that falling between the end points of the arched 'wings', had been swept clear. But instead of the typical grey metal surface that I had expected to see I found myself looking at a patchwork of black plates, roughly rectangular, and each about six feet by four feet, curved as though to fit snugly about the length of the spar. The plates were fitted together almost seamlessly, and served no obvious purpose. What was most startling about them, however, was the fact that they could not be prised away from the central spar: the metal of which the airframe was constructed was so smooth as to be virtually frictionless, and nothing could be made to adhere to it. The wooden frame of Droxus's ship had been anchored in only eight places, by being built snugly around the end points of the four wings. How, then, were these plates clinging to the metal beneath? The frames were not, so far as I knew, magnetic, and their substance was so dense that it could not be penetrated – even assuming anyone would be so foolish as to try drilling into so volatile a material.

'It's a mystery, no?' S'nam said.

'A mystery, yes,' I said. 'But one that, hopefully, will resolve itself once we're finished digging.'

S'nam nodded and put his team back to work.

As the construction of our ship's driveshafts progressed, I found myself faced with the problem of training P'nad's people in how to use them. It was already accepted that P'nad's followers would make up our crew, along with such of the people of Uhrgratz who wished to accompany us and who had the aptitude for the work involved. I had tried to keep the design as simple as poss-ible, sacrificing certain innovative and sophisticated subsystems in favour of a powerful main drive that could be easily maintained in flight. And, too, one that was robust enough to hold up under combat conditions.

The 'oars' that would turn the twin shafts were simple pull/push devices, the rate of rotation directly related to the speed with which the oars were worked. I had considered employing some kind of gearing system, but given the necessity of working in wood I had abandoned the idea. By making the oars fairly long we would be able to generate a tremendous amount of torque for relatively little effort, and still allow ourselves a broad spread of useable power. Or, at least, that was the theory.

Using a mock-up of the full-size device I spent hour after hour putting P'nad's people through their paces. This improvised training device, which amounted to little more than a lash-up compared to the real thing, offered none of the resistance that the rowers could expect to encounter when driving the ship itself but my principal concern at the moment was to get a physically balanced crew who could row in time with one another – whether or not they would eventually have the muscle power for the task was not a question I needed to ask, not given the kind of people I was working with.

One man, halfway through a training session that was going particularly badly, voiced a question that I suddenly realized had been in many people's minds.

'Shaw,' he said, standing up behind his oar, 'is this not a task better suited to slaves than free men?'

I heard mutters of agreement around me, and knew that I had been too preoccupied with other matters to spot this unrest as it developed.

'There are no slaves in my camp,' I said simply.

I waited for the mutterings to die down and for every eye to be on me before I continued.

'We were all slaves once,' I said, speaking calmly and keeping my voice low so that each man would have to strain to hear me. 'I will accept no man in my company who would see his fellow men in chains. I remember K'nen, whom you all knew. K'nen was no friend to me, but were he here today I would permit no man to make him a slave. This task of ours, whether the will of the gods or not, is a task worthy only of free men. You have all agreed to follow me, but I say now, if any man would have a slave take his place then let that man leave my company, because he and I do not fight the same fight.'

I looked from face to face slowly, and although I could see confusion on some and a degree of disapproval on others, no man stood to leave.

'I will give you a new word,' I said, voicing an idea that had been in my mind for some time now. 'In my land, for many centuries, there has been a tradition that, among fighting men, is one of the most honoured. It is the concept of a group of warriors who provide their own transportation from place to place, who go wherever the fighting needs them, not in vessels powered by slaves, but in their own vessels driven by their own hands. These men are the greatest of all warriors, the mightiest of the mighty, and to be accepted into their ranks is the highest honour a warrior can aspire to. These men are called Marines. Will you be my Marines?'

A murmur of surprise went around the group of men, as this new concept was discussed in hushed tones. I knew that the notion was unknown among the Vinh, to whom slavery was an institution as old as civilization itself, and where menial labour of any kind was regarded as beneath the dignity of a free man. But these men had known slavery from the other side of the social divide, and their perspective would be unique. I hoped that that would be enough.

One man, a leader of one of the work crews, stood up.

'I will be a Marine,' he declared.

Another arose. 'I will be a Marine,' he said.

And another. 'I too,' he said.

In moments they were all on their feet, and I felt as though I had won the greatest victory of my life, because I knew that never again would these men regard slavery in the way that they had been taught to regard it.

'In that case,' I called out, almost deafened by their shouts, 'I will give you *another* new word!'

They laughed, and I knew that before the day was done I would have the whole of P'nad's group beating a path to my door to be made into Marines.

I walked among them and picked out a particular individual on whom I had had my eye for several days. He was not the largest of the ex-slaves, but his rowing was the most regular and his timekeeping excellent.

'This man,' I said, 'will be given a special task, and the name we will call him from now on is "hortator".'

I heard interested mutterings at this new word, and although the individual in question had no idea what his new title meant it was clear that he already felt immensely proud of his achievement.

I produced a pair of wooden mallets that I had appropriated from the Ladden and a barrel that would serve as a drum. And for the next few hours I went through with them the ways in which our new 'hortator' could help keep their rowing in time by pounding out the beat with his mallets. The man I had chosen did not let me down, and before the day was done we had successfully worked out four completely different cadences, and with boisterous good humour my new Marines had put their backs into rowing in time to the pounding of the mallets.

Things went well for the next few days: the Ladden worked like demons, and needed very little input from me; the training had weeded out those who were not really suited to the task of rowing, a task that was now much sought after; those who were destined not to become oarsmen did not lose out, however, as our ship had need of many men of varying skills and abilities; and the excavations had now advanced so far that we had slung ropes over the visible portions of the airframe in readiness for its final release.

I suppose that all of this should have warned me that a disaster was imminent, but I was getting carried along by the sheer impetus of it all and I failed to spot the danger signs until it was too late.

The first hint I had that something was amiss came as I was settling down to a few hours' sleep in the hours just before dawn. My head had barely touched the pillow before I heard a great many voices raised in panic and anger; and then a terrible scream pierced the night, followed by a sound like the tearing of a thousand sheets of canvas.

I was on my feet and out of my tent in an instant, trying to locate the source of the sounds. It didn't take long to locate it, because it was right in front of me. The airframe had not waited for us to finish digging it out; with half of its last wing still buried it had finished the job all by itself.

The terrible rending noise I had heard had been the sound of the buried arch tearing itself free from the ground, and the scream that had preceded it had been that of a man who had been trapped by the shifting bulk of the thing.

Something about what I was seeing didn't make sense, and it was several seconds before I could work out what it was. I had already observed that, in some way, the airframes were balanced so that, in flight, they always presented a particular aspect; seen from the front or rear, they resembled a large 'X' with a thick dot in its centre. This frame, we had all assumed, had been buried with the 'X' tilted through forty-five degrees, so that one of its upper wings had protruded through the topsoil to form the entrance arch to the temple. Only now did I realize how dangerously wrong we had been. The frame had been buried tilted through more than one hundred and eighty degrees: one of its two upper wings was the one most deeply planted in the earth, so that when it was released it did not merely rise, it *rolled*, and that was what I was now witnessing. It was like watching some prehistoric creature rising up from the grave that had held it for millennia.

With a sinking sensation I realized that the ropes we had used to secure the thing were not holding it. One by one I saw them snap like lengths of frayed cotton, and as the frame began to rise from its pit I had a sudden premonition that we were going to lose it.

I raced forward, tripped and fell, and was on my feet and running again without really knowing what I was doing or why I was doing it.

The airframe, which had been briefly halted in its mighty roll by a slightly stronger rope, suddenly lurched as the rope parted, and completed its turn, in the process catching one of the labourers with its swinging lower arch and reducing him to a bloody smear on the grass where he had stood. The thing's momentum was not reduced by its seeming weightlessness, since its mass must have been measured in the hundreds of tons.

It began to lift, and not slowly, and as it presented its cross-section to the light breeze it began to drift.

I was almost under it now, and scarcely ten yards in front of me there trailed one end of a rope whose other end was attached to the thing's upper left wing. Without a thought for the consequences I broke into a furious sprint and hurled myself at the dangling end of the rope. To my own amazement I caught it, and at that moment the last of the restraining ropes that were still anchored to anything broke, and the airframe lurched skyward with me still dangling uselessly underneath it.

I cast a glance below me, intending to release my hold and, hopefully, land on some soft and yielding surface. It took only the most cursory of observations to realize that any such plan was already out of the question. The airframe had gained over fifty feet in a matter of seconds and was still climbing. It spun dizzyingly about its vertical axis as the winds increased with the higher altitude, making it a full-time occupation for me just to hang on. My grip on the rope was perilously close to its end, and I was being whipped along so rapidly I didn't dare to try to climb higher. All I could do was to hang on and hope that whatever it was that governed the height at which this airframe would hover would soon decide that we were high enough above the land for it to cut in.

Chapter 39

DISASTER

The frame must have ascended to a height of a thousand feet or more before I sensed its upward motion had ceased. It was now travelling towards the east at a good ten or fifteen miles an hour, so I was hardly in a position to feel particularly safe, but ascending the rope to find a more secure perch now seemed like my first priority.

It was a slow and torturous process, but long, agonized minutes later I had climbed high enough to be able to gain a meagre purchase on the central spar. The frictionless surface offered little in the way of a foothold, but the rope was anchored around the rearmost foot of the arch and with much struggling and slithering about I managed to tuck myself up under the incline of the tilted leg, the rope looped around my waist to hold me in place and my legs braced around the less slippery surface of the black plates that lined the central part of the main spar.

And from the dubious security of that vantage point I was able to ponder the truly desperate nature of my predicament. I was now more stranded, more utterly isolated, than I had ever been in my life. I was beyond the reach of any aid or assistance, and unable to do anything myself to remedy my plight. It took me all of ten seconds to arrive at this conclusion, and all that was then left to me was an increasingly bleak depression.

The minutes became hours, and the airframe drifted on east-wards, sometimes gaining speed as the wind increased, sometimes slowing almost to a standstill as it fell. I passed through a brief rainstorm that soaked me to the skin and left me shivering against the cold metal, my sense of desolation increasing even further.

Day gave way to night and I found myself drifting in and out of a fitful sleep; it wasn't long, however, before my exhaustion took its toll and I sank into a dreamless oblivion. I awoke in a blind panic only minutes later; I had slid sideways off the central spar and was dangling from it by the length of rope which had come partially untied. Shaken and shaking, I crawled back into place and retied the rope more securely.

Morning came with more rain, but soon after that the sun came out from behind the clouds and I was bathed in its golden warmth, and foolishly I felt my spirits lift a little.

I was already beginning to feel hungry and thirsty, and logic dictated that a death by starvation was the most probable fate that awaited me. I decided that if it came to it, I would untie the rope and fall to my death instead. It was not much of a choice, but at least it would be my own.

By the second morning I was half-delirious, and even if I had had the strength to carry out my resolution I no longer had the wit to remember it.

Dark shapes seemed to fill the sky close to me, but my eyes had already begun to play tricks on me by then and I wasn't prepared to trust what they seemed to be telling me. When a claw struck my shoulder and a beak dug into my neck I changed my mind pretty quickly, and feebly tried to beat off my avian attacker. It was a carrion bird of some description, and took a lot of persuading that I wasn't dead. In the end, and after I'd been raked by its talons all across one arm and half of my chest, it finally got the message and sailed off away from the airframe, filling the sky with its screeches of disappointment.

I tried to pull myself together at that point, since the bird clearly had not been alone. Several of its brothers were squatting on the far end of the spar, watching me closely and occasionally squawking in dismay as the frame tilted in the wind and they slithered across its smooth surface. At such times I found myself laughing maniacally, and forced myself to stop.

The sun was baking my head and back when a huge, flapping creature suddenly reared up in front of me. It was ten times the size of one of the carrion birds, and its wings seemed membranous, like those of a bat. Silhouetted against the sun as it was I could only see it as a monstrous shadow looming over me, but it was obvious that resistance would be futile against such a nightmarish beast. Nevertheless, I prepared to sell my life as dearly as I could.

'David!' a voice called, shrill above the flapping of the creature's wings.

I looked around foolishly: had one of the birds suddenly acquired a voice? And how did it know my name?

'David Shaw!' came the cry again, and I seemed to know the voice. But how was that possible? Or was I simply going mad?

The creature circled out of the sun, and my befuddled brain suddenly saw it for what it really was. It was an airframe, a miniature version of the one to which I was tied, and its flapping wings were two makeshift sails strung between its wings. And, most incredible of all, seated between them upon a wooden platform was Ailette!

I gave a cry of joy, though it came out as more of an inarticulate croak.

'Take this,' she said, tacking against the wind. She handed me a water flask, which my weakened fingers fumbled open and from which I drank with relish.

'Eat,' she said, handing me a small bundle of provisions.

I ate ravenously, and while I did so Ailette swung her vessel around and cast a line around the leading edge of the arch to which I was bound. Then, letting out her sails to their fullest, she towed the vast airframe around and began to lead me back the way I had come.

In a matter of hours we were joined by two other tiny vessels, virtually identical to Ailette's, that quickly went to assist her in her task.

As my strength slowly returned I found my mind filling with

questions, not least of which had to do with where my saviours had come by their incredible vessels. Conversation was impossible under the prevailing conditions, however, so I was forced to bide my time.

We reached Uhrgratz five days later, and Ailette airlifted me off the large airframe and lowered me to the ground. If I'd intended to question her there and then – and, to be honest, that is exactly what I had intended – I was destined to be disappointed. Because no sooner had my feet touched terra firma than the cumulative effects of my ordeal finally hit me and I passed out in her arms.

Chapter 40

LEGACY OF THE PAST

Despite my exhaustion, I was on my feet again several hours later. I ate a substantial meal, but I did so on the hoof; against her protestations, I made Ailette give me a guided tour of the incredible place in which they had found the small airframes.

It had clearly been a workshop of some kind, as well as a storage chamber. Its age was impossible to calculate, but certainly it was on the order of centuries – perhaps millennia.

When the large airframe had torn itself loose from the earth it had carried with it a slab of stone that all the former slaves and villagers together could not lift. This slab had been the airframe's principal anchor, and also the roof of the main part of the underground chamber.

In the chamber they had found five Y'nys lecterns, and a host of devices similar in construction to the mutahiir. Two of the lecterns were smashed, and a third could not be made to function. The remaining two were active, but their screens would display only gibberish. I suspected, from having looked at them, that the language was the same as that to be found on Librarian clothing. Neither lectern appeared to recognize the contemporary written form of the High Tongue.

Of the mutahiir-like devices, about two-thirds were inactive, their crystalline structure decayed and full of black impurities. The functions of the other devices could not be deduced from simple observation, and knowing how deadly the mutahiir had been no one felt like experimenting with them to learn more.

In a side-chamber they had found the four miniature airframes. The chamber had been just deep enough to take them, and the frames were resting against its ceiling, there being nothing else to hold them down.

Attaching heavy rocks to one of the frames with long ropes, they had pulled it out of the confines of the chamber and waited to see what would happen. What happened was that it rose into the air for about sixty feet and then hung there, bobbing in the light breeze.

They repeated the exercise with a second airframe, but this time they tied someone to it first. They also provided longer ropes for the weights and made sure that they could be reeled in by the frame's 'pilot'. This time the frame rose about ten feet short of the first one and stayed there. The pilot reeled his weights in a little and the frame rose to match the height of the first one.

Much experimenting followed.

The only principle that could be derived from their observations was that somehow the mechanism that controlled the airframes' altitude was sensitive to weight – or, more likely, to mass. Any weight added to the frame that stayed within the ambit of its four 'wings' caused the frame to rise in proportion to the amount of weight: the greater the weight, the higher it rose. Stripped bare, the frames all tended to rise to about a thousand feet, give or take a hundred feet or so. Weight that was added that lay outside the ambit of the wings, namely on long ropes, would have the opposite effect. And the greater the weight, or the further the distance it was lowered from the frame, the lower the frame would descend.

With one of the smaller frames, a pair of man-sized stone weights lowered to a distance of thirty feet from the frame's central spar would bring the frame low enough for the weights to trail along the ground. To get the frame lower would have required shorter ropes, and unmanageably heavy weights. I suspected that some kind of inverse square law was in operation here, like that governing electromagnetic effects.

As soon as was humanly possible, the Ladden had rigged up one of the small frames as a sailing vessel. Ailette was the only person in the camp who had had any experience on controlling a sailing ship, so she had immediately set about teaching three of my Marines how to handle one. I think P'nad had intended that she should teach four of them, but apparently she had insisted on taking one of the vessels herself. Given her greater experience, P'nad had been forced to agree reluctantly.

All four vessels had departed within an hour of one another, but Ailette's greater expertise had allowed her to take and then maintain a substantial lead. No one knew which direction my own larger frame had followed, so Ailette did the only thing she could: piled on every square inch of available sail and let the same winds propel her that were propelling me.

'I almost missed you,' she said. 'You were about thirty metres below me, and maybe a quarter of a kilometre off my course. Luckily the sun was reflecting off your airframe so brightly it was blinding; that was how I spotted you.'

I nodded, studying one of the two surviving lecterns in the chamber.

'I wonder what the connection is between the Y'nys and the airframe builders?' I mused. 'I can't believe they were the same race – the technologies seem light years apart.'

'Perhaps Celebe will know,' Ailette said.

I nodded.

'She should be back soon,' I said. 'We'll ask her then.'

Chapter 41

TOO DEEP A LOSS

It was ten days after my return to the camp and almost sixty days since Celebe had left for Benza, and her return was now overdue. I had been keeping my fears in check for several days, trying to think up plausible excuses for her being delayed, but with each new dawn that broke with no sight of her I was beginning to fear the worst.

The work on the airship was long past the point at which my presence was needed, and the training of my Marines and other crewmen had now been delegated to a handful of the most promising of P'nad's followers. I was beginning to feel superfluous, and with time on my hands my worries began to nag at me relentlessly.

I voiced my concerns to Ailette, who had even less to occupy her time than I did, and tentatively broached a subject that had been on my mind for several days.

'I think I should go after Celebe,' I said,

Ailette looked at me as though I had lost my mind.

'I'm not needed here,' I told her, 'and this waiting is killing me.'

'Not needed?' she repeated incredulously. 'David, if you left now

this whole project would fall apart. Don't you realize how vital you
are to it? It's your presence that keeps everyone going.'

'Now you're being ridiculous,' I said. 'These days I'm lucky if
anyone says ten words to me, they're all so busy.'

'And without your presence,' she replied, 'how long do you think
all that industry would last? This is your mission, David, and these
are your people. If you leave now, Hareg will stir up trouble among
the Ladden, P'nad will oppose him, and both sides will down tools
until one or the other wins the argument. And since no one *can*
win, that means the project ends right there – forever. And with it,
the freedom of P'nad's people – again, forever.'

I squirmed under the intensity of her gaze, not wanting to place
too much credence in what she had said, but recognizing the truth
of at least half of it.

'And just out of interest,' Ailette added, 'how did you propose
to follow Celebe anyway? Benza is months away on foot, and that
would be the only way you could get there. You can't use the
Libraries without her, can you?'

I had in fact been considering taking one of the smaller airframes,
but since none of them was yet airworthy for so long a journey that
notion seemed best left undisclosed. And, too, I did not want to give
away the secret of our airship to Droxus's followers by having one
of the smaller vessels spotted while I was overflying the Kingdoms.
Leaving aside the more advanced aspects of our ship, our greatest
weapon against our enemy's vessel was going to be surprise.

And so I chafed and fretted for another two days, my mood not
much lightened by the ever more frequent consultations now being
requested by the Ladden – it seemed as though the construction
was so well advanced that they now needed my input on certain
aspects of fine tuning. It was both frustrating and at the same time
perversely satisfying to be the only 'experienced' engineer in the
whole group.

I was examining one of the rowing bays on the skeletal framework of the vessel, itself now partially attached to the airframe,
and debating with two of the Ladden on the need for additional
strengthening, when a cry went up from the edge of the camp; in
among the general hubbub I clearly heard Celebe's name being

called. I raced from the ship's hull, descended one of the numerous ropes that anchored it to the ground, and ran towards the source of the cry. The sight that greeted me provoked the most mixed reactions I had ever felt, for it filled me simultaneously with horror and joy.

Celebe was walking slowly into camp: her armour was lacerated in a dozen places and caked with dried blood, her helm split open along one side, and the usually translucent substance of which it was made now looked strangely dull and lifeless. That her wounds were mortal seemed a certainty, yet it was impossible to tell how long ago she had sustained them.

She was dragging her left leg, which was flayed open to the bone from hip to knee, and would surely have had to drag herself along the ground were it not for the fact that she was being aided – almost carried – by an armoured companion whose identity was instantly known to me, and whose presence it was that had so delighted me. It was Tor Taskus.

In an instant the two were surrounded by villagers and ex-slaves and Ladden. Celebe was lifted to a half-dozen willing shoulders and borne towards the camp of P'nad's people, where those among us most skilled in medicine were to be found. Other hands went to Tor's aid, and only now did I realize that my old friend was himself badly injured.

I forced my way to his side, crying out his name. He gazed at me with a wry grin, his face bruised and his mouth bloody.

'I thought never to see you again,' he said through a throat that sounded as dry as dead leaves. 'When the Knight told me . . .'

His voice gave out, and a flask of watered-down wine was thrust into his hands. He drank deeply before attempting to speak again, and when he did so his voice was grim.

'My friend,' he said sadly, 'our city is fallen. Benza is razed all but to the ground.'

His words left me stunned with disbelief and a grief that was so intense it was an actual physical pain within me. Benza – gone . . .

'Then all is lost,' I said numbly, 'and all we can do is seek revenge—'

'No, my friend,' Tor said, 'all is *not* lost. Our city is no more, that much is true, but Benza herself – the people, the lands – those prevail. In a thousand villages and hamlets, and in war camps in the hillsides, we carry the battle to our enemy. Our efforts are no more than the bites of insects against the might of that vast army, but while hope survives in the heart of a single one of her sons, Benza lives on.'

The fire in Tor's eyes as he spoke was the living proof of his words, and I felt my despair give way to a fragile hope,

'Is the army of Droxus still in Benzan territory?' I asked.

It seemed to me that this alone might give us some hope for success, if true.

'It is, though barely,' Tor confirmed. 'It moves northward towards Carmalt, the present capital of the Kingdoms. If that city falls, and the King is taken captive, I fear it would spell the end for the Vohung peoples. It is for that reason that we are attempting to delay the army in Benza for as long as possible. Riders have been sent to Carmalt and a dozen other cities to the north and west to summon aid, but you yourself know how our reports of the invasion were met at court. If your own plans to defeat this army do not succeed, I think nothing will.'

I could see that Tor was virtually dead on his feet and I decided to save any further debate until after he had had a chance to rest. I left him in the hands of the villagers and went to see how Celebe was faring.

I found her in one of the tents, being ministered to by a group of P'nad's people and with Ailette kneeling beside her and apparently speaking with her in hushed tones. In the confines of the tent, I realized that Celebe's wounds were even more serious than they had appeared outside: I could smell something that I took to be the stink of gangrene.

I moved slowly towards her, not wishing to intrude on what appeared to be a very private conversation, but as soon as Celebe saw me she beckoned weakly for me to approach. I kneeled beside Ailette and stared into the ruby lenses that served Celebe as eyes. The light that had always seemed to shine within them was almost gone.

'David,' Celebe gasped, grasping my arm in a grip that was unbreakable despite her obvious weakness, 'I have met the real enemy, and I know his measure. He is not invincible, but to destroy him will demand of one of your followers the ultimate sacrifice. One of them must become a Knight of the Thirteen.'

I stared at her silently, not understanding what she was saying.

'The Librarian,' she said, obviously sensing my confusion, 'he is your enemy, not the puppet Droxus nor his bully Hol Krexus. It is the Librarian you must defeat, and to do it someone must take up the Y'nys armour after my death.'

'You won't die,' Ailette said, her tone giving the lie to her words.

'Hush, child,' Celebe said, not unkindly, 'nothing can save me now. But the armour will repair itself, and only with it can you defeat the man who calls himself Rohc Vahnn.'

'The Librarian?' I prompted. She nodded. 'Celebe,' I said, 'what do you know of him?'

'All,' she said, her voice fading to an almost inaudible whisper. 'He passed me in a street in the city of Coiz, so close I could have touched him, and he did not see me. I surprised him; I accessed the information storage in the Y'nys armour he wears beneath his robes. I discovered the means to destroy him, but I underestimated his strength. He—'

Her body convulsed in pain, her teeth bared and grinding together as the spasm intensified and then slowly passed. Her grip on my arm became slack, and for a moment I thought she was dead. Then she reached up and grasped my tunic, pulling herself up to face me.

'Your woman lives, David,' she said, her voice a quavering whisper, 'and is safe. They fear her, after what happened over the Valley. The Librarian is no fool. He knows the power of the gods. But he knows, too, how fickle they are, and because he has defeated me – their emissary – he believes they will not aid you in defeating him. But he is wrong, David. The gods favour you; that I have lived to pass on what I have learned is proof of this. Do not lose faith, do not . . .'

She sagged back, her hand falling to the bed. One of P'nad's people pushed me aside and bent over her, but neither Ailette nor I needed anyone to confirm what we already knew. Celebe had breathed her last.

I arose slowly; somehow, Celebe's death seemed even more terrible at that moment than the destruction of Benza. There was an immediacy, a personal aspect to it that struck to the heart of my belief in the rightness of what I was doing. Was any cause worth the loss of a single life? It seemed to me that with the stakes we were all playing for I should have been able to answer that question in an instant. The fact that I couldn't frightened me very badly.

Ailette was standing at my side, and I was startled to see tears pouring down her cheeks, tears not merely of grief but of total anguish.

'I was so wrong about her,' she sobbed in French. 'We should have been friends. And now—'

I pulled her into my arms and held her while she wept uncontrollably against me. I wondered what Celebe had said to her in the moments before I had arrived that could have so changed Ailette's feelings for her.

In the tent behind me I heard the footsteps of several people. I turned my head and saw P'nad and Hareg and Tor Taskus and the leader of the Uhrgratz villagers and about half a dozen others all crammed into the tent entrance. They were staring at Celebe's body, some of them visibly shaken by what they saw. I knew that to many of the people in our camp Celebe's status as a Knight of the Thirteen had made her seem as immortal as the gods themselves.

'Tor,' I said, 'if you're up to it, we need to hear everything you can tell us.' I glanced at Hareg. 'We are out of time,' I told him. 'How soon can the airship be launched?'

He studied his feet for several long seconds, then looked up at me – it was the first time, I think, that he had ever done so without resentment in his eyes.

'If we complete some of the non-essential work during the flight,' he said, 'we can be ready in three days.'

'I had not intended taking any of the Ladden on the flight,' I told Hareg. 'My agreement with your people . . .'

'Shaw,' Hareg said, 'I will be blunt. I care nothing for your agreement or your mission. But I am Ladden, and the work we do here is the work we were born for. Many of my people have expressed a desire to accompany you – not to fight, though if it came to it we are not cowards – but to observe their creation in operation. I, myself, would welcome such a chance. And, if you so chose, we could be disembarked after the work was done and before you went into battle – although a handful of us would prefer to remain on board even then, should maintenance be required that only we could undertake.' He held out his hands in a gesture I had seen his people use when negotiating with potential clients for their work. 'The offer is there, Shaw,' he said. 'How do you respond?'

'I accept it gladly,' I said, without hesitation.

Hareg nodded, and turned and left the tent.

I gently eased Ailette from my arms.

'I must go,' I said softly.

'I understand,' she said.

'You should try to rest,' I told her.

'I will stay by Celebe,' she replied. She looked up at me. 'She will have to be . . . prepared. And – her armour will have to be removed if someone else is to take it up.'

That was a prospect to which I did not look forward with any pleasure. That it was a necessity seemed certain, but the price it would exact from whoever took it up was too terrible to contemplate. Celebe had not spoken lightly when she said that to become a Knight of the Thirteen Gods was to abandon one's humanity.

'Do nothing until I return,' I said to Ailette.

She nodded, and I left the tent with Tor and P'nad and the others.

Chapter 42

TOR TASKUS'S TALE

Tor's story was one of incredible good fortune wedded to ever-present disaster. The small troop of men he had led out of Benza towards Sjaadok had sighted Droxus's airship and recognized it immediately for what it was – the 'giant lalantha' of which the madman had spoken. Realizing that they could not outrace it back to Benza they had pressed on; Tor had been certain that ground troops were marching through the Kingdoms and intended to confirm his suspicions before returning to the city.

He had encountered the army of the Librarian, Rohc Vahnn, two days later. Only his own familiarity with the territory through which it was advancing had enabled him and his men to avoid capture or death. It was at this point that Tor had made what I knew must have been one of the hardest choices of his life. Every fibre of his being, every ounce of training he had ever had, was telling him to get back to Benza and join his people in the defence of their city. But Tor was an intelligent man, and had not become a high-ranking Captain simply on the strength of his sword arm. The city of Benza alone, even with a full garrison, could not hope to match the manpower of the invading army; even leaving aside the threat of Droxus's airship an extra dozen men were not going to tip the balance. And so Tor had done the only logical and sensible thing in the circumstances. He had split his force and sent his men in twos to Benza's other cities to summon reinforcements. The idea of going outside Benza for help did not at that time occur to him – intelligent or not, Tor was still a slave to his upbringing.

The call to arms resulted in several hundred men taking the field in defence of their Kingdom, but by the time they reached the city it was encircled by Vahnn's army. They succeeded in splitting the army's attention, and probably bought Benza a few precious days, but in the end their efforts could only delay the inevitable. Benza was overrun, more than half of her warriors slain, and the city put to the torch.

But, as Tor had said, the fight was far from over. Fleeing their homes, the city's Captains had set up hundreds of war camps throughout the Kingdom, arming the peasants and promoting long-standing militia men to the ranks of full soldiers in order that the peasant bands should not want for leaders.

When Celebe arrived in the Kingdoms she was almost immediately confronted by one of these bands, only her status as a Knight of the Thirteen granting her unquestioned admittance to their company. She travelled with them for several days, until a chance encounter with another group, this one led by a Captain, revealed to her that Tor Taskus still lived. Because I had been Tor's friend I might, in relating my adventures to Celebe, have made him out to be a more important figure in Benza than he actually was. Perhaps because of this, or perhaps for personal reasons that we would now never know, Celebe asked to be taken to Tor, or at least given directions to his camp. The Captain of whom she made this request was unwilling to divulge matters of a military nature, even to someone like Celebe, but he readily agreed to provide her with an escort.

And thus it was that Celebe and Tor Taskus met, a meeting that was, in many ways, a crucial turning point in the affairs of Benza. Each was possessed of knowledge that, once pooled, pointed clearly to a means of saving the Kingdoms. A joint attack, comprising our airship on one side and Tor's army on the other, if timed correctly, could bring this war to a swift and unequivocal conclusion.

The remains of the city of Benza, now deserted by the enemy army, were still being used as a meeting place for the leaders of Benza's army, and it was there that Tor and Celebe headed. Tor's idea was that they would put their joint plan before his leaders and then he would accompany Celebe back to Uhrgratz. This wasn't strictly necessary, but I think Tor was eager to see me again, and to see for himself the work we had done.

Everything went according to plan until their route to Uhrgratz took them through the city of Coiz in Grammenia, the southernmost of the Vohung Kingdoms. They had planned a brief overnight stop in Coiz, which is a small city by Vohung standards with little in the way of strategic importance – for which reason, I presumed, it had escaped a visitation by Rohc Vahnn and his army. It was therefore a major source of astonishment to both Tor and Celebe when, making their way to a boarding house that had been recommended by the keeper of the tavern in which they had eaten supper, they were passed in the street by Vahnn himself. He had been, according to Tor, deep in contemplation, and had not seen Celebe standing motionless in the shadowy doorway of a house she and Tor had been passing at that moment.

(Although Tor could not know it, I believed this to have been the moment Celebe had spoken of on her deathbed, the moment when she had used her armour to access the data storage in Vahnn's own armour and thus learned the secret of defeating him.)

Vahnn had seen Tor, but apparently had not ascribed any importance to his being there. This was not too surprising, since the Benzan Captain was now wearing the uniform and armour of a common Grammenian soldier, even having abandoned his beloved sword in favour of the long knife more common in those lands.

No sooner had he passed than, according to Tor, Celebe had seemed to go mad. She leaped from her place of concealment and cried something that Tor could not understand, and then the alley in which they stood was full of lightning and fire and a sound like the clashing of a thousand swords. Tor had been flung aside by the display of energy and almost knocked unconscious, so ferocious had been the force that struck him.

Shaking his head, he had looked up in time to see both Vahnn and Celebe awash with multicoloured bands of energy, the Knight apparently directing the flow of power around her while the Librarian writhed in agony on the receiving end of her attack. Tor had had scant prior experience of the powers possessed by Librarians, and certainly had never seen a battle such as this before. Yet even to his untrained eye it was clear that Celebe was winning, for the Librarian was offering no resistance whatsoever. He was therefore amazed when, an instant later, and with no visible warning, the tide of battle suddenly turned in Vahnn's favour. The energy that had been lashing him so mercilessly was flung back at Celebe, the alley echoing with a crack of thunder, and her armour was rent open in a dozen places, the terrible forces striking through the fissures to ravage the flesh beneath.

In an instant, the battle was over, and the alley was plunged back into darkness and a silence through which Tor could hear his own blood pounding in his ears.

The Librarian now seemed totally unaffected by the duel, although in its earlier stages he had clearly been suffering. He walked calmly to where Celebe lay moaning on the cobbles of the alley, her armour streaked with blood, and looked down at her briefly.

Then, as though she were of no consequence, he had turned on his heel and walked away.

Tor paused in his narrative to down a goblet of wine, the first he had had since beginning. Clearly the memory of that battle had shaken him.

Staring into the empty goblet, he said, 'I could scarcely believe it when I discovered that Celebe yet lived. I tried to bind her wounds, but her armour offered no purchase to bandages and in the end I was forced to abandon the attempt. She seemed driven by a need to return here, and I think it was that need that kept her alive throughout the remainder of the journey.' He smiled grimly. 'It was no easy ride either, my friend. We lost our gryllup to bandits in the foothills outside the Asmina Valley, though two of them did not live to enjoy their victory and I think a third may have been denied the chance of future progeny. Yet it was fortunate for us that they had not struck sooner, for if they had I think we would not now be here. The walk to the nearest Library, hidden in the mountains of the Valley's northernmost boundary, almost killed her; we had to rest for many hours before she dared use the device to transport us to this land, and when she did so she emerged unconscious and bleeding badly from many of her wounds. I tended her as best I could, knowing from what she had said that without her to guide me I should never survive the journey through the swamps of that region.' He sighed and accepted another drink. 'She has the heart of Gazig, that one,' he avowed. 'Twice I thought her dead, only to have her claw her way back to life. When she eventually regained consciousness I all but carried her through the swamps. It was a journey of four days from there to here.'

He sagged back on the cushions he had been sitting on, as though completing the story had drained him of whatever strength he had had left.

I took the flagon of wine and poured myself a generous measure.

Celebe had had the opportunity to go anywhere once she had reached the first Library. She could have gone to the city of Asmina, where surely she could have been made well. Perhaps she had not trusted the Thirteen to do so, yet even with her life at stake she had not taken the risk. Instead, she had come here, to be certain her message of hope was delivered.

I drained the goblet, my hand shaking. It seemed to me that I owed Celebe something, something that I could not now repay. Yet there was still one last thing I could do for her, however little it might have been under the circumstances and, rising slowly to my feet, I set out to do it.

Chapter 43

CELEBE

To describe what happened next is something for which I have little stomach. Yet as a testimony to Celebe's bravery, and to the price she was prepared to pay in order to be able to return even a few of her fellow humans to their own lands, it is something that very much needs to be told.

I reached the tent in which she still lay and found Ailette kneeling at her side.

The Knight's Y'nys armour was now cold and grey, but for all its lifeless appearance it was clearly far from inert, since the terrible rents that had marred its surface had now closed, leaving only whitish seams to mark their passing.

The armour had changed in other ways. It had split open along its outer edges, dividing much as conventional armour would have done. It could now, I assumed, be removed.

Ailette looked up at me.

'I will take her place,' she said simply.

I was taken aback. This was something I had never anticipated.

'I can't ask you to do that,' I protested.

I had, in fact, intended to take Celebe's place myself. I was the

395

only one to whom the mission was important enough for such a sacrifice – or so I had thought.

'You have not asked it,' Ailette said. 'I know what is in your mind, David, but it is not the path for you. Your destiny lies a different way.'

I looked at her speechlessly.

'Come,' she said, 'let us remove the armour.'

I watched in silence as the young French girl addressed herself to the task. For all her obvious trepidation, her hands were steady as she reached for Celebe's right ankle. 'The . . . feet first,' she said. 'Celebe told me—'

I put my hand over hers. She flashed me a look of gratitude as together we eased the covering from the Knight's right foot. It came away easily enough, revealing skin beneath that was ghostly pale, almost as translucent as the armour itself had formerly been. Although the sight was not a pretty one, it gave no indication of the horror to come.

We removed the armour from her right shin next, and the sight that greeted us caused us both to step back in surprise and dismay. I cast a fearful glance into the segment of armour I now held, and felt my flesh crawl at what I saw there. The inside of each half was not smooth as the foot coverings had been; each section had two protuberances, crystalline and razor-sharp, that, when the armour was in place, would have pierced the lower leg right through the bone. The protuberances had come free of Celebe's body with no hint of resistance, and the wounds they left were clean and neat and utterly horrible. I heard Ailette sob as she stared at the pale expanse of Celebe's calf, the wasted muscles and the inch-long incisions.

We moved woodenly to the larger sections on her thigh, and found similar disfigurements, this time three to each leg. The protuberances were each about six inches long; they had passed almost completely through each leg.

The armour on her arms and body told a similar tale, her torso pierced by a dozen crystal knives that were far longer than those in her extremities. Her heart and lungs and most of her other vital organs had been cut through by the protuberances, the most wicked-looking of which had severed her sternum in two places.

Her spine had been cut through once for each of the major vertebral regions.

But the worst we had inadvertently saved till last. When Celebe's helm was removed we found it to be full of crystal knives, all pointing downward. Without the helm, there was little or nothing of the skull beneath that could be recognized.

Ailette collapsed at the side of the bed upon which Celebe's pitiful remains lay, her body shaking with great sobs, her head buried in her arms.

I heard movement at the tent entrance.

'Stay out!' I yelled, my voice not steady; I didn't know who was there, and I didn't care. I wanted no one to see Celebe as she was at that moment, so . . . naked.

Ailette's voice, trembling and small, came to me from behind her arms.

'Quickly, David,' she sobbed, 'before I lose my courage.'

'Ailette, no!' I cried. 'I can't let you—'

'Help me, David,' she pleaded, 'I have to do it – for her. But I can't do it alone—'

'She wouldn't want—'

'She understood,' Ailette said, 'and now I do too. The greater the gain, the higher the price. The gods do not bestow their armour lightly, but Celebe was worthy of it, and I am to be her successor.' She looked up at me. 'Please, David,' she whispered, 'don't let me disappoint her.'

I wiped tears from my eyes and heard myself say, 'Get out of those clothes.'

She was naked an instant later, shivering in the half-light inside the tent even though the air was warm.

'The helm first,' she said.

'Are you sure?' I asked.

'Celebe told me,' she said. 'Without the helm in place, fitting the rest of the armour would simply kill me.'

I picked up the broad, parabolic shell with its monstrous contents. Only now did I notice the multicoloured lights that danced inside it.

'Will it—' I began, '—will it hurt?'

'Let's find out,' she said.

I lifted the helm over her head. For an instant – the last instant – our eyes met. Ailette leaned impulsively forward and kissed me clumsily on the lips.

'I loved you,' she said in a rush.

'I—'

'Now, David,' she urged, 'in the gods' names do it swiftly.'

I lowered the helm over her head. There was no resistance, but the air was suddenly filled with the sweet scent of honey. Ailette gasped, and the helm became warm in my hands. Its surface sparkled with buried light, and then it was again the silvery, translucent crystal that it had been when first I had seen it.

'David,' she gasped, 'David, is *that* you?'

'Of course it's me,' I said, a little afraid. 'What makes you doubt it?'

'You're . . . you're beautiful!' she said. 'I never dreamed, never imagined . . . It's like I've never seen you before, but only a shadow of your true self. David, if only I could tell you . . .'

'Ailette—' I said.

'No, David,' she said, 'not Ailette. Celebe.'

'Celebe is dead!' I snapped.

'Chantal Clavalle is dead,' Ailette said. 'Chantal Clavalle, whose every thought and memory I now share. Celebe is not one person, David, she is a composite entity, and Ailette Legendre is now a part of her. While ever I wear this armour it will be Ailette whose consciousness drives it, but as an entity I *am* Celebe.'

I stared at her in a mixture of horror and wonder. If what she said was true then both she and Celebe – or rather, she and Chantal – had achieved virtual immortality.

'Help me with the rest of the armour,' said the new Celebe. 'The helm is drawing my life from me too quickly. My mortality must be sealed within the Y'nys and preserved.'

We fitted the breast- and back-plates into place, the wicked projections entering her body as painlessly as had those in the helm. The scent of honey intensified, becoming almost overpowering. The former Celebe, Chantal Clavalle, had possessed a fuller figure than Ailette, yet the armour moulded itself effortlessly to the contours of its new wearer. It was slightly disconcerting to see this incarnation of the Knight of the Thirteen standing before me, her eyes barely level with my own, whereas before they had stared over the top of my head.

In moments Celebe was encased in her Y'nys crystal, and although the operation had left me feeling strangely troubled and not a little queasy she seemed delighted with the transformation.

She looked slowly around the tent.

'So,' she breathed, 'this is how the gods see the world.'

'They aren't gods,' I said quietly.

'Perhaps not,' Celebe agreed absently, 'but neither are they men.'

I looked down at the sad thing that had once been a French woman named Chantal Clavalle. It was difficult to be sure, but I thought that she might have been beautiful.

'The others must see her,' Celebe said.

'No,' I said.

'They will honour her,' Celebe said.

'They will pity her,' I said. I didn't want that.

'Yes, they will,' Celebe agreed. 'But the pity will pass, and then they will think of what she has done and they will celebrate her bravery and her sacrifice. But they cannot do that unless they see her as she is. They must know the full price that has been paid for their victory.'

I looked at her sharply.

'Is victory that certain, then?' I demanded.

She laughed.

'We speak of different things,' she said. Then, in a voice that was undeniably that of Ailette, 'I am sorry, David. My perceptions have changed so rapidly that I am losing sight of why I have done this, why you are here. Your victory is not yet assured, but all the elements necessary to it are now in place. It is for you to put them to their best use.' She glanced at Chantal's body. 'Let them see her, David,' she said quietly. 'She deserves to have the extent of her sacrifice known.'

I nodded, and together we moved slowly towards the entrance of the tent.

Chapter 44

FLIGHT OF THE *MARINER*

On the morning of the third day following Chantal's death we began boarding the airship.

Much had been accomplished during those three days, and I think everyone in the camp – those who would crew the ship and those who would be left behind – felt a sense of grim optimism for the outcome of our mission.

The Ladden, and those of P'nad's people and the villagers who had sufficient skill to aid them, had worked night and day to complete enough of the vessel to make it airworthy, and although it remained very basic in some respects there was no denying that they had lived up to Hareg's promise.

Those of us not involved in the building work, principally P'nad, Tor, Celebe, the ship's crew, and myself, spent our days in ever more intensive training and our nights in long planning sessions.

According to Celebe, the reason for her inability to defeat Rohc Vahnn had been simply the relative strengths of their armour. The armour of a Knight was the finest that Y'nys technology could produce, but because the Y'nys had never been a warlike people – making them, perhaps, unique in the planet's history – the armour had no overt offensive capability. It did have an almost unlimited ability to defend its wearer, and a capacity for the manipulation of power sources external to itself. It was this capability that Celebe had used on Vahnn. She had tapped into the power of his own armour and used it against him. Vahnn's armour, like that of all Librarians, differed from Celebe's in two major respects. Firstly, it possessed a wide range of offensive capabilities – some of which I had experienced personally – and, secondly, it was made of a slightly different type of Y'nys crystal. This variant was less sophisticated than the armour of a Knight, but had a much greater capacity for storing and directing energy. Had this not been the case, Vahnn would now be dead. Unfortunately for Celebe, although her attack upon him had been perfectly timed and executed, the energies she had unleashed from within his own armour had been too potent for her own Y'nys to withstand. Vahnn had survived by the simple expedient of actually increasing the potency of Celebe's own attack and then waiting for her armour to overload from the strain. As a display of his own personal strength and the extent to which he was prepared to go to ensure victory it was both impressive and daunting. Such a man would never concede defeat; only with his death would this war be ended.

I had puzzled over the apparent extent of Celebe's knowledge of Vahnn's affairs; her brief contact with him had left her knowing far more than would have seemed possible. The explanation in itself revealed another potential weakness in Vahnn's armour. The Y'nys crystal's most basic function is to act as a data storage system. Unless specifically designed to perform this task in a set manner – as in the case of the Libraries – it will simply record every bit of sensory information to which it is exposed until its memory capacity is full. Since a block of Y'nys no larger than a house-brick can store upwards of a hundred years' worth of input this meant that Vahnn's armour contained a complete record of his entire life from the day he had first donned it. That Vahnn himself was unaware of this fact seemed obvious – had he known it, he would surely have obliterated Celebe completely when he had had the chance, for he would certainly have known that she must have accessed his armour's data. That he did not do so suggested to me – and to

Celebe – that this aspect of his armour's powers was one of which he knew nothing.

It was when she gained access to all this information that Celebe learned the one thing that boded ill for our plans, for it not only served to explain an old mystery but also hinted at powers that Vahnn possessed for which we would have no counter or defence. Somehow, and even Celebe could find no explanation of how, Vahnn had discovered how to use his armour to duplicate the Libraries' instantaneous travel facility; this meant that he could, in effect, transport himself – at will – to any point on the continent, possibly on the whole planet. How developed this ability was we could not determine, nor if it was limited to Vahnn himself or if other Librarians knew how to utilize it. I thought this last unlikely – Sonder, for example, had shown no evidence of possessing such a power. That Celebe had been able to gain only an inkling of this talent of Vahnn's concerned me greatly; if his armour could hide *this* fact from her – even if only partially – what else could it hide, and what else had it hidden? It cast a shadow of doubt over all her conclusions about the man, and this late in the day doubts were something we had no use for.

I wondered about Vahnn's presence in Coiz at the same time that Celebe and Tor were there. Had it been mere coincidence? The question was fatuous. So what had he been doing there? I recalled the meeting I had had with the intelligence in Asmina, and the things Celebe had said about the 'gods' and their non-linear view of time. Were they playing with me? Or did Vahnn himself have some access to their perceptions, allowing him to intercept elements of my plan and undermine them? Yet if that were so, why had he not simply come to Uhrgratz and destroyed us all?

I slept badly during those three nights, my mind tormented by doubts and uncertainties. I was careful to keep the majority of them to myself, for whatever problems lay ahead of us we were now committed to a course of action, and sowing seeds of defeat among my own people was an added burden that this mission did not need.

There were other things to occupy our minds during those few days, some only peripherally connected to our mission, yet important enough in their own ways. Chantal's remains were carefully prepared for her funeral, which Ailette, in her new identity, advised us should be in the form of a cremation. Whether this suggestion came from a Knightly tradition or from her new access to Chantal's own memories I did not know. Many impromptu meetings seemed to be taking place among the various social groupings in the village, a great many, it seemed, being initiated by the villagers themselves. The death of Chantal, I knew, had affected the people of Uhrgratz more than anyone else in our camp, for they had known her long before we had and in rather a different capacity. The final upshot of all these gatherings was that the strongest of the villagers were presented to me for inclusion in my crew. My initial reaction was one of surprise, and not a little reluctance to accept their offer. They remained to me a largely unknown quantity, and I did not want to jeopardize the mission by having on board the ship people whose behaviour I could not predict and whose motives I only vaguely understood. My reservations were overturned, however, when the existing crew gave the villagers their unqualified support. In the face of such unanimous approval I could only accede to the request, and to be perfectly honest I did so with a sigh of relief. Even with all P'nad's people pressed into service we were going to be running the ship on what amounted to a skeleton crew by the demands of the task ahead of us. With these new recruits, however, I would feel a lot more comfortable about the way I had decided to split the workload. I had decided some time earlier to work on a three-watch rota, with my best men on the command watch for when the actual battle took place. These extra hands would help fill the gaps with which my schedule would otherwise have been littered.

And thus it was that on the morning of the day Hareg had promised me for departure we began to assemble beneath the hull of the ship where it hung some fifty metres above our heads. No matter how much 'ballast' we added, the vessel could never actually be brought to ground, possibly due to the mass of the hull and drive train it was now carrying. That it could, theoretically, be brought lower was certain – otherwise it could never have been buried – but to do so would have meant using heavier ballast than our vessel could, at present, accommodate.

Carrying last-minute provisions, tools, weapons and, in some cases, half-finished sections of the vessel's interior, we all ascended the single tower which the Ladden had constructed beneath the ship in order to make their own tasks easier. This tower, broad and largely hollow, had been used to ferry raw materials up from the village and also the completed but sectioned components of the drive. It had taken the Ladden days to build, and at the time I had protested its necessity; but it had, I had been forced to concede, saved much more time than its building had consumed.

Most of the Ladden were accompanying us on the first leg of our journey in the hope that they could complete those portions of the ship that were still unfinished. We would deposit all but a handful of them in Benza before pursuing Vahnn's ship in earnest; that handful, volunteers all, would be my 'engineers', and would stay with the ship until victory – or defeat – was ours.

The ship itself was a fascinating mixture of the Ladden aesthetic and brutal necessity. The basic shape of the hull was a copy of the curved 'wings' of the frame, but lower and shallower. It had a single interior deck that would be used on this journey for every conceivable purpose other than flying and fighting. There had been no time to divide it into cabins, nor for the building of furniture or stowage space. Everyone had brought a sleeping mat on board with him and his personal 'space' would be encompassed by it. The upper deck, which was partially open but whose sides curved up and over to afford protection to those seated at the rowing benches, was designed as both command centre and launching platform for the two smaller airframes that we had brought on board. One of these was rigged with a large, mastless sail, an improved version of the one Ailette had flown some weeks before. Steering it required a lot of diving around on its narrow deck and the manipulation of two heavy sail boards: I was not looking forward to the task I had set myself where it was concerned. The second frame was totally bare except for a pair of looped ropes that had been tied around its upper wings. It had been brought aboard at Celebe's request, and although I had some suspicion of her plans for it I had not pressed her.

We spent a good hour getting the feel of the ship. We'd all been on board it many times before, but today the atmosphere was different. Today marked the end of all the planning and waiting, and the beginning of the end for either Rohc Vahnn or the Thek continent.

I let each watch take ten or fifteen minutes on the main deck, the oarsmen getting the feel of the mechanism for which they had trained for so long, the hortators practising their beats on the leather-topped drums, the Ladden inspecting the tool pits that lined the deck for running repairs in flight, and our hand-picked archers trying out the arrow ports that lined the bulwark around the upper deck. I would have liked a couple of dozen muskets and some kegs of powder, but the only firearms within a hundred miles were the pair of ceremonial muskets belonging to the people of Uhrgratz. They were aboard, but since only Celebe was versed in their operation they were not likely to see much action. I intended to have her train two of our men during the flight, but I wasn't setting too much store by them where the actual battle was concerned.

When the command watch finally took its place on deck I ascended the sterncastle and surveyed my crew. The second and third watches were lined up around the edges of the deck. P'nad was commander of the second watch, which meant that when we went into battle he would take charge of the two-thirds of the crew who were free for combat. The third watch was under the command of S'nam; on the sterncastle with me stood Tor Taskus, who was not actually a member of the crew – I would not have felt comfortable having Tor under my command – and Celebe, whose status remained necessarily vague. With us were our steersman and Hareg, who was in command of all the Ladden on board. Hareg was one of those who had volunteered to remain with the ship during the battle, and although I still felt a degree of resentment both towards him and from him I was glad to have him with us.

Standing looking down at the sea of faces below me I suddenly realized that they probably expected me to say something at as momentous a juncture as this. I wondered what would be appropriate, and expected that whatever it was I'd only think of it an hour from now.

I saw a couple of enigmatic glances passed between members of the crew and then the hortator of the command watch, the man whom I had first elevated to such a task, stood up and faced me.

'If you will permit it, Shaw,' he said, 'we have given your vessel a name.' He looked around a little sheepishly, adding, 'We did not think it right to embark on a mission such as this in a soulless machine. We think the name is an appropriate one, but the final decision we leave to you.'

It had never occurred to me to call the airship anything, but knowing that the Ladden were artists first and craftsmen second I thought I saw their hand in this. I had no objections to such a notion, and I told the hortator that I would gladly sanction any name the crew were happy with.

'Then the name we have chosen will surely meet with your approval,' he said, 'for it was from you we gained it. You have called us your Marines, and we chose to know this ship as the *Mariner.*'

As though on cue, two men stepped forward with a long plaque that had been secreted beneath their rowing bench. Emblazoned across it, in cursive Vinh script, was the single word which in English would have been read as 'Mariner'.

'This pleases me greatly,' I told them all.

A great cheer went up, and the plaque was hoisted into place at the rear of the sterncastle.

Recognizing that this little ceremony had been far better than any pep talk from me I wasted not another second in getting under way.

'Cast off mooring lines,' I called.

Men moved to the task, and in seconds the ship was beginning to drift slowly away from the tower beneath it.

'One-quarter beat,' I told the hortator.

'Ready oars!' he bellowed.

Men grasped their oars firmly and waited for his next command.

'On the third beat!' he yelled.

His hammers began to beat the time, and on the third stroke the oarsmen drew back, heels straining against footrests and muscles bunching. The ship shuddered, and every throat let out a little gasp as the sound of her propellers came to our ears.

'Hard about,' I told the steersman. 'Set a course for Benza.'

He spun the huge wheel that controlled the ship's steer boards and the massive bulk of the vessel tilted almost imperceptibly as it began to turn.

I heard muted cheers from beyond the confines of the ship's deck and knew that they came from those we had left behind in the village. I felt a smile come to my lips.

'One-half beat,' I told the hortator.

He picked up the pace and the oarsmen matched him perfectly.

The ship straightened its course as the steersman aimed us northward.

'Ship ballast,' I called.

Large wooden capstans were turned at eight locations along the deck and the stone weights that had anchored us were winched up into the lower deck. The airframe rose smoothly, the wind ruffling the hair of everyone on deck.

'Three-quarter beat,' I said.

The ship seemed almost to leap forward, its beams shuddering with the passage of air.

'Full beat,' I said.

The hortator called out, 'Full beat on three!' and I saw men move their lips silently as they counted the beats.

Wood groaned as the oarsmen took the ship to its maximum cruising speed; I smelled scorched timber as the two shafts that turned our propellers began to heat up.

'Hareg,' I said, 'have your people watch the drive constantly until we're sure of exactly how it will perform.'

He nodded and moved quickly down to where the Ladden of this watch stood on the main deck.

'P'nad,' I called, 'I want everyone below decks who is not on this watch. We all need to get as much rest as possible.'

P'nad waved his acknowledgement and the men of the second and third watches filed slowly below decks.

Tor leaned on my shoulder.

'You seem to have everything under control here,' he said, 'so I think I'll join your men below.'

I grinned at him.

'If I've fooled you so completely,' I said, 'then I *must* have fooled everyone else.'

He laughed and headed towards the stairwell at the rear of the sterncastle.

I looked down at the oarsmen: they were still pulling to the maximum beat. I saw sweat on faces and naked chests, and knew that not a few hands would be nursing blisters in a very short while. One or two of the men cast me questioning glances; maximum cruising speed could not be maintained for long. I stared back at them for minute after minute. The beat of the great drum was as regular as the pendulum of a clock.

Presently, I said, 'Hortator—'

'Shaw—?' came back the reply; the man sounded as breathless as the oarsmen.

'Attack speed,' I said.

He almost missed his beat. His recovery was a masterpiece of self-control.

'On the third beat!' he yelled.

The oarsmen picked up the pace; the ship groaned and creaked around me; I could hear some of the oarsmen gasping. The wind was flapping my garments around me, bringing moisture to my eyes.

I leaned on the short railing that overlooked the main deck, not hurrying.

'Hortator—' I said.

'Shaw—?' he gasped.

'Ram speed,' I said.

'On the third beat!' he bellowed breathlessly. 'One . . . two . . . three!'

The beat of the drum was now that of a heart on the point of seizure. In thirty seconds the first man to succumb to the pace collapsed over his oar with a gasp; ten seconds later, almost a quarter of the men had ceased to row; some looked at me with hate in their eyes. I let the beat go on; in a minute, barely half of the oarsmen were still pulling. The ship was shaking like a leaf in a hurricane, and the lack of hands on the oars was making it impossible to maintain ram speed.

'All stop,' I called to the hortator.

'Stop rowing!' he yelled, a command that, under the circumstances, brought an involuntary smile to my lips. I smothered it quickly.

I made my way down to the main deck. My popularity, I judged, had known better days.

'Well rowed,' I said to a man who had been one of the last to quit.

'Well rowed,' I said to a man who had been one of the first to quit.

'Well rowed,' I said to all of them.

I turned to the hortator. He was red and sweating.

'Excellent timekeeping,' I told him.

I stood on the raised walk between the banks of oars; beneath it, visible through the widely-spaced boards, were the twin driveshafts. They were still turning under their own momentum. Coming to all stop from ram speed, it would take minutes for them to wind down.

Most of the rowers were still looking at me with puzzlement or, at worst, resentment, but not quite so much hatred.

'In ten days, if all goes well,' I said, 'we engage the enemy. When that time comes this watch will take the oars. You men will fly this ship into battle. And I have absolute faith in every one of you.'

I walked up and down a bit, hearing rasping breaths being drawn around me. The men were all strong – ex-slaves, villagers, and a couple of iconoclastic Ladden – and although I had just pushed them to their limits they were recovering quickly.

'But—' I said, letting the word hang until every pair of eyes was on me, 'the training you had before today was only the beginning. From now until the day we engage the enemy you must train and train and when you think you can train no more you must train again. Today you have worked hard. I'd like to make a prediction: in seven days' time, you will remember today and be amazed at the change those seven days have made.'

I walked back to the hortator's place just below the sterncastle.

'You are all Marines,' I told them, 'and this is *your* ship. You named her, and I know you will do her justice.'

I could feel the ship starting to drift slightly; it had lost its forward momentum and the cross-wind was catching it.

'Shall we rest a while longer,' I asked, 'or shall we row?'

'Row!' someone shouted.

'Ram speed all the way to Benza!' another optimist offered.

Everyone laughed.

'One-quarter beat,' I told the hortator. 'Increase to half at your discretion.'

I ascended the sterncastle as the quarter beat began; behind me, I heard a couple of men in the front rows urging the timekeeper to go faster.

Chapter 45

CONFERENCE IN THE RUINS

Time passed quickly in the days that followed, for there was much work to occupy the time of every man on board.

A friendly rivalry sprang up between the three watches, with each trying to outdo the others in their rowing practice. The command watch took an early lead in these contests and held it resolutely despite the best efforts of their fellows; this came as no surprise, of course, since I had placed the strongest men in this watch. The main aim of the contest, then, became a race for second place, and thanks to the efforts of P'nad and S'nam this seemed to change hands not merely daily but from one watch to the next. One side effect of this rivalry, unexpected but greatly welcomed, was that our average speed increased by over five miles per hour. This meant that we could now expect to sight Benza in less than six days, and probably engage Vahnn's ship in less than eight days.

(We could have cut this time in half – maybe even more – had we been able to run at full speed all the way. But wood is not metal, and it was necessary for us to give the drive regular rest periods, for cooling and shrinking. Thanks to the ceaseless work of Hareg and his people these rest periods grew fewer in number and shorter in duration as time went by, but we were never going to eliminate them entirely.)

The Ladden not directly involved with the drive system worked like demons during the voyage, completing their work on the hull and even finding time to section off the crew's quarters to afford everyone some measure of privacy. In an effort to maintain a relaxed and friendly attitude between everyone in the ship's complement I made sure that no one gained preferential treatment in this respect. I had no desire to see an 'officer class' élite spring up, still less for the crew to imagine that there was one. The *Mariner* had not been built to furnish me with a military career, but to accomplish a specific purpose. I did not expect even to be allowed to remain on this planet once the mission was accomplished, much less to be in a position of authority over its inhabitants.

Celebe was fairly uncommunicative during the journey, spending long hours in silent meditation. On the few occasions she could be drawn into conversation it was only on the most banal level, and presently I gave up the attempt. It came as a surprise, then, to find myself approached by her one night as I stood a late watch on the vessel's forecastle.

We were approaching the southern boundary of Benza now, and my watch crew needed only minimal overseeing at their rowing. The hortator kept up a steady three-quarter beat, but so practised had everyone become at their respective tasks by now that he actually beat only the first stroke, counting the second, third and fourth silently to himself. If we had to face the enemy tonight, I thought, we would be ready.

I was leaning over the handrail that circled the prow, gazing into the moonlit depths below, when I heard the sound of Y'nys-shod feet behind me.

I half-turned and said a casual hallo, not expecting any more than that in reply.

Instead, Celebe said, 'May I speak with you, David?' and the voice was Ailette's.

I turned my back to the railing and said, 'Of course. Is this the Knight of the Thirteen I am addressing, or my friend Ailette Legendre?'

Her lips smiled; I wondered if, behind their opaque triangular shields, her eyes joined in.

'We are both here, David,' she said softly, 'but it is principally as your friend that I wish to speak with you.'

'In that case,' I said, 'you have my undivided attention.'

She leaned on the railing at my side, gazing out into the darkness. Small sounds drifted up to us, the cries of night birds hunting their nocturnal prey, or occasionally the more distant noises of animals howling at the moons. What little of Ailette's expression I could see seemed, in that moment, very human.

'When this is over,' she said, 'and if we are still alive, I shall have to stay on this planet. I think I am right in saying that you would like to stay also.'

I said nothing. Ailette knew how I felt.

'What of your Mrs Catlin?' she asked. 'Do you think she would stay?'

I didn't know the answer to that. Mrs Catlin's motivations had seldom been clear to me.

'If she did not wish to stay,' said Ailette, 'would you remain without her?'

'Does that question even arise?' I asked. 'I thought the Thirteen had already ruled on that issue.'

'Hypothetically,' Ailette persisted, 'would you stay here without her?'

'I don't know,' I said. 'I don't think I would.'

'Then she means more to you than the kingdom we go to liberate,' Ailette said.

I frowned.

'Not exactly,' I said. 'It's just – I don't know; staying here without her just wouldn't seem . . . right.'

'Suppose,' Ailette said, 'you had to choose: save Mrs Catlin, or save Benza. Which would you choose?'

'That's idiotic,' I snapped. 'It couldn't possibly come to such a choice.'

'If it did,' Ailette said, 'which would you choose?'

'I couldn't make such a choice,' I said. 'No one could.'

'A true Benzan could,' Ailette said. 'With them, loyalty to one's city overrides all personal ties.'

'Then I guess I'll never make a true Benzan,' I said angrily. 'But under the circumstances that doesn't make much difference, does it?'

She straightened up beside me, and once again she was Celebe, Knight of the Temple of the Thirteen Gods.

'Thank you for your time, David,' she said. 'Good night.'

Without another word she turned and walked away, and I had the distinct and disturbing impression that something of significance had just happened.

I was sharing the early evening meal with some of the men from my watch and a few of those of the third watch when a lookout came charging down the ladder from the upper deck and announced breathlessly that Benza had been sighted on the horizon.

I arose slowly. Conscious of the eyes of my men on me, and knowing that the second watch still had over an hour left before going off duty, I said to the lookout, 'Please tell P'nad I shall join him on deck in a moment.'

The man nodded and ascended the ladder like a cat. He was an Uhrgratz villager, and all of them seemed to have uncanny climbing abilities. That was one of the reasons for employing them as lookouts, since such a task meant being willing to scramble out onto the outer extremity of the ship's two uppermost wings. (The wings were now equipped with a kind of rope ladder for this purpose, but it was a brave man who ventured up them without some kind of a safety line.)

To those of my watch seated around me I said, 'Rouse all the men. I don't anticipate trouble, but let's not be over-confident. Remain below decks until I call for you.'

Leaving them to their task, I ascended the ladder to the upper deck.

P'nad nodded to me as I joined him on the sterncastle and said, 'We are at three-quarter beat and should reach the city within the hour.'

'Bring us to one torbik,' I said, 'then slow to half and circle the city.'

I descended to the bulwark surrounding the rowing deck and

made my way forward. Ascending to the forecastle I stood in silence and watched as my city grew larger in the distance.

My city. I had known, of course, from Tor's description that the city had been badly damaged by Vahnn's army – that it had, in fact, been all but destroyed. But that knowledge had not prepared me for the actual sight of it now. Nothing, I think, could have prepared me for the sight that loomed so grimly before me.

As we came to within a torbik of the outer wall, P'nad turned the ship to port and began to circle. I covered my eyes briefly, scarcely able to bear what I was seeing. I felt a hand on my shoulder and turned with a start. Tor Taskus stood at my side, his face hard and set, but his eyes still holding a warmth that I wished I shared.

'Do not grieve, my friend,' he said. 'A city is only bricks and mortar without the hearts of men, and the hearts of the men of Benza shall yield only in death. When this fight is over, we shall rebuild, better than before. Or,' he added with a shrug, 'we will all be reunited in the halls of Gazig where the Lord of Blood will judge our efforts. I think he will be satisfied with the answers you and I shall give.'

I almost wished I shared Tor's fatalistic belief, but before I could answer him a call went up from the starboard lookout.

'A crowd is gathering in the city!' he called.

Catching P'nad's attention on the sterncastle I gave him the hand signal to take us down.

'Run out ballast!' he called.

He turned and said something to the steersman and the ship began to spiral downward towards the city. Leaning over the railing beneath which the hortator sat, P'nad gave the order to slow to quarter-speed.

We descended unhurriedly, trying to give the impression of being on a peaceful visit. I knew that Tor and Celebe had prepared the rulers of Benza for our visit, but after the Kingdom's previous experience of an airship I wanted to take no chances.

We came to a halt over what remained of the gate house in the outer curtain wall; it was the highest structure still standing, and would be useful to use as an anchor point.

Tor and I joined P'nad on the sterncastle. Celebe was already there, as were Hareg and S'nam.

To P'nad I said, 'I want you to keep a crew at the oars the whole time we're here. Vahnn's ship should be miles away right now, but he's surprised us too often in the past for us to be able to take that for granted. If he shows up, take no chances – this ship is our main weapon against him, and we can't afford to jeopardize it.' I turned to Celebe. 'I'd like you to remain on board,' I told her, '—unless you can give me a good reason for your doing otherwise.'

'I shall remain on board,' she said.

'Then Tor and I will go and confer with his people,' I told them all. 'We should be back before dawn, and all being well that's when we go after Vahnn.'

There were nods of approval all around so Tor and I headed below decks to the belly hatch through which we would descend to the city. Moments later, we were climbing slowly down a knotted rope towards a crowd of over a hundred heavily-armed men.

Despite the dubious glances our vessel was receiving Tor and I soon found ourselves getting a boisterously friendly greeting from the assembled soldiers and townspeople. I recognized a few of them, Captains I had known from so many months before and a few common soldiers, but the majority were strangers to me.

Guards were quickly posted below the *Mariner* and then Tor and I were led away to the command centre of Benza's scattered army. It proved to be a tavern within the outer ward of the castle, and although the ale was in short supply what there was was good. I felt a brief flash of nostalgia for that other tavern I had so often frequented in the middle ward, and I found myself wondering what had become of the girl who had worked there.

I was brought back to the realities of the present situation by the arrival of the man who was currently the acting ruler of the Kingdom of Benza. He was a man whom I had only met once before but whose power in the Kingdom was, at any time, second only to that of the Duke himself. This man was the Warlord of Benza, the supreme military head of her armed forces. Under any other circumstances than these his position was a purely advisory one, since his rank carried with it no executive authority. It was only when the Duke himself was physically incapable of leading his forces that the Warlord's role became an active one, and that usually only until the Duke's successor could be elevated to the position. I suspected that it had been centuries since a Vohung Warlord had actually had to lead an army in the field for more than a single engagement, but with Joshima and most of his family held hostage this was one Warlord who could remain in office for the duration of the war. Under any circumstances his task would have been an unenviable one; faced with a war such as this it was positively daunting.

The Warlord was a slightly-built man of medium height and with an unremarkable face. He was, I judged, perhaps sixty years old in earthly terms. His hair, which was cut very short, was white and was, perhaps, the most striking thing about him.

He sat down at the head of the long table around which we were gathered and the tavern was instantly cloaked in silence. However minor the impression the man himself may have created, the sheer power of his office was a tangible presence in the room. No authority on the planet could take from this man his present status, not even that of the King himself. It was a uniquely Vohung convention that ceded such power to one man and left it solely to his own discretion when, and if, he should elect to pass it on. That no Warlord had ever exceeded his legal right to the office was similarly uniquely Vohung.

'Runners have been dispatched,' the Warlord said without pre-amble. 'Every fighting man in Benza will shortly fall upon the army of the Librarian Vahnn. If the other Kingdoms are to be believed, their own armies will take this as their cue to join us.' He looked directly at me, and I felt as though I had been pinned in place by a lance. 'Is your war vessel ready to engage that of our enemy?' he asked.

'It is,' I replied.

'Then let us get down to details,' he said.

For long hours after that we all went over every aspect of the battle ahead. The men around me, some Captains, some soldiers of lesser rank, and some former militiamen, were clearly struggling to encompass the concept of the kind of war they were facing, and it was to their credit that they achieved even a fractional understanding of what was involved. Their tactics were straightforward and, in some ways, simplistic. They had no idea of how to mount a siege, nor of the tactical and logistic differences between a battle of hundreds of men and one involving tens of thousands. It was my hope, vain though it might have been, that if Vahnn's airship could be destroyed, or at the very least seriously disabled, then the loss of that symbol of his power would so dishearten his followers that they would abandon their plans and be scattered before the smaller force of men in the Vohung contingent.

It was long after dark when the event occurred that was to throw all of our plans into disarray.

It began, from the point of view of those of us on the ground, with a flash of light that burst through the windows of the tavern like a bolt of lightning. And as though it had indeed been such a natural discharge it was followed almost immediately by an ear-splitting peal of thunder. But I had heard that sound too often before not to instantly recognize it for what it was.

Chapter 46

BATTLE OF THE TITANS

The slowest man in that room was out of the door in less than twenty seconds; the fastest was barely on his feet as I reached the street.

With a sense of utter despair I looked up at the airship. It was swaying wildly, tugging on its anchor line, a cloud of black smoke billowing from somewhere around its upper deck. I could see the lurid red glow of flames licking over the upper wings, hear the angry cries of men.

I ran towards the gatehouse, and from above came a second crash of thunder. Lightning danced around the metal frame of the *Mariner*, and to my horror I saw one of her great propellers suddenly tilt crazily on its shaft and then tumble slowly towards the ground. Six feet of propshaft came with it, the shattered end of which was charred and smoking.

Feeling as though a part of myself had just been torn away I raced up the stairway to the top of the gatehouse. I reached the battlements in time to see the ship's anchor line suddenly go impossibly taut and then snap like a single strand of cotton. As I stood and looked on helplessly the ship began to drift away from the gatehouse.

Given a moment of quiet reflection I might have questioned my desire to reach the airship. P'nad was a capable leader and would be doing everything possible to save what was left of the *Mariner*, and my presence would, in all probability, be of little further assistance. But despite all my protestations to the contrary I had come to think of the *Mariner* as *my* ship, and if she was in trouble then *I* should be with her.

I was abruptly knocked flying by a very heavy, very solid object striking me a glancing blow across the left shoulder. Scrambling to my feet I saw one of the ship's ballast weights slowly trailing past me, the large stone block turning on its line following its impact with my now aching shoulder. In an instant I was hurling myself on the weight, my hands clutching the thick rope from which it hung.

The rope had not been designed for climbing, and was uncomfortably thick, making a secure handhold difficult to obtain. But I was running on adrenalin now and I scrambled up the line with a haste that left no time for thoughts of personal safety.

It was a tight squeeze through the access hole into the ship's hold, and once there I found the place filled with smoke. Taking the best swallow of clean air that I could I stumbled blindly forward to where I remembered the nearest ladder to be. Whether from the random pitching and rolling of the deck beneath my feet or the disorientating effects of the smoke my memory proved inadequate to the task. Instead of finding what should have been the central port-side ladder I blundered into a painfully substantial supporting beam. The impact jolted the air from my lungs and when I involuntarily inhaled I felt my senses swim as my lungs filled with smoke. Coughing and gasping, I tried to feel my way along the angled beam, only to lose it as it passed overhead and out of arms' reach. Logic dictated that it must have been the rear structural member that I had been following, and that therefore there was a ladder less than ten feet away from me. Logic, sadly, had little to do with my jumbled thoughts at that moment, and the next solid object I ran into was one of the newly erected dividing walls of the hold. My eyes were burning in their sockets now and consciousness was gradually deserting me, my lungs labouring loudly for a single gasp of clean air. The muscles in my legs were twitching and jumping, and with a curse of sheer frustration I felt myself sinking to the deck.

I remember thinking that it couldn't end like this, not so senselessly, with not a blow struck in anger. Images washed across my mind – Benza in flames, Mrs Catlin a slave of the brute Hol Krexus, the *Mariner* a gutted wreck floating forever over the green hills of the Kingdoms, Droxus leading his armies victoriously into Carmalt to claim the crown of Vohung for himself – and all of it – all of it – my fault. My fault for not having the sense not to climb into a smoke-filled hold.

Consciousness must have left me at some point, because the next rational thought I had was one of stark disbelief that I could suddenly breathe again. I opened my eyes to a scene of utter chaos. I was on the upper deck, with men running and shouting all around me. I was not the only one lying amid the confusion, and I guessed in that moment that several of the crew had been trapped in the smoke-filled hold and someone – probably either P'nad or S'nam – had engineered their rescue.

Struggling to my feet, my head still spinning from the prolonged lack of oxygen, I tried to make some sense of the pandemonium all around me.

The focus of the action was easy enough to find, and simultaneously the cause of the fire that was still raging. Rohc Vahnn was standing on the ship's forecastle, and scarcely ten feet away from him was Celebe. She was on her hands and knees, her body sparkling with energy, and seemed to be in agony. As I watched, Vahnn gestured at her and lightning seemed to flash from his body and into Celebe's. She screamed with pain, her body writhing on the deck. Flames licked the wooden boards all around her; a gaping hole in the deck some yards to one side of her billowed smoke from the hold beneath. All the rimwood fixtures on the sterncastle were aflame, and even some of the sardwood structural members were starting to smoulder.

Dismissing all other considerations from my mind, I tried desperately to think of some way of helping Celebe. I knew that the desire uppermost in her own mind would be to reach the miniature airframe that she had had brought on board in preparation for precisely this encounter, and that lay on the main deck directly below her. If I could gain her a few moments' respite from Vahnn's attack there was every chance she could reach it. But to even attract Vahnn's attention was to court instant death and, worse, to die to no good purpose. I had survived one meaningless death today and I had no intention of placing myself in the path of another.

Amid the general air of chaos on the deck, I was suddenly aware of purposeful activity all around me. I caught sight of P'nad on the rowing deck, leading a fire-control party around the still-smoking remains of the starboard propeller shaft. Elsewhere, S'nam and Hareg had assembled the remainder of the crew and were busily counting heads – I prayed that everyone was present, since further forays into the hold would be as dangerous for the would-be rescuers as for any unfortunate enough to be still trapped there.

A sudden thought came to me and I acted on it instantly. One face in the crowd of assembled crewmen had stood out because of an association it had in my memory: he was one of the two men Celebe had been training with our pair of muskets. In a moment I was at his side and seconds after that we were both racing for the weapons locker on the aft section of the main deck. I gave silent thanks to whatever Providence had been watching over me when I had so positioned that particular locker, for had it been situated below decks it would have been almost certainly out of our reach.

My own familiarity with muskets was limited to an understanding of their operating principles and a few hours of casual observation when Celebe had been giving her lessons on the deck of the *Mariner*. I was no stranger to handling firearms, however, and when we reached the locker I snatched up one of the muskets and began to load it – and if my efforts were not so proficient as those of my companion he was diplomatic enough not to mention it.

As soon as both weapons were ready we separated to opposite sides of the deck and each took aim at the figure of the Librarian. I had had only seconds in which to explain my plan to my crewman, but as I had instructed he held his fire and waited to follow my lead.

I knew that Y'nys armour could not be penetrated by a musket ball, and that in any case Vahnn's defensive shields would be able to turn one aside before it even made contact. But from conversations

I had had with both Celebe and her predecessor I knew that there was a limit to how many different ways the energy put out by such armour could be simultaneously employed. I was counting on the fact that Vahnn could not launch the kind of attack he was now engaged in *and* hold his screens in place at the same time – if, indeed, it *was* a fact, and not merely wishful thinking.

I aimed directly at Vahnn's head, drew a breath to steady myself, and fired.

The musket kicked back more than I had expected, but not so much that the ball hurtling from its barrel went entirely off target. It struck Vahnn squarely across the temple, and although he was visibly startled by the occurrence he was not injured by it. He whirled towards me, his right hand coming up to launch his lightning in my direction – but his left hand remained focused on Celebe, holding her pinned to the deck. I had no cover behind which to hide, and closed my eyes before the inevitable flash of heat and pain. Instead, I heard a second crack of musket fire, and opened my eyes to see Vahnn staggering to one side, clearly in pain, his left hand clutched tightly in his right; blood poured through the clenched fingers of his left hand, and I realized that my sharpshooting colleague had followed my own reasoning but had chosen his target more prudently. Readied to attack, Vahnn had had to remove the shielding from his hand, and had instantly paid the price.

I found myself galvanized into frantic action – if one of us could reload fast enough, we might finish the Librarian for good!

I was still priming the pan on my weapon when I heard the barking report of my colleague's musket and realized that he had beaten me to it. I looked up, and saw Vahnn glaring at my musket-wielding crewman with a degree of hate I would hesitate to call human. That his shields were now fully restored was evident, as was the fact that my valiant companion was a second away from death. I yanked back the hammer on my musket and yelled, 'Rohc Vahnn, you son of a bitch! *I'm* the one you want!'

Vahnn half-turned, and I gestured menacingly with the musket. I didn't fire – I wanted to give my colleague as much time to get to safety as I could. The Librarian smiled coldly, his eyes burning into mine. I knew that there was no power that could save me this time, and that the weapon in my hands was of no more use against a man like him than a fly swat would have been against a rhinoceros. But blind optimism is a difficult thing to crush, and I was still determined to let Vahnn have a musket ball between the eyes even if only for my own personal satisfaction.

I was lining up the weapon's sights when, from the lower deck some yards away, I heard a voice that sounded like muted thunder.

'Librarian,' it rumbled, 'you have claimed your last victim.'

Vahnn and I turned simultaneously towards the source of the voice – as, I think, did everyone standing on the deck at that moment.

The whole purpose of distracting Vahnn had been to give Celebe time to reach the bare airframe that lay below the ship's forecastle and, even weakened as she had been by his attack, she had used the brief respite to do just that.

Vahnn stared in startled dismay at the sight of her now. She was standing astride the frame's central spar, her hands clutching the ropes we had attached to its upper wings and her feet braced in a knotted rope we had tied around its midsection. And, to the astonishment of all present, the airframe was floating above the deck, suspended there by some unknown power.

'This is the end, Vahnn,' Celebe's amplified voice said. 'The gods have tolerated your insane pride for long enough.'

Vahnn took a step backwards, wary but not as frightened as he should have been. I sensed a gathering of energies in the air around him, and at the last moment I realized what was happening: he was going to transport himself away.

I opened my mouth to shout a warning to Celebe, and then my eyes saw something that human eyes were never meant to see: I saw the spatial distortion that preceded the Librarian's intended escape. It was like looking into an exploding mirror, except that the sight was actually physically painful. I threw my arms over my eyes, and was startled to hear Vahnn let out a wail of agony. I looked, and saw the distortion effect engulf him. His body seemed to shatter into a million fragments, some unseen force holding him together in a recognizable shape even as he was blasted to atoms.

The effect subsided, and Vahnn was whole again, but badly shaken and weakened by what had happened.

Celebe's voice said, 'There is no escape, Librarian.'

And I realized what had happened. She had used *her* armour to override his, cancelling its ability to transport him away.

I glanced at her again, and saw the airframe rise slowly above the deck. It was alive with energy now, and in the moonlight I could just make out a faint trail of what looked like fireflies being drawn out of Vahnn and into Celebe. She was tapping his energy reserves, draining his Y'nys armour and powering up her own, just as the former Celebe had done on that night in Coiz when he had defeated her. Only now, Celebe's armour was augmented by the airframe to which she had attached herself. I knew now that her armour was somehow controlling the flight of her airframe, that although the two devices were the products of wildly differing technologies there was some common bond between them, some similarity that allowed them to interface and operate as one.

Vahnn was no fool, and he saw the extent of his plight in an instant. Anyone else might have given in to blind panic, or perhaps launched a last-ditch, all-out attack in the hope of overwhelming Celebe with his sheer ferocity. To his credit, Vahnn did neither, but instead turned and ran purposefully for the front of the forecastle. I saw – belatedly – the flaw in Celebe's plan. If the smaller airframe could be used to augment her own power, how much more powerful could Vahnn make himself if he could but make contact with the larger frame upon which the *Mariner* was built?

Celebe caused her own frame to follow Vahnn, but with such painful slowness that I knew she would never overtake him before he could leap from the hull and onto the bare metal of the central spar.

The energy that was draining out of Vahnn now was a solid column of light joining him to Celebe, and every step he took seemed to weaken him further. Static discharges leaped randomly from the forms of the two combatants, grounding themselves in the upper wings of the *Mariner* and illuminating the deck beneath.

Feeling such helplessness as I had never known before, I willed Celebe to move faster, to catch Vahnn before he reached the railing at the front of the forecastle – if necessary, to impale him on the forward spike of her airframe.

Vahnn reached the railing, which was still flickering with flames from the now largely extinguished blaze, and collapsed over it, his robes catching fire and burning away to reveal the armour beneath.

He half-turned, gazing malevolently at Celebe who was still ten feet or more away from him. His face was reddened and scarred from the flames of his burning robe, and his body seemed to seethe with the energies that flowed all around him. He bared his teeth in a hideous grin and smashed the railing with a single blow of his armoured forearm.

I cried out as he fell from view, and suddenly the whole ship rocked under the force of a terrific explosion. The forecastle was blasted to matchwood, and something like a miniature sun seemed to have engulfed the forward spike of the ship's frame. A shock wave of wind and noise hit me and carried me twenty feet along the deck, leaving me bruised and battered and only half-conscious. The force of the blast hurled the *Mariner* backwards through the air, her nose tilted at an angle that threatened to pitch all of us from her deck. She wheeled around, rocking from side to side as the system of forces and energies that controlled her attitude tried to regain control of her.

All around me, I saw men clinging to the deck for dear life; the ship was littered with clamps to which men could attach safety lines in time of combat to prevent them from being accidentally thrown overboard but most of the men were not wearing their lines and those that were were too far from the fixtures for them to be of any use. I made a mental note: from now on, *everyone* would wear his safety line at all times, and as soon as possible I'd have Hareg's people rig up more fixtures on every deck. The thought almost made me laugh out loud; there was scarcely any deck left, and it was highly unlikely that what little remained of the *Mariner* would ever see combat now.

I looked around for any sign of Celebe, but both she and her airframe were gone. The second miniature airframe, that to which we had fitted the sail, was still lashed to the deck, but so badly had it been battered about that it would need an almost total refit before it was airworthy.

The *Mariner*'s internal stabilizers finally did their mysterious work and the ship began to rock gently in the breeze, its equilibrium restored.

I looked to where P'nad stood on the rowing deck; he was already rounding up his men to douse the last of the fires and would probably be kept busy for several hours yet. S'nam and Hareg were still on the sterncastle, and it was to them that I quickly made my way.

'Will the *Mariner* steer?' I asked of Hareg.

He looked at me as though I were demented, then shook his head and said ruefully, 'Steer, yes; but how will we move her?'

'We've still got one propeller,' I said, 'and the rowing stations for it look relatively undamaged. See what you can do with them – but go easy, Hareg; we've drifted about two torbiks from Benza, and right now all I want to do is get us back there. We can worry later about running the drive up to full speed.'

His expression told me what he thought of that suggestion, but he made his way to the lower deck without another word.

What could I have told him? That I knew the *Mariner* was finished? What good would that have done? Right now, all I wanted was to keep everyone too busy to think about the realities of our situation. And the realities were that as far as the war in Benza was concerned we were now little more than casualties. The knowledge that somehow we seemed to have destroyed the threat of Rohc Vahnn himself was scant consolation when his army still occupied the country.

I was still puzzled by what had happened to Vahnn, and I needed desperately to talk to Celebe about it. I was confident that she still lived, and that when she saw our heading she would easily make her own way back to Benza.

It was almost an hour before Hareg appeared on the burned remains of the lower deck once more.

'The ship will steer,' he informed me. 'And you may risk quarter-speed on the oars – but I offer no guarantees.'

'I ask for none,' I told him. I turned to S'nam, who had stood at my side while we waited for Hareg's report. 'Man the oars,' I told him.

The men on the sterncastle gave a mighty cheer, and all of them rushed to be first at the oars. There were far too many of them, and as soon as the benches were full the remaining men took up places behind their colleagues, whether to provide moral support or in the hope that someone might need replacing I wasn't entirely sure.

The hortator's drum was a blackened shell, but the man was not to be done out of his job. He took up his place and called the beat verbally.

I glanced behind me; the steersman of the second watch stood ready at the wheel, and I was pleased to note that his safety line was fastened.

I called out to P'nad, who was directing clean-up operations all over the ship.

'Ready to make way!' I advised him.

He waved his acknowledgement.

I leaned over the railing below which the hortator stood.

'One-quarter beat,' I said.

'Quarter time,' he bellowed, 'on the third beat: one . . . two . . . three . . . beat! . . . beat! . . .'

The ship groaned. A wooden deck spar, one of its ends weakened by fire, snapped loudly, flying up to clang against the ship's port wing. It sailed over the side, trailing smoke and cinders. Not a man at the oars missed his stroke.

'Steersman,' I said loudly, 'hard about.'

'Hard about!' he yelled back, spinning the ship's wheel.

The vessel banked slightly, beginning its slow, wide turn. Smoke billowed from the holes in the hull that the Librarian's attack had created, and I felt the boards of the deck shift disconcertingly under my feet. The Ladden-built hull held, however, and in minutes we were facing back towards the ruins of Benza.

I saw Hareg and his people moving about below, checking the propshaft and the rowing stations. He looked pensive, but not worried.

'Hareg of the Ladden!' I called out.

He looked up at me.

'I salute your workmanship,' I told him. 'This is a fine vessel.'

He looked around at the destruction wrought by Vahnn. It was some kind of miracle that the *Mariner* had not been reduced to a bare airframe. If Hareg doubted my sincerity – which was entirely genuine – his expression did not show it. He finally returned his gaze to where I stood on the sterncastle and I saw an expression in his eyes that I had never seen there before.

'And I salute your crew,' he told me, and not a man there could miss the implication of his words – most of the crew had originally been Ladden slaves, and by Vinh law still were. 'There are no better free men in the world,' he said, adding, '—Captain.'

Such a cheer went up then that the whole ship rang with it. Men stamped their feet and pounded their hands together, and I marvelled at what Hareg had said. It was a statement from which there could be no going back, and one that must ultimately alter the entire future history of the Ladden race.

Over the din of the impromptu celebration I heard the steersman call, 'We're over Benza now, Captain!'

I waved my arms for quiet and didn't quite get it.

'All stop!' I called to the hortator.

He made himself heard long enough to bring the ship to a standstill and we quickly made her as secure at anchor as was possible under the circumstances.

Then I hurried below to make my way down to the city.

Chapter 47

PURSUIT

Chantal Clavalle – Celebe – had lied to us. That the lie had been a tactical necessity did not make it any less of an annoyance, but did prevent that annoyance from turning into full-blooded resentment.

The energies contained within an airframe were not, as we had been led to believe, compatible with those of Y'nys armour, but were in fact their exact opposites. Bringing the two together could only result in destruction for one of the agencies involved, as we had seen so graphically demonstrated when Rohc Vahnn had attempted to tap into the power of the *Mariner*'s airframe. Had he done so while in full control of his own armour it is possible that the whole ship would have been destroyed in the joining, but the battle with the new Celebe had so drained him that he was no longer a match for the power output of the vast airframe. And it was that selfsame battle that had prevented Celebe herself from being destroyed when she attached herself to the smaller airframe. The constant augmentation of her armour's energies by those of Vahnn's allowed her to maintain a precarious equilibrium within the miniature airframe, balancing the rising tide of forces while at the same time draining Vahnn to the point where his destruction by the larger airframe was possible without placing all our lives at risk.

Chantal, in one of those rare moments when the Thirteen had allowed her to share their seemingly omniscient overview of time, had predicted just such a possibility. But realizing that Vahnn had it in his power – whether he knew it or not – to access the data storage in her armour, just as she had accessed his, she dared not commit such knowledge to the Y'nys itself. And so, somehow, she had retained the knowledge in the part of her brain that remained detached from its armour, and had taken it to her death with her. Only now, with Vahnn obliterated, was Ailette able to gain entry to certain parts of the armour's memory banks, parts that hinted at all of this, and that had been guarded by multiple-nested protocols – the highest of which was that the Librarian should have been utterly destroyed before those protocols could even be discovered.

The battle with Vahnn had left several questions still unanswered, the most pressing of which, to my way of thinking, was how he had known where we were. From the eyewitness accounts of my crew, he had materialized directly onto the ship's main deck, virtually in front of Celebe, and launched his attack seemingly without even the necessity for a moment's pause to take aim. That suggested to me a degree of precognition or of surveillance: neither facility, so far as I knew, was within the powers of a Librarian. It was, however, within the powers of the Thirteen, and that was what gave me the greatest cause for concern. Several times before, I had wondered at the involvement of Vohung's 'gods' in this battle, but this last piece of evidence seemed to me irrefutable proof of their meddling.

Casualties from the battle were relatively light, but too heavy to let my conscience rest easy. Two men had died, both of smoke inhalation, and five more had sustained minor injuries. Three of them would be fit for duty in a few days, but the others would not be able to row for several weeks. I was loath to leave them behind, and was relieved to find that both had other talents that could be put to use on the *Mariner* – if, indeed, the *Mariner* could be made fit to sail.

The damage to the *Mariner* was, to no one's surprise, bordering on terminal. There was no way, with the tools that were to hand, to repair or replace the starboard propshaft. The rest of the damage to the hull was severe, but could be fixed given enough time. And time, of course, was what we had very little of.

I asked Hareg if he thought the ship could be flown effectively on one propeller. His answer surprised me.

'The propeller is not our main problem,' he said. 'It is the structural integrity that concerns me. But if that can be guaranteed, you should be able to fly with only perhaps a thirty per cent reduction in speed.'

'Only thirty per cent?' I said, startled. 'Not fifty?'

I had, in fact, expected more than a fifty per cent loss in power, and more than a little difficulty in steering.

'My people and I have now had ample opportunity to study the propulsion device in operation,' Hareg told me, 'and have already concluded that there are many ways in which we can improve upon it. Some of those would require a total rebuild of the mechanism, but there are several that can be accomplished here and now. Once completed, they would allow the single remaining propeller to almost double its efficiency – almost, and I would advise against pushing too hard under circumstances such as these.'

'Hareg,' I said, 'if you can get the *Mariner* airworthy, I will settle for any degree of efficiency that will allow us to intercept Droxus before he overruns Carmalt.'

'That,' Hareg assured me, 'you will have.'

'How long will it take?' I asked.

'To secure the structure, and complete the modifications to the propeller shaft that I have in mind,' Hareg said thoughtfully, 'ten days.'

'I don't have . . .' I began.

'But you do not have ten days,' Hareg told me, 'so we will do it in three, and complete final repairs in flight.'

I grinned at him. 'Hareg,' I said, 'you are a born engineer.'

'Another new word?' he said, and with an enigmatic smile went back to work.

I conferred with Tor Taskus and Benza's Warlord once more during the next three days.

435

Celebe, who had reached Benza barely an hour later than the *Mariner*, was also present, a fact that seemed to afford some moral and spiritual comfort to the city's occupants. I knew that worship of the Thirteen Gods was a serious business to most Vohung, which was not too surprising since these gods actually lived on the Kingdoms' doorstep. What was surprising, and somehow strangely human, was the fact that the fickle nature of the gods did not make them any less loved. Gazig, for example, was seldom far from the prayers of most soldiers, but invoking his name was to risk summary destruction if he decided that your foemen were more worthy of his aid than you were. Given their devotion to their deities, the Benzan people looked on Celebe's presence among them as the best of all possible good omens.

Our conference was brief and, it must be admitted, largely an exercise in morale-building. Both the Warlord and I swore mighty oaths to one another; he to engage Droxus's army in the field until not a man in Benza was left to fight and I to blast Droxus's airship from the skies or face death myself in the attempt. I'm sure that, had she been there, Mrs Catlin would have disparaged our promises as so much macho posturing, but as unlikely as it now sounds in the cold light of day we were each utterly sincere, and the meeting left us all feeling that we not only had a chance for victory, but that Droxus's defeat was now little more than a formality. The truth, of course, was to be a very different matter.

After the meeting, and mindful of the need to gain every advantage we could for the coming battle, I asked Celebe about the bizarre flight she had taken in the miniature airframe. If she had been able to control it with her armour then perhaps she could do the same for the *Mariner*, increasing our manoeuvrability incredibly. Unfortunately, she was as much in the dark about what had happened as I was.

'There is undoubtedly a means of "flying" the airframes using Y'nys technology,' she said, 'but I would not risk such a thing with the *Mariner* until I have had time to study the phenomenon in considerable detail.'

The three days that it took Hareg and his Ladden to rebuild the *Mariner* were not as frustrating for me as had been those other three days when we had been making ready to leave Uhrgratz and I had found myself superfluous to the activities going on around me. This time, every available hand was needed to help with the refitting, and the whole crew was kept busy, sometimes for up to eighteen hours a day. The time passed rapidly: Tor Taskus and the army of Benza had departed on the morning of the first day, yet if all went according to plan we would pass them within hours of setting off in pursuit.

One advantage, if advantage it was, to having a single propeller was that I now had twice as many crewmen as I needed. I had no intention of leaving them behind, and instead rearranged the rowing watches into shorter shifts; this would allow each watch to row much faster, increasing our real speed considerably. I was relying on Hareg to hold the drive together under such punishment, and had every confidence that he would do it.

We did not bother attempting to retrieve the airframe Celebe had used to attack the Librarian, partly because I did not feel we could spare the time but also because I did not feel we could trust it – how had interfacing with Celebe's Y'nys armour affected it? If we entrusted some special mission to it and it suddenly began behaving erratically we would have bought trouble for ourselves that we did not need. If we survived the encounter with Droxus we could return and retrieve it then, and Celebe could study it to her heart's content.

There was no ceremony when the ship finally departed. We simply put ashore the majority of the Ladden and bent our backs to some serious rowing.

The *Mariner* had changed in subtle as well as gross ways. There was a different feel to it now; it had had its baptism of fire, both figuratively and literally, and somehow it had acquired a character of its own in the process. It was no longer simply a vessel: it was one of us.

We flew at three-quarter beat for two-thirds of each of the new shorter watches, ending the watch with a short burst of full speed. Hareg and the other four Ladden who had remained on board nursed the mighty propshaft night and day, fussing over it and occasionally smiling knowingly at one another. If they felt a special pride in their handiwork I wasn't about to begrudge them it. The original design may have been mine, but the thundering device that was hurling us through the air above the Thek continent was entirely theirs, as far removed from my original conception as a grown man is from an embryo.

The days and nights came and went as we chased Droxus's army, each one the same as the last, the landscape below us changing little as we headed north, until the peace of an early-morning watch was suddenly shattered by the cry of a lookout. His words, which I am sure came instinctively to him, had probably not been heard on this planet in millennia.

'Vessel on the horizon!' came the excited cry.

I was below decks when the cry went up, but I was on the sterncastle seconds later.

I took a brief moment to study the terrain below us, and to make out the faint 'X' on the far horizon, its sails billowing around it, before making my next decision.

'All stop!' I called to the hortator.

'Cease rowing!' he yelled.

Our forward momentum would carry us for several hundred yards, but that didn't concern me particularly.

This watch was under S'nam's command, and although he showed no irritation at the way I had usurped his place I felt annoyed with myself for having done so. S'nam was a good watch commander, and deserved better treatment.

'My apologies, S'nam,' I said. 'Please take us down to fifty metres and resume rowing at whatever speed is necessary to keep Droxus's ship in sight – but no faster than that.'

'Yes, Captain,' he said, and added with a grin, 'And no apology is necessary, Shaw.'

I returned the smile and went forward.

I could just make out the sailing ship as we began to descend, and S'nam had the hortator take us first to quarter-beat and then to half. Our quarry remained in view, occasionally drawing slightly closer and forcing us to reduce speed, occasionally pulling away and necessitating a few minutes at three-quarter beat to close the gap once more.

I was confident that Droxus's ship had not spotted us. Despite Vahnn's presence at Benza I did not believe he would have acquainted Droxus with the existence of our ship – if, in fact, he had known of its existence, which I doubted: the moment of his arrival on deck would have been the first time he would have seen it. Yet even if he had known in advance, his contempt for lesser creatures, so typical in a Librarian, would have precluded his informing Droxus of what he knew. And with no expectation of airborne pursuit, Droxus would not have posted lookouts to watch the sky.

We followed Droxus until sunset, at which time I returned to the sterncastle where the watch was now under the command of a young man named Halke. He was a competent enough fellow, but looked a little overawed at being in command at such a crucial time.

'Halke-jin,' I said, 'please set the ship for stealth.'

'Yes, Captain!' he said. To the hortator of the watch he called, 'Silent beat!' and the timekeeper switched his regular mallets for a pair with specially muffled heads. The beat could still be heard in the confines of the rowing deck, but even on the sterncastle it was almost inaudible.

'Lights out!' called Halke.

Every light on the ship was promptly extinguished, including those of the inner hull that led onto the ladder ways to the main deck.

'Silence on deck!' Halke called, although with Droxus's ship so close no one was much engaged in casual conversation.

'All stealth rules now being observed, Captain,' said Halke.

'Very good,' I said. 'Increase speed to one-half and bring us to within one torbik of the enemy's vessel and then hold at that distance.'

'Yes, Captain,' he said. He leaned over the rail and said, in a stage whisper, 'Go to one-half.'

The hortator repeated the command, his gravel voice an all but inaudible murmur over the sound of the ship's propeller.

There was little that could be done to silence the moving parts of the *Mariner*'s drive, but at a torbik's distance and with almost

439

a thousand feet difference in altitude, I thought there was little chance of its being heard by our quarry.

The ship picked up speed with the increased beat, and would be in place in a little over an hour.

'Halke-jin,' I said, 'please summon me when we are at one torbik from the enemy.'

'Yes, Captain,' he said.

I went below and found Celebe and P'nad.

'How far are we from Carmalt?' I asked Celebe.

'We will be there before noon tomorrow at our present speed,' she said. 'For maximum effectiveness as a propaganda victory, that is when we must engage Droxus's ship.'

Sometimes, even though the voice was that of Ailette Legendre, I couldn't distinguish between this incarnation of Celebe and its predecessor. I found the thought a chilling one.

'Droxus's army,' P'nad observed, 'will already be ringing Carmalt.'

'If the city still stands at all,' Celebe observed.

'Tor's intelligence said it did,' I reminded her.

'Intelligence that was many days old and suspect to begin with,' she pointed out. 'And on the subject of things suspect,' she added, 'I will once again voice my objections to your plan to rescue the woman Catlin.'

'Objection noted,' I snapped, 'and unless you have some new argument—'

'You have never satisfactorily answered my original one,' she said.

'Rescuing Mrs Catlin isn't the only reason for what I've got planned,' I told her. 'We need to know how many of Droxus's prisoners are still on board his ship, and anything else that will help us to attack it successfully. The last thing we need is to kill half the ruling families of Vohung in the process of "liberating" them.'

'A fine-sounding rationale,' Celebe said, 'but merely a smoke-screen to hide your true intent. The only thing that truly prompts this idiotic rescue is your infatuation with the Catlin woman.'

'Do not call her "the Catlin woman",' I said angrily. 'And whatever I feel for her – not that it's any of your damned business – it is not an infatuation.'

'You would jeopardize our whole mission to save one woman,' Celebe said. 'How else would you describe your feelings?'

'I don't suppose the word "love" enters into your programming, does it?' I snapped.

'It does,' Celebe replied. 'But I was beginning to wonder if it existed in yours.'

I looked at her angrily, and to my amazement a slow smile spread across her lips.

'You still cannot admit it,' she said softly, 'not even to yourself – can you?'

'Damn you, Celebe,' I said, flustered. 'Are you playing games with me?'

'What you propose to do,' she said, 'is fraught with risks – for yourself, for your woman, and for all of us. I would ask of you only that you understand your own motives before setting out, for if you fail to do so you sow the seeds of your own failure.'

I frowned at her. 'Deep,' I grumbled, 'very deep. And do I take it this is Celebe who now speaks?'

'More Ailette than Celebe,' she said.

P'nad was looking at us both as though we were talking a foreign language, which wasn't surprising. It seemed as though everyone who had ever met Mrs Catlin had evolved their own notion of how I was supposed to feel about her. The fact that my true feelings didn't fit any of their convenient little fictions seemed to distress them not at all.

'My objections,' Celebe said, 'are genuine. But you lead here, David, and I will not openly oppose you. That said, I would rather your mission was a success than a failure. And if I have been, as you say, playing games with you, it is only to make you face the realities of what you do. To undertake this rescue at all is perilous; to do so with no clear understanding of why you are doing it is madness.' She stared at me from behind her red eye lenses, the crystal dimly lit from behind. 'I have voiced my fears,' she said, a fatalistic shrug in her voice. 'Now I will follow your lead.'

I couldn't deny that much of what Celebe had said had struck a nerve with me. I had struggled for months to work out what I truly felt for my former teacher – struggled, in fact, for years if I was being honest. And while I have never been a great believer in sudden revelations there had been a single event in recent weeks that seemed to have confirmed for me a suspicion I had been entertaining for some time.

Chapter 48

REUNION

At the risk of being accused of introducing a note of melodrama into what I have tried to make a historically accurate document I must now confess to something I have not previously mentioned.

Ever since the death of my father, I had been plagued by recurring nightmares. I have not mentioned them previously because they had no bearing on my narrative – also, and perhaps more truthfully, the mere prospect of reliving them in print filled me with dread, and with a sense of guilt that, however misplaced, was never far from my thoughts.

The nightmare follows a set pattern, but minor details change from time to time. Essentially, it is a replay of my father's suicide, but when his body falls at my feet, his blood splashing across my boots, fact gives way to fantasy. Because in my nightmare, my father is not dead. With a hole in the back of his skull the size of a fist, and pint after pint of blood pumping from the rather smaller hole in his throat, he is not dead. As I kneel at his side, retching, he lifts his head and looks at me. There is no reproach in his eyes, and none of the bitterness that had consumed him towards the end of his life. Instead, there is only a desperate, wordless pleading, and the guilt that consumes me is born of my complete inability to comprehend what it is that he wants. He looks at me with that pitiful, inconsolable expression, and then he speaks. And with each word, his blood gushes from his mouth, more blood than a human body could possibly hold. And it is this small fact, this one incongruity, that dispels my suspension of disbelief and brings me awake. In my nightmare, I hear my father's words, yet on awakening I cannot remember them.

Details change: sometimes he shoots himself through the heart; sometimes he doesn't shoot himself at all, but cuts his throat – that is one of the worst; sometimes Mrs Catlin is standing between us and my father's blood stains her boots instead of mine; sometimes – this happened increasingly more often during my separation from Mrs Catlin – I try to stop him from pulling the trigger, and fail by the tiniest fraction of a second.

And then came the sudden departure from the usual scenario that has prompted me to set all of this down. Because in this nightmare, on this solitary occasion, it is not my father who dies. It is Mrs Catlin.

I hear him utter his tirade about teaching me the meaning of death, a tirade which I now know by heart, so many times have I relived it, and then, instead of taking his own life, he points the gun at Mrs Catlin a..d fires. She dies in hideous slow motion, and unlike the former nightmares concerning my father her death is final. Irrevocable.

I awoke from this nightmare with my father's voice ringing in my ears, a new speech from him which I had never heard him give in life.

'That's death, boy,' he says, laughing and weeping hysterically, 'and there's no coming back from it!'

I had sat in the darkness of the hold of the *Mariner*, bathed in sweat and shaking from head to toe, and it had been a very long time before I was able to re-establish my grip on reality sufficiently for me to be able to tell myself convincingly that Mrs Catlin was not dead, that she was still very much alive, and that no matter what else happened I must rescue her from Droxus and see her returned safely home. For more than that I had not dared to hope, although the feeling with which I had awoken, when for those few moments

I had truly believed her dead, had dispelled any doubts I might ever have had about my true feelings for her. The only mystery now remaining was how I had been able to hide from that simple truth so effectively for so long.

At one torbik from Droxus's ship I climbed aboard the miniature airframe that was lashed to the *Mariner*'s deck and, with scarcely a word of farewell, launched myself into the night.

The airframe was sail-powered, and its sail dwarfed it. It was fashioned of black-dyed canvas, and because of the load ratio enabled me to make far better speed than could Droxus's larger, slower vessel. With luck, and a stiff tail wind, I would overhaul him in less than an hour.

The tiny craft, its only concession to comfort being a narrow wooden board upon which I sat, rose into the darkness with breathtaking rapidity. It caught the breeze as it rose and fairly raced along its course.

Sailing was a pastime I had had little experience of on Earth, and it took all my meagre skill and concentration to hold the vessel on course. Much of the steering was done with the sail, although a rudimentary sailboard offered a little fine tuning. Since Droxus was directly upwind of me, I was relying on holding the sail full on to the breeze to keep me on course.

In far less time than I would have anticipated I saw the sterncastle of the mighty sailing vessel looming ahead of me. With my vast black sail acting as a shield I had approached in unseen silence, but I could already make out figures on the decks and knew that such good fortune could not last.

The ballast arrangements on my vessel were as rudimentary as everything else about it. A heavy stone slab, presently on the bench behind me, was attached to a stout rope that could be played out in measured lengths. I played it out to its first stop by the simple expedient of shoving it off the bench. It dropped like . . . well, like a stone, and the airframe jolted with the force of it. Then it began to descend. I manoeuvred alongside the hull of Droxus's ship and, taking a grappling iron from its place next to the ballast weight, slung the metal hook at the handrail below the larger ship's sterncastle. I hadn't taken much of an aim, and as the hook caught on the wooden rail I realized how fortunate I had been. My small vessel was descending so quickly I would not have had time for a second cast.

The rope attached to the grappling hook played out until it became taut and there I hung, suspended between Droxus's ship and the swinging ballast weight below me. I was hanging just below the keel line of the big airship, my own craft swaying slowly from side to side.

I furled my sail quickly to keep it from tearing me away from my mooring and then steeled myself for what I knew must come next.

Unclipping my safety line, I began to climb up the grappling rope towards the deck. The rope was provided with strategically placed knots, yet even so it was a nerve-racking experience. I could feel my garments flapping about me, hear the rustle of the sails on the ship above me, the occasional muted voices of its crew. I think I had never before in all my life felt so totally alone.

The climb can't have taken much above two minutes, yet it seemed as though I hung there for hours, my arms straining against the force of the wind produced by the larger vessel's passage through the air. It was with a feeling of considerable relief that I reached the handrail to which the grappling hook had attached itself.

My relief was short-lived, for no sooner had my left hand closed around the wooden rail than a figure loomed up before me. My grappling iron had not landed unnoticed, it seemed, and this particular member of Droxus's night watch had clearly intended to increase his own stature among his crewmates by capturing me single-handed.

That one small fact, that he had not yet raised the alarm, gave me a tiny glimmer of hope. The primed crossbow that he was slowly levelling at my temple went some way towards dispelling that hope, but after that psychologically dispiriting climb I was in no mood to take any more setbacks.

Not giving myself time to think about what I was doing I lashed out with my right hand, a brutal slashing blow that caught the

446

man across the throat. His eyes went wide in pained and startled shock, and the crossbow, jostled off target, went off in his hand. The quarrel tore a furrow through the left shoulder of my tunic before disappearing into the darkness, but I had one foot on the edge of the deck now and enough leverage to spring forward. I caught the man by his already injured throat and yanked him over the rail. If he cried out now then all was lost, but as I dangled from the railing with my fingers still tightening around his neck I knew that he would not cry out. He thrashed madly for long seconds, his arms windmilling as he sought some purchase from which to launch a counter-attack, but there was too little time and he was too disorientated. When he finally went limp in my grasp I continued to squeeze until I was certain he was dead and then I let him fall into the darkness below.

Shaking from the effort, I pulled myself up to the railing. I glanced about, but there was no one in sight. Droxus's security was lax, a result of his own overconfidence. For the sake of Benza, and the *Mariner*, and Mrs Catlin, I hoped it would remain so.

Staying low so as not to form a silhouette against the railing I edged forward.

In the brief time I had been on board Droxus's ship I had seen most of it and could guess at the parts I had not seen. My plans now were to check the prison level and determine how many were being held, warn those that were of the battle to come, and then, if Mrs Catlin was not among them, locate her and, if humanly possible – and without alerting Droxus – liberate her. Or, failing that, to ensure that she was in a safe place when the attack began. It distressed me greatly to consider it, but I was already coming to believe that the latter course of action would prove to be the only practicable one.

It took only a matter of moments to gain the interior of the ship, and so totally secure was Droxus in his belief in his ship's impregnability while in flight that I found not a single sentry at any hatchway. It seemed to me now that being spotted as I had been while boarding had been the height of bad luck.

I quickly made my way to the level where the prisoners were kept and, keeping to the shadows, observed the passageway between the pens where a jailer was usually to be found standing watch. There was indeed a jailer in evidence, but he was sound asleep and, by the looks of the empty and overturned wine flask at his side, dead drunk.

I moved swiftly forward. A dozen stifled cries of astonishment greeted my appearance. The jailer stirred fitfully, grunted noisily several times, then settled down as before.

I scanned the faces around me. Most of them were known to me from my time aboard the ship, but a few new additions were visible also. I was delighted and relieved to spy the Duke of Benza among them.

'There is little time for explanations,' I told him, his fellow prisoners crowding behind him at the bars of their cell, 'but this vessel will be attacked some time tomorrow. If the chance presents itself, I recommend you make whatever break for freedom you can.'

'Fear not,' said the Duke, 'we shall.' He smiled warmly at me. 'It is good to see you alive,' he said. 'When this is all over, and Benza restored to her people, there will be a place for you in her court, if you will have it.'

'Nothing would do me greater honour,' I told him, and the words were not merely empty. 'Now quickly, tell me the whereabouts of the female I was captured with.'

His face turned grim.

'She is held captive by the traitor Hol Krexus, may Gazig burn his soul,' he said bitterly. 'She is unharmed, so far as we know, but since the recent disappearance of the Librarian her fate may change at any moment.'

'Where is she being held?' I asked.

'We don't know for certain,' the Duke replied, 'but when we first came aboard, supposedly to negotiate trade agreements, we saw several cabins on the same level as Droxus's. Logic dictates she is in one of them.'

That was bad news. A lengthy search would soon see me discovered, a circumstance for which I would be able to offer no plausible explanation – other than the truth, which Droxus must never suspect until it was too late.

Realizing that I must, in all probability, abandon my intended rescue, I determined to risk one foray into the upper decks on the off chance that some clue might lead me to Mrs Catlin. It was a slim hope, and a mark of my desperate state of mind that I was prepared to risk everything on so slight a possibility.

I left the prison level immediately, unwilling to risk the guard's awakening and discovering me, and leaving a host of unasked questions from the captive Vohung nobles similarly unanswered. I felt strangely guilty about rushing away like that, as though perhaps I owed these adoptive kinsmen of mine a little more than the short shrift I had given them. I rationalized it to myself as the need to avoid detection by the sleeping jailer, but the truth was somewhat less selfless. My desire to liberate Mrs Catlin was overriding not merely my good sense but also my sense of proportion. And I kept getting a naggingly elusive memory of a conversation I'd had with Celebe recently, a conversation in which she'd asked me which one I'd choose if it came down to it, Mrs Catlin or Benza. It seemed to me that there had been more to that conversation than had at first met the eye. Likewise, and perhaps more pertinently, I remembered the conversation we had had about why I was really making this rescue attempt, and the need for me to be more level-headed than I had been so far tonight.

Outside the prison level, I found myself in the narrow passageway leading to the ship's armoury. This was perhaps one of the least-frequented areas of the ship under normal circumstances, and I took a few moments to pull myself together in the semi-darkness. Standing there, with no real idea of what the rest of the night would hold, I was seized with a sudden, totally irrational idea. Before I could question the notion, I found myself at the door to the armoury. It had been seriously damaged during the earlier prison break, and the repairs that Droxus's men had made did not extend to the rebuilding of the lock. In fact, the door was now little more than a rectangle of wood wedged into the hole. (I had noticed, in the hold, that the damage to the ship's structure done by the 'bird' over the Asmina Valley had been almost invisibly mended, as had the damage on deck; presumably such extensive repair work had left no time for minor repair details like interior doors, even when those doors gave access to all of Droxus's weapons.)

I eased the door open and slipped inside. And discovered that Droxus was not quite so careless as I might have thought him to be. The armoury was virtually empty, only a handful of battered old weapons that looked barely serviceable being still in residence.

I leaned heavily against one of the room's benches, slowly regaining my grip on reality. I had come here to retrieve my sabre, and faced with its absence I was forced instead to see the sheer absurdity of my actions.

All right, I said to myself, *enough is enough*. My very presence here was jeopardizing all the people who were depending on me. I knew now where Mrs Catlin was being held and I would plan my attack accordingly. She was a born survivor, and would come through this – she would, in fact, have a better chance for life under those circumstances than she would making a reckless bid for freedom with me tonight.

Feeling as though I had just had my first intelligent thought since deciding to undertake this ridiculous rescue mission I slipped out of the armoury and headed towards the forward deck hatch.

The sound of footsteps approaching from ahead brought me up sharply. I glanced quickly about me for any sign of a hiding place and was slightly amazed at my good fortune in finding one. The corridor was lined with storage lockers of some kind, each one scarcely eighteen inches wide and none of them locked. Even so I had to try three in rapid succession before finding one that was sufficiently empty to accommodate me, and ducked inside. I kept the door slightly ajar; it opened away from whoever was approaching, so I would not get a view of them until they had passed by.

I heard the footsteps, made, I now judged, by naked feet, as they approached the door. They sounded oddly familiar as they drew nearer, and I peered intently through the tiny crack in the door as the walker moved past. I almost cried out with joy as she did so, for it was Mrs Catlin. I began to open the door, then froze as I heard a man's voice from the forward end of the passage.

'What are you doing down here?' it demanded.

450

For an instant I thought I had been spotted, but then I realized he was addressing Mrs Catlin.

She turned to face him, her expression imperious, and I felt a great weight leave my heart as I realized that whatever had befallen her in the past months had done nothing to crush her spirit.

'I am taking water to the prisoners,' she told him.

'If you are taking water to the prisoners,' he said, 'then where is it?'

'The water store is on the other side of the prison level,' Mrs Catlin said caustically, 'as you would know if you ever ventured there yourself.'

There was an uncomfortable silence following this remark and then the man's voice said gruffly, 'Very well, go about your business. But swiftly.'

Mrs Catlin did not deign to reply but simply turned on her heel and marched off. I recalled something Celebe had said, that Mrs Catlin was feared aboard Droxus's ship because of what had happened over the Asmina Valley.

I waited as long as I dared before venturing out again, not wishing to be seen by the man who had spoken to Mrs Catlin. My former teacher's walk was as brisk as ever, making it necessary for me to leave the storage locker sooner than I would have liked in order to overtake her before she reached the prison level. But fortunately the man had departed and I emerged unnoticed.

It took only seconds to overtake Mrs Catlin, but I had already been on this ship too long and there was no time for formalities. I came upon her unheard and grasped her from behind, my hand over her mouth to keep her from crying out and my other arm around her to pin her own arms at her sides. She gave a muffled shriek and then I was carrying her, kicking and struggling, back towards the empty armoury.

I nudged the door open with my shoulder and wrestled Mrs Catlin inside before pushing it to with my foot. I spun her around in my arms and, keeping my hand over her mouth, turned her face up to mine. She was still struggling and it was several seconds before I saw the light of startled recognition dawn in her eyes. Her struggles ceased abruptly, her eyes widening in disbelief, and I took my hand slowly from her mouth.

She mouthed my name silently, her eyes suddenly bright with tears, and before I knew what I was doing I had lifted her in my arms and was kissing her. It didn't take long for me to realize that she was not responding in kind – was not responding at all, in fact – and I drew back, embarrassed and angry with myself.

She stared at me without speaking, and I was conscious of the fact that my arms were still around her, and that, for some reason, she hadn't tried to push me away.

With the greatest difficulty I forced myself to meet her penetrating gaze, and was surprised to find no trace of censure in it. If anything, she looked pleased – stunned, but pleased.

Throwing caution, and what little remained of my sanity, to the winds, I mouthed the words 'I love you' and waited for her to laugh in my face.

She didn't laugh, but a smile as bright as summer sunshine lit up her face. She raised herself up on her tiptoes and placed her lips next to my ear. In a whisper I could barely hear from even that tiny distance she said, 'I know that, Shaw. I've known it for years. I just wondered when you'd realize it.'

She drew back, her eyes shining with a gentle, rather familiar mockery.

'Are you laughing at me, Catherine?' I whispered. She hadn't dismissed my feelings out of hand, as I'd half expected she would, but she hadn't given me much to be hopeful about either.

She chuckled silently.

'Of course I am, David,' she replied. 'Isn't that how you and I communicate? And do me a favour, would you? Don't ever call me "Catherine" again!'

There was a childlike, boundless happiness in her eyes as she looked at me that I'd never seen there before, and as far as I could tell there was only one possible explanation for it. But she still hadn't said the words.

As though reading my mind, her face suddenly became serious.

'I'm glad you love me, Shaw,' she whispered. 'Because I've loved you for years, loved you more than I've been able to bear at times.

I don't know what you want to do with the rest of your life, but I hope there's a place in it for me.'

I swept her up in my arms, kissing her fiercely, and this time she responded with an enthusiasm that took my breath away.

After a considerable time our lips parted and I told her, '*You* are the rest of my life.'

She hugged me, giggling like a schoolgirl, and I said, 'Now let's get out of here. There's still the small matter of a war to win.'

Chapter 49

HOME TRUTHS

Getting off Droxus's ship proved scarcely more difficult than getting on it had been, but one more thing of significance occurred during our escape that I will now record.

With the death of the Librarian Rohc Vahnn, many questions had remained unanswered. Most of them found answers in the sight that met my startled eyes as we emerged on deck. Glancing towards the sterncastle, I was stunned to behold a figure that at first glance I thought to be Celebe. My reactions had barely had time to sort themselves out before I realized that it was not Celebe, but another Knight of the Thirteen. Now I understood how Vahnn had been able to intercept us so accurately: this Knight, whoever she was, had the same limited access to the perceptions of the Thirteen that Celebe had, enabling her to tell Vahnn where he needed to be at a given time in order to be able to strike us where it would do the most damage. It was only the fact that a Knight's perceptions *were* limited that had saved us from total destruction.

We had to wait a nerve-racking fifteen minutes or more for the Knight to quit the upper deck and go below. That still left the steersman, but I had been careful in planning my route to ensure that the anchor point for my vessel was out of his line of sight. It would probably have been out of the Knight's line of sight too, but where one of her kind was concerned I didn't feel like risking it.

Those fifteen minutes were a strain on both my patience and my self-confidence – seeing the Knight like that had really shaken me – but they were also among the most satisfying fifteen minutes of my life.

Mrs Catlin and I had had a communication problem with one another for years, yet crouched in the shadows on the middle deck of an enemy ship, a thousand feet above an alien world, and totally unable to speak, we communicated more effectively and more freely than we had during the entire time we had known one another. It was astounding to me then, and remains so today, to realize how little I had appreciated the wealth of information that can be transmitted by a single touch. And touch, unlike language, cannot lie. A caress, if insincerely meant, is as damning as a blow. And, if sincerely meant, is more effective than a thousand verbal vows of love and fidelity. Mrs Catlin's hand on my shoulder, her body pressed against mine, her face brushing my cheek, all spoke volumes of the truth of her feelings for me. I seemed to understand now why displays of affection between us in the past had always been awkward, had always stirred up feelings that I had not understood. It had simply never occurred to me that what I was feeling was love, and it was that inability that had led to puzzlement and confusion and, ultimately, resentment.

I was almost sorry when the Knight finally went below.

As soon as she was out of sight, we slipped out of the shadows and made our way to the forecastle. Mrs Catlin glanced over the railing and stifled a gasp of surprise. She looked a thousand questions in my direction but I simply slid over the rail and began to descend. As familiar as I was with Mrs Catlin's climbing skills I knew she would need no assistance in following me.

As soon as we had made it to the deck of my tiny vessel I slipped the knot that held us attached to Droxus's ship and we dropped away into the darkness, the ballast line of my ship pulling us down.

'Shaw,' Mrs Catlin gasped, 'this is fantastic! But – what do we do now?'

I was deriving a little perverse pleasure from being better informed on something than she was, and was secretly glad that the more abrasive aspects of our relationship would probably not vanish entirely because of our new-found romance – in many ways, it was our arguments that I had always enjoyed the most.

'We wait to be picked up by the *Mariner*,' I told her.

She didn't bite, so I said, 'The *Mariner* is *my* ship.'

'Isn't this your ship?' she asked.

'I guess so,' I replied, 'but the *Mariner* is . . . a bit bigger.'

She looked up at the receding outline of Droxus's ship and I saw the light of understanding in her eyes.

'There's going to be a confrontation, I take it,' she said quietly.

'A battle,' I said.

'When?' she asked.

'If all goes according to plan,' I said, 'about noon tomorrow.'

'Why then?' she asked.

I told her about the siege of Carmalt – it transpired she already knew about the destruction of Benza, which wasn't too surprising. I asked her about Hol Krexus, and she looked at me sharply.

'He hasn't bothered me since you were taken by that "bird" creature,' she said. 'But when the Knight came aboard—'

'When was that?' I interrupted.

'When we put in for repairs at the Librarian's home city,' she said. 'Anyway, when she came on board Droxus and the Librarian and Krexus all had a long meeting with her. After that I was kept pretty much under open arrest, so to speak. Droxus talked to me a lot about his plans – he's quite insane, you know? A sociopath?' I nodded. 'Well, I listened and nodded a lot but I think he knew I wasn't taking any of it in so he eventually gave up. After that I was just given slave duties to perform, but Krexus avoided me like the plague. I think he was scared of me.'

'That's what Celebe said,' I confirmed. 'But I wonder why she didn't know about the presence of another Knight.'

'Who's Celebe?' Mrs Catlin asked.

And I settled down to tell her everything that had happened to me since the incident over the Asmina Valley. Mrs Catlin went into teacher mode and an hour that could have been spent more enjoyably (to my mind, at least) was instead consumed with a frequently interrupted monologue.

By the end of it the *Mariner* was in sight on the horizon and any hope of continued privacy was lost.

Mrs Catlin saw the approaching silhouette and said, wistfully, 'I'm sorry, Shaw, I guess all of that could have waited till later, couldn't it?'

I was sitting on the narrow board that served as the deck of my vessel, Mrs Catlin facing me. I reached over and pulled her, unresisting, into my arms. She smiled up at me and, her arms around my neck, kissed me with an enthusiasm that was not forced.

'This is still difficult for you, isn't it?' she said at length.

'Not difficult, exactly,' I said. 'I think I'm just finding it hard to think of you as, uh, well . . .'

'A woman,' Mrs Catlin said, eyes sparkling with gentle mockery.

'To put it biologically,' I said, 'yes.'

'It's been difficult for me too,' she confessed. 'I have to keep reminding myself that you aren't my pupil any longer, that you aren't just a boy. But then, I've found it difficult to think of you as a boy since I first met you.'

I gave her a puzzled look.

'Do you believe in love at first sight?' she asked.

'I don't know,' I said. 'Perhaps – under the right circumstances, with the right people.'

'I fell in love with you the first time I saw you,' she said, which I found frankly incredible. 'I thought you were a sixth-former at least, you were so mature, so confident in everything you did. I couldn't believe it when I found out you were only just turned fourteen. I mean, OK, I was barely twenty-two, but—'

'What?' I exclaimed. 'You were twenty-two when you came to teach at our school?'

'Well, I was twenty-one, actually,' Mrs Catlin said. 'I came straight from teacher training college.'

I was astonished. 'We all thought you'd been teaching for centuries,' I said. 'You were so in control, so, uh, poised—'

She laughed.

'Do you know what I majored in at college, as the Americans say?' she asked.

I shook my head.

'All-night poker sessions,' she said. 'I learned very early on how to bluff my way out of tricky situations. When I was faced with my first real class of screaming fourth-formers I just did the same, and it worked. So I kept on doing it.' She looked at me searchingly, her arms around me. 'Do you remember the first time we actually met?' she asked.

'Vividly!' I exclaimed. 'You hauled me out in front of the class and destroyed me. I hated you for months after that.'

'I had to,' she said. 'I wanted to be with you so much it hurt, but I knew that if you even had a hint of how I really felt it would be impossible. So I set out to make you hate me. Once I'd done that, being with you was safe. Agony, but safe.'

I laughed.

'I never knew you were so devious,' I said. What she had just told me was amazing, and gave me fresh insight into how strong she could be when she had to.

'Then when I found out who you were,' she went on, 'that you were the son of my childhood friend, and that coming here, to this place, was your deserved heritage, it all seemed to make a kind of sense. It was like fate, or destiny. We'd been brought together for a purpose.'

I remembered things I'd heard in the Asmina Valley and suppressed a shudder. 'Fate' no longer had the abstract connotations for me that it had for Mrs Catlin.

Further conversation was forestalled by the arrival of the *Mariner*. I winched in enough of the ballast line to rise above the larger ship's deck and then lowered it again to bring us down beside the mooring post to which the smaller vessel would be made fast.

P'nad and Celebe were waiting for us on deck, and I could see that both were surprised and visibly pleased that Mrs Catlin was with me.

'It is good to see you again, Linna,' P'nad said to Mrs Catlin.

'I am pleased to see you recovered,' she replied.

Then they both smiled and embraced.

459

'Celebe—' I said, intending to introduce Mrs Catlin; then I thought better of it and said, 'Ailette?'

The Knight gave a faint smile.

'I am here, David,' she said.

I turned to Mrs Catlin.

'Mrs Catlin,' I said formally, 'may I present Ailette Legendre, also known as Celebe, Knight of the Temple of the Thirteen Gods.' Turning to Celebe I said, 'Ailette, this is Mrs Catlin—' I glanced at my former teacher, who was looking at me and clearly wondering what I was going to say next. I said, '—the woman I love.'

Ailette laughed, a purely human sound with no trace of Celebe in it.

'This is news to me?' she said, slapping me good-naturedly on the back and probably dislodging a couple of ribs in the process. 'I am truly pleased to meet you at last,' she said to Mrs Catlin. 'But, please – how should I address you? This fool,' she grinned, indicating me, 'has yet to tell me.'

Mrs Catlin slid under my arm and stood at my side as naturally as though she had done so a thousand times before.

'P'nad calls me Linna,' she said, 'and I count him my friend. I would be pleased if you would do the same.'

It was said with a smile, but no one doubted that Celebe had just been put in her place.

Before anything unpleasant could develop I said to Celebe, 'There is a Knight of the Thirteen on Droxus's ship.'

I was hoping to surprise her, thus defusing the situation, but she merely said, 'I suspected as much.'

'And you didn't tell me?' I said, dumbfounded.

'You had enough to concern you,' she replied. 'It seemed best to say nothing.'

Recovering my composure I said, 'What made you suspect it?'

'Vahnn always struck at me,' she said, 'never at you or the *Mariner*. A Knight's perceptions are especially sensitive to other Knights, to sensing their involvement in certain events. Thus, Vahnn's Knight was able to deduce when he must strike to be certain of finding me. In that way, he could attempt to remove me from the battle – and you must remember that having no knowledge of the existence of the *Mariner* Vahnn would consider me your greatest weapon. Using me as a rallying figure, you would be able to convince anyone that you met that the gods favoured your cause. Naturally, Vahnn would wish to prevent such a thing.'

I nodded slowly.

'He just missed you at Vraks'has,' I said, 'then he battled you at Gaahak and left you for dead. He almost missed you then, too, and would have if you hadn't attacked him. And then, finally, he confronted you on the deck of the *Mariner.*'

'Where his own overconfidence in his armour defeated him,' Celebe said. 'He should have returned to Droxus as soon as he realized we had our own airship, but he did not do so, and with that error he forfeited his own life and the success of his mission.'

'Yes, well,' I said slowly, 'that last is still in doubt. So we'd better start getting this ship ready for war.'

P'nad said, 'We have not been idle in your absence, Captain. Everyone knows his duties for the coming battle, and Hareg and his people assure us the ship is ready.'

I felt Mrs Catlin stiffen at my side.

'Hareg is here?' she asked; her hatred of him, it seemed, was undiminished.

'Hareg is my ally,' I told her, 'and a trusted member of my crew.' She looked at me, not a little angrily. 'Things have changed in the past months,' I said gently. 'Wait until you know all the facts before passing judgement.'

She disengaged herself from my arm.

'You have a lot to do,' she said stiffly. 'I won't keep you.'

She walked quickly away.

I sighed.

'Some things,' I said, 'haven't changed.'

Chapter 50

VICTORY OR DEFEAT

We sighted Carmalt better than one hour earlier than anticipated. It was a surprise, but a welcome one. The command watch was at its rowing station, every other crew member waiting anxiously below decks or around the bulwarks of the main deck. No one was in much of a mood for waiting.

We were still shadowing Droxus's ship at treetop height, and had passed over several of his army's patrols. Their responses had been suitably frantic, but the vast majority of his followers seemed to take us for an ally, actually cheering us as we passed. I could only attribute this reaction to the belief among his men, no doubt consciously fostered, that his own airship was a device he himself had invented. It would then come as no surprise to them to find that he had built a second ship, his own deception keeping them from seeing the real truth of the situation.

No sooner had Carmalt achieved a recognizable size and shape on the horizon than Droxus's ship began to pull ahead of us.

'He's been running with only a light sail,' Mrs Catlin said; she was standing at my shoulder on the sterncastle, dressed now in the garments of an Uhrgratz villager. With a thousand and one other things on my mind, I still found the time to notice how attractively she managed to wear the roughly woven yet colourful costume, her reddish-brown hair, a mass of curls and tangles from the long months during which it had not seen a comb or brush, giving her a wild and untamed appearance. If I lived through this day, I vowed silently to myself, I would never again fail to take full advantage of the feelings she and I had discovered in one another.

'There was some damage to one of his main masts,' she continued, 'and the repairs were never satisfactory. He's up to about three-quarters sail now, which is probably the best he can manage.' She looked at me. 'Can you catch him?' she asked.

'We could,' I said, 'but we'd be in no condition to fight afterwards. But it isn't a problem – once he reaches Carmalt he'll circle, and then we'll have him.'

'Once he starts to circle he'll see you,' she said. 'Then what?'

'By then,' I said, 'it won't matter.'

I leaned on the railing; the oarsmen were pulling half-beat, which they could comfortably have kept up for hours.

'Three-quarter beat, timekeeper,' I said.

I saw grim smiles light a dozen faces. The waiting, they knew, was over.

'Three-quarter beat!' the hortator bellowed, his own enthusiasm evident in his voice.

The gap between the two ships ceased to grow, then began very slowly to narrow.

The land below us gave way now to mile after mile of open fields, a vast tract of cultivated farmlands that circled Carmalt. It was an irregular chessboard of variegated colours, the golds and browns of grass crops mixed with the greens of root vegetables, and among them the occasional patch of what looked like heather, but was, I knew, a uniquely Vinh food source that was undoubtedly a distant cousin of the earthly soya bean. I could have been looking at the environs of any Vohung city, except for the scale of the undertaking around this, the Capitol of all the Kingdoms, and so prosaic did the landscape appear that I might have been fooled into thinking that all was peaceful in that mighty, never-conquered fortress.

But I was not fooled.

Because I could see, in the distance, the tents, the wisps of smoke, the clouds of dust, that marked the camp, the vast, almost city-sized encampment, of Droxus's army.

If the farmlands of Carmalt circled her like a great patchwork quilt, then the army of Droxus circled her like a noose. And with each passing day, perhaps each hour of each day, that noose closed tighter and ever tighter, wringing the life from her as surely as the hangman's noose steals the life of a man.

I could make out details in the city itself now – not fine details, not from this distance, but details enough to be able to imagine the rest. Her outer walls were broken in a handful of places: crude and inefficient siege machines – more of the handiwork of Droxus – had chipped away at them for weeks, so that now those areas had to be constantly defended, drawing manpower away from other areas where it was sorely needed. Gutted buildings could be made out in the centre of the city, and I guessed that somewhere in the camp of the enemy would be ballistae for hurling burning coals over the besieged ramparts. I imagined the panic that such an attack would have engendered – and wondered at the resourcefulness and determination of the people of Carmalt that had somehow enabled them to keep the destruction as limited as it was. Every trick of defending a city under siege – a concept unknown in the living history of the Vohung – would have had to have been reinvented day by day, night by night, by a people with no natural talent for such an undertaking. If any city was worthy of saving, I thought, it was a city peopled by men and women such as these.

Droxus was almost over the city now and was beginning to furl sail, coming round to circle. He was also losing altitude, his ballast weights visible at perhaps half extension. Of course, he would not want to descend to within bowshot of the city, however ineffectual such a defence would have been.

I looked around me. Celebe was standing to the rear of the sterncastle, seemingly unconcerned, her enigmatic gaze fixed emotionlessly on the forward horizon. P'nad and S'nam were at opposite sides of the steersman, ready to move forward to take command of their respective watches. The steersman between them, his hands on the *Mariner*'s great wheel, seemed dwarfed by their broad, muscular frames. In his eyes, however, was the same determination that I saw in theirs. On the deck below, moving rapidly to and fro beside the moving parts of the propshaft, were Hareg and the other four remaining Ladden, all their attention fixed on the product of their inventive genius. Forward of them, clustered around the handrails that lined the lower deck, were upward of a score of crewmen, all armed, waiting for the signal to go into battle.

I drew a deep breath.

The waiting was over.

I looked at P'nad.

He nodded.

'All crew to battle stations,' I said.

Both he and S'nam moved forward, calling out the order to their men. No one cheered, but somehow it felt as though they had.

Bowmen swarmed on deck, taking up their places on both upper decks and the lower main deck; most of the men carried longbows, only a handful possessing crossbows, and I suspected that if all went as planned today no one in Benza would ever again look with disdain upon a longbowman. The arrows of the bowmen were mostly bodkin-tipped, for greater depth of penetration, but each man also carried a small supply of crescent-tipped shafts that could be used for cutting ships' rigging lines. The concept had been alien to the archers, and to their metal workers, but once explained to them had been readily grasped and acted upon. My own knowledge of how a crescent pile should look had been sketchy to say the least, but I think our efforts had been successful – at any rate, we would soon know.

My two musketmen were placed one on the forecastle and one on the sterncastle, in the hope, however vain, that if the opportunity arose one of them might be able to dispatch Droxus himself. Each man was also armed with a longbow, since our supply of musket balls and gunpowder was limited.

The remainder of the crew was divided into three. Two-thirds lined the outer deck in readiness to board Droxus's ship should it prove practicable, or to repel boarders should the plan backfire. The remaining third sat at the vacant rowing stations that had once operated the starboard propeller; if Droxus's own archers and musketmen fired upon us there was every possibility of our oarsmen being hit, and having a full complement of reserves was a bonus I had never counted upon. In addition, these men carried large shields with which they could protect the working oarsmen should it prove necessary.

Men were still taking their places when I leaned once more over the hand-rail and said 'Full speed' to the hortator.

The ship surged forward, the men barely waiting for the command. I hoped their eagerness would not get the better of their discipline.

I turned to the men at the windlasses that operated our ballast.

'Raise ballast by ten,' I called.

They began to turn their wheels, and the *Mariner* rose smoothly higher. At ten revolutions they stopped, and we were still some hundred feet or so below Droxus's ship. The distance between the two vessels was diminishing rapidly as he turned broadside on to us, but not so rapidly that, if his lookouts were alert, he could not evade our attack.

'Hard to port,' I called to the steersman. 'Put us in front of him.'

'Yes, Captain!' he cried, spinning the great wheel.

The vessel leaned into a shallow turn, its boards creaking, Hareg's make-shift repairs protesting the strain. I hoped this was one time he and his people would live up to their reputation.

'Attack speed,' I called to the timekeeper.

'Attack speed on three!' he yelled.

And with an audible groan from the propshaft the *Mariner* raced ever more swiftly towards its target.

From the top of the starboard wing a lookout yelled, 'He sees us!'

All eyes on the starboard side turned to peer at Droxus's vessel, and no one could doubt the lookout's claim. Activity on the deck of the sailing ship became frantic as men gazed in disbelief at our own craft, only half of them retaining the wit to do something about it.

'One-quarter starboard,' I called to the steersman; Droxus was reacting more slowly than I had expected, and if we weren't careful we'd overshoot.

The *Mariner* straightened up; we were flying like a spear towards the other ship, and would take her amidships in less than a minute.

'Ballast up another ten!' I called.

We were still below Droxus, but if my timing was right another ten turns on the ballast wheels would bring us level with his upper deck. I wanted to avoid striking his lower decks at all costs, since that was where his prisoners were.

To the steersman I said, 'Straighten up!' and he spun the wheel to centre. The *Mariner* was rising nose first, which was just what I wanted.

'Ram speed!' I called over the handrail.

No command was necessary; the hortator raised the beat and the oarsmen matched it. I felt my heart pound to the rhythm.

'Brace for collision!' I yelled, and the cry was echoed all over the ship.

Men clipped safety lines to snap rings at their stations as the bulk of Droxus's ship raced sideways towards us.

And Droxus proved, in one single, devastating moment that whatever else he was, he was no fool.

At the last possible instant his ballast weights were lowered to the end of their lines and his ship went dropping below us, our steel-like central spar missing his wooden hull by yards and, a second later, narrowly missing the open arch of his upper port wing. Our own lower wings crashed against his vessel, but the damage they did was minimal, and the impact almost rolled the *Mariner* onto its back, sending men flying to the length of their safety lines and too-loosely held weapons clattering across the deck. With that one simple manoeuvre Droxus had not only proven himself to be a natural master of airborne combat, but had – more importantly – denied us the easy victory we had hoped for.

I saw stunned and frightened faces all around me – this was a debacle no one had even thought to consider! That my own expression was a mirror to that of every man in my crew was a certainty, and equally as certain was the fact that if I didn't regain some kind of control – and quickly – this setback would turn into a rout.

'Ship ballast!' I yelled, clinging to the handrail and bracing my feet to keep from falling over it. 'Steersman, hard to starboard! Timekeeper, ram speed! Now!'

The ship was swaying from side to side like a cork in a hurricane, but the familiar-sounding orders seemed to cut through the chaos and as rapidly as it had come the panic began to recede.

I heard the hortator bellow, 'Rest oars!' and gave silent thanks for his cool-headed logic – going from chaos to ram speed without a moment's pause would have been insanity; in all probability the uncoordinated rowing that would have resulted would have wrecked the drivetrain. 'Half-speed!' he yelled, which was the fastest that a man could pull from all-stop. In seconds, he had us up to ram speed. And the steersman already had the wheel hard over to starboard. The *Mariner* heeled into the turn, banking so sharply I almost lost my footing on the deck.

I looked around me; I wasn't the only one struggling to stay upright. Behind me, Mrs Catlin was clutching one of the newly erected posts that lined the sterncastle, her safety line clipped to it. I hadn't realized she was still on deck.

'Go below,' I told her. It was hard enough to concentrate without having her to worry about.

'Forget it, Shaw,' she replied, predictably enough.

Cursing silently, I turned back to the job at hand.

I had intended circling behind Droxus's ship, desperate to keep him from doing to us what we had just tried unsuccessfully to do to him, but as I looked back to where I had expected him to be he was nowhere to be seen. I realized immediately that he must still be below us – but where?

'Lookout!' I called. 'Give us a bearing!'

All the lookouts were peering over the railings, and in seconds the answering cry went up.

'Coming up behind us off the starboard side!' one of the aft lookouts cried, a note of fear in his voice.

I cursed Droxus's skill. He had let us pass him and was now upwind of us. He would be piling on sail in the hope of ramming us.

And at this altitude, there was no way we could survive such an attack.

I was also dimly aware of the fact that we had now overshot the bulk of Droxus's ground-based forces, and that even if we should succeed in defeating him, few people on the ground would be able to see it. Victory was one thing, but the blow to the morale of his ground troops was what was needed to rescue Carmalt.

I thought furiously, wishing I knew whether Droxus was a gifted amateur or a genuine professional. If the latter, I didn't give much for our chances. But if it was the former, then eventually he would make a mistake. All we had to do was to survive long enough to capitalize on it.

I leaned over the handrail, and in the calmest voice I could muster I said, 'Slow to one-quarter.'

I sensed the brief hesitation before the timekeeper yelled, 'Rest oars! Quarter-beat on three! One . . . two . . . beat!'

The ship slowed, and I felt dozens of pairs of eyes on me.

I turned to the steersman. 'Hold the turn,' I said. 'Be ready to straighten up on my order.'

'Yes, Captain,' he said, his face covered in sweat.

I called to the starboard lookouts, 'Where is he?'

'Directly off the starboard wing!' they all cried.

'How far?' I demanded.

'Less than a torbik,' called out the man amidships.

'Run out forward ballast by ten,' I called.

The men at the forward ballast wheel turned it through ten revolutions and the ship's nose dipped. Now everyone facing forwards could see Droxus's vessel rushing up to meet us. In an instant we were pointing directly at one another, and I yelled, 'Straighten up!'

The steersman spun his wheel and we were flying nose-to-nose at Droxus's ship.

'Full speed!' I said to the hortator.

'Maximum beat!' he yelled.

The distance between the ships shrank with frightening rapidity.

'Run out all ballast!' I cried.

The *Mariner* dropped like a stone, never losing its forty-five degree nosedown pitch.

Droxus's ship flashed past overhead, and the loudest cheer I had ever heard erupted on the *Mariner*'s deck.

I smiled grimly. We had played Droxus at his own game, and restored our own self-confidence in the process, but we were no nearer victory now than we had been a moment ago.

Unless—

'All stop!' I called. Then, 'Steersman, hard to port!'

Droxus was riding the wind; turning a sailing ship at that speed would be a laborious process, and he would lose most of his momentum in doing it.

'Ship all ballast by twenty!' I called.

The *Mariner* began to rise slowly, turning in the air on inertia alone.

'Quarter speed,' I said.

We began to move faster, the circle tightening.

'Half speed,' I said.

I could see Droxus's ship above us; he was taking in sail and turning to starboard. He was coming broadside on to us, but he was fearfully far away, and he had the advantage of altitude.

'Full speed,' I said. Then, 'Steersman, straighten up.'

What would I do in Droxus's place? Would I try the rapid-descent trick again, or would I credit my enemy with enough intelligence not to fall for it a second time? Or would I assume – perhaps rightly – that as a defence it was unanswerable?

And suddenly two thoughts hit my mind simultaneously.

The first, a memory: Droxus, standing on the sterncastle of his ship, saying to me, 'These people haven't had a single original thought in generations—'

The second, a realization: Droxus couldn't know that David Shaw commanded the *Mariner*! As far as he knew he faced a Vinh opponent who had somehow happened upon another flying vessel. A moment's cool reflection would give the lie to such an assumption, but such a moment Droxus would not have had. And even if that were not the case, would his own egotism, his mad desire for conquest, have allowed him to believe that he was facing an opponent who could defeat him? I was gambling all our lives on the assumption that it would not.

471

'P'nad!' I called.

The giant ex-slave was beside me in a moment. In as few words as I could I explained to him the mad plan that I had just conceived. He made no comment – for which I was deeply grateful – but returned to his men and began issuing orders.

I leaned over the handrail.

'Attack speed,' I said.

I called out to the men at the ballast wheels.

'Ship all ballast!' I cried.

The *Mariner* levelled off and continued to rise.

I knew that the timekeeper was waiting for the call to go to ram speed, but I had other ideas in mind.

I turned to the steersman. 'On my command,' I said quietly, 'turn hard to starboard.'

He glanced over my shoulder at the onrushing broadside of Droxus's ship and, though clearly confused, said, 'Yes, Captain.'

We were almost on top of the sailing vessel now, and I knew that Droxus would drop his ballast at any second. I tried to recall the exact sequence of events from our first attack, so that I could outmanoeuvre him, and realized that if I succeeded it would be more by luck than judgement.

At the last instant I said to the steersman, 'Now!' and he spun the great wheel.

'Drop ballast!' I cried.

The *Mariner* began to descend.

'All stop!' I called to the timekeeper.

Every oar stopped, the ship's momentum carrying her on.

And Droxus had made his first mistake.

At the instant we had turned he had run out his own ballast and made the turn to port – an exact repetition of his tactics during our first attack.

Both vessels were now descending, but we were twenty feet or more below him and running parallel to his starboard side.

I heard P'nad cry to his archers: 'Loose!'

And a score of crescent-tipped shafts flashed upwards.

I felt Mrs Catlin's hand grip my arm.

'Shaw!' she gasped. 'That was brilliant!'

One of Droxus's ballast weights was already plunging into the distance below us, its rope severed. In rapid succession, two more followed it. And his ship began to rise.

'Ship ballast by ten!' I called.

We rose after him, our archers taking out another of his weights, then another. His ship was listing badly now, and he was drawing in the remaining ballast to protect it. Already we had made it impossible for him to descend to ground level; if we took out any more of his weights he would be stranded at a thousand feet until he and his men died of starvation. It was a fitting end, but not one I could afford to allow him.

'Half speed,' I told the hortator. And to the steersman, 'Hard to starboard.'

We began to peel away from Droxus's ship, now almost a hundred feet above us, when the *Mariner* was suddenly rocked by a terrific explosion. I was flung to the deck, conscious of bits of deck planking flying through the air all around me; I could hear the cries of injured and terrified men. A second explosion, this time in the air off our port bow, knocked the ship onto its side, sending it spinning crazily through the air. And before anyone had time either to recover or even guess what was going on the air around and above us was suddenly thick with arrows. The sound of them thudding into the wooden parts of the ship, or clanging off the metal air-frame, was a deadly staccato above all the other sounds around me.

Too late I saw what had happened. Rather than accepting his defeat gracefully, Droxus had initiated an immediate counter-attack. The explosions had been powder kegs, probably already on deck for the bombing of Carmalt. We had been unspeakably fortunate that he'd only had time to drop two on us, and not a dozen or more. The activity of his archers, however, was no less deadly, and was still going on.

'Drop all ballast!' I cried over the medley of sounds around me. We had to get out of range, and fast!

The ship began to descend, but too slowly. And not evenly. One of the capstan men was dead, spiked with arrows, and had fallen over the wheel, making it impossible for his colleagues to turn it.

'Shield men,' I called down into the rowing deck. 'Cover the oarsmen!' To the hortator I said, 'Best speed, as fast as you can.'

He nodded and at barely half speed we began to limp away. But Droxus was turning with us, and the hail of arrows was now accompanied by the crackle of musket fire.

'Hard to port,' I called. 'Take us under him.'

The 'shadow' of an airframe, the blind spot beneath it as seen from its top deck, would be huge at this distance. If we could get into it and keep descending, however unevenly, we would be safe.

But the ship did not turn.

I looked quickly back and saw the body of the steersman lying on the deck beside the wheel, a single arrow protruding from his forehead.

Before I could stop her Mrs Catlin had released her safety line and was behind the wheel, spinning it to port for all she was worth. An arrow thudded into it, and was instantly snapped off as it passed the wheel's axle post. Mrs Catlin blinked several times, very quickly. It was her only visible reaction.

In a moment we were under Droxus's ship, its real shadow falling over us and creating a gloomy setting to match our situation.

There was a small fire burning to one side of the forecastle where the first bomb had hit us, but S'nam was already getting men forward to control it. There were bodies everywhere, some beyond help but many others in need of medical assistance. P'nad, whose men were now redundant as soldiers, began the painful task of attending to the wounded and dying. On the rowing deck below me, injured men were being helped from their places on the benches and being replaced by uninjured members of the reserve.

For all the chaos, no one was panicking. And amid the confusion, order was being restored. I felt a fierce, exulting pride: with men such as these, no task was hopeless, no goal beyond reach.

I leaned on the handrail, resisting an urge to leave the sterncastle and take a more active part in things. No one down there needed me, and the best thing I could do for them right now was to keep out of their way.

That, and one other thing. Decisions had to be made, hard

decisions, and they had to be made quickly. We had dealt Droxus a painful blow, but he was still a long way from being defeated. And as bitter a truth as it was to face, I couldn't allow our own casualties to deter us from accomplishing that task.

The fire was out now, and the *Mariner's* uneven attitude had been corrected. The decks had been cleared of casualties and all the rowing stations were full. Behind me, a steersman from another watch had replaced Mrs Catlin at the wheel and she was once again standing at my shoulder.

I looked at her.

'Go below,' I said.

She hesitated.

'You're needed there,' I said.

She nodded briefly and was gone. I smiled; once, she would not have let so obvious a chance for a sarcastic rejoinder pass her by.

Behind me, a voice said, 'She has fire, that one.'

I half-turned. Celebe had been on deck since before we had engaged Droxus's ship but this was the first comment she had seen fit to vouchsafe. I noticed the wry smile on her lips and returned it doubtfully.

'Enough to burn down a small city,' I replied dryly.

I turned to see P'nad climbing to the sterncastle. S'nam was not far behind him.

'Casualties?' I asked.

'Eight dead,' P'nad said. 'Thirteen injured, nine of them too badly to serve. Other than that, we are ready.'

S'nam said, 'One of Hareg's people is among the injured. Hareg does not think it will affect his ability to care for the ship.'

'Then let's get this over with,' I said. 'Droxus is trapped at a thousand feet now, which gives us all the advantages. But I've underestimated him once today and I don't intend to repeat that mistake. Here is my plan—'

I spoke quickly and simply, and P'nad and S'nam nodded in all the right places.

'Any questions?' I asked. Neither man spoke. 'Then let's do it,' I said.

A moment later both men were stationing their archers along the forward edges of the lower deck and all around the sweep of the forecastle.

The timekeeper had been regulating his beat to keep us in Droxus's shadow, and the steersman had foiled all of Droxus's attempts at shaking us loose, but now it was time for a change of tactics.

At my command, the ballast weights were lowered to their fullest extent and we dropped rapidly out of range of Droxus's archers and musketmen. Then, at a steady three-quarter beat, we turned and headed upwind of him. I took us more than a torbik before calling out for the ballast to be shipped once again. With the wind now blowing against Droxus, we rose to his altitude and prepared for what I hoped would be the final act in this grim drama.

'Full speed,' I told the hortator.

Droxus would undoubtedly spot us in time to try some evasive manoeuvres, but with most of his ballast gone he would not be able to drop out of range in time to avoid us.

We were half a torbik distant when he began to tack into the wind. His skill was impressive to see, but this time it wasn't going to be enough.

'Attack speed,' I said.

The *Mariner* flashed towards the sailing ship like an arrow, the replacement steersman holding us on course despite all Droxus's efforts.

'Ram speed,' I said.

At the last instant Droxus did the only thing he could. He turned nose on to us and readied to take the impact full frontal, thereby avoiding having his hull torn in two by a hit amidships.

Across the rapidly shrinking divide between the two ships flew a hail of arrows, our own aimed primarily at Droxus's rigging. We did some damage, reducing his ability to manoeuvre, but in another moment I did not think it would matter.

Braced as I was, the impact of the two vessels nonetheless threw me violently to the deck. There was a hideous rending sound, as of inch-thick steel plate being torn like tin foil, and a crunching, splintering *crack!* that went on and on as the forward spike of each vessel tore through the wooden hull of the other. Our own ship, designed as it was with airborne combat in mind, came off best, its streamlined shape deflecting the worst of the impact. Things did not go so well for Droxus, however. His blocky, deep-sided vessel was slashed open like a rotten log, the spike of the *Mariner*'s airframe spearing it from its bow to a point somewhere aft of amidships.

As staggered as I was by the sheer enormity of the damage we had inflicted, and horrified by the possible consequences for anyone caught below decks at the moment of impact, I knew that I couldn't afford to waste an instant before capitalizing on our success.

The hulls of the two ships were now scarcely ten feet apart, a silver expanse of airframe being all that separated us.

'P'nad! S'nam!' I cried. 'Get ready with your boarding parties!'

An instant after the impact, Hareg and his people had rushed to the huge flange which joined the propshaft to the propeller housing. They had not waited for instructions, since this was one manoeuvre no one needed to be told about. Using huge levers, they had separated the hub and, in a matter of seconds, reattached it with its mechanism reversed. They had rehearsed that operation a thousand times, and I don't think they had ever done it faster.

'Timekeeper,' I called, 'half-beat.'

To the pounding of his wooden mallets the *Mariner* inched slowly backwards. Arrows flashed from the shattered deck of Droxus's ship, sporadic and poorly aimed. Our own archers returned fire, and to better effect.

'Full speed,' I told the hortator.

We pulled free of the sailing ship and, once clear, hurtled away from her.

'All stop,' I said. Then, 'Hareg!' No other order was necessary.

In moments the vast hub had been reversed again and we were swinging around Droxus's ship to take her from the side.

I shuddered at this first clear view of the destruction the *Mariner* had wrought. The front of Droxus's ship was ripped open along a jagged line, the upper deck peeled back like the skin of some giant fruit. The lower deck had, in places, been smashed completely away, leaving the remains of the hold open to the sky. Even now, supplies could still be seen tumbling out of it, a streamer

477

of dried meats, vegetables, and other ship's stores that drifted away on the wind.

I tried to make out the location of the prison level. It had been near the stern, but I had never seen the ship from this angle before. Had I destroyed Benza's rulers, and the rulers of her allies? Or had our attack broken open their cells and given them freedom? There was no way to know.

'Steersman,' I said, 'I want to take out the enemy's forecastle. Can you do it?'

He peered along the length of the *Mariner's* forward spike, as though sighting along the shaft of an arrow.

'No problem, Captain,' he said.

'Do it,' I said. To the hortator, I said, 'Ram speed at your discretion.'

'Yes, Captain!' he said. To the oarsmen he cried, 'Full speed on the third beat.'

The impact this time was less ferocious, but it sheered the forecastle of Droxus's ship cleanly in two, and the *Mariner* didn't stop until our own hull was crushed up aginst the shattered remains of his.

P'nad and S'nam didn't wait for my order, but instantly led their men over the starboard handrail and onto the main deck of the sailing vessel.

I turned to Celebe.

'You will be needed over there,' I said.

She nodded slowly. No one else would stand a chance against Droxus's Knight. Yet I think the prospect of battling one of her own order was repugnant to Celebe, and was making her hesitate.

'They need you!' I cried.

She shuddered, and abruptly raced forward.

I climbed down to the main deck.

'Hareg,' I said, finding the Ladden standing beside the time-keeper's station, 'you're in command until I return. If the battle goes against us, get the *Mariner* to safety.'

'No man on board would obey such an order,' Hareg said.

'It's up to you to see they do,' I told him. 'This ship is more important than any of us. You see she's kept safe.'

Without waiting for him to reply I turned and ran for the forecastle.

In an instant I was standing on the ruptured deck of Droxus's ship. And, immediately, I knew that my order to Hareg would not have to be carried out. My fears for the safety of the Vohung prisoners had been groundless, for they were even now fighting on deck alongside my own men. And the crew of Droxus's ship were outnumbered by almost three to one.

I skirted the battle on the main deck and headed for the sterncastle. There was only one man I wanted to get my hands on now, and that was Droxus himself.

I found him where I had expected to, but he was not alone. Between him and me stood Hol Krexus, and beside him was a Knight of the Thirteen.

I don't know who was most astonished at seeing me, but the former Benzan Captain went quickly from surprise to pleasure.

'I have dreamed of this moment,' he said bitterly. 'Now will my honour be avenged.'

I couldn't believe he thought he still had any honour left that was worth avenging, but nor did I have time to waste with him. I, too, had thought long and hard about what I would do when this confrontation came, and I had played out all the possibilities too many times to want to re-enact any of them now. Krexus was beyond redemption, and I was content to leave his punishment to his gods. All I wanted to do was to make sure he never hurt anyone ever again.

Behind him, Droxus was pale, though whether from fear or anger I couldn't tell. The Knight, who seemed aloof, unconcerned, stood impassively at her side. I didn't expect her to intercede on Krexus's behalf, but once he was dispatched she would undoubtedly act to protect Droxus. I wondered where Celebe was; I hadn't seen her since crossing from the *Mariner*.

Krexus drew his sword. I already held mine, a straight-edged one from the Ladden armoury. It was a good weapon, well balanced, with a damascened blade. But I would gladly have traded it for my sabre.

Krexus came at me. He had learned from our two previous

encounters, and had apparently been doing some intensive training between then and now.

I took his blade in a circular parry and stabbed him through the throat.

Stepping past his crumpled form I advanced on Droxus. He was, as ever, unarmed, and I had little desire to do murder, but one way or another he had to be destroyed.

'Come no further,' said the Knight, seeming to acknowledge my existence for the first time. 'This man is under my protection.'

'Then you and I must do battle,' I said, wishing I felt as confident as I was trying to sound.

'Do not be foolish,' she said, almost laughing. 'Your puny weapon cannot harm me. Although I am curious to know how you managed to defeat the Librarian Rohc Vahnn.'

'It's a long story,' I said, stalling for time.

This time she did laugh.

'In truth,' she said, 'it is of little consequence. Vahnn was a mortal who aspired to the power of the gods. I am one of the chosen of the gods. Their will protects me. I need fear no mortal foe.'

I saw movement behind her, the silvery glint of sunlight on armour. A figure arose from behind the sterncastle: Celebe.

'What, then, of an immortal foe, sister?' Celebe asked softly.

The Knight began to turn, but Celebe moved like lightning. I had wondered how she would combat one of her own kind, one whose armour was as strong as her own and who had no offensive powers that could be manipulated against her, as Vahnn's had been. The answer proved to be as simple as it was gruesome. With a strength that no living creature could have duplicated and a speed that almost defied the eye, she snatched the helm from her opponent's head. The Knight died instantly, yet even so there was time for her to utter the most hideous scream I had ever heard. I almost turned away, sick to my stomach. Watching the armour being removed from Chantal Clavalle had been bad enough, but at least she had been beyond all feeling. This . . .

I faced Droxus, conscious of Celebe casting the other Knight's helm over the side.

'You are my prisoner,' I told him.

480

He looked about, a hint of madness in his eyes. Then he smiled unexpectedly, almost ruefully.

'A minor setback,' he said, his equanimity forced yet with an underlying confidence that I found disturbing. 'Return me to Earth if it pleases you,' he said, 'but never doubt that I shall return. I know the location of several points of contact between our Earth and this world, and I will not hesitate to use them. And I learn from my mistakes, David – you will not find me so easy to defeat a second time.'

I considered killing him. The stakes were high enough for it to be justified, yet murder is still murder, whatever the justification.

I considered letting Celebe kill him. I knew that she would do so without hesitation if I but turned my back, yet to do so was merely to substitute one weapon for another: the guilt would still be mine.

I could, of course, have left him to the mercy of the people of Vohung. But whatever his crime, Droxus was not a part of their culture, and if judgement was to be passed on him it should not be their brand of justice. On Earth, with luck, he could be treated for his condition, which was almost certainly pathological in origin.

I said, 'Order your men to surrender.'

He laughed. 'Very well,' he said.

I watched him closely for any sign of trickery but he seemed genuinely reconciled to his defeat. This, if nothing else, seemed to me to prove the unbalanced nature of his mind.

Even with their leader ordering their surrender, it took most of an hour before we were able to subdue the last of the opposition. With the ship secure, I ordered Droxus's followers taken down to the prison level, where a constant armed guard was kept over them.

Then, with P'nad taking command of the captured vessel, we disengaged the *Mariner* from her erstwhile foe and prepared to take the sailing ship down. This we did by 'docking' the two ships – the forward spike of the *Mariner* threaded through the upper wings of Droxus's vessel – and using the *Mariner's* ballast we brought both ships down.

It would be a pleasure to record at this juncture that the sight of its leader in defeat had such a disheartening effect on the army besieging Carmalt that it laid down its arms and surrendered. If this were the work of fiction that, to earthly eyes and minds, it must surely appear then that is what I would record. Sadly, the truth is seldom so tidy.

That Droxus's followers were demoralized by what they saw is undeniable, but the sheer size of their force made it almost impossible for it simply to disband and surrender. There were too many ambitious sub-commanders, all willing to step into Droxus's shoes for Carmalt to win so easy a victory.

Yet if the blow to Droxus's troops was less than mortal, the boost that our victory gave to the defenders of the city of Carmalt was a hundred times more telling. Their spirited defence became a wild counter-attack, and the *Mariner* assisted them – using the weapons captured from Droxus's own arsenal.

The battle went on for days, and when Droxus's supply of gunpowder and musket balls had been used up it settled into a collection of smaller battles, many of them wars of attrition, that dragged on for weeks. In the end, it was almost three months before Carmalt could truly claim that it was liberated, with not an enemy force active anywhere in its environs.

By then, winter was setting in, and we were discovering that the *Mariner* was not an effective all-weather vessel. The damp air got into her drive and made parts swell that had no room for such swelling. Hareg and his people worked hard to keep her mobile, but in the end we realized she would not be capable of transporting the disparate elements of her crew back to their home lands until the following spring.

Surprisingly, no one seemed too concerned.

Chapter 51

AFTERMATH

And so the greatest adventure of my life had come to an end. There were, of course, postscripts. There were more postscripts than can be comfortably accommodated here. But one or two were particularly worthy of note.

On a personal level, I was deeply honoured, and highly delighted, to be made a genuine 'Captain', this time in the court of Benza. The rulers of several of the Kingdoms wanted my allegiance, and the King of Carmalt even offered to *adopt* me. But I had started this because of my feelings for the relatively small land that had once made me feel so welcome, and her honours were the ones I cherished the most. No one disputed my ownership of the *Mariner*, though the Duke of Benza was clearly very happy to make my command of her a condition of my new rank, thus ensuring that even if he did not hold actual title to the vessel he did have authority over its crew. It was an interesting precedent, and one that I felt would make for enthusiastic competition in the locating and securing of other airframes in the future. The captured sailing vessel, incidentally, I presented to the Duke of Benza as a prize of war. The King of Carmalt night have felt a touch snubbed by this gesture, but if he was he concealed it behind a mask of diplomacy that I, at least, never penetrated.

The Ladden ex-slaves had all been promised a home in the Kingdoms, and while I may have overstepped my authority in making that promise the rulers of the various Vohung lands were only too eager to honour it. An official manumission ceremony was held, with Hareg representing his people and approving the procedure.

There was much celebrating during the early winter months, although the soldiers of the outlying Kingdoms had departed soon after Carmalt's liberation in order to return home before the first snows. The days had barely begun to shorten before I, too, felt that it was time to make a move.

I had enjoyed the time in Carmalt, especially since it gave Mrs Catlin and I time to get to know one another on a whole new level. We still fought – I think it had become a way of life for us – but we now had a new way of making up afterwards.

And so there came a night, not long before the first snows, when neither of us had had the time or the inclination to sleep, that she lay at my side with her body wrapped around mine, her red-brown hair spilling over my chest as her head nestled in the hollow of my neck. She was humming softly, something classical, and seemed utterly content. It was a feeling I shared. It was a feeling I was getting very used to.

'Shaw—' she said lazily.

'Hmmm?' I replied.

'Why are we still here?' she asked.

It was a question I'd asked myself several times lately. I could find only one answer.

'The worlds haven't come back into phase,' I said. I knew it was true. The Thirteen weren't giving us a holiday, they just weren't yet able to send us back to Earth. (I could no longer think of it as 'back home': a part of me would always be of the Earth, but that part seemed to be growing smaller by the day.)

'What will happen when the worlds *are* in phase?' she asked.

'Celebe will tell us,' I replied.

Celebe had been touring the towns and villages for hundreds of miles around, spreading the Word of the Thirteen. We hadn't seen her for weeks now.

Mrs Catlin sat up, her elbows propped on my chest.

'Let's not wait,' she said.

I gave her my best puzzled look.

'Let's fly away,' she said. 'If we're not here when she gets back—'

I put my finger to her lips, silencing her.

'It doesn't work like that,' I said gently.

The Thirteen weren't dependent on following a sequence of cause and effect. They already knew what we would do: if we fled to the ends of the Thek continent we would arrive there just in time to be sent back to Earth – and Celebe would already be there, waiting to send us. But I couldn't tell Mrs Catlin that. There was too much about our past that I now found myself questioning; there was no need to burden her with it as well. Also, no one who had not been inside the 'city' of Asmina could hope to appreciate the scale of the power of the Thirteen, or the fact that what they did had little to do with manipulation, and much to do with understanding. I did not believe that the Thirteen had created my feelings for Mrs Catlin, nor hers for me; I *did* believe that they had engineered a scenario in which those feelings could find their true expression. But only my experiences in their presence supported that belief. To anyone else, the precise opposite would almost certainly seem to be the case. And that was the last thing I wanted Mrs Catlin to think.

She slid out of bed and crossed the richly carpeted stone floor to the narrow window that overlooked the city. We were quartered in a high tower of the central castle of the city, and the view, even by moonlight, was breathtaking.

I watched her in the semi-darkness, the silver light through the window playing over the outline of her body. It was incredible to me now to realize how much I loved her, as though all the feelings I had suppressed for most of a decade were surfacing in a vast tidal wave, one that could swamp all my reason in an instant if I let it. Sometimes, I was happy to let it.

She turned to face me, a smile unexpectedly on her lips.

'Let's fly anyway,' she said. 'If we have to be sent home, let's at least have some kind of a honeymoon.'

'Is that a proposal?' I asked, startled.

Her face suddenly became very serious, and perhaps a bit afraid.

'I think it is,' she said, her voice trembling.

'Then I accept,' I said.

She rushed into my arms, and there were tears in her eyes.

'Gods, that was stupid,' she whispered, holding me tight. 'If you'd said no—'

'If I'd said no *I* would have been stupid,' I told her. I pulled her under the covers with me. She was still shaking.

'Tomorrow,' I said.

She looked up at me.

'Before you change your mind,' I added.

She kissed me fiercely, her nails biting into my shoulders.

'I'll never change my mind,' she vowed.

And the next day, in front of most of the citizens of Carmalt, Mrs Catlin became Mrs David Shaw.

EPILOGUE

It occurred to me that I might not say any more, that I might end my story there and leave its inevitable conclusion to your own imagination, that I might even, perhaps, delude myself into believing that the Happy Ending we had prayed for had, in fact, come to pass. Yet to do so would be to turn this history into a fairy tale, and the sheer reality of all that Mrs Catlin and I had seen and done would cry out in protest at so gross a misrepresentation. So the true ending to my story shall now be told.

I write these final words as I have written all that precedes them, in the gloomy confines of the house that had once been my home, at a table where my father and I had shared many meals together and over which he had told me tall tales of his youth and had forged my character and my beliefs. I write them alone, more alone than I have been in all my life, and if the purpose of writing was to exorcize the demons from my soul then the effort has been a wasted one.

Mrs Catlin – I think I would always call her that, even now – had got her wish, and in the repaired sailing vessel of Droxus, now christened the *Freedom* by her new crew, we had made the long journey to the Asmina Valley. The winds had favoured us all the way, blowing against the natural trend for the region and the time of year, and a journey that should have taken weeks took only a matter of days. The Breath of the Gods—

Celebe met us on a road cutting through the centre of the Valley, perhaps the same road on which I had met her armoured predecessor and her own human self so long ago. The Valley appeared, to me, as I had last seen it, in what I was told was its true aspect. From the mutterings of the crew I suspected the view was one I had all to myself.

'It's so desolate,' Mrs Catlin breathed at my side, peering over the railing that ringed the repaired forecastle. 'Beautiful, in a bleak kind of way, but forbidding.' She glanced at me. 'I can almost believe it is the home of the gods,' she said. 'Certainly nothing human could live here.'

I put my arm around her, saying nothing.

Celebe was brought on board and we continued on to the city.

After that, events grow vague in my mind. I know that we went into the city, and I know we traversed those hideous corridors and vast chambers that I had passed through on my last visit, but when I try to recall the specifics of our visit I find myself remembering that other time instead, as though the two were somehow a single occurrence.

Our confrontation with the Thirteen sticks in my mind as only a handful of sentences, words heard and remembered yet their source forgotten, as though they had been inscribed directly into my memory without ever passing through the medium of my senses. The words were few and brief, and their consequences devastating.

'The woman will integrate. Her soul is not closed. Her presence changes nothing.

'The man she calls Droxus is diseased by his own standards. On any plane he is a threat. He will remain with us until a place can be found.

'The other is fluid, but his time is not yet. He will integrate, but only after growth. He will be returned through the rift for a time.'

As with my previous experience of the Thirteen, the 'audience' was followed by blackness, by an oblivion that lay somewhere between sleep and death. And when it lifted I found myself lying face down in a cave, naked, and very confused. Behind me was a crevice, through which I could see only blackness, and ahead was a rough passage at the end of which I could see a patch of daylight. I crawled towards it, and emerged into the chill air of the Yorkshire Moors. I was home. But Mrs Catlin was not with me.

In a state of sheer desolation I trudged through ice-cold grass to where I remembered leaving the bike, and was not surprised to find it gone. How many months – years – had I been away?

I was eventually picked up by a passing motorist; I was suffering from exposure by then and would gladly have died, except that a single phrase kept hammering away in my brain: *He will be returned through the rift for a time.* For a time. But how long was that? How long was a 'time' to the gods?

It has been four years now since I was returned to the Earth. I visit the cave regularly, but so far it has been only a cave. One day, perhaps, it will be more. I have never given up hope, although on each visit despair attempts to claim me. On such occasions I make myself believe it was all a dream, that there never was a woman called Mrs Catlin, that all the things I have written in this manuscript were found in the bottom of a bottle. That there are no gods, and that reality is a lie. But there *are* gods. And reality is never a lie. And one day I will face those gods again, and on that day, somehow – somehow – there will be a reckoning.